LOVE AND PUNISHMENT

Susan Mac Nicol

www.BOROUGHSPUBLISHINGGROUP.com

LOVE AND PUNISHMENT
Copyright © 2014 Susan Elaine Mac Nicol

ISBN 978-1-941260-7-91

This book is dedicated to my wonderful husband and family, who have been a constant source of support over the past rather eventful twelve months. It's also a big thanks to my publisher, Boroughs, for understanding that a lady sometimes needs time to wind down and take things slower.

ACKNOWLEDGMENTS

To the brilliant John Trevillian, for suggesting the word 'punish' in the first place when I was looking at a book title, and whose comment sparked the title for this book. He's always such a good source of advice.

And to my buddy Geoffrey Wakeling, who was the first person to ever read this story as my beta reader, and who had a major man-crush on Anthony as a result—thanks for your support and unwavering confidence in me and this book.

And to the various people who helped me with the Italian translations and the workings of the London Police Department—a great thanks to you too.

LOVE AND PUNISHMENT

Susan Mac Nicol

Table of Contents

Chapter 1

By the time he reads this, you'll be mine. Inside and out.

The words loomed eerily off the page as Flynn Parker re-read the message on the cream-coloured notepaper. It was seven p.m. on a chilly February evening. He'd gotten back into his basement flat in Chelsea after a sweaty and energetic game of squash at the gym. All he wanted to do was have a warm shower then wait for his boyfriend, Anthony, to arrive for a drink. They'd been together six months now and Flynn already knew he was in for the long haul. He had a fervent hope for tonight: that hot, raunchy animal sex would be on the menu and Anthony wouldn't be too tired to participate. Flynn needed to alleviate some of the tension that still racked his body from the gym and the tough day he'd had at the newspaper with deadlines and angry interviewees. He hadn't anticipated the official-looking cream envelope lying in wait in his hallway—an envelope that had obviously been slipped under the door. He frowned.

Who the hell would send me something like this slipped under the bloody door? It's so damn cloak and dagger.

As an investigative crime journalist for a mid-sized independent newspaper, he was used to the weird things that life had to offer. He felt a frisson of unease trickle down his spine as he laid the note down on the kitchen top. As he busied himself making coffee, absorbed in the task, some small shadow to his left made him turn in curiosity. Something cold and acidic was pressed against his face. He struggled as he tried to take in air, but only gulped in the noxious fumes of whatever was being pressed against his nose. It happened so quickly that he had time only for a fleeting moment of terror before everything went dark.

He awoke in blackness. His head felt stuffed with cotton wool. He could see nothing, feeling only the crinkle of something silky lying across his eyes.

I must be blindfolded. At least I hope to shit that's what it is and I haven't actually gone blind.

When he tried to move, he realised he was flat on his back on a rough, yielding but scratchy surface. He was cold, his skin prickling with goose bumps as cold air lapped at his body. He didn't even want to *think* about what that might mean. His arms were stretched above his head, bound to something he couldn't see. Flynn's mouth was dry, his throat scratchy and sore as he called out.

"Hello?"

The room was silent, though he sensed someone watching him. Flynn's breathing deepened as he listened for a sound, any sound. He started as a hand brushed against his bristled cheek, a soft and loving caress. He felt a swell of fear then panic at the unseen person. Flynn didn't mind being taken control of, but only by one person. This wasn't him.

The voice, when it spoke, was almost lazy, hypnotic in its tones, almost mocking. "So Flynn, you wanted to talk to me. I suppose this is a game of sorts, just not the one you were hoping for. I know you and your detective lover like to play blindfold and bondage games. I've seen you at it."

It was a man's voice, amused and chilling. Flynn felt sudden despair grip him. Not only at the fact that this person knew them both and that he and Anthony had been watched in their most intimate acts, but at the sheer confidence in his captor's voice. He took a deep breath. Perhaps he could talk himself out of this situation.

Being exposed to monsters and interviewing them on a regular basis on his crime beat had definitely hardened him. He also thought he'd developed some really good negotiation skills.

"What do you want with me? Do I know you?"

The person moved closer. A gentle hand caressed his torso, lingering on his stomach. "You look beautiful naked, do you know that? You have the body of an athlete, all broad shoulders and slim hips. Must be all that calisthenics you do with your boyfriend."

Flynn swallowed with difficulty as his throat tightened at that confirmation that he was indeed nude. He shivered in disgust as a warm, wet tongue slowly licked at the wolf tattoo he had on his left pectoral muscle.

"You may know me, somewhere deep down inside, how would you know? You can't see me, you can't touch me…" The voice trailed off as the figure traced his fingers across Flynn's groin, brushing his flaccid dick and wiry curls. The fingers squeezed his prick gently. Flynn closed his eyes in mortification at the fact that this stranger was touching him so intimately.

"I bet he loves what you have inside your trousers, doesn't he? I know I would. Does he appreciate you, I wonder, like I would? Suck you and fuck you like I would?"

Bile rose in Flynn's throat as he realised that perhaps this wasn't just a simply mistaken identity or garden variety kidnapping. He tried to move his lower body away from the exploring fingers and moaned in pain as savage fingers gripped his balls tightly, digging in and sending a jolt of pain down his spine.

"Stay still when I touch you, Flynnie baby." The voice was rough, husky. "Or else I'll send you back to Anthony minus what he seems to enjoy."

The thought of this person making good on his threat made Flynn lie still, as his breathing got sharper with fear. The man stopped his exploration and bent down to whisper in Flynn's ear. Male cologne assailed his nostrils.

"Neither of you ever look behind you, do you? All that time, you never looked behind you. I was there, watching you both, seeing the sweat on both your bodies all those times you fucked each other and you didn't think anyone was watching. So confident you were all alone. Dirty boys, both of you."

Flynn cried out as the speaker bit down viciously on his ear lobe then bit again further up the ear. The pain was agonising. The metallic tang of blood scented the air.

"What the fuck is it that you want? Tell me." Flynn gritted his teeth, eyes smarting with pain, frustration and shame.

The figure chuckled. "It's too late for that, sexy. You got your wish. Are you sure you still don't who I am?"

Flynn swallowed.

It couldn't be him, could it? The man they called the Bow Tie Killer?

If that was true, he knew he was in great danger. He'd heard from Anthony what had happened to BTK's other victims.

"I see the penny dropping, along with your jaw. Yes, it's me. The Bow Tie Killer. BTK." The voice grew angry. "Who the fuck comes up with these asinine names anyway? They make me sound like some sort of sandwich, like a fucking BLT."

The voice was mocking. "Just because I like to tie people up whilst I fuck them? That makes me some sort of scary monster?"

Flynn felt despair in his heart. "No, it's because you slit their throats when you've finished with them and tie a scarf around their necks. And yes, I wanted to talk to you. To see what your story was, find out what makes you tick. I saw the letters you sent to the police."

Inside Flynn was silently screaming. He had never been so fucking scared in his life. Not even when he'd been a young rookie reporter many years ago, and a twelve-year-old boy from one of the London gangs had pointed a loaded revolver at him and threatened to blow his head off. He closed his eyes and tried to calm his inner self, marvelling at the fact he was having a fairly coherent conversation with a known killer.

The man the press called the Bow Tie Killer, or BTK, was the man Anthony Parglietto, Flynn's lover and a Detective Inspector with the CID had been hunting for the past six weeks. The first murder victim, Katherine Dodd, a nurse at the local hospital, had been discovered in a secluded area of Hampstead Heath, raped, her clothing slashed and her throat slit. Her hands and feet were tied together with black silk ties and around her neck. Hiding the terrible gaping wound of her slashed throat, the killer had gloatingly tied a cheap silky black and white spotted scarf, fashioned like a bow tie.

Four weeks ago, the killer had struck again. Roger Treave, a school teacher from a local secondary school, had been found on Parkland Walk in Haringey. He'd gotten the same terrible injuries, the same bindings and a similar bow tie around his neck. This killer definitely didn't have a preference when it came to gender, something Flynn knew Anthony hoped would narrow down his search somewhat.

The figure moved closer and Flynn felt the trail of something soft and silky across his stomach. The hands moved caressingly across his hips as the voice spoke musingly.

"You said on TV you wanted to talk to me. I've granted you your wish."

Flynn felt sick and in hindsight he wished he'd never made that throwaway comment on air. Anthony had been incensed when he'd seen it on the news report. He'd growled that Flynn was playing right into the killer's hands by encouraging him. It looked like he'd been right.

"I said that, yes. I wanted to write your story first hand. Maybe we can talk—"

The man laughed harshly. "I'll tell my story when I'm ready." He moved around to the other side of Flynn and trailed his fingers again down his stomach.

"If you like, we can go one step further. I'll let you experience it all first hand. First I'll fuck you, and then I'll kill you. Of course that would mean no story." His voice was cutting. "I'll watch that light drain out of your eyes, and see blood spew out of you like a regular chocolate fountain at a wedding. Who the hell has one of those things at a wedding anyway? It's tacky and cheap. Champagne's a much better idea."

Flynn felt his breath deepen in fear.

What in fuck's sake was he supposed to say to that?

When he spoke, he was surprised his voice was so steady. Inside him, the turmoil threatened to make him sick. "Then the world wouldn't know who you are. Wouldn't get to talk to you." He took a deep breath, trying to quell the fear. "You need me to do that."

The voice laughed harshly. "I can do all that without *you*, sexy. There's a myriad of you nosy reporters out there just gagging to talk to me. You all gag for it. But I did like your interview style and you're a real looker. Plus Anthony seems very fond of you."

There was a moment of quiet then the voice spoke musingly. "No, I think I'll just kill you. Once I've had you, of course. You have a really nice body. All that squash and gym and bedroom calisthenics with your tame detective really keeps you in shape. I'm going to enjoy this."

Flynn heard the sound of a zip being undone and tried desperately to free his hands, his wrists chafing at the bonds.

The voice chuckled again. "You won't get free so don't bother trying. Just lie back and enjoy it. I'm quite the lover, so I promise you won't be disappointed. You should be used to this situation anyway, given with what you get up to with Anthony. And the beauty of it is you don't even have to do anything; I'll do all the work. But feel free to writhe a little. It'll make it that much more satisfying for me."

Flynn's fear intensified as the voice carried on gloatingly. His mind tried desperately to think of a way out that didn't involve being raped and butchered.

"Yes, I know a lot about the great Detective Parglietto, your little bit of Italian rough. I suppose in his way he's fairly attractive, if you like tall, dark and brooding. And of course, he's looking for me, isn't he? He's a real tenacious bastard. I admire that trait, even if he does want to rip my heart out for what I'm doing in his city."

The man ran run his hands up the inside of Flynn's legs, caressing his balls. A hot wave of shame flooded Flynn's body as he wriggled in vain to escape the greedy hands.

"You motherfucker," he shouted in anger and terror. "Why not let me free and we can do this like real men? Give me a chance to at least fight back, you bloody coward."

The man chuckled. "Now, now, Flynn. Where's the fun in that?"

A hot mouth surrounded his nipple. Fingers slid inside his arse, rough and cruel, and Flynn cried out in pain, all reason and thoughts of courage gone.

"God," he groaned, hating the pleading sound of his voice, "Please don't do this."

"Anthony does this to you." The voice was flat as the man continued his assault on Flynn's channel, and a hand gripped Flynn's cock and stroked it roughly. To his overwhelming desolation, Flynn's cock was already semi-erect with the attention it was being given and he hated himself for responding.

This was nothing like Anthony's tender gestures and caresses. This was hard, rough and made him feel dirty and used. His legs were spread-eagled and tied, and he could do nothing. Finally the fingers withdrew and the hand was lifted from his cock. Strong hands lifted Flynn's hips. Something that felt like a pillow was slid beneath his buttocks.

"It makes it a little easier to get inside you this way when you're all hog tied down like this. More on offer, so to speak. A little easier access to the 'dominion of pleasure.' Do you like that description? I used it in a dissertation once and everyone was very impressed. They said it was sheer poetry." The voice grew angry. "Stupid fuckers. They had no idea about anything." He laughed. "Are you ready? I promise I won't be gentle, I know you like it rough. I'll take the ropes off your ankles to make it easier, as long as you promise not to try to kick me with them. Deal?" The voice was gloating.

Flynn nodded. He had every intention of kicking out however he could to try and defend himself, to strike back at this psycho tormenting him. He already knew begging wouldn't help; it would only serve to give this bastard more satisfaction.

Perhaps I'll land a lucky blow and knock the fucker out.

He waited with a heart soaked in fear, his throat dry. Minutes went by and Flynn wondered why the other man hadn't done anything yet, even as he was grateful for his captor's inaction. Then the voice gave a chuckle.

"God, this is fun. I'm just kidding, Flynn. I have no intention of doing anything to you. Not this time. I just wanted to play a little game of my own."

Flynn's relief was short lived as fear struck again that the guy was just playing with him. "You fucking bastard."

The man giggled, a chilling sound. "Careful, Flynn. That sounds like an invitation. And I know who my parents were."

Flynn clamped his mouth shut.

The voice continued lazily. "I like to see the fear in people's faces. I quite like you. It's why I haven't hurt you as much as I could. And you're right. You *are* going to tell my story. Exactly the way I want it told, and when. I want the great Parglietto to know I could have shoved something inside you, my cock or one of those dildos you both like so much. I could have even slit your throat. It'll take that arrogant bastard down a peg or two." The voice grew even more vicious. "I saw the ceremony on television a few months ago where he graciously accepted his Professional Contribution award for 'outstanding achievements and contributions to the world of policing.' He stood up there all noble and I wanted to knock his teeth down his throat. He has no fucking idea what that did to me."

His captor moved around to Flynn's side. "I'm going to put you to sleep now. Then I'll take you home. I'm sure that by now your policeman lover will have found the note I left at your apartment. He was due over there tonight, wasn't he? He'll be bloody frantic by this time."

The voice sounded viciously satisfied. "I left a little present for him there too, so he knew something bad was going to happen to you. I wanted to shake that smugness off his rugged face." The figure pressed the same foul-smelling stuff he'd used in the apartment over Flynn's nose.

"Good night. I'll be in touch soon. Keep an eye out for me."
Flynn fell down into a spiral of blessed darkness.

Chapter 2

Detective Inspector Anthony Parglietto strode around the kitchen in Flynn's home. He ran a large, tanned hand through mid-length, curly black hair as he growled into his mobile phone.

"Jesus, Rupert, I've told you already! He's fucking gone, and all I have is this bloody cryptic note signed BTK, and we all fucking know who that is. Yes, *that* one. I've just sent a picture of Flynn off to your phone. His satchel is still here, the front door was open—that's not like him at all. He's normally ultra-cautious. You know how bloody paranoid he is."

Anthony looked down at the note on the kitchen table, pinned there by a full tomato sauce bottle, a condiment he knew Flynn refused to have in his kitchen. Anthony had never even been able to get him to buy it for his own bloody fish and chips, for God's sake, so the bottle must mean something.

As he'd arrived at Flynn's basement flat off the street around eleven-thirty p.m., Anthony had seen the open front door. He'd made his way inside. Flynn's old, beaten satchel in which he stored all manner of things was sitting on the kitchen counter, with his mobile in it. His laptop bag was at the side of the kitchen table. Flynn's house keys were on the tabletop. The note had been sitting on the table and Anthony had glanced at it, thinking Flynn had to dash out quickly and left him a note. The handwritten words on the cream note paper had frozen his blood.

Anthony. I have your little fuck buddy. I'll send him back once I'm finished with him, but he might not be in the same mint condition. Sorry about that. You might just have to have sloppy seconds tonight. Your buddy, BTK.

He'd not touched the note, just called the station and told them to get the Scene of Crime team down here fucking quickly, midnight or not. Once he'd hung up, he'd had time to process the chilling words, fearing what they meant. Then he'd found another note, addressed to Flynn on the same cream-coloured notepaper, lying on the floor by the sink.

By the time he reads this, you'll be mine. Inside and out.

The two bits of paper had sent Anthony spinning into a spiral of frustration and fear. He stood now in agonised helplessness, his broad-shouldered figure gazing out into the darkness beyond. Anthony Parglietto was forty-two years old, six-foot-four and muscled like a boxer, with an explosive Italian temper just like his mother's.

The Criminal Investigation Department—the Homicide and Serious Crime unit, in fact—had been his home now for the past nine years. He grimaced as he gazed out of the window. All he could think about now was that the monster he was hunting had Flynn in his clutches. Flynn of the cheeky smile and pale blue icy eyes and a nose for trouble—both causing it and getting into it.

He strode impatiently to the front door and peered out into the street above. It was quiet. Still no SOC team. SOC were usually quick to get to the crime scene but Anthony had no time to wait when Flynn was in mortal danger. Street lights flickered and ebbed undecidedly. Anthony muttered an expletive as he stalked back into the kitchen, tapping his fingers impatiently against his thigh. Close to ten minutes later, he heard the sound of a commotion outside. He walked impatiently over to the door, once again looking up into the street. The detective saw the fat, waddling form of Joe MacGrew, dressed in his white pull-on suit, and his assistant, Maddy Glover, exit their van. Anthony double-timed to the top of the stairs and waved his arms at the pair. They looked at him and Joe nodded. The couple approached, both looking tired and bleary eyed.

Joe clapped a hand on Anthony's shoulder as he walked down the stairs and past him into the flat. "Anthony, don't worry. We'll find him. The rest of the team are on their way."

Joe walked past Anthony and into the kitchen and looked around, shrewd eyes assessing the situation.

Despite his dread, Anthony felt reassured. Joe and Maddy were among the best at what they did and they'd find something. They had to.

"Is this the note?" Joe asked quietly. He took a swift look around the room, keen eyes noting the layout and no doubt documenting the tableau set before him. "Have you taken a look around yourself? Find anything you want to tell me about?"

Anthony nodded. "Just the notes and the sauce bottle. It doesn't belong to Flynn. He won't have it in the house. And there's another note too. I found it on the floor." He frowned at Joe's look. "Don't worry. I picked it up with a piece of cling wrap. My prints aren't on it. I'm not a fool, Joe. I've been doing this for a while."

He watched as Joe and Maddy did what they did best, all the time feeling a sense of complete helplessness that he could do nothing useful himself yet. Joe laid his kit out on the kitchen table as Maddy picked up the tomato sauce bottle in her gloved hands, examining the bottle.

"It's not a new one. It's been refilled from the looks of it." She twisted the cap, lifting the bottle to her nose. Her face paled as she looked at Joe grimly.

"This is blood."

She dipped a cotton bud in the substance and took out her little spray bottle of luminol. Anthony watched in trepidation as the bud turned a greenish blue. He knew all too well what that meant. He paled, bile welling up in his throat that he swallowed, feeling its acidic sting as it went down.

"Jesus Christ. Human blood?"

She shook her head, her face grave. "I won't know until we get it back to the lab for microscopic analysis. But even if it is, that doesn't mean it's Flynn's. You need to keep calm."

But her voice sounded uncertain. Anthony passed a shaking hand over his eyes. It was one thing investigating a crime when someone you didn't know was involved, but it was another altogether when the victim was someone you loved. He watched as the two investigators moved around the kitchen purposefully. Anthony felt useless at his inactivity and looked blindly out into the back garden, his helplessness choking him. Ten minutes passed as he paced up and down the flat, with Joe swearing rudely under his breath when Anthony got in his way. Joe was especially annoyed that his team hadn't arrived yet. Apparently there'd been a traffic accident and they were held up.

Anthony scowled and backed off. He knew he'd hate anyone getting in the way of him doing his job. Finally he gave up watching in sheer frustration and stood there, knuckles white as he leaned on the sink, gazing at the blank wall. His back was tense and his stomach churned with fear. He heard low murmurs as Joe and Maddy talked to each other. Suddenly he heard someone call his name from outside.

"Anthony?"

He turned in sheer relief, his heart jumping on hearing Flynn's voice. His look of welcome at Flynn's return faded into shock and fear as he saw the pale and drawn face of the man he loved at the entrance to his home. Flynn's clothes were dishevelled and stained with grass. Anthony noticed idly that the buttons were done up all askew. Flynn's dark blond hair was matted with sweat, and clung to his pale cheeks like strands of hay from a bale. Blood crusted his left ear and cheek. But it was Flynn's eyes that haunted Anthony the most. The deep blue sparkle he loved so much had gone, leaving nothing but dark, empty holes in his face. He moved over to Flynn swiftly, seeing Maddy and Joe's horrified glances. He caught Flynn's lean form as he fell to the floor. His eyelids fluttered.

Anthony knelt down beside his lover. "Christ, what has that bastard done to you?" His voice was anguished and he pulled Flynn to him, folding his arms around him protectively as he leaned into him. Anthony's voice was rough with anger. "Call an ambulance, Maddy. Get them here ASAP. He needs a checkup."

Maddy nodded, her eyes wide, and disappeared to make the call. Joe waddled over, his brown eyes full of concern for the man who lay in Anthony's arms, his body shaking and cold.

"He said he was the Bow Tie Killer," Flynn whispered, his voice flat. "He said he was going to kill me." His eyes were unfocused and his speech was slurred. Anthony had a suspicion he'd been drugged. His heart exploded in fear as he held Flynn tighter and fury threatened to choke him.

Joe grasped his shoulder, a firm grip that was both a warning and a comfort. "Tony, stay with him whilst the ambulance comes, son. Maddy and I will finish processing this crime scene."

Anthony knew Joe was only about three years older than him and the endearment threw him. His eyes prickled and he fiercely blinked back the tears that threatened to come. He couldn't show his emotions now, not with Flynn lying limp and shaken in his arms and a psychopath to catch.

"Baby, it'll be all right, *amore mio*. The ambulance will be here soon. Just hold on," he murmured as Flynn shivered in his arms. His shirt was torn, with buttons missing.

"He tied me down," Flynn whispered brokenly. "He told me he was going to rape me then kill me. He stuck his fingers inside me."

"Jesus, babe." The tears that Anthony had been holding back came to the surface at Flynn's obvious distress. He wiped his hands across his eyes quickly.

"But he didn't. When he finished playing his game, he told me he was taking me home," Flynn said softly. Anthony felt sick at his matter-of-fact words. "He drugged me and he must have dressed me because I was naked when I was with him. The next thing I knew I was in the field down the road, laying on the grass. I managed to get up and come home. I just wanted to get home to you." His voice broke.

Anthony held him close and wished with all his heart that he could squeeze BTK's throat being tightly beneath his fingers.

Chapter 3

Flynn lay on the hospital bed at the University College London Hospital, stiff white sheets covering up the ignominy of having to wear a blue hospital gown with his arse gaping out the back. Anthony sat beside him on the hospital chair. Much to Flynn's disgust, Anthony and the doctors had insisted he be swabbed and inspected for any trace evidence his violator may have left behind. Flynn hated it, but he'd gritted his teeth and let them get on with it. His ego was shaken, his chest tight with embarrassment and he'd been glad when they'd taken their swabs and instruments away and left him alone to well in his shame. They'd also taken photographs of his bitten ear.

He'd given his statement to two sharp-eyed, world-weary policemen and he was exhausted. The fact that he hadn't even seen the man who'd taken him had made the police sigh in disappointment. Anthony's watchful eyes had been on him for every word he spoke but he hadn't said a word during the interview.

Flynn watched Anthony as he sat with his hands between his legs, looking down at the floor. He looked far too big for the chair, Flynn thought inconsequentially. His shoulders were hunched over and his long legs looked uncomfortably contorted. The crown of his head, that thick spot of jet-black hair that Flynn loved to run his hands through, was shot through with strands of silver. Anthony's normally olive complexion was paler than usual and there was a nervous tic in his jaw as he clenched it. Anthony must have felt Flynn's gaze as he looked up at him, his eyes anxious. Flynn quickly averted his stare.

"Don't *do* that," Anthony said quietly, regarding him with a narrowing of his hazel eyes.

"Do what?" Flynn muttered, knowing full well what he was referring to.

"Look away. Why can't you look at me?"

"It's nothing," Flynn said hoarsely as he picked at the covers with nervous fingers.

But Flynn knew what his lover meant. Anthony had been with enough victims in his twenty-plus years on the force to know when one of them felt ashamed at being unable to do anything against their abuser or captor. Flynn was by nature not a self-pitying person and had a very strong character. It could have been much worse and he could be one of the victims currently lying in the morgue. He could have been raped, for God's sake, something that still made him want to hurl. But he still didn't want Anthony to see his face and look deep into his eyes, knowing that he'd see a man who hadn't been able to protect himself.

"Do you want to see a trauma counsellor?" Anthony's face was set as if he knew what his answer would be.

Flynn shook his head. "No, I don't. I need to deal with it myself."

"Flynn," Anthony began.

Flynn cut him off with a wave of his hand. "I know you mean well but just don't. Please."

His voice sounded steady but inside rising hysteria threatened to bubble over if he concentrated too deeply on what he'd been through or what he'd managed to escape from. *Best to suppress it. Bury it so deep that it never saw the light of day. Isn't that when men do?*

"Then look me in the eyes and tell me that." Anthony's voice was resolute. "Look at me. I'm still here for you if you need me. So if you're feeling all gung ho, then at least fucking look at me."

Flynn heard the tone of desperation in Anthony's voice. Slowly he raised his eyes to those of the man who sat fidgeting beside him. He expected to see a reprimand in them, a disappointment for not fighting harder, for not being a victim. But all he saw were Anthony's concerned and loving strangely coloured green-brown eyes, the same ones he'd looked into when they were making love or sharing an ice cream popsicle at the beach. Anthony nodded slightly and seemed to relax. Flynn dropped his glance and looked over at the door as the nurse entered.

"We're all done, Mr. Parker," she said softly. "We have everything we need from you. If you'll just sign this discharge form, you can go home. I assume you have someone to go with?"

She glanced at Anthony who nodded. "I have a car waiting," he said. He threw a stern glance at the nurse. "The powers that be have told you that this isn't public knowledge, haven't they? We don't want this getting out into the press."

The nurse nodded as she watched Flynn sign the release form. "Yes, I've been formally threatened with the thumbscrews." Her voice was dry. "I'm glad he has someone. No one should have to go through what he's been through and go home alone. That killer out there is a bloody psychopath."

She briefly brushed Flynn's shoulder with a comforting hand and disappeared out of the room. Flynn swung his legs off the bed and stood up. Anthony moved to help him. He was going to refuse then relented in fatigue. He was just too fucking tired to be all prickly and independent.

"I'm all right. I just want to get home and have a long hot shower. I need to feel clean again. Then I want to crawl into bed and just sleep."

Anthony looked across quickly and Flynn knew he was wondering whether he'd been included in the plans or whether Flynn was going to turf him out the minute he got to his home.

Flynn reached out and caressed his cheek softly. "I want you to stay. I'm not going to go all, 'don't be with me,' and push you away. I don't want to be alone tonight."

Anthony's face cleared in relief. Flynn closed his eyes, swaying a little on his feet. It was nearly three-thirty in the morning and he was bone tired. The bite wound had been cleaned and dressed and he'd had a tetanus shot.

They left the hospital and walked over to a parked police car in the road outside. Anthony nodded a hello to the driver of the police car and climbed in the back beside Flynn. The police driver nodded back and the car started and drove away. Anthony reached out a large, warm hand and squeezed Flynn's gently.

"I'll be fine," Flynn murmured. "I was lucky to get away with my life if it was the real BTK killer."

Anthony put warm arms around him. "You've been through hell. You've given your statement despite me saying it could wait until tomorrow." He scowled fiercely. "Now you need a good night's sleep. Then in the morning we'll get you some police protection."

Flynn moved and looked up at him, his heart lurching
Am I that damned pathetic that I need a bodyguard?
"I don't need anything like that," he said mutinously.

Anthony waved his expressive hands in agitation. "Christ, you didn't think I was going to let you have no protection, did you? This is the goddamn Bow Tie Killer we're talking about here, not some petty criminal. This is a man who's already murdered two people and could have easily made it a third. He took you from me and that's not going to happen again, by God."

His body trembled with suppressed violence and Flynn knew better than to argue with him when his hot Italian blood was up. He sighed heavily.

Anthony's voice was firm when he next spoke. "Then tomorrow you're coming to stay with me for a while. My place has better security than yours." Anthony had a large one-bedroom apartment in Finsbury. His building had security, and key cards for the lift.

"We'll get your clothes and your laptop in the morning and then you can move in with me for a little while so I can keep an eye on you."

Flynn wanted to play the macho card and tell Anthony he could look after himself. But if truth be told, he wanted nothing more than having company somewhere that wasn't home, where someone had managed to sneak in. So instead he leaned into Anthony's warm, muscular body with quiet assent. He laid his head against a broad chest and slid his hands under Anthony's jacket, smelling the Lacoste aftershave he wore.

"Fine," he said, wanting to hibernate like a bear and not wake up until it was all over. "I don't feel like arguing with you tonight."

Anthony's chest rumbled as he replied. "You've got your own amazingly sexy Italian stud and you might as well make use of him on his home turf."

Flynn knew he was trying to distract him and for a moment, things seemed almost normal and he could forget he'd been kidnapped and tormented by a psychopath who was still on the loose.

Chapter 4

Anthony stood in the cold early morning darkness of Valentine's Day and looked down at the body sprawled before his feet. He pulled his windbreaker closer around his body as he shivered, both in cold and in disgust. The woman lying before him, eyes open, and mostly naked, having only a pair of bloody blue silk panties on, had dark red hair which was spread across the cold ground like dying flames. Her lower jaw was smashed and bloody, her hands bound in front of her with thin blue rope and her ankles tied. Around her neck, soaked in dry crusting blood, was tied a flamboyant black-and-white silk bow tie. In the distance he saw his partner, Sergeant Rupert Gregg, interviewing some of the crowd around the scene.

The detective turned as a grim-faced Graham Manning strode up beside him, his long greatcoat flapping as he walked. The pathologist from University College London Hospital—known as UCLH—did not look happy. That could have been because it was three o'clock in the morning. It could also have been that the man was getting sick of having people's bodies turning up, savaged and abused, on a regular basis. The tarmac parking area around the industrial neighbourhood was quiet and deserted except for the officers on the scene, busy taping it off to some curious vagrants who were anxious to see what was happening.

"Tony, this is another fucking Bow Tie kill?" The older man's voice was rough with anger. "Christ, he didn't waste any time, did he? It's only been five days since he took Flynn and his last killing was three weeks ago. This animal has no pattern. He just seems to do things as they take his fancy. Even his dump sites and his victimology vary like the blazes." He frowned. "And this one still has panties on. The others were totally naked. That's different as well." He knelt down beside the dead woman. "No doubt about cause of death," he muttered. "Her throat's slit, just like the others. Much more viciously too, her bloody head's almost severed. Poor girl. Do we know who she is yet?"

Anthony nodded as he gazed blankly at the corpse. "Her name is Christine Donovan. Twenty-seven years old, according to her National Insurance card. The team's running down last sights, finding out where she lived so they can tell next of kin." His face was grim. "I think this one was intended as a Valentine's present to us. This person has a fucking sick sense of humour."

Graham looked at his set face. "I'd tend to agree. It's his style."

Anthony watched as the pathologist gently turned the woman over. He heard Graham hiss loudly and leaned down in curiosity to see what had caught the man's attention. The detective could see the woman had a large open wound just before the panty line on her lower back.

Graham frowned as he examined it. "Something's been cut out of her. A large piece of skin is missing. About three inches across by an inch. I'd hazard a guess it was a tattoo. It's a popular spot for someone to have one."

Anthony was puzzled. "Why the hell would he remove a tattoo? Generally that would only be to keep us from identifying someone, yet he left her wallet and NI card here. That doesn't make sense."

He watched as the pathologist carefully rolled the woman onto her back and peeled the panties down over her hips. Both of them exclaimed in disgust and disbelief at the same time.

"Jesus Christ!" Graham recoiled in disgust at what had been hidden beneath the blood-soaked panties. Anthony's nostrils flared in anger at the desecration of the woman's body. The missing tattoo, with its ragged edges, had been inexpertly tacked across the woman's pubic region, covering her pubis and looking like a soiled piece of grey cloth that was trying to hide something immodest. The stitches were child-like, untidy and jagged, looking like a parody of an inexpertly sewn smile on a home- made rag doll.

"*Merda!* This is one sick animal." Anthony spoke through clenched teeth as he regarded the handiwork of the Bow Tie Killer. "What the hell did he hope to gain by doing this? I'd hazard sheer pleasure myself. No real reason." A thought crossed his mind and he felt sick. "Hell, I hope she was already dead when he did this."

Graham was looking at the killer's creative patchwork with some trepidation. "I hope so too, Tony, but I'm not so sure she was. I'll find out more when I do the post mortem." He gently rolled the panties back over the abomination beneath and stood up, grimacing as his knees popped. His face was pale as he looked at the detective.

"He's done something different and sick to each one of them. Katherine was viciously sodomised and Roger was found with a thong stuffed inside him. God, compared to what I think this woman went through before she died, Flynn was lucky to get out alive."

Anthony scowled darkly. "This was no man. This wasn't even an animal. Whoever's doing this is sub-human and doesn't deserve either title."

The pathologist smiled tiredly. "The famous Anthony Parglietto view on humanity and what makes someone human. You have an interesting viewpoint. I heard you and the rest of the crew debating it in the lunch room the other day. It certainly seemed to get a bit heated, especially with Rupert. That man has a fairly high moral compass and he isn't good at seeing the shades of grey in between. It must make for interesting discussions between the two of you, being so different." He stretched and yawned, pulling his coat closer around his body. The wind had picked up and it was chilling to the bone. He looked at Anthony sympathetically.

"How's Flynn anyway? How are you both coping?"

Anthony thanked his lucky stars each day that his work team, colleagues and friends were accepting of him being a gay man on the force. Sure, there had been some teething troubles with a couple of policemen who'd not been happy working with a "fag," but after a few sparring matches and more than a couple of threats from Anthony to rearrange their faces, it had become work as usual. Most of the time everyone was accepting of his sexuality, and if they hadn't been, Anthony couldn't have given a fuck. He wasn't about to get back in a closet and close the door. Anthony had learnt some valuable lessons about being the man he was and to hell with the rest of the world if they didn't like it.

"Flynn is Flynn." Anthony's voice was resigned. "He internalizes everything and tells you he's fine when you know damn well he isn't. He isn't sleeping that well and is pretty nervous still. This fucking monster has made him crazy. Yet he's determined to keep on the story despite what happened to him."

"I don't know how you managed to keep it out of the newspapers but I'm glad you did."

Anthony nodded. "We managed to control the situation." He winced.

"Managed to control the situation." This is my boyfriend's *kidnapping and assault by a psychopathic killer, for God's sake.*

"I've got a man on him, trying to watch out for him. But I won't be able to do it for much longer." He heaved a huge sigh. "God knows what'll happen when they get called off because they no longer think he's in danger. I have a buddy of mine from the SAS. He offered to keep an eye on him afterward but Flynn point blank refused. I'll do it anyway. He's not being given the bloody choice." His voice was fierce.

"Has BTK been in touch with him since he let him go?" Graham's voice was quiet. "I know he said he wanted him to tell his story, it's why he didn't kill Flynn. Is anything going on?"

Anthony frowned. "Not that he's told me. He'd better bloody well tell me if he does."

Privately he wasn't so sure this was the case as Flynn had been very cagey lately with his phone and laptop, and Anthony had noticed that both of them were now password protected. He wasn't sure how to broach the subject with Flynn though. His lover's mood tended to be fairly explosive at the moment. Anthony knew from past experience dealing with trauma victims that shame, guilt and the feeling of being helpless played havoc with the ego—especially for a man.

The pathologist stood up, wincing at the movement. "BTK has been too busy desecrating people, it would seem. We need to get this one back to the lab for a proper post mortem. I'll go get the guys to take her away." He looked at the detective ruefully. "I can't promise when that'll be. I'll try get to it as soon as I can but we're a little backed up at the moment."

Anthony nodded. "Call me when you've managed to finish it. If I haven't heard from you by end of tomorrow, I'll chase you. I really need to find this guy. He's going to do it again, have no doubt. I don't want another dead body on my patch."

Manning nodded. "Was Flynn able to tell you anything about him? Anything that might help you find this sick bastard? How the kidnapper got him out of the flat without anyone seeing?"

Anthony shook his head in frustration. "He could tell me how he smelled, how he sounded, how he felt," his voice deepened in disgust, "But nothing substantial. The sicko blindfolded him." He gazed vacantly across the grey parking lot. "His flat is pretty secluded and below street level. There'd be no problem really for someone to park on the street and get someone into a car, even if it was dead weight. It's a quiet neighbourhood; it was late at night. I think it was just a mix of good planning and the right opportunity to move without being seen. Flynn's offered to have hypnosis with a therapist to see if we can unlock anything hidden away so we're going to try that. But other than that I have sweet fuck all." He sighed. "Other than the fact BTK seems to have a beef with me for whatever reason, from the little conversation Flynn had with him. I've done something in the past to upset him, I think. I've had the team go over all my previous cases trying to get some indication of why he's mad with me." He smiled twistedly. "But it could be any one of the guys I've arrested or even put away. They may have someone on the outside getting revenge."

He scowled. "I wish the bastard would target me directly rather than people I know. But that's not this one's style," he mused thoughtfully. "This one thrives on psychological torture. Fear and power." Anthony stood and gazed down absently at the dead woman at his feet. "Joe's team found nothing of forensic help on the first body. They're still working on number two. Now they can add this one. I'm hoping they'll be able to give me something soon that'll point me in the right direction. He has to have left something behind." Even in his own ears he heard the desperation in his voice.

Graham smiled sympathetically and patted his arm. "You'll get there. You know you have a sixth sense when it comes to these psychopaths. It's a true gift." He grinned faintly. "Your solve rate is the best in the department. Have faith."

Anthony looked down at the dead woman at his feet. "I hope you'll have something to tell me about this bastard, Christine. I promise you I'll find him, eventually. I won't let you down like I did Marco."

His face darkened when he thought of the murder of his brother just over a year ago. His younger brother had only been thirty-three when he'd been butchered and left to die in an alleyway behind a gay sex club. It was the one cold case Anthony wanted more than any to solve.

"You've never gotten any new leads on Marco's killing then, Anthony?" Graham looked at him in sympathy. "You always thought it wasn't just some random gay bash killing that the press made it out to be, didn't you?"

Anthony passed a tired hand over his eyes. "My gut's always told me there was something more to it. There was a conversation we had shortly before he died that made me feel uneasy. But I could never get to the bottom of it. Marco was promiscuous, sure, and we argued about it. But he had the same sixth sense I have for judging people. He was pretty good at telling what people were like. We used to call it, the Parglietto Presence. "He smiled sadly. "But it failed him this time. I helped him come out when he was fourteen, supported him through the bullying at school, and still I couldn't protect him from a sick killer."

He felt the familiar wave of guilt and grief swell through him at Marco's death. His mother and father, Rosa and Domenico, had been devastated at the killing of their youngest son. Soon after Marco's murder they'd moved back to Italy, not wanting to live anymore in the same country that had killed their child. Marco's ashes had left with them, as had Anthony's other brother, Paulo, and sister, Marietta. As the eldest son, with a steady job and a career in the police force, Anthony had elected to stay. He would always remain hopeful that one day he'd find Marco's killer.

Graham reached out and squeezed his arm. "You can't keep everyone safe, Anthony. You're only human, my friend."

Anthony shrugged. "I guess." He glanced over into the distance. "Looks like Rupe needs me. I'll speak to you later, Graham."

He left the pathologist with the body and turned and trudged across the empty parking lot toward his sergeant, Rupert Gregg. They'd been together nearly four months now, ever since Anthony's last long-standing team member had taken up a new position abroad.

Anthony was finding Rupert hard work as he was a man who tended to see things in black or white, right or wrong. Anthony was definitely a middle-of-the-line man at times. But he was trying to make it work. Rupert was very good at what he did, being reliable, diligent and persistent with witnesses, victims and perpetrators alike. Anthony preferred to have a more casual relationship with his sergeants, one where they weren't both too officious and rank conscious, and with Rupert, this seemed to work well.

His sergeant was putting away his leather notebook into the top pocket of his dark grey Paul Costelloe suit. He tended to think of himself as a fashion aficionado and had a great admiration for the clothing label. Rupert himself was lean, swarthy, with close-cropped dark brown hair and a smile that always made Anthony think of a *Friends* episode he'd seen in his early years when Ross had tried to whiten his teeth. The man was a veritable fashion plate with a dazzling grin. The grin was definitely missing now as he looked up at his DI.

"Anthony. No one's bloody seen anything. No car, no van, nothing suspicious. Par for the course. One minute she wasn't there, the next, she was. No one pays any fucking attention to anything in this place. Too busy crawling into their cardboard shacks with their bottle of cheap brandy." His tone was disgusted.

Anthony ran a hand over his tired eyes. "BTK really outdid himself this time. He carved the woman's tattoo out of her back and sewed it onto her pubic region."

Rupert regarded him with an open mouth. "Jesus, that's sick! Why the hell would he do that?"

Anthony shrugged. "With this guy it was probably for fun. He gets off on this sort of stuff." He yawned widely. "God, I'm knackered. I can tell you we need all the help we can get on this one. Graham's going to get her back to the morgue and hopefully we'll have a PM as soon as we can. We need a lead. We can't have another bloody death. The press is already killing us on this one and the DCI is taking a lot of flak, which in turn is going to hit us. We've got to get a break soon."

Rupert shrugged. "The press will give us shit no matter what we do. DCI Winslow is a tough bugger. He'll find a way to make the crap flow downstream to us, I've no doubt. So we can expect to get covered in it at tomorrow morning's briefing." He looked at his boss quizzically. "How's Flynn? Is he coping with the abduction?"

Anthony nodded. "He's shook up but starting to get angrier, which is good. I just try to keep my head below the parapet when he gets a little stressed."

Rupert nodded. "You're a good man. You'll both be fine. You know if either of you need anything, I'll be there for you." He reached out and clasped his superior's shoulder.

Anthony smiled tiredly. "I know. Thanks for that. Come on, let's make a move. I want to get home and crawl into bed. The briefing's at nine so that doesn't leave all that much time for sleep."

Chapter 5

Marshall Cunningham sighed as he let himself into his two-bedroom flat in the centre of Battersea. He laid his car keys down on the small table in the entrance. He closed the door behind him and leaned against it, his eyes closed. He loved getting home. This flat was his refuge from the stresses of dealing with people every day of his life. He'd bought it three years ago because it was in the right area and it was one of the rare few that were serviced, with a concierge and a bevy of cleaning ladies who kept the corridors and his apartment spotless. It was like living in a swanky hotel and he enjoyed the feeling. He paid extra for the privilege though—a lot extra. The only downside was he was fairly close to the service elevator which tended to be quite noisy when in use.

He'd had one of the worst days of his life at UCLH today and he was glad to be home. His job as an orthopaedic surgeon meant he'd seen enough injuries today to write a thesis on the incredibly stupid things people do to themselves. Broken femurs, ankles, and injuries that were mostly sports related, as sports were his specialty. He'd even had one large young man who'd sustained a dislocated elbow playing football and had cried solidly the whole way through being examined. It had been a fairly trying day, he had to admit.

He ran a hand through his thick, unruly auburn hair and sighed. He was looking forward to sitting down with a large gin and little tonic, putting his feet up on the coffee table and perhaps indulging in some relaxation activity later when Blair came over. Marshall grinned as he thought of his hot lover, eight years younger than himself. He still had no idea why the incredibly sexy Blair Malcolme was with him but he thanked God every day for the last two months that he was. Having a hot, younger, dirty-blond-haired man in his life, with the most amazing green eyes he'd ever seen, the body of a hot male model, all muscles and curves and a cock the size of the London Gherkin, was something he could only have dreamed about.

Marshall was already on his second gin and tonic of the evening when his lover arrived, letting himself in with his key. The doctor heard the front door open. He watched as Blair walked into the lounge, his face breaking into a smile when he saw Marshall sitting in his chair.

"Marsh! You're home early." He leaned over the back of the chair, kissing Marshall fiercely from behind, his lips warm and soft. Marshall closed his eyes as his man's tongue slipped into his mouth. The two men stayed entwined together until Blair finally broke free and walked over to pour himself a drink. Marshall watched him avidly, loving the taut round cheeks of Blair's backside, and the way his polo shirt clung to his broad shoulders and accentuated his perfect pecs. The surgeon was already hard in his trousers, his cock pushing against the front of his chinos, the friction almost unbearable. God, this man did things to him he'd never experienced with anyone else before.

"I can feel you looking." Blair turned around slyly. "Do you like what you see?" he asked teasingly.

Marshall grinned. "I love it. I plan on getting up close and personal with all of it later." He saw Blair's quick smile and the narrowing of his eyes as he sat down beside Marshall and took a sip of his vodka tonic, a drink he seemed to thrive on.

Blair looked at him. "Talking of up close and personal, I have an idea I want to shoot past you. It's something I've been thinking about for a while."

Marshall looked at Blair quizzically. "Okay. Tell me about it." He reached out a hand and stroked Blair's cheek gently, feeling himself harden more as he did so. God, this man was sex on legs. Blair had that air about him, an air of insouciance and devil-may-care, interspersed with something just that little bit dangerous and unknown.

Blair reached over, looking knowingly at the bulge in Marshall's trousers and caressed the front of the older man's groin. "I met this really sexy young man at work today. He looks just like Brad Pitt and he's pretty hot." Blair worked at a fairly high-class gym as a personal trainer. He wasn't particularly pumped, as he hated body building, but his body was strong and toned. Marshall frowned, not sure where this was going but not really liking the direction.

"He's really into the whole threesome thing and I wondered, maybe, if we could do something with him." Blair took a large gulp of his drink and Marshall could see his pupils dilate at the idea of the threesome. He was obviously quite turned on by the idea.

"A threesome? Where the hell did that idea come from?" Marshall felt agitated at the thought of having to share Blair with anyone. "I'm not sure I fancy that idea."

"You're a red-blooded gay male. What's not to like about the idea?" Blair's eyes were flat and not as flirty as they'd been earlier. Marshall sighed. His young man hated being thwarted. He was used to getting his own way ninety-nine percent of the time.

"I honestly don't feel comfortable with the idea. Christ, the man's a stranger. We don't know who he is or who he's been with." Marshall shook his head. "I don't think I'd want to do it."

"Come on." Blair wheedled. The doctor could see he was using all his considerable charm to get him to agree. The younger man's oh-so-kissable lips were pouting, actually pouting, and his green eyes were darker than usual. He looked so deliciously decadent with his tousled blond hair that Marshall had to use all of his considerable willpower not to simply bend over and let Blair do him right there. Blair caressed his cheek tenderly.

"It's only a little deviation from the norm and you might enjoy it. I mean, having two hot guys fuck you at the same time? Surely that's a real turn on?"

Marshall shook his head vehemently as he stood up. "Christ, what part do you not understand about? I'm really not into threesomes, even if the other guy does look like bloody Brad Pitt. When will you get it into your thick skull that you alone are enough for me? It makes me feel I'm not enough for *you*, to be honest."

He hated the sulky tone of his voice even as he said the words. He was a forty-year-old surgeon, for God's sake, not some college kid about to blow his first hot guy. Blair's eyes narrowed as he too stood up, his icy glint telling Marshall perhaps he'd struck a nerve as he moved into him like a cat about to pounce on an unsuspecting sparrow. He could see the faint sheen of sweat on Blair's forehead.

"Are you doubting that I like you?" Blair asked softly. Marshall felt the first swell of rising excitement and a little fear as his lover gazed into his eyes, his lips slightly parted and his body still. The younger man had an uncanny knack of making the room feel small and enclosed with his presence.

The surgeon swallowed. "You want another man to be involved in our sexual relationship. What would that say to you if the shoe was on the other foot? Are you bored with me?"

He could see Blair's sultry stare even as he moved closer to Marshall, wrapping his hands around his backside and pulling him closer. Marshall closed his eyes as he felt Blair's erection pressing into his own, feeling faint with his need for this man. He pressed his own cock tighter against Blair's through their clothing, rubbing himself against the other man's slightly as he felt the breath leave his body.

"I could never get bored of you. Have you seen yourself? Those abs, that washboard stomach and that tight ass, not to mention that amazing cock of yours. Always so hard and ready for me, aren't you? I just thought perhaps we could have a little experimental activity. Now I know you're a spoilsport and you don't want to do anything like that, I suppose I won't suggest it again."

Blair trailed his warm lips down the side of Marshall's neck, then back up to his ear, where he slowly stuck his tongue inside. Marshall felt himself growing impossibly big in his chinos. Blair moved against him suggestively, his growing arousal evident. He licked the beads of sweat off Marshall's top lip, sweat that he was sure was forming due to the intense heat he felt building up inside him. He moaned softly as Blair pulled down the zip of his trousers and reached in and grasped him, sliding his hand up the silky length of him. Marshall groaned loudly, his eyes closing in sheer want.

"Unzip me and take me out," Blair whispered into Marshall's ear as his fingers squeezed Marshall none too gently. "Right now. I want you to touch me. Then I'm going to bend you over and fuck you—hard. I want to come inside you."

Marshall needed no urging. His hands fumbled at Blair's jeans, the tight, ass-hugging jeans that were his stock in trade, and he gasped when he found the younger man had no underwear on. He wrapped his hand around Blair's impressive erection, one of the many other reasons Marshall desired this man, and stroked him gently, hearing Blair's hiss of pleasure at his touch. Their lips met greedily, tongues meeting teeth, voraciously devouring each other's mouths. Marshall moved his arm and ran one hand down Blair's arm, feeling something bulky beneath the sleeve. He heard the younger man hiss in pain. He stopped his exploration of Blair's mouth and pulled away, frowning, still holding onto the man's cock.

"Blair? What's underneath your shirt? I feel a bandage or something. Have you been hurt?"

His lover regarded him with smoky eyes. His lips were wet from their kisses and his eyes were unfocused. "I got bitten by a dog. Some idiot let their bull terrier run loose whilst I was lying down on the grass in the park at lunchtime. Damn animal took a nip out of me. Don't worry. I went to have a tetanus shot. I was going to ask if you could write me up some antibiotics, just to make sure. I'll be fine. Now come here. I haven't finished with you yet. I need to taste you some more. A lot more."

He roughly grasped the other man's face and thrust his tongue once more into Marshall's mouth, his lips voracious. Blair's hands slid round Marshall's waist, pulling him closer, groaning as the other man dry humped himself against his hips, their cocks pushing into each other. Finally Blair pulled away, leaving Marshall bereft.

Blair's eyes were dark, his breath coming in deep gasps as he roughly pulled Marshall's trousers and boxers down to his ankles. He motioned for him to step out of them and pushed Marshall onto his knees in front of the high-seated couch.

"Bend over." Blair commanded hoarsely as he reached into his jeans pocket and took out the small tube of lubricant he always carried with him. He slid his trousers off and slid his hand up and down his cock slowly, his face filled with sheer satisfaction at his self caresses. Marshall did as he was told, kneeling down on the floor and placing his upper body on the wide canvas couch, his arms either side of him. He felt cool air on his bare arse, which was now stuck up in the air, waiting for Blair to take it. He felt his lover move in behind him and apply the lubricant to his crack, and Marshall shivered in pleasure as the man lightly inserted his finger while he did so then caressed his balls softly.

Blair was a great advocate of an online homosexual manga Kama sutra website. He found a lot of inspiration there for his very creative ways to propose new sex positions. It was another thing Marshall loved about him—his creativity and exuberance, although sometimes it did go a little far. At times he was almost a little scared of his lover and his intense and, to be fair, mostly dictatorial behaviour in anything he did. Blair didn't like being challenged and could be fairly vindictive when he wanted to be. Marshall had found a small part of himself that he hadn't thought existed—the part that went out of his way to irritate Blair so that the younger man could punish him in some fashion. He supposed it was some sort of masochistic streak in him but he did love it when Blair got forceful and a little out of hand. The man was very inventive in his revenge. Marshall sensed Blair standing behind him and he closed his eyes in anticipation.

"Ready for a good rogering?" the younger man whispered as he positioned himself behind his lover. Marshall heard the rustle of a condom packet as Blair opened it. "I feel like going in rough, deep and fast, so you'd better be prepared. If you're not going to let me have another man screw you whilst I fuck your mouth, then you'll have to take the consequences. I was really looking forward to that threesome and I intend making you pay for that refusal. But you knew that, didn't you, and still you refused me. What does that say about you?"

Marshall heard Blair's soft and not-altogether-pleasant chuckle as he set about punishing him for not agreeing to his anticipated threesome. All Marshall could do was bury his face in the couch and wait for both his pleasure and his pain to be over.

Chapter 6

Flynn sank down onto the couch, his glass of Chardonnay clasped in one hand. He leaned back against the soft cushions with a sigh as he sipped the wine, rolling the liquid around his mouth. He listened to the soft strains of Anthony's favourite John Coltrane album, *Coltrane's Sound*. The soothing sounds of the sax and bass filled his ears, calming his troubled spirit. His mobile rang. He smiled when he saw who it was.

"Kieran? Hi. How are you?"

Kieran Weslake was Flynn's ex-lover. They'd been together for eight months before Flynn had broken up with him six months ago when he'd met Anthony. He and Kieran had been more friends with benefits than the hot, scorching sexual relationship he and Anthony had. He been sick with dread the day he'd planned what he had to say to break it off and move out of the house they'd shared.

Kieran was a good man, a gentle man worth loving. But Flynn needed more than that. He needed Anthony Parglietto and his passion, his overwhelming desire. He needed his strength, his sheer sexiness and the fact that he made love to Flynn like no one ever had.

The soft tones of Kieran's voice echoed down the line. "I'm fine, thanks. I called to let you know there's still mail here for you. The postman still hasn't gotten used to the fact you don't live here anymore despite me telling him every chance I get." His tone was wry.

Flynn laughed. "That postie was never the sharpest tool in the shed. Thanks for letting me know. Next time I'm out your way I'll pop in and pick it up."

Not for the first time he felt relieved they'd managed to stay friends. No longer close but at least civil to one another.

"Good. Otherwise, how have you been? How is Anthony and his case?" Kieran's voice was wary. Flynn knew he blamed Anthony for the breakup, even though it took two of them to do the horizontal—or vertical—tango.

Flynn took a deep breath. He didn't like lying to him. "I'm fine. The case is driving Anthony mad as you can imagine. He gets impatient and frustrated at not getting closer yet to catching this sick bastard." His voice faltered slightly.

"He seems very single minded. I'm sure he'll catch him soon." There was silence. Flynn tried to deflect him away from asking anything else about the case. He wasn't sure he could talk about it and not show what he was feeling in his voice. "How are you doing, Kieran? Are you still travelling so much all over the world?"

Kieran sighed. "I'm afraid so. The hotel industry is growing and there's new ones going up all the time." Kieran worked for a hotel chain and was sent all over the globe to project-manage new builds and renovations. "I'm off to Turkey next week. No rest for the wicked."

"Well, at least you'll get some sunshine even if it's not too warm. Maybe we can get together for a drink when you get back and catch up."

"I'd like that," Kieran said softly. "Anyway I'd better go. I have a plane to catch in the morning to Liverpool and I really need some sleep. Look after yourself, Flynn. Speak soon."

"Good night, Kieran. Safe journey tomorrow." The phone disconnected and he laid his down on the table. He took another sip of his wine. As he drank, the mail notification on his mobile pinged. His heart jumped.

Christ, what if it was another message from *him*? God, if Anthony knew what was happening in there, he'd be incandescent with both anger and fear. The fact that Flynn was being contacted by the killer he was looking for would definitely not go down well. But he had his reasons for not telling Tony yet, his safety mostly, if BTK's threats were anything to go by. Kieran had also been threatened with bodily harm if Flynn said anything to anyone. He pushed those thoughts out of his head, not wanting to dwell on them right now. Not for the first time he wished he had a family member he could talk to. Flynn's parents were both dead, nearly four years now after a car accident, and he'd been an only child. He had an aunt somewhere in the boondocks of Scotland who he hadn't seen in over twenty years, and that was it as far as family support went. Anthony was everything he had and he was damned if he was risking him for a minute.

Flynn risked a look at his phone and heaved a sigh of relief when he found a rather mundane text from his bank giving him an update on the dwindling state of his bank account.

As he deleted the text, he heard the front door open. His body went cold. Since being abducted from his own flat, any entrance into his own private world was suspicious until he knew for sure who it was.

Anthony walked through the door, his hair mussed and untidy, falling in curls around his face and the nape of his neck. Flynn relaxed, seeing Anthony grimace and shrug his shoulders wearily. His lover looked tired, his face drawn.

Flynn stood up and walked over to him, wrapping his arms around his neck and pulling his mouth down to his. Anthony sank into him gratefully, his strong arms encircling his waist as he pulled Flynn to him, his mouth searching and almost desperate. Flynn wondered what had happened today to make him feel so needy.

When they drew apart, Anthony sighed tiredly, taking off his tie and laying it on the hall table. He loosened two of his top shirt buttons and walked over to the minibar in the lounge to pour himself a large whiskey.

"Were there any developments today on the case?" Flynn asked quietly. Anthony shook his head in frustration as he took a large gulp of his drink.

"The SOCO guys and Graham have been over the scenes and the bodies and not found a fucking thing that's really useful, other than the fact he's an animal and likes to mutilate people. Nothing that can lead us back to this guy. He leaves no trace of himself that we can find. I've got them having a third look. I know what weapon he uses to slice open their throats—something similar to a Stanley knife, Graham thinks. I know what kind of silk he uses to make his bow ties, and I know that the guy can't fucking sew to save his life. But anything that tells me who he is or what he might be doing? I don't have a clue. I've got Rupert going over all the information we have in case we missed something. I don't even know how he transports the victims to dump them. He has to have a vehicle, yet no one's seen anything remotely suspicious at any of the dump sites."

He slumped down on the couch, his face brooding. Flynn sat down next to him, running his hands through Anthony's thick black hair. His boyfriend sighed in satisfaction and sat back, his eyes closed.

"I have the appointment with the hypnotist tomorrow morning. Maybe that'll trigger something you can use." Flynn murmured and saw Anthony's eyes open, his dark gaze anxious.

"Already? Are you going to be all right with all this? Do you need me to come with you—?"

Flynn leaned forward and kissed him, stopping his words, and he groaned softly in the back of his throat as their lips met. Anthony's hands pressed into the back of Flynn's head, as his tongue slid wetly into his mouth. Flynn felt his need for him in the way he kissed. If truth be told, he was feeling extremely horny himself tonight.

It wasn't the first time they'd made love since he'd been taken by BTK. He'd needed Anthony's closeness in the following days, his intimacy to try and keep away the memories of being tied down to a table or a bench and threatened with rape and death. Sex with the man he adored was a great distraction.

Their kiss grew in intensity and Anthony's hands strayed over his backside, pulling Flynn onto his lap, their hardened cocks pressing against each other. Flynn pressed back, his hands impatiently tugging Anthony's shirt out of his trousers. Anthony stopped his assault on his mouth to look at Flynn with darkened eyes.

"Hell, *tesore mio*, you taste so good." His words tailed off as Flynn stroked his stomach, feeling the hardened muscles of his abdomen as he finished the job he'd started, unbuttoning the shirt completely and sliding his hands across his lover's broad chest. Anthony groaned softly.

"So do you," Flynn murmured against his mouth. He chuckled softly as Anthony's fingers slid under his loose tee shirt and caressed his nipple, one of Flynn's really needy erogenous spots, which caused him to take a deep breath.

Flynn was addicted to Anthony's kisses. His lips were always warm and sensuous and the slight stubble on his chin a welcome sensation as it brushed against Flynn's skin. Anthony's hot, slick tongue darting hungrily into Flynn's greedy mouth was one of his favourite things to suck on. They kissed for a long time, changing positions, intensity and spit with abandon. Finally Anthony released Flynn's mouth, his own lips swollen and wet, his eyes black as he took a deep breath and stared into Flynn's face.

"I think we need to move this into the bedroom."

Flynn nodded, breathless. "We have far too many clothes on." He lifted his tee shirt over his head and threw it down on the couch. Anthony gripped his arms, pinning them at his sides, and then leaned forward to lick languorously at Flynn's tattoo, following the lines with a wet, pink tongue. It was one of *his* favourite things to do. Lick Flynn like he was a gourmet lollipop then move the action downward to his cock and do the same thing but with a lot more vigour.

Flynn tried not to think of another tongue that had intimately touched the baying wolf on his body. "It's a lot comfier on that down duvet and I can examine every inch of you in detail to make sure it's still all there. It has been a while. A day at least."

He grinned wickedly as he got to his feet and held out his hand. Anthony took it and then pulled him close as they stood, pressed together, Flynn breathing in the scent of Anthony's sweat and Joop! Splash cologne.

God I love to just breathe this man in. I want to bottle his scent and keep it with me all the time.

Flynn pulled Anthony impatiently toward the bedroom. The room was dimly lit, with only the bedside lights illuminating it, casting shadows on the wall. The bed itself beckoned, Anthony's choice of deep bronze and yellow linen inviting them to get on it. Flynn dropped onto the bed, undid his jeans and tugged them down over his hips to his feet then kicked them off impatiently to land beside the bed. He smiled as Anthony realised Flynn hadn't been wearing any underwear and his cock sprung free and proud. Flynn gently stroked himself, smearing wetness down his shaft and Anthony blinked rapidly.

"Slut," Anthony murmured as he shrugged his shirt off his shoulders, and took off his shoes and socks. Flynn chuckled and watched greedily as he unzipped his trousers and stepped out of them. He slid his boxers off, and Flynn revelled at the sheer maleness of him, the musky scent he exuded and the hooded look in his hungry eyes as he looked down at Flynn. He lay back against the pillows in wanton invitation, hands above his head, as Anthony settled down beside him, hands wandering over his hips, down his side, trailing down his stomach, and then bending down to once again roughly tongue his already sensitive nipples. Flynn arched his back, hands clasping together, eyes closing in pleasure as Anthony's hand encircled his prick, stroking it firmly, then reached down to cup his balls. Soft, warm breath teased his ear as Anthony bit Flynn's earlobe.

"You look like you were made to be ravished, *amore*," he whispered, as his hands grew more demanding with Flynn's cock. "Like a man who needs a really good fuck." And definitely *un pompino*."

Flynn hitched a breath. He'd been with Anthony for just over six months and definitely knew the Italian word for blow job. From the way Anthony kissed his way down Flynn's body, it looked like he was about to get one. He moaned softy and lowered his hands to grasp the covers as a hot, wet mouth engulfed his cock and proceeded to drive him through the roof. It was given some of the most lovingly heated and sucking attention it had ever experienced and by the time he had come in Anthony's mouth, he was drained and limp. He was only able to loll back on the sweaty sheets as Anthony pushed Flynn's legs back, up over his shoulders. From the sight of Anthony's blown pupils, the sheen of moisture on his face and the slickly lubed fingers that pushed their way into Flynn's arse, he was more than ready to let loose too. Anthony's broad chest was matted with sweaty hair, his breathing was deep and laboured and the Leaning Tower of Pisa he had jutting out from his groin definitely looked as if it were ready to make a trip into the depths of Flynn.

"You are the sexiest man I've ever known and you drive me crazy," Anthony gasped as he readied himself for his invasion. His urgent cockhead pushed at Flynn's puckered entrance and Flynn's stomach muscles tightened in anticipation. The heated flesh pressing at his entrance, sans condom, as they both agreed there was no need, was like heaven.

"Good to know. Now stop talking and do me." Flynn took a deep breath as Anthony slid inside him, and he grasped his shoulders as their hips began synchronising, thrust and push, the feeling of his man filling him with pleasure. Flynn's mouth found Anthony's, as their wet, open-mouthed lusty kisses made the intimate act they shared even better. Anthony's breathing was ragged, his low groans making Flynn hard again. There was a sense of power at having him at his mercy like this. Flynn panted loudly as he ground into him. His fingers dug into the firm muscle of Anthony's shoulders. Their mouths separated as they both came up for air and then Flynn's teeth dug in, biting the top of his lover's shoulder violently.

Anthony exclaimed in pain. "Jesus, I know you're horny but watch what you're doing. I don't want to have to have a bloody tetanus shot after a night of raunchy sex with you."

"You wanted it, you got it. Should I stop?" Flynn teased. This was exactly where he wanted to be. Forgetting the events of the past days, close and safe with Anthony, secure in the knowledge they were together.

Anthony laughed, a low, sexy sound that made Flynn's stomach tighten. "Jesus, no, don't stop. Just don't bite me to pieces."

He continued with his hard, hot length filling Flynn with silky smoothness. He gasped at the sensation as he thrust his hips against his, the slap of skin on skin a complete turn-on. Flynn's legs wrapped around his waist as he moved above him. His mouth once again found his in desperation, his tongue slicking into his mouth. He murmured softly, words in Italian, something that never failed to arouse Flynn. He felt the heat in his groin, the warm sensation that heralded his climax and he gripped him tighter. He heard himself moaning loudly as the sensations rocked his body, turning his groin into a flaming rage, his cock tightening and throbbing as he came against Anthony's skin.

Flynn loved that incredible feeling that coursed through his thighs and belly, those spasms of pleasure that made him gasp, and gave him release from his sexual tension. He also loved watching Anthony's face as he climaxed, his eyes screwing shut and his breath exhaling in a puff of warm air as he clasped Flynn tighter and his body trembled against his. Flynn saw that look now and as his warm semen coated his stomach and Anthony's with the force of his release, Anthony moaned loudly as he came, burying his face in Flynn's sweaty neck. His dark, curly hair tickled Flynn's cheek. They held each other tight, heavy breaths wafting against each other's sensitive skin. They stayed that way for some time, both content to simply let their bodies relax and their hearts slow down from their fast-paced beats. Finally Anthony rolled off Flynn and lay beside him, pulling him into a warm and sweaty embrace. Flynn forgot the past, forgot the fear and the guilt and closed his eyes as he tucked his body against his lover's, draping his arm across Anthony's stomach. It was still there when he drifted off to sleep.

Chapter 7

The next morning, Flynn watched Anthony trying to tame his mussed hair and reflected wryly that they both looked like they'd had a rough night of debauchery. He shaved while Anthony took a shower, then watched him dress and try to smooth down his unruly curls whilst they were still damp. It was a woebegone attempt and Anthony finally gave up in exasperation.

Flynn grinned and reached up a hand to stroke his cheek. "You and your hair. You look like a gypsy with that "just got out of the shower" look and the stubble on your chin. Very sexy, I have to say." He reached up and clasped Anthony's face in his hands, kissing him softly and then wrapping arms around his middle.

"I love you," he whispered softly.

Anthony nuzzled his neck. "I know and I love you too, *carissimo*. Just promise me you won't overdo it today at the hypnotherapist. If it gets too much for you, stop."

Flynn nodded. "I will. He's supposed to be a really good practitioner. I'll be in good hands." He grimaced. "I just hope something comes out of it that you can use to catch this sick bastard."

Anthony nodded as he leaned down and kissed him deeply. "All we can do is try. Now I need to be off. I have a briefing this morning on the BTK case and Winslow will kill me if I'm late."

Flynn watched as he left the bathroom. He waited until Anthony was out the door and he heard the ping of the lift. Then he went to the lounge, curled up on the sofa and lifted his laptop onto his lap. He hit the power button and felt bile rise in his throat as he waited for it to boot up. He clicked on the email programme and held his breath as the messages came sailing in. They entered the inbox and pinged into different folders he'd created. When the send and receive finally stopped, Flynn heaved a sigh of relief. He had nothing new from *btkman@hotmail.com*. The psycho bastard hadn't sent him anything. He'd hoped against hope that the killer had grown tired of baiting him and would leave him alone. But his brain said he was simply messing with him.

Flynn moved the mouse and hovered over an email folder he'd created simply called BTK. He hesitated then clicked the folder open.

A string of email messages revealed themselves and he started with the first one and re-read it for about the hundredth time.

Flynn. I hope you enjoyed our little get-together as much as I did. I hope you told Anthony all about it. He deserved to know. I notice the story didn't make the newspapers; are you feeling a little ashamed about our tryst? Tsk-tsk. No matter. We know what happened don't we? BTW did he find my bottle in your kitchen? The dog that came from didn't need it anymore. But he served his purpose. Anyways, I'll be in touch as promised. You said you'd tell my story. I don't want you to say anything to anyone yet. And I mean anyone. That includes Detective P. If you do, I will kill him. I'll also kill your other fuck buddy, Kieran. Just as an extra. You know I will. So keep that pretty mouth of yours closed or I'll cut your lips off too. See then if you can give Detective Italy a blow job. This is the plan. I'll send you a little bit of information each time and you can add it to your scrapbook. If I hear of anything leaking out before I want it to…well, let's just say you'll have to find someone else to screw you. If they still want to when you're all disfigured. I know you can do it, Flynn. So make sure you fucking do. Or I'll be standing behind you one dark night and you won't ever see me coming. Your admirer, BTK.

Flynn had been physically sick when he'd read it for the first time. He'd known this man was psychopathic but the sheer chilling, conversational words in the email had sent shivers of dread down his spine. Keeping this from Anthony had been difficult but Flynn's options seemed limited. He wasn't prepared to take any chances on his safety or Kieran's so for now he was playing along with the perverted bastard. The police presence he'd had assigned to him since the incident was a comfort factor but he also knew it wouldn't last forever. Flynn had heard Anthony on the phone speaking quietly to someone about what was going to happen when they eventually pulled the protection detail off.

He'd received close on ten emails from BTK in the past few days, all giving small snippets of information about himself. The first few were nothing too revealing, just minor items of what Flynn thought looked like irrelevant information. Which village BTK had lived in as a boy (Great Dunmow); what the name of his first pet had been (Buffy); the name of his favourite secondary school teacher

(Mr. Armandsone); and how many times BTK had masturbated each day (in Flynn's opinion, the rather alarming figure of six).

Hell, even at my peak I only did it about twice a day. Maybe there was something wrong with me*!*

Then BTK had started giving random names and cryptic comments, disgusting in their description.

Mandy was the first. Redheaded, 34C. Blended her ass till she was creamy and ready to blow.

Elliott. Aah, Elliott. He was a lovely boy. Tight, willing and very limber. Pity. I liked Elliott. It was dreadful what happened to him.

Rachael. Blonde. Nothing up front but God, what lips. I loved them round my cock. But she needed to be taught a lesson. And I'm a really good teacher.

Sandy. Did her every which way but Sunday till she screamed for me to stop. But I couldn't. I was having far too much fun. I think I might have shagged her to death.

There were others along a similar vein, all very dark and disturbing, eight in all. Flynn had logged them all in a spread sheet, chronologically, separating each element so he could isolate it if necessary later. Flynn was really scared that this killer would come after Anthony or Kieran. As Flynn also had an email application on his phone, he'd had to protect that too, just in case. So this was his deep dark secret, communicating with a man who'd kidnapped and assaulted him, and killed a lot of people. A man who'd threatened to kill both of his lovers and cut his lips off. It was a wonder he was still bloody sane. Flynn knew he was a strong character but this was definitely taking its toll on him.

He closed the laptop and frowned. He was worried about the whole hypnosis thing. What if he said something when he was under that he shouldn't? Flynn knew the whole doctor-patient privilege thing applied…but still. He sighed as he stood up and went to take a shower before his appointment. He still smelt of sex and Anthony's aftershave.

No use worrying about that now. I have enough on my plate. Best get this appointment over and then see what happens.

*****

Anthony sat at his desk opposite Rupert, scowling as he sorted through the mound of paperwork on his desk. The morning's press interview had gone badly for his superior, DCI Fred Winslow, and he just knew that the man's frustration and irritation was going to find its way to him sooner or later. It was the way things worked. The press had been relentless in their criticism of how the case was going and the fact that the Bow Tie Killer was still out there after murdering three people. Anthony couldn't really blame them. The public was scared, there were very few leads that were turning out to be something good and he was still no closer to finding the animal behind the murders. He slammed the file he was holding down on his desk and muttered a fierce expletive. Rupert looked up from the file he was reading and raised an eyebrow.

"We'll find him, Bulldog."

As much as Anthony hated his nickname in the office, he was resigned to the fact it would always be his. His nickname had been given after the bulldog, Max, in the old American TV show *Jake and the Fat Man*, which was a staunch favourite in the detective's common room. Anthony was always being told of his passing resemblance to the young Joe Penny and his own Italian ancestry and he was teased unmercifully about it by his team. The fact Anthony held the views he did and had a tenacity to surpass anyone else in hunting down criminals was part of it too.

Rupert laid his own file down and leaned back in his chair, sighing heavily. "We just have to keep going, turning over every scrap of information we have in the hope we get a decent lead. This bastard isn't really giving us much to go on. But I did hear that Graham and his team had found something a bit strange on this latest body. That young lab tech down at UCLH, Angie Green? I saw her in the canteen when I was there for the last results and managed to prise it out of her." He grinned.

Anthony's ears pricked up. "What did she have to say?"

Rupert glanced at him. "She said they'd found some skin in the woman's teeth. Graham thinks that was the reason the jaw was all smashed up. The killer wanted to destroy any evidence and also smash the jaw so we couldn't use it for comparisons later."

Anthony's gaze narrowed. "The killer's skin?" he shot back sharply.

His partner shrugged. "Maybe. They were doing some tests and she said she'd let me have the report later on what they think happened tomorrow. She thought perhaps the woman had bitten the guy."

Anthony's face darkened. "It'll be something if we can find a match in the DNA database. It would be a real coup." He sighed. "But that will take weeks and this guy is clever. He would have known we might have found something, even with a smashed face. He's not too worried about it or he'd have made sure he'd never left anything behind."

"He might be clever but he's only human. He might be losing focus, getting arrogant." Rupert leaned forward in his chair. "Maybe we get lucky and get a break."

Anthony regarded his colleague thoughtfully. "This guy is nowhere near human. He doesn't even feature in the human stakes."

Rupert sighed. "I knew as soon as I said those bloody words that you'd jump on them. I'm my own worst enemy in starting this conversation again. It always leads to trouble."

Anthony scowled. "I'm sorry I get on the old hobby horse. But after killing three women and molesting my boyfriend, believe me, if I ever get the chance to put this guy down like a rabid dog, I will." He saw his sergeant's face darken and he waggled a finger admonishingly in front of him. "I know we disagree on this one. But shit, even you have to admit this guy is a real psycho. Surely you must believe in that whole 'eye for an eye' thing that's mentioned in the Bible?"

Rupert shook his head vehemently. "I'm not getting into this old chestnut debate. You know I believe everyone can be redeemed and deserves a fair trial. I'm no priest but I have to believe that. Or else this whole world will go to crap in a handbasket and we'll have anarchy and dissolution on the streets to such an extent that no one will ever be safe from each other."

"I'd rather have the crap off the streets and six feet under so they can't bother anyone ever again," Anthony muttered fiercely. "There's no such bloody thing as human rights when you're not even fucking human. Being human means having compassion and concern and giving a damn about your fellow man, and this BTK fucker does none of that."

He grinned slightly as Rupert lifted his hands and placed them firmly over his ears, in a monkey-hear-no-evil gesture.

Anthony raised his hands in supplication. "Fine, I'll get off the soap box. Your ears are safe, so you can remove your hands now," he said drily as Rupert slowly took his hands away. The two men smiled at each other in shared camaraderie but Anthony couldn't resist a parting shot.

"Even the Catholic priest Thomas Aquinas said, 'Although it be evil in itself to kill a man so long as he preserve his integrity, yet it may be good to kill a man who has sinned even as it is to kill a beast. For a man is worse than a beast, and is more harmful.' Aristotle even agreed. So my views aren't that far out if men like them believed it in too."

He chuckled at Rupert's glare. His colleague scowled.

"Hell, Bulldog, you just have to have the last bloody word, don't you?"

Anthony shrugged. "I'm Italian. We like to make sure we get our point across. Blame my mother. She's the one who taught me never to give up. God knows she never does."

He stood up and picked up his jacket, shrugging into it.

"I'm going to go down to the path lab at the hospital myself and see if I can charm anyone into giving me the report sooner rather than later." He smiled at his partner, feeling a slight sense of relief at having thread of hope to work on. "Maybe I'll run into Angie and she'll share more with me." He waggled his dark eyebrows.

Rupert sniffed. "Good luck with that. She knows you're gay." He smirked. "Now I, on the other hand, am a straight man with a lot of charm and a great fashion sense."

Anthony smiled and shook his head. "You never fail to amaze me. You have this irresistible attraction for the young ladies in that lab. Don't you remember what happened with that last one? Sheena Montague? I'd have thought you'd have learnt your lesson after her."

Rupert frowned. "I had no idea she had a boyfriend who was a body builder. She never told me."

"Well, you found out soon enough when the guy tried to punch your lights out on the way home from dinner. Thank God he was a little drunk and uncoordinated or he might have done some serious damage to that lovely face of yours." Anthony grinned at his colleague as he raised a middle finger at him in a rude gesture. Then he grew serious again.

"I know we won't get DNA confirmed yet, but if there's anything they find, no matter how small, I want it now. We need everything we can get. If Winslow gets hold of us—"

"*Winslow* is standing right behind you, DI Parglietto."

The droll tone of his superior caused Anthony to sigh heavily as he turned, spotting Rupert's wicked smile as DCI Winslow regarded them both with a flat stare. Fred Winslow was a barrel of a man with the stance of a gorilla. He was short, stocky and in English vernacular, built like the proverbial brick shithouse.

Anthony nodded at him. "Sir, we were just talking about the case. I was on my way over to UCLH to see if they had any tangible information for us yet on the Christine Donovan case."

Winslow scowled fiercely. "I'm glad to hear someone's finally doing something on this case. It's about bloody time. I've had my arse kicked a dozen ways round Sunday for the lack of progress so far. Did you hear about the fucking press interview this morning? I really didn't appreciate having to stand there looking like a fucking idiot in front of a bunch of press piranhas whose only intention was to sink their teeth into my fairly meaty dick and rip it off. Am I making myself clear, *Bulldog*? Sergeant?"

"Crystal clear, sir. You'd like to keep your dick just where it is." Anthony said and heard Rupert's snort of laughter behind him. He grinned as his boss turned a deeper shade of pink.

"Christ, Parglietto. You're lucky I give you the time of bloody day. Otherwise I'd crack you one for that comment." Winslow's face was set but Anthony could hear the tone of amusement in his superior's tone. "You have to be one of the most annoying sods on this team, Anthony. Now fuck off and go find me a lead we can use to catch this psycho killer that's terrorizing my city."

Anthony nodded and made a move to leave until his boss's quiet voice stopped him in his tracks.

"How's Flynn? Is he getting over what happened? Are you both okay?" Fred Winslow regarded his detective with some concern.

Anthony turned. "We still have bad nights when he wakes up in a cold sweat but we're dealing with it. He's a little better." He scowled. "I'll be better myself when we have this bastard behind bars or even better, dead."

Winslow sighed heavily. "Anthony, enough of the rhetoric. God, you know I already have my doubts about letting you work this case given what happened. Don't make me change my mind."

Anthony scowled. "You know I'm the best man for this job. I haven't failed you yet, have I?" His face darkened as he remembered the one case he hadn't yet solved.

His boss waved a hand in his direction. "You're the best. But the minute you step out of line, you know your balls and your arse are mine." He grinned wolfishly. "And not in any way on this green earth that you'd like. So keep personal feelings out of this investigation." He glanced at Rupert who was sitting looking as if he wanted to interject but not daring to. "Your partner has his concerns too. So make sure you don't let either of us down."

Anthony gritted his teeth. "My job is cleaning up the streets and keeping society safe from the monsters that prowl around. That's exactly what I intend doing." He turned, clearly indicating the conversation was over. "Excuse me, sir. I'd better get going. Rupert, I'll see you in a while. Keep ploughing through those case files and see whether we missed anything. I'll take anything you can give me at this stage."

Chapter 8

The monster Anthony was looking for carefully replaced the bandage around the upper part of his left arm and secured it with a butterfly clip. He'd had to clean the rather nasty wound he'd incurred on his latest jolly. When he'd seen the teeth marks and his torn skin he'd wished the woman was here so he could kill her all over again, with even more violence than before. The bite had made him angry so he'd really gone to town on her throat. The stupid bitch had managed to get her teeth sunk into his arm whilst he was on top of her, pounding away. Normally he was very careful, but this one had caught him unawares in his final throes of his rather intense orgasm. She'd been particularly juicy, with breasts like a Page Three girl and the dark tunnel between her legs had been tight. He liked that in a woman. God, he liked that in a man.

But he'd made her pay. He'd seen something in a video game a while ago, some first-person shooter game where you got a chance to perform a range of enjoyable actions. One of them he'd particularly enjoyed had been cutting away skin from someone while they were awake. It appeared to be quite a skill. As he'd managed a fairly high score on the game, he'd thought it might be time to try it for real. He grinned. Tattoo removal really wasn't that difficult. Hell, perhaps he should set up shop for people who'd got theirs in a fit of drunkenness and then regretted it afterwards.

He looked into the bathroom mirror and allowed himself a wolfish grin. His deep green eyes gazed back at him, his square jaw straight, his even teeth the perfect match for the rest of him. Blair knew he was something special. He saw it every time he looked in the mirror or caught a glance of himself in a shop window. He'd seen the admiration in both men and women's eyes as they'd wondered how best to get him on their side so they could screw him. Ever since he could remember, he'd used his looks to his advantage and it made no difference to him if they were male or female. He'd enjoy sex any way it was offered; it was the reason he did the job he did. Working as a personal trainer at Gucci's Gym in the city gave him access to the equipment he needed to keep his physique, the constant admiration to keep his ego going and the never-ending supply of gullible and needy prey to work on.

It was how he'd met Marshall. Blair had to admit he was as fond of Marshall as he could be, given the fact that he might one day have to kill him. The man had a certain *je ne sais quoi* about him. It wouldn't be the first time he'd killed a lover he'd been quite attached to and it probably wouldn't be the last either. Although it would be the last time he ever tried to train a lover in his special line of art. He couldn't go through that pain again, the agony of destroying something he was trying to create. Last time had really messed him up for a while. He'd never thought he could get that attached to something—*sorry, someone*—in his life.

Marshall had been working out in the gym late one night. Blair had seen the man's incredible body, those auburn locks and his tight butt cheeks that looked as if they needed someone between them. The man was older than him too, which was another complete turn-on for him. He quite liked the idea of fucking someone who wasn't a callow youth, someone who had more maturity. And when the guy had smiled at him across the room, a shy and incredibly sexy smile, he'd just had to have him. So he'd sauntered up beside him, given him the full wattage of his amazing smile and the man had been smitten. Blair had made sure he was into anal and happy to be a bottom, taken him to the sauna, fucked him until neither of them could walk and then gone home with him to the man's rather trendy home in Battersea.

He'd seen Marshall now off and on for about two months and it suited his purpose having him in his thrall. You never knew when you might want something from a doctor's stash. Like a script for antibiotics for a bite, or tranquilizers stolen from the drawer in Marshall's consulting room at the hospital, the one where he kept all his free samples from pharmaceutical reps. It had been easy enough convincing Marsh to get naked and bend over the desk one morning when he'd gone to visit him unexpectedly. When Marshall had gone off to the bathroom to clean himself up, Blair had simply opened the unlocked drawer and taken what he needed. Marshall was a trusting soul; lucky for him.

His lover hadn't suggested he move in with him, something he was pleased about as Blair wasn't ready in the least for that. He had his own apartment in the city, one that allowed him unfettered access, privacy and his own personal space and was also close to the abandoned shop that he took most of his women to. The last thing

Blair wanted was any questions on his whereabouts or his sudden disappearances.

Marshall was a good lover, prepared for the most part for anything Blair wanted to do to him and was a definite sucker for punishment. Blair appreciated that. Marshall's refusal to the proposed threesome still rankled and Blair thought he'd have to work on him. He really liked the idea of someone sucking Marsh off whilst he went in at him from behind. Blair liked the thought of someone sucking *him* off whilst Marsh did them from behind exciting too. Blair wasn't a man who would ever bottom. He needed the control being on top gave him, the fact that he could pound at a man's arse until they begged for mercy. There was no way he was letting anyone have that level of control over him, no matter how good it might feel. But any which way you looked at it, he fancied the idea of having his threesome. He was going hard just thinking about it.

The killer rolled his sleeve down and popped two more antibiotics into his mouth. The last thing he needed was an infection from the bitch's teeth. He thought his lover had bought his story about the dog. Marsh knew he liked to go and lie in the sun at the park and watch everyone walking by but he doubted his lover knew why. The Bow Tie Killer smiled. He usually liked to watch for the right woman to walk past to attract his attention. It was nothing in the way they looked; it was all about the way they carried themselves, their smile, and their sexiness. But he already knew who his next woman would be.

She was Asian. A ripe, luscious, tiny, long-haired woman who looked like a porcelain doll. He'd had his eye on her for a while and he was close to having the final plan in place to bring her back to the shop and do to her what he did so well. His smile grew cold, his eyes flat. He knew someone—*two someones in fact*—who wouldn't like the idea, apart from the woman herself. But it was time to send another message or two and mess with their heads a little more. They'd got off easy and it was time to ramp up the pressure. He was having so much fun. It would be a pity to let it lapse.

Chapter 9

Flynn heaved a deep sigh as he walked out of the lift into the bustling seventh floor newsroom where he worked. His session with the hypnotherapist had gone well, although they hadn't really come up with much more for Anthony to use. It had left him drained as he'd revisited his ordeal, but talking about it to someone had helped. And Flynn *was* getting over it. His innate toughness in being put in compromising positions and walking away had come to the fore.

As he walked over to his work station, he thought guiltily about what he had on his laptop. That would probably go much further for Anthony to find this sick bastard than what he'd just managed to dredge up from his subconscious. But he just couldn't take the chance on anything happening to either Kieran or Tony. Not yet.

"Flynn, how did your interview go?" Masumi Teragaya looked at her colleague with an enquiring glance.

"It went well; thanks, Sumi." To cover his absences, Flynn had told everyone he was conducting an interview with a potential confidential informant on a real story he was working on. A fairly sordid story, one of money laundering, murder and family intrigue. "We'll see how it pans out when I check out the information they've given me. How about you? Is your story about the child abuse scandal at that children's home taking shape?"

The little Japanese woman's eyes darkened. "You cannot believe the stories I am hearing. It is terrible. Those poor children. I cannot believe a person can do such things to another human being, let alone children. The perpetrators should be taken out and have their extremities and all their limbs cut off whilst they still live." Her face crinkled in fierce frown. For someone so small, Sumi could generate quite a lot of menace when her temper was up.

"God, you and Anthony should get together." Flynn tossed his jacket down over the chair back. "He has the same sort of idea. Only with him, it's just 'put the buggers down where they sit so they don't leave a ripple.' If Anthony could have a ray gun that just disintegrated bad people, he'd be the happiest man in the world."

Sumi smiled, her tiny hands waving in the air animatedly. "I cannot disagree, after hearing what I have today. Tell your handsome man he has a fan." The Japanese woman regarded her friend carefully. "You look a little peaked. Is everything all right with you? Do you need anything?"

Flynn shook his head, grateful for the other woman's concern. "No, I'm fine. I just need to focus on this story and get it finished. It's pretty complicated and I need to concentrate."

"Do you want to have a drink tonight?" Sumi smiled. "We could go to that tequila bar on Oxford Street and watch those hunky male waiters with their shirts off."

Flynn chuckled. "God, you're incorrigible. Sorry, no can do. We're meeting friends later tonight for dinner."

Sumi nodded. She turned as someone called her name. "I have a meeting now. I'll speak to you later." The diminutive reporter waved a small hand in Flynn's direction and disappeared.

He heard his mobile ping as a message came in. He picked up his phone and smiled when he saw the text from Anthony.

how did it go? did they find anything in that brain of yours? A

He sent a text back and then switched on his laptop, waiting for it to power it up so he could get to work.

not much, just those fantasies of you naked and tied up on my bed.

His mobile buzzed moments later.

like the idea of the whole tied up thing tho lol
2nite buster i will rock your world, I promise.
I look 4ward to it after dinner tonight. ti amo. A

Flynn spent the rest of the afternoon in anticipation of what he hoped would be a raunchy evening with Anthony. First tasty Italian meal, then tasty Italian man. He loved eating continental.

*****

Flynn sighed as he looked around the bustling restaurant he and Anthony sat in. His beer stood untouched in front of him. Anthony leaned over, covering his hand with his. It was one of the things Flynn loved about his boyfriend. He had no aversion to PDA; in fact sometimes it was Flynn who felt a little uncomfortable in public when Anthony nuzzled his neck, kissed him or pulled him in for a hug. Anthony would tell the world to go fuck itself if they ever interfered in his demonstrations of affection to his lover.

"What's wrong, *amore*?" Anthony asked him. "You've been very quiet tonight. I thought you were looking forward to seeing Graham and Judy for dinner."

The couple had agreed to meet the pathologist and his wife at the Italian restaurant they often frequented. Tonight though, Flynn felt uneasy and fidgety. Anthony had told him earlier tonight as he'd pulled him close for a tongue searching kiss that Flynn was one of the strongest men he knew and he was very proud of him for not letting himself get overwhelmed by his ordeal. Flynn thought that might have been the trigger for the mood swing to the black side of the dial. The knowledge that he was keeping secrets from Anthony, that he didn't deserve his praise and his admiration, still weighed heavily on his conscience.

He trailed his fingers across his lover's big hand, tracing the slight scar on the top of his right hand where Anthony once been sliced by a junkie with a piece of glass.

"I'm fine. I was just thinking about the session with the hypnotherapist."

"*Amore*, you did what you could. The fact that you couldn't remember anything else we didn't already know isn't your fault."

"I know. I was just hoping they'd find something you could have used. Instead all they found inside my head was this deep dark desire to ravage you in every way possible." His voice turned husky and he leaned forward and kissed him softly. Anthony's lips parted to allow his tongue in as he kissed him back. Finally they heard a throat clearing at the side of the table.

"When you two come up for air, you might see that your friends have arrived for dinner as planned." The gravelly tone of Graham Manning interrupted their session. Anthony stood up, a wide smile on his face.

"Sorry, we were just amusing ourselves. You're late as usual, Graham. Judy, lovely to see you." He hugged the short, attractive blonde woman standing next to the pathologist. She had a look of pleasure on her face at being embraced.

"I swear, Anthony, you get bigger every time I see you."

Flynn chuckled. "It's all that junk food he eats. I keep threatening to phone his mother and tell her, but Rosa would be on the next plane out so she can stop him getting all podgy. Probably not a good idea." Personally he thought Anthony had been losing weight but then Judy hadn't seen him in months. Graham laughed as he sat down next to Flynn.

Half an hour later they had food in front of them and were tucking into fragrant and steaming Italian cuisine.

"So, Anthony, did you hear back from the lab today after all your efforts to charm my team with that Italian temperament of yours?"

Graham smirked as Anthony scowled fiercely. Flynn grinned, knowing how his lover tended to become very Italian with both sexes when he was trying to court favours or get his way. It seemed that whether it was at home, work or in the bedroom, nothing changed. Anthony could still charm the opposite sex with his rough-hewn good looks and sexy accent. Sometimes Flynn wanted to throttle him out of jealousy.

"No, the pathology lab told me I had to wait until tomorrow." Anthony shook his head in frustration. "You need to tell them to get a move on. I really need anything they've got for me yesterday if I'm going to catch this bastard."

Graham shrugged his shoulders. "Hey, we can only do what we can. We're none of us miracle workers down there. These things take time and results can't be rushed. Not if you want it done properly." He raised an enquiring eyebrow. "You *do* want it done properly, don't you Anthony?"

"Of course I fuck—" he glanced over at Judy with a slight hint of apology, "Yes, I want it done properly. I'd hate for it to be rushed then the evidence gets thrown out for some bollocking reason and the case is tainted. It's tough enough getting these bastards behind bars and into their cushy cells without having that hassle as well."

"Cushy cells?" Judy laughed softly. "I didn't think the jails here are that luxurious, Anthony."

"If I had my bloody way, they wouldn't be in cells at all." Anthony's tone was unflinching.

Flynn saw Graham sit back with a wicked smile as if things were about to get interesting. He rolled his eyes at the grinning pathologist. Graham shrugged his shoulders in enjoyment. Flynn sighed in exasperation. He needed to head his lover off at the pass. Once Anthony got on his pet subject he was nothing less than a speeding freight train looking for somewhere to stop.

"Should we order more drinks?" he said desperately, looking around for the waiter.

Graham guffawed. "Nice try, Flynn." He too knew there was no stopping Anthony.

"Criminals like the one I'm looking for should never see the inside of a prison cell. They should be six feet under where they can't hurt anyone again." Anthony's voice was quiet but determined and he toyed with his wine glass. Judy looked at him speculatively.

Flynn closed his eyes in resignation.

And here we go.

"You believe in corporal punishment? The death penalty?" Judy's voice was not judgemental—simply curious.

Graham leaned forward. "Our Anthony here is a retributivist. He believes the punishment should fit the crime and he says so rather vocally at any chance he gets." The pathologist grinned. "It makes for an interesting discussion at the station when you have a bunch of policemen and lawyers in the same room. It can be very entertaining."

Anthony raised a rude middle finger at his friend who laughed loudly. Flynn sat forward, still hoping to stop the train.

"Does anyone want dessert? I saw some lovely looking cheesecake on the cake stand earlier—"

"I believe criminals who kill should in turn be killed," Anthony said, interrupting his lover softly. "It's the only way they can really pay for their crimes and the only way people can be safe. Why house these people at taxpayers' expense in places where they simply develop their own hierarchy and kingdoms and where punishment simply becomes a byword? Instead they create their own little world inside the prison, their own rules and just live out whatever time they have inside in making other people's lives a misery to enrich themselves. Then they get released after some bunny-hugging do-gooder decides the buggers have had enough. I don't call that justice of any sort for the victims or their families."

Flynn sat waiting for the train to finally stop. It was on the downhill stretch now and wasn't losing speed any time soon. Better wait it out.

"But what about their human rights—" Judy's question was rudely interrupted as Flynn's heart sank. Graham laughed explosively.

"Jesus, now you'll really get him going, Judes. My God, you couldn't have picked a better turn of phrase to set him off."

"I'd like to hear Anthony's views." Judy said quietly.

Anthony sat back. "It's pretty simple really. I don't believe that being born human makes you a human being. I believe you have to earn that right. Compassion, sympathy, empathy and love. These emotions all make us human beings. And if at any time you lose them and take life or dignity away from another person, you forego your right to be seen as one."

He shrugged as Judy stared at him in fascination. Flynn had heard it all before. He wasn't a hundred percent sure he agreed with Anthony and his very rigid black-and-white outlook. Flynn was definitely more of a grey person. But Anthony, fierce policeman and staunch protector of the victim, was not. Admittedly, Anthony had seen things in his life that he could never fathom—violence, death and destruction—that in his eyes, gave him a right to feel so strongly about his beliefs.

He leaned back as Graham and Anthony got into a debate about the death penalty. Something Anthony was all for and Graham was on the fence about. It turned fairly heated and finally Judy leaned forward and laid a hand on her husband's, stopping him mid-sentence.

"Come on, you guys. Tone it down," she said laughingly. "The whole restaurant is looking at us." She cast a curious glance at Anthony. "If you caught this serial killer, Anthony, what would you suggest his punishment be?" Judy sat back after having asked her question, her eyes searching. Anthony regarded her for a while before leaning back as he answered.

"He should be put to death," he said quietly. "He doesn't deserve to live after what's he's done and the hurt he's caused." His dark eyes flickered in Flynn's direction. Flynn caught his breath at the implacability in that look. "I'd personally like him to suffer a long, drawn-out and agonizing death but I guess that wouldn't happen. So I say a quick injection of something similar to what you'd use to put an injured dog down and it would be all over."

He stared down at the table, his face dark. "That way I know he's not coming after anyone ever again and the people who have to get on with their lives can do so without fear."

The people around the table were quiet, as if absorbing his words. Judy nodded thoughtfully.

"What do your colleagues at the station think about your views?" Judy asked quietly. "I imagine there's a few there that probably feel the same way you do."

Anthony nodded. "There are, although they might not say it out loud too much." His face darkened. "My partner and I tend to have a little bit of a difference of opinion—"

Graham laughed again explosively. "That's putting it mildly! Rupert Gregg is a good enough policeman but God, he's narrow minded and self-righteous. His family are from a pretty religious background and I think it's been drummed into him that the only person able to make those sorts of decisions on life and death is God." The pathologist waved a hand. "Not that I don't think it's probably the best way to do things. But there are definitely extenuating circumstances to any situation."

"Rupert is pretty black and white," Anthony remarked softly. "But that's what he believes so I can't fault him even if I do disagree." He frowned slightly as if remembering something not very pleasant. His eyes flicked toward Flynn and Flynn felt a little unnerved at the speculation he saw in them. Then Anthony's face cleared and he was back to his usual self.

Flynn smiled, trying to put his strange expression out of his mind. "I'd love to be a fly on the wall when that happens. Rupert with his Calvinistic view and you with that rather extreme thinking and that fiery Italian way of doing things." He smiled wickedly. "I think it would be such a turn on. Perhaps you can tape it, Tony, and bring it home for us to watch. I think it would definitely get me in the mood."

Anthony reached over and caressed Flynn's cheek. "I'll have to consider that," he said huskily. "Although normally, just the sight of me in the—"

Flynn reached across and laid a finger on his lips. "Enough of that," he said firmly. "Let's not traumatise Graham and Judy."

The others laughed. Flynn reached over and caressed Anthony's face. "Are we done with the serious topic of conversation for the time being?" he asked jokingly. "I only ask because I really want some of that cheesecake."

Anthony chuckled as he rubbed his thumb over his hand gently. "I think that's over for now," he agreed. "Perhaps we should rather turn the subject to the one Graham loves the most—the fact Chelsea are getting their arses kicked."

Graham looked up indignantly. Chelsea was his football team and Arsenal was Anthony's and they had many a debate about the capabilities of the two teams. The conversation soon turned to heated discussions about football and Flynn and Judy sat and watched in amusement.

Chapter 10

It was almost midnight when the couple finally got home to Anthony's flat. Anthony loosened his tie as he threw his keys down on the hall table. He'd found half a dozen messages on his home phone from various members of his team. Some of them he'd returned as he knew they'd still be awake, others could wait until tomorrow. One of the calls was from his superior telling him quietly and almost apologetically that the police detail for Flynn was being pulled the next day. The powers that be had decided that there was no further justification for spending taxpayer money to protect a man who might only be slightly at risk. Anthony was expecting it but still it worried him that Flynn would be unprotected when he was not with him. He sighed. He'd see what he could do tomorrow to sort that one out. Right now he had an awkward question to ask of his lover.

He walked through the bedroom to see Flynn sitting up in bed, his laptop already on his lap. He looked up at Anthony walked in. He saw Flynn immediately flick the screen off and close the top. Anthony felt a sense of disquiet at the expression on his face. Flynn looked better than he had before but he still had dark shadows beneath his blue eyes.

Flynn was three years younger than Anthony at thirty-nine but he was starting to develop crow's feet in the corner of his eyes. Anthony thought it was sexy. Flynn's lean, muscled frame was continually tensed as if ready for battle. His short, dark blond hair stuck up constantly like unruly spikes from where Flynn ran his hands through it with regular abandon.

"Can I ask you something?"

Flynn nodded. "Of course."

"All of a sudden you've password protected your phone and your laptop. Why would you do that? Is there something on your laptop you don't want me to see?"

Flynn's face paled and Anthony's skipped a beat at his expression. He knew someone about to lie when he saw it; he was a seasoned policeman.

Flynn shook his head fiercely. "Of course there's nothing on here. Why on earth would you think that?"

Anthony shrugged as he got undressed. "I just get the feeling you're being secretive, that you're trying to hide something. Rupert mentioned he thought it was strange that BTK would say he wanted you to tell his story and then you never hear from him. It's been on my mind too and tonight's conversation just made me think of it."

Flynn flushed. "You think I'm in touch with that bastard and keeping it secret? How could you think that?" His hands clenched the bedcovers as Anthony watched him closely.

"I just wanted to make sure I knew what was going on. Is that bastard contacting you? Is that why all of a sudden I'm persona non grata on all your gadgets?"

"God, you're being a pain. Of course not." But Anthony heard the defensive tone in his boyfriend's voice. His stomach clenched. Flynn *was* hiding something.

"If that sick fucker is contacting you, you need to tell me. This is a murder investigation, not a one-man journalistic crusade to tell the bastard's story. You could be had up for aiding and abetting a criminal or obstructing justice, and believe me, you don't want that. Is he in touch with you?"

Flynn stiffened. He shifted in the bed, his eyes glittering and teeth clenched.

"No, he is not fucking in touch with me! Don't you think I would tell you if the man who kidnapped me, stuck his fingers up my arse and threatened to slit my throat was 'in touch with me?' Christ, give me *some* credit!"

Flynn's chest heaved with anger or fear; Anthony wasn't sure which. "Then why the secrecy, why all the bloody encryption?"

Flynn glared at him in apparent fury. "Because the newspaper has had some leaks and someone managed to get some sensitive information out of the editorial office. So the company put in extra security controls with our equipment so they can protect themselves. I imagine it's the same that the bloody police department does to protect their information. Is that all right with you?" he asked him scathingly.

Anthony drew a deep breath. That reasoning seemed logical enough. Perhaps he'd been wrong.

"I only ask because I'm worried about you." He saw Flynn's unrelenting posture and raised his hands. "I'm sorry if I was badgering you but I want to make sure you're okay."

"I'm okay, I've told you before," he said between clenched teeth. Flynn lifted the laptop off his lap with an exasperated sigh and placed it on the bedroom table. He lay down, pulling the covers up to his neck and switched off the light. Anthony sighed as he got into bed. He thought with a pang that any thoughts of lovemaking were now definitely off the table. The best thing to do now was go to sleep.

*****

The following morning they sat together at the kitchen table in uneasy silence. Flynn felt Anthony's eyes on him as he sipped the strong espresso made from the fancy coffee machine he had installed in his kitchen. It was Anthony's first Friday off in a long time on his duty roster and they had both intended making the most of it today. Of course, there was no guarantee his phone wouldn't ring and he'd be called into the station. Flynn broke the awkward silence.

"I suppose I should be thinking of going back to my place," he said frostily. "Your place is getting a little cramped and I think I might have overstayed my welcome."

He needed to allay any suspicions Anthony had about him and having contact with BTK once and for all, for all their sakes. Going on the offensive might help.

Anthony sighed. "Don't be stupid. I'm sorry I had to ask you those questions last night. I only had your best interests at heart. You know that. I want to keep you safe."

Flynn's guilt at the fact that he *was* lying through his teeth to Anthony and that he had every right to be suspicious of him made his stomach clench. He'd *thought* that Anthony had bought the cover story about the office leak that he'd carefully concocted for such an eventuality. His acting skills were obviously better than he'd thought. Anthony was adept at sniffing out lies, ferreting out the truth and incredibly sensitive to people's tells. It was what made him so good at his job. But recently his emotions *had* been operating at a higher level even than usual and his usual cynicism and suspicion was a little easier to overcome.

"You know you're welcome to stay here as long as you want, right?" Anthony said softly, his dark eyes watchful as he gazed at

Flynn over the rim of his cup. "You don't have to go home if you don't want to yet."

Flynn laid the paper down on the table with a frustrated sigh. "I know that. But this place is too small for the two of us."

"We could move into a bigger place together?" Anthony's face was hopeful. "I have no problem giving this place up and we can find something else you like."

Flynn frowned even as his pulse raced at his suggestion. It was the first time either of them had mentioned a longer-term solution to their living arrangements. "I thought you loved it here? You've always said you never want to move." He felt a slight hope that perhaps Anthony might not be as immoveable as he'd thought in giving up his bachelor pad. He knew he'd be able to rent this place out within a day, the demand was so high.

Anthony nodded, his dark hair falling over his forehead, and he brushed it away absently. "I know what I said. But that was before all the craziness happened. My perspective has changed since then. You are what is important to me. Not this place. I want you to feel safe again."

Flynn felt a surge of love for him as he contemplated the suggestion. In truth, before the abduction, he'd been absolutely certain that he wanted his own place, his own space. Now, he wasn't so sure. It would be good to have someone to come home to, someone who would know if he wasn't around when he should be. He wanted someone to hold him when he woke up in a cold sweat, after dreaming about what BTK had done to him and his other victims. It was silly, he knew, but then what had happened to him, the vulnerability he'd been left with as a result, that someone could take him and do what they wished with him, had changed his perspective somewhat.

"Are you sure? I know what you're like when it comes to home and hearth. You like stability and I know this place has been a haven for you."

Anthony chuckled quietly. "You make me sound like some old fart that's stuck in his ways. I'd hope I'm not that bloody bad." He face grew more serious. "Yes, I like stability. It's about the only time I get it in my job. But I love you. So if that means finding a bigger place for us both to live, where I can keep an eye on you, of course I'll do it."

Flynn stood up and walked over to him, straddling his lap as he hugged him then kissed him gently. "Then I shall be gracious and say I accept your offer."

"It'll be safer too," Anthony muttered quietly. His hands encircled Flynn's waist protectively. "They've called off the police detail that was watching you. I couldn't justify it anymore and the DCI said it had to stop."

"Personally, I'm surprised you got away with it for long. It's been ten days. They've been very good to let it get this far." Flynn felt a slight discomfort at the fact that the ever-present and comforting shadow he'd had following him was being let go, but he knew they had no choice. As much as he'd moaned about it originally, he had to admit the comfort factor had been high.

"I have someone else lined up you keep you safe. A mate of mine who's ex-SAS is in town and he says he'll be your unofficial bodyguard for the next week. Ernie's a tough SOB. He won't let anyone near you." Anthony's voice was fierce.

"Anthony, I don't need a personal bodyguard. The police detail was one thing but this? I'm not a fainting maiden. I appreciate the concern but you do know that you can't do this forever, don't you? Protect me?" Flynn's voice was quiet.

Anthony stared into Flynn's eyes, his own darkened with resolve. "I'll take what I can get if it gives me a little more peace of mind for the next week. Please let me do this, Flynn. It will make *me* feel better even if it doesn't matter to you." He leaned back on the chair and Flynn stood up, taking his empty coffee cup to the sink.

With Anthony in this mood there is no point in me arguing. The man is as stubborn as they come.

"Are you any closer to finding him?" Flynn turned to face him.

Anthony nodded cagily. "We do have something but I'll only get the report later today if I'm lucky. I said I'd pop in later to see what they have."

He didn't elaborate and Flynn knew better than to ask. After the last fiasco when he'd told him something he shouldn't have and Flynn had ended up on the wrong end of the BTK's violence, the policeman in Anthony was now very cagey now about sharing anything with him. If Flynn remembered, Anthony's exact words, uttered in an implacable tone, had been, "The less you know, the better off you are. I can't risk you going off half-cocked and inviting this motherfucker to another party with you. So don't even ask me to tell you anything about the case anymore." He'd been good to his word.

Flynn felt the chill of both guilt and fear as he thought of what currently resided on his laptop. He'd received another message last night, a few hours before Anthony walked into the bedroom. BTK had sent him another email. It was a fairly innocuous one by BTK standards and Flynn still had no idea what it meant.

The flesh seems to weep

Her throat red, no life, no sound

I come, feel alive

He'd puzzled over for it for a while then filed it in the BTK folder. He thought it was about the disgusting fact that BTK had killed someone and then had sex with them, or done both at the same time but he couldn't figure out why it was written the way it was. Flynn realized Anthony was speaking to him, his head cocked enquiringly at his lack of response. He smiled. "Sorry, I was miles away. What were you saying?"

"I said I'll contact that woman I know that runs the estate agency, see if she has anything on her books we can go look at. Ginny normally gets the really good properties before anyone else."

"That's because she sleeps with anyone that will give her a listing." Flynn remarked drily. "She's also the one who tried to get off with you at that party we were at a while ago, isn't she? Said if anyone could turn you straight she could."

Anthony scowled. "Well that's never going to happen, is it?"

Flynn quirked an eyebrow. "I'm not sure I like the idea of you two playing 'hunt the house' together. She clearly had ideas about playing 'hunt the sausage' with you. And perhaps she has gay--to-straight super powers."

Anthony's face flushed. "Jesus, don't remind me. That woman was a bloody leech with hands like an octopus. I had a hard time fending her off without decking her one. She just couldn't accept I wasn't into women. But she knows everyone in town and she still has the hots for me, which is in our favour." He shook his head at Flynn's splutter of laughter, a slight grin on his own face. "Okay, so she's a bit of a bicycle. But if she can find us a decent place, I'm all for it. I'll pretend she can turn me."

Flynn waved his hand. "Fine, go for it. Just don't promise anything in return that you can't deliver, sunshine. We want at least a two-bedroom—preferably three if we can get it as I need a study—decent area, close to tubes, great coffee shops around and no bloody kebab shops anywhere in the vicinity or you'll gain twenty pounds!"

Anthony's predilection for greasy, late night and, in Flynn's opinion, disgusting hamburgers and kebabs, was well known.

Anthony nodded, satisfied at the request. "I'll give her a ring and let her know."

Flynn thought he sounded quite excited about the prospect of moving in together. He had to admit he felt a sense of peace he hadn't felt in a while. For a fleeting moment, the email he'd been worried about was put to the back of his mind. Flynn also had an overwhelming urge to make up his secret transgression to his man and he knew exactly how to do that tonight. It had been a while since they'd done it because Flynn didn't like the vulnerability it had made him feel after being taken, but tonight he wanted to give it a whirl, to make everything up to his sexy and domineering lover. Just the way they had in the past before BTK had made it all go to hell. Damn him and his little games. Flynn would show him that his psyche was still fine and he could still enjoy a game of bondage without feeling scared and out of control.

Chapter 11

That night after work Anthony let himself into his flat. The apartment was quiet, only the ticking of the clock in the hall breaking the silence. It was in darkness save for the light on in the lounge. An uplighter shone softly in the corner, highlighting the Matisse print on the wall, a picture he had bought when they'd been in Provence two months ago. Flynn had been ecstatic at its softly muted colours depicting the mother and child in a field full of flowers and Anthony had caved in and bought it for that certain spot on his wall.

He was about to call out to Flynn that he was home when in the dim light he saw the clothing scattered on the floor, laying a trail to his bedroom. His blood heated up, his groin swelled and his cock immediately leapt to attention. He knew exactly where this was going. A surge of delight suffused his body. He just *knew* Flynn was in there, waiting for him, ready to tease him. It was a bit of a surprise to him actually as Flynn hadn't been partial to this particular game since being taken by BTK. In the past it had been one they played often but now Flynn seemed a little wary. Anthony supposed it was to do with the fact that he'd been bound and blindfolded at the mercy of a crazy killer. But whatever had led him to decide the game tonight, Anthony was very pleased about it.

He walked down the hall. He reached the bedroom and gently pushed the door open. It was then that he saw Flynn framed in the light of the lamp shining from the lounge. He lay, apparently asleep, on the leather and wood divan Anthony had brought over from Italy. Its dark burgundy colour contrasted with what Flynn wore, which was nothing but a black thong lying stark against his pale skin. The divan was under the window. The bedcovers were rumpled, as if Flynn had been sleeping. His robe was draped across the foot of the bed. Anthony moved toward the gleaming body of his supine lover.

Flynn's face was turned away toward the back of the sofa. His dark hair was tousled and his arms stretched above his head to the right. He wore a blindfold. Anthony felt a stir in his groin seeing those lean, hairy legs stretched out wantonly, inviting him to run his hands up and over his groin. Even appearing asleep, Flynn had the power to excite him, to make Anthony hard and ready. He stepped toward him, watching the rise and fall of Flynn's chest with their already hardened nubs. Anthony wanted to run his tongue over that chest, with its smattering of fine hair, to take Flynn's nipples in his mouth and suck them until Flynn groaned in pleasure. As he got closer in the dim light he saw the hands with their bonds of silk. Green bonds lay dark against Flynn's wrists, fastened to the wooden struts of the upright chair arm. His hands were tight fists. Anthony chuckled softly, a noise that sounded loud in the stillness of the room.

"Been waiting long?" he whispered as he took off his jacket. "I tried to get home as soon as I could."

Anthony knew the bonds would be loose so Flynn could break free if needed but he also knew he wouldn't. It was the way the game was played.

At the sound of his voice, Flynn's body relaxed. His hands unclenched. Sometimes no words were spoken when they played this game but after his recent ordeal, Anthony knew Flynn would need reassurance that there was no stranger outside the blindfold he wore.

Anthony took off his silk tie, trailing it gently along the length of Flynn's leg, over his barely covered groin. Flynn shivered. Anthony grinned, knowing by now how these games were played and what signs of excitement to look for. He loosened his shirt buttons slowly with one hand as he watched the rise and fall of Flynn's chest quicken, getting deeper with the slow caress of the silk on his skin. Anthony's hand slowly brushed against his lover's stiff cock. Flynn stirred restlessly, a slight moan escaping his lips, lips that looked inviting and that Anthony wanted to feel on his mouth, around his own cock, sucking him dry until he was spent.

"I would have told them all to go hell if I'd known what was waiting for me here. *Uomo sexy,*" he mouthed against Flynn's ear, as his tongue flicked slowly in and out of it. Flynn gasped in pleasure and the sense of power that this game brought made Anthony breathless. He loved to make this man so dependent on him, to take this normally totally self-controlled individual and make him beg him to end it.

"I should just walk out of here and leave you for someone else," he murmured, unfastening his trousers, letting them slip to the floor. His erection bulged in his boxer shorts, and he reached down and ran his hand along it, enjoying the sensation of the silk against his penis. He turned Flynn's face toward him as he stroked himself gently.

"What have we here?" he questioned softly, knowing all the while what he would find. Flynn's unseeing eyes were in their velvet prison but Anthony knew Flynn was watching him. He slid his finger softly across the brows of Flynn's eyes and down the curve of his cheek.

He cupped his face in his large hands, pushing it against his groin, making Flynn smell the musky scent of him, letting the bound man feel his excitement against his forehead. Flynn groaned softly, speaking for the first time since Anthony had got home.

His voice was husky, his quick breathing interfering with his words. "You love this game, don't you?"

Anthony knelt down beside Flynn. His tongue licked him from the top of his knee, slowly making its way toward that soft smooth spot of his body, the groove between Flynn's hip and thigh. Anthony bit the skin gently, teeth nipping, causing Flynn to cry out slightly in both pain and pleasure.

Anthony knew Flynn would be frustrated at his arms being bound, as much as it turned him on. From experience he knew that all Flynn would want him to do was climb on top of him and thrust into him with a passion that would only be spent with the two of them being joined together and mixing bodily fluids in a final rush. Flynn's impotence at not being able to force Anthony, to guide him, was all part of the game. The blindfold added to the mystery. He'd sense the sweat on Anthony's body, feel his heat, but he couldn't see his face. That for Flynn had always been the ultimate aphrodisiac.

Sometimes Anthony spoke no words, just took him violently. But tonight Anthony was in the mood to play and tease. They both needed the release that this game brought with it. Anthony trailed his finger across Flynn's leaking prick, flicking it softly. Flynn moaned and writhed on the divan, his hips thrusting upward.

Anthony laughed. "Steady on, *tesoro mio*. I'll get there in a moment. For now I'm just enjoying this beautiful spectacle of manhood any way I can." He knelt down at the side of the divan then mouthed the leaking cock in front of him, lips playing against the flesh, enjoying the taste of musk on his lips. Flynn groaned louder and once again his hips pushed upward.

"Christ, Anthony, that feels so good." His voice shivered, the desire in it plain, the need an aching plea.

Anthony slid a soft finger over the sensitive spot between Flynn's legs. Flynn's prick twitched and he moaned louder. Anthony's own erection was ready to pound nails. He hardened even more and groaned softly at the sensation building up in his groin at seeing Flynn so turned on. He licked his lips, his breathing deepened and his lower stomach grew tighter with desire. He slowly ran a finger over Flynn's opening and his lover's body tensed in anticipation of him sliding his finger inside, filling him and finding that secret spot with his fingers. But tonight the game rules had changed. Anthony teased Flynn, making sure he stayed away from that most sensitive part. He chuckled as he heard his groan of sheer disappointment as he moved away.

"You can't always get what you want. Sometimes you need to be left wanting," he whispered as he stood up and stepped out of his underwear. He groaned softly as he sprang free, the air caressing his erection.

Then Anthony covered Flynn's body, his cock pressing against his. They both grunted at the feeling of smooth flesh against flesh, wet, slick heat that made them both rub against each other in sheer need. Anthony kissed Flynn hungrily, his tongue sucking his as his fingers caressed Flynn's cock, smearing fluid over the shaft, rubbing the tip as Flynn wrapped his legs around Anthony's thighs.

"*Ti desidero,*" he whispered against Flynn's heated neck. "I want you."

"Anthony, please," Flynn gasped. "I need to feel you inside me. I've been waiting ages and I don't want to wait any longer. Make me come, please."

Anthony chuckled softly as his tongue slid into Flynn's ear. "I intend on making you come. I want to see you squirm. I love being inside you, you know that. You feel so tight and hot." His own desire was peaking to get inside Flynn and thrust until they both came. "Let me just get you ready, then I promise I'll fuck you into next week."

"You don't need to do much," Flynn gasped. "I was working on myself just before I put the cuffs on so I'm pretty open. Just use some of our own sticky stuff. That should do the job."

Anthony bit Flynn's bottom lip, tugging it between his teeth as he slid slick fingers inside Flynn's eager hole. Flynn cried out, his body pushing back, trying to push Anthony's fingers deeper inside himself. Anthony loved this wantonness of Flynn's, this need to be filled.

Flynn was muttering loudly now, a steady dialogue of "Fuck me, for God's sake, what's the matter, you not up to the job?" and a constant stream of profanities and jibes at Anthony's apparent inability to do the job that Flynn wanted him to do.

With a snarl, Anthony did what he was told and thrust inside Flynn, sliding forcefully in past the folds of hot, taut muscle, revelling in the tightness of Flynn. Flynn cried out and gripped Anthony around his shaft with muscles well practiced in the art. His thrusts grew fiercer as Flynn pounded his pelvis against him. Anthony felt the tight walls of Flynn's passage tightening around him. His groin felt as if it was about to explode and he knew he wasn't going to last long. From the sounds and pants Flynn was making as he attempted to impale himself even deeper on Anthony's engorged cock, neither was he. Their lips found each other as they duelled with wet, swollen tongues, fucking each other with their mouths as well.

"God, you drive me crazy," Anthony whispered in his ear. The fact Flynn was sightless and all Anthony could see was the silkiness of the binding around his eyes was an aphrodisiac. He imagined Flynn's eyes beneath the covering, pupils dilated in lust, deep blue eyes staring into his in a frenzy of want.

Flynn's called his name out loud, "Tony" over and over again, as Anthony muffled his cries with his kisses. The slick feel of their mingled sweat against their torsos, the friction he felt as he drove into the man beneath him— these were all senses heightened by the erotic scenario that they played in. Anthony licked the beads of sweat from Flynn's top lip as he heard his deep grunt as waves of Flynn's warm come shot across his belly and chest. Anthony loved the feeling of Flynn's internal muscles wrapping around his cock as he came, squeezing every last shred of defence from him. Anthony's cock gained momentum, and then he was releasing the heat that had built up in his balls. The musky rush delighted them both in an expulsion of sweat, semen and juices, and they both cried out. Their limbs shuddered and twitched, still entwined, as they blended together, spent of their passion for the time being, breathing heavy and laboured in the aftermath.

Chapter 12

Marshall Cunningham sat in the UCLH hospital canteen, idly flicking through the latest copy of GQ someone had left it on the table while he ate his rather mediocre chicken Kiev and salad. He'd thought he might as well see what the magazine had to offer. He was very taken with a rather delicious picture of some hot American actor on the front looking like a million dollars in his suit. He looked up as someone plonked themselves beside him, smiling widely when he saw who it was. Angie Green regarded him with sheer lust and avarice. He'd never quite had the heart to tell her he was gay. He wasn't all that obvious and the admiration in her eyes pandered to Marshall's need to be desired and noticed. It was good for his ego.

"Angie, good to see you here, away from Death Valley. How's Graham treating you? Last time we spoke, you said he was a right slave driver."

Angie rolled her blue eyes and flicked back her dark blonde hair in a gesture of vamp archness. Marshall thought it a pity that such a work of art was wasted on him.

"Graham's still expecting everyone to work twelve-hour shifts and then some. He's a bastard, I can tell you. But he's so good at what he does and I need the experience so I suppose I'll just have to put up and shut up like everyone else." She reached over and touched his arm gently. "How are things with you? Still spending all that time at the gym, keeping that gorgeous body of yours in shape?" She smiled at him and he grinned back.

"Yup, I still spend a lot of time there. It's become my second home really. There's nothing like having a good workout to clear the mind. You're looking good too, Angie. Are you doing anything to keep that shape you've got?"

She flushed in pleasure at his words. "I swim sometimes, but I'm not a big gym person. Perhaps you should introduce me to your gym sometime and we can work out together?"

Marshall deftly sidestepped her invitation. "I heard you guys down in Path were having a right nightmare with this new serial killer—the Bow Tie Killer. He must really be keeping you guys on your toes."

He thought Angie looked a little peeved at him changing the subject. She shrugged.

"He's a real freakazoid. This guy is nasty, I have to say. He even—" she broke off as she realized she was probably about to tell him something she shouldn't. Marshall was morbidly curious about the whole serial killer thing. He had probably watched every available movie he could on the crime channels on TV. He turned up the charm.

"I don't know how you do it, Angie. How you manage to stay so calm and keep sane when you see all that grisly stuff you do. You must be an incredibly focused person. But this sicko must really be taking a lot out of you. Who do you talk to when you go home? Have you got anyone you can confide in? If not, you know you can always talk to me." He reached over and covered her hand with his, seeing her face light up at his words.

"Jeez, that's great to hear. I haven't got a boyfriend at the moment, so when I get home the only thing that greets me is my cat. I do get a bit spooked sometimes at what I see in the Path lab." She leaned forward conspiratorially and lowered her voice. "The poor girl who was his latest victim? He actually carved her tattoo off her back and sewed it onto her pubic region!" She nodded at Marshall's grimace of disgust. "I know. That's really sick, isn't it? And the worst thing is, she was alive when he did it. But she got her own back."

Angie sat back in her chair, and Marshall could see she was dying to tell him more. "Really? What did she do?"

"She bit the fucker." Angie's voice was satisfied. "She took a great big bite out of him. We found his skin in her teeth. We're running it for DNA now but it will take a few weeks for the results to come back. We haven't even given the police the report yet. Some guy is coming down later to pick it up. At least it might be something for them to work on. They at least know the guy has a bite somewhere."

Marshall nodded. "He sounds like a real prize. What the hell motivates someone to do that to another human being? They have to be really mixed up." He felt a distinct sense of distaste at this individual's lack of humanity. As a doctor himself, it went against everything he believed in. He sighed and stood up. Angie's face dropped at his leaving.

"I need to get off. I have a patient to see in twenty minutes. It was great chatting to you though. I'm sure we'll see each other again here soon. Take care."

He waved slightly at her as he made his way out of the cafeteria. He wasn't lying. He did have a patient to see, a young girl who'd developed a severe case of carpal tunnel syndrome, possibly from playing too many computer games. Her file said she spent close to seven hours a day on her gaming equipment. He'd been astounded when he read that. Seven hours a day constituted a severe case of obsession or obsessive-compulsive disorder in his opinion. It was also complete stupidity to do something so repetitive for so long. He'd definitely be having words with her when he saw her later.

He got home later that night to find Blair already busy cooking pasta in his kitchen. Marshall smiled at the sight of his lover dressed in nothing but a pair of tight black jeans, bare-chested with an apron around his waist. He had to admit the sight was extremely alluring. He kissed the younger man hello as his eyes wandered over the kitchen work top and his hands cupped his lover's backside, loving the feel of the taut muscles beneath.

"This is a lovely surprise." He grinned as he lightly touched the bandage on Blair's left upper arm and frowned. "How's that bite doing? Have you taken the bandage off and checked that it's not inflamed? Perhaps I should take a look—"

Blair shook his head and moved his arm away. "There's really no need. I cleaned it earlier and put a fresh dressing on." He leered at his partner. "Later I can pretend I'm a cop, shot by a sniper in the line of duty, and you can be the sexy medic that comes to my rescue. I can think of a couple things you can do for me that will make me very happy. One that involves your mouth and my cock."

Marshall shook his head in amusement. "Christ, you have a one-track mind! Not that I'm complaining. I quite like that idea." He lifted the lid of a pot and smelt the aroma coming out. His nose wrinkled in appreciation. "It smells really good. Is it ready yet?"

"Give it about ten minutes. Why don't you go shower and by then it'll be all done."

Marshall grinned and disappeared into the hallway to take his shower. He turned the water on as hot as he could stand it and climbed into the large wet room in his en suite bathroom. He stood under the jets of steaming water, simply enjoying the sensation of the liquid on his skin. It soaked through to his muscles, easing the strain of his day. He heard a sound and turned to see Blair standing behind him, naked. He smiled as he stepped into the shower, pulling Marshall closer to him, his cock already erect and just begging to be sucked. Marshall enjoyed giving oral and prided himself on being pretty good at it.

"I thought you might need a little soaping down," Blair murmured huskily as he picked up the shower gel and poured it onto his palm. "Dinner can wait a little while longer."

Chapter 13

Anthony flicked through the pages of the report he'd been given by the Path lab at UCLH, his nose wrinkling in disgust as he read the contents. Rupert watched him, his fingers drumming on his desktop.

Anthony looked up at him with a frown. "Christ, would you stop that bloody racket? I'm trying to concentrate."

Rupert's fingers stopped their steady beating as he sighed loudly. "I want to know what the hell the report says too," he muttered. "You've been reading it for bloody ages."

"That's because I'm the man in charge here so stop being so bloody impatient and I'll fill you in soon." Anthony scowled and returned to his reading while Rupert glowered at his superior. After a few minutes, Anthony laid the file on the desk across from Rupert and passed a tired hand over his eyes.

"Christine managed to get a good bite out of the guy. They found some very small chunks of skin in her teeth and in her mouth. They've sent it for DNA testing against anyone currently in the database but they don't think we'll have a result for a couple of weeks. A couple of fucking weeks! This psycho could kill more women before then."

Rupert was glancing through the file himself, and as he reached one section of the report, he gave a low whistle. "Jesus, the guy actually cut that tat off her whilst she was *alive*? He's a bloody animal." His tone was grim.

Anthony nodded. "All the more reason to find him. So we have skin and DNA, just nothing to match it with yet. I doubt this guy will be in the database already. And we know our guy has a bite somewhere, probably on his upper arm. The lab said the hair follicles were not as dense which apparently has significance. They're still testing the skin for lotions, anything they think might give us any clue. Hell, maybe they'll tell us he uses something very rare on his skin, and we might get lucky."

Rupert looked up from his reading. "He probably thought he'd destroyed all the evidence bashing her jaw in like that but he slipped up."

Anthony nodded tiredly. "The DNA will be our best bet if we can find a suspect to match it against. He uses a condom when he rapes them too. So nothing there either. The man's a phantom. A fucking ghost. But we'll find him. We have to."

He turned as DCI Winslow shouted from his office across the floor. The man's face was set and his voice boomed out over the constant buzz of the room.

"DI Parglietto. I need a word. In my office, now."

Anthony glanced at Rupert who raised an eyebrow.

"He's got a definite bug up his arse," Rupert said quietly. "I wonder what the hell's happened."

Anthony stood up. "I guess I'm about to find out."

He walked across the floor, conscious of all the eyes on his back and entered his boss's office. Fred Winslow looked at him from eyes that were flinty. Anthony wasn't sure whether the glare was for his benefit or for the man who stood beside his superior, looking out into the street below. The man turned as Anthony came in and gave him a frosty smile.

"Detective Parglietto. Good to see you again."

His tone was sarcastic. Anthony felt his temper rise simply at the smirk on the man's face. Eddie Bowminster was a reporter on the *London Chronicle*, a weekly crime magazine with a fairly large following, much to Anthony's disgust. The magazine was, in his opinion, one that sensationalised the crime and the horrific events of the victims, laying it bare to speculation and often giving away too much information, information that put the police force on the back foot sometimes. God knows where Eddie got his information, but he always seemed to be abreast of everything going on.

"Bowminster. I should have known that you'd come crawling out of the primordial shit ooze at some stage." Anthony regarded the man flatly. "Shouldn't you be off somewhere trashing someone's life?"

Eddie looked hurt. "Detective, are you still pissed at me for that article I wrote about your brother's death? I told the story as the facts presented themselves."

Anthony snorted explosively. "Yeah, of course you did. My brother as some gay tramp trawling the gay bars and ending up being butchered behind one of them."

"I'm sorry you saw it that way." Eddie said primly. "I did my research. I wrote that story the best way I could."

"Fuck you, Bowminster," growled Anthony, his temper rising. "That was my little brother you demeaned in your crappy rag of a newspaper."

"I told it like I saw it. Your brother was in the wrong place at the wrong time and met the wrong man. It's a sad story but not a new one."

Anthony clenched his fists. He saw his boss move forward in his chair and knew sooner or later he'd stop the discussion.

"It wasn't just some random gay murder splatter fest. Something else was going on there and I will find out what it was one of these days. Then I'll take your bloody newspaper article and shove it—"

DCI Winslow scowled. "That's enough, Parglietto. Let's be civil. I know you two have a history but put it behind you both. We have a killer to find. And it looks like Mr. Bowminster here might be able to help us with that."

Anthony looked at his boss with narrowed eyes. "In what way could this slime ball help us? It's never bloody happened before."

He muttered under his breath. *"E' una testa di cazzo."*

Winslow gave a fierce frown, no doubt knowing Anthony had said something rude in Italian. Anthony didn't think he'd understand he'd just called Bowminster a fucking idiot.

Eddie tut-tutted. "Honestly, Anthony. All I do is report the truth. And as it happens, I do have something to offer you. For a price, of course."

Anthony shook his head in disgust and looked at his boss. "Are you really going to let this wanker get away with this bullshit, sir? Pardon the French but he's a complete tosser that likes to make himself out to be more important than he is. We shouldn't be pandering to his—"

"Anthony, shut it." DCI Winslow's tone was threatening. Anthony bit back the words he'd been about to say. Fred Winslow had his limits and Anthony thought he might have just reached them.

"Bowminster has something to share with us. Go ahead and tell Detective Parglietto about the note." The DCI waved a hand in Eddie's direction and Anthony could almost see the reporter's chest swell with self-importance. He wanted to punch him in the face then kick him where he fell.

"I received a communication from the Bow Tie Killer himself."
He stopped, obviously enjoying the look of disbelief Anthony felt
sweep across his face.

"How do you know it's BTK? And why the fuck would he send
anything to you?"

"I am a well-known reporter, Anthony. I have my following.
And your superior here has confirmed the authenticity of the note I
got which clearly tells me something that hadn't been in the public
domain. The fact that Roger Treave had his own thong stuffed up his
arse." The reporter's nose crinkled in distaste.

Anthony stared at him. "Where's this note?" he asked quietly.

Eddie grinned and pulled out a small plastic folder with a piece
of paper inside it. "This is a copy. I've already passed the original to
DCI Winslow here and he's sent it to your forensics lab. I was very
careful when I got the note. The minute I saw who it was from, I put
on a pair of latex gloves when I read it." His voice was smug. "You
see, Detective? I'm a crime reporter following crime scene
procedures."

Anthony ignored him as he read the note. A shiver of cold ran
down his spine as he noticed the writing was the same distinctive
flowing cursive he'd seen on the note he'd found in Flynn's flat.
This was definitely the same man.

Mr. Bowminster

I'm a great fan of your work. You have an ability to tell a story
in a way that really grasps at the essence of things. So bearing this in
mind, I thought I'd share a little something with you. Ask Detective
P about the item of clothing they found stuffed inside poor Roger.
Calvin Klein, I believe. Quite a risqué item of clothing for a
schoolteacher to wear. Perhaps he was having it off with the gym
teacher? Anyway, I digress. I'd also like you to pass on another
message for me to DI Parglietto. The same message I've given to
another one of your professional colleagues. He's not as fortunate as
you though in being able to share.

The flesh seems to weep,
Her throat red, no life, no sound
I come, feel alive

If you or those miscreants at the CID can figure this one out,
good on you! However, it will be too late of course. But at least I'll
feel I've provided you with a small challenge to keep the little grey

cells working. I'll be back in touch as soon as I have something more to say.

The Bow Tie Killer aka BTK (Really? You media hacks couldn't come up with anything more creative?)

Anthony looked up at the two men watching him. His skin crawled at the mention of the "he" in the missive "being given information he couldn't share." His instincts screamed again that Flynn was withholding something from him. "He's taunting us, obviously. Telling us something that even if we figure out what he's saying, he knows it will be too late to do anything anyway. It's been three days since we found Christine Donovan. This bastard has already chosen his next victim. He may even have them already. We know he keeps them, that the day the bodies were dumped wasn't necessarily the day he killed them. Christine was killed the day before Valentine's Day according to the autopsy report. Some poor woman could already be in his clutches and we haven't got a fucking clue who she is or where she might be."

He slammed the note in its plastic casing down on DCI Winslow's desk and paced the room, running his hands in agitation through his hair.

"Maybe we'll get something from the note," Fred Winslow regarded his detective with sympathetic eyes. "Maybe he's getting cocky. He might make a mistake. But I have no bloody clue what the poem's about. It just sounds like a load of bullshit to me."

Anthony stopped his pacing as something suddenly struck him about the note. He frowned as he moved forward to pick it up again.

"You're right, sir. This is a poem, isn't it? A special type of poem. I think it's a haiku of some form."

"A what?" Eddie Bowminster moved across to peer over Anthony's shoulder at the note.

Anthony gazed at him scathingly. "I'm just an uneducated policeman and you're a reporter yet you don't know what a haiku is? A Japanese poem. Five, then seven, then five syllables again. The cadence is the trick. What the hell does that mean? That he's going after a Japanese woman? And if so, how the hell would we know which one? Fuck, this is frustrating!"

Once again he slammed the note on the table and DCI Winslow reached out a cautionary hand and grasped his shoulder firmly.

"That's not a bad call, Detective. It might just be something we need to consider. And stop that damned pacing, will you? It's wearing out the carpet tiles."

Anthony stopped and regarded the other two men. "If he does intend taking somebody Japanese, then how can we find out who it might be? Christ, he could just have had a bloody shiatsu massage and is feeling all laid back so he thought he'd write a poem. How do we know?"

Eddie Bowminster rubbed his chin thoughtfully. "As it's a fairly personal message to you, Anthony—can we not perhaps assume that this maniac might have targeted someone you know, closely or by association? Do you know any Japanese people?"

The detective stared at Eddie as if he'd just grown a third eye.

"That's probably the most intelligent thing I've ever heard you say, Bowminster. No, I don't know anyone Asian, but Flynn might. It's an international news agency that he works at. It's a place to start anyway. We have nothing else as a lead yet. We can't check out every fucking Japanese person in the city so we have to start somewhere."

Anthony looked at the reporter grudgingly. He could see Fred Winslow biting back a smile at his consternation that the reporter had actually come up with something solid, even if it was a shot in the dark.

"I'll get hold of Flynn, see if he knows anyone that's Japanese. At least we can feel we're trying to figure this out instead of sitting around with our fingers up our backsides."

He left the two men standing and disappeared to his desk to get his mobile. Rupert looked at him quizzically as he sat eating a huge sandwich with what looked like chicken and salad. Anthony scowled, realising he was starving and hadn't yet eaten at all.

"Trust you to take care of your bloody stomach," he growled at his partner as he picked up his phone. "Christ, I'd kill for a double-decker now."

Rupert smirked. "Just as well I got you one then, isn't it? It's in your desk drawer. I had to hide it from Victor. He was on the prowl for something to cadge."

Anthony gave him a thumbs-up as he dialled Flynn's number. "You're a good man, Rupe. Tell Victor if I find him anywhere near my sandwich, I'll rip his bloody arms off."

He heard Flynn answer on the other side.

"Flynn Parker."

"Flynn, listen, this needs to be quick. Do you know anyone who's Japanese?"

Flynn chuckled on the other side and despite his agitation Anthony smiled at the sound.

"Lover, only you could ask me such random questions. Yes, I know someone who's Japanese—why?"

"Who do you know? It's important." He could hear the anxiety in his own voice and when Flynn spoke next, he could tell he'd picked up on it too.

"Masumi Teragaya. A work colleague here. What's going on?"

"Can you see her? Is she near you?"

"Masumi hasn't come in yet. She's late. She's normally here by now."

"Can you try phone her, see if she's okay? It might not be anything, but we have reason to believe BTK might have targeted someone Japanese. It's a long shot but I just want to follow it up. Let me know when you've spoken to her or not."

Flynn's voice was subdued. "I'll call her now. I'll call you back in a while."

He rang off and Anthony sat down at his desk, and opened his drawer. A large, plastic wrapped double-decker—ham, cheese, sausage and pickles—sat there, just waiting for him to sink his teeth into it. But all of a sudden he didn't feel that hungry. He closed the drawer.

"What's going on, Tony? Why are you looking for somebody Japanese?" Rupert leaned forward, crumbs on his chin. Anthony filled him in on the recent events and Rupert sat back, stunned.

"Jesus! He's contacting the press now? Or what loosely constitutes the press anyway. And he mentioned you? And what did he mean about telling someone else 'that couldn't share?'"

Anthony felt a sense of disquiet at that reminder. His worried expression caused Rupert to look at him knowingly.

"Do you think maybe he's telling Flynn stuff and telling him not to say anything? After all, that's the reason he let him go, wasn't it? And yet he's never made contact with him after all that. It always seemed a little off to me. Why would he do that?"

Anthony shook his head vehemently. He had to cut this off at the pass. He didn't like it either. And now with BTK's last little sarcastic dig, he had no idea what to think. "He'd tell me if he was contacting him. I've asked him about it already. He said he wasn't."

"But then why did he let Flynn live then? He must have had a reason. And if he is in touch with him and he's keeping it secret, why? I thought he wanted his story told. Why not tell it?"

"Jesus, give it a bloody rest, will you?" Anthony stood up as his mobile rang and he glared at his sergeant. "I need to take this call. It's Flynn."

He answered his phone, ignoring Rupert's sigh and his rolling eyes as he finished the rest of his lunch.

"Did you manage to get hold of your friend?"

Flynn's voice sounded scared. "No. She's not answering her phone which is unlike her and her boyfriend hasn't spoken to her since last night around seven o'clock. He's been worried; he can't get hold of her this morning but he thought her phone battery might be flat. She has a habit of letting it run down. What the hell is going on? Is Sumi in trouble?"

"I'm not sure. I thought it was a long shot when we started this, but now I'm beginning to think there might be some substance to it. Can you get your employer to text me her address, tell them it's a police matter and to stuff the whole employee confidentiality thing. I want to send a unit round to her house to check it out. I need it quickly."

"I'll go see Grace now and get it from her. I'll text it soon. God, please tell me this isn't him." Flynn's voice trembled.

"Get me that address." Anthony said softly. "It might be nothing. Just text me."

He cut the call short and put his phone in his pocket. Hopefully it was a false alarm and Sumi would be fine. His gut told him that he was being too optimistic.

Chapter 14

It was dark outside, the late evening drawing in. Flynn sat at the dining room table, laptop open in front of him, gazing blankly at the screen and the tiny cursor as it winked on the last line of the poem he'd recently been sent by BTK. His hands were frozen, his skin felt clammy and he felt like being sick again. He'd already vomited up the barely digested remains of a tuna salad only half an hour before.

Anthony had called just before his upchucking session. He'd quietly told Flynn that Masumi's apartment was empty, but her colleague's handbag and house keys were on the dining room table. It was déjà vu, similar to Flynn's own abduction, and he could tell from Anthony's gentle tone that he feared the worst. Even more gut wrenching was the fact that he'd told Flynn about the so called Japanese poem they'd received leading them to think someone Japanese was in danger and that they'd made the connection from there. The same Japanese poem that Flynn had received the night before, the one he'd told no one about. If he had, perhaps the connection would have been made earlier and Sumi would still be safe.

Flynn now had a difficult decision to make: he could tell Anthony about his secrecy and underhandedness in keeping things from him and risk being possibly arrested and having him leave him for his duplicity, or keep quiet and hope they caught BTK before he killed anyone else. Flynn knew deep down what he needed to do, but the mere thought of risking his relationship with Anthony broke his heart.

Flynn started when he heard Anthony's key in the lock and he entered the room. His boyfriend's face was drawn, his greeting smile faint and barely there. He looked exhausted and Flynn knew that the fact that another woman might be dead or dying was eating away at his soul. His stomach was knotted with fear for what was about to happen.

"*Sera, amore,*" Anthony greeted him softly. He often spoke to Flynn in Italian when he knew he was stressed but tonight his loving words simply made Flynn's gut wrench and his throat swell with dread.

Anthony's brow furrowed at seeing his face. "Flynn, there's still hope. Masumi hasn't come home, but we haven't had any other bad news, so maybe it's still okay…." His voice tailed off as Flynn shook his head blindly and tried to get the words out. Anthony moved swiftly over to him, placing a warm, strong hand on his shoulder.

"What's wrong? I know you were friends but this is a little extreme, isn't it? We don't know what happened yet."

"It's not just that. I have something I need to tell you and you won't like it. I've made a terrible misjudgement. I think I might have got Masumi killed."

Anthony pulled away from him, his face paling. "What the hell are you talking about?"

Flynn waved at the dining room chair, "Sit down, please," he said quietly. "I need to tell you something and you're going to get fucking angry. You may even have to arrest me, so I need to do this quickly."

Anthony stood in confusion for a while, staring at him, until finally he moved to the chair and sat down, his elbows on his knees as he leant forward and peered intently at Flynn's face.

"What the hell have you done, Flynn?" His voice was quiet but Flynn could hear the apprehension in it.

He swallowed. "I've been getting emails from BTK for the past week. He keeps sending them to me. He said he would kill you and Kieran if I talked about it. The last one I got was that poem you mentioned. I got it last night."

His voice sounded dead even to his ears. Flynn watched Anthony's face dully, his wonderful, expressive face, as it moved from shock, to anger, to resignation and then finally a mixture of all three. The explosion he'd expected didn't come. Instead, he buried his face in his hands and was quiet. Flynn watched him in silence. When Anthony finally looked up, the look on his face was of sheer despair.

"Jesus, what the fuck have you done?" His face was ashen, his voice was defeated, so unlike his lover that Flynn felt more scared of this reaction than the sheer explosive fury he'd expected. He thought he'd prefer the fury. It wasn't too long in coming.

Anthony stood up angrily, his hands flexing at his side, his brown eyes dark with anger. "Exactly how many emails has this bastard sent you? I need to see them. Now."

He walked over and loomed over behind Flynn in silent demand. His tone brooked no argument. Silently, Flynn refreshed the screen of his laptop then entered his password and clicked on the BTK folder. He was aware of Anthony's eyes on everything he did and he knew he was remembering Flynn's impassioned argument the other night about why all of a sudden he'd been password protecting his gadgets. He knew now that he'd lied point blank to his face. That certainly wouldn't sit well when he'd finally got to grips with this betrayal.

Flynn sat back and motioned to Anthony to do what he needed. He pulled up a chair and wouldn't even look at Flynn. He simply sat down, pulled the laptop toward him and with a frown of concentration, he began clicking his way down the dozen or so emails in the folder. His face went greyer with each click and occasionally he closed his eyes as if in pain then opened them again to stare fiercely at the screen. He muttered in Italian and Flynn's stomach tightened further with dread as Anthony spat the words out. Finally he closed the laptop and regarded Flynn with a cold stare that made his bones chill.

"You fucking lied to me. Point blank to my face. I know you think you were protecting me and Kieran by not telling me about this. And I know you were scared about him coming after you again. But I could have protected you and Kieran if I'd known. Somehow. You know I would have. As for me, I can take care of myself. There's some information in these emails that may help us in finding out more about this guy if we'd had the chance. Instead he gets to be all cosy and pally with my boyfriend, laughing at me behind my back, making fools of the people I work with who put their fucking lives on the line every time they go out on the job." His voice was hard and terrible to hear.

Flynn swallowed. "Anthony—" His hands were freezing cold and he put them between his jeans-clad legs for warmth.

"Don't you dare try and make fucking excuses. You lied to me. Cold, stone-faced lies. Rupert said he didn't feel comfortable with the fact that BTK hadn't tried to make contact with you after he let you go. He was right. How do you think that makes me feel, knowing that my partner seems to know my boyfriend better than I do? That I let my feelings for you get in the way of the job? And now someone else is dead because we both fucked up. Because you know what? Masumi is dead. I can feel it. And tomorrow or the next day, I'm going to be the one who has to stand over her mangled and violated body and apologise to her for not catching this psycho sooner." His voice was bitter and Flynn could only sit there as the guilt and hurt caused his chest to swell painfully. He stared down at the table top.

Anthony stood up, his face bleak. "Give me your phone. Un–password protect it first. The laptop too. I'm taking them to the station so I can have a real look at them. I'll have to talk to the DCI as well if he's there, see if I can try and convince him not to arrest you for obstruction of justice. Luckily you're a reporter." His voice was sarcastic. "He's used to you lot being underhand and protecting your 'sources.' Although I doubt I'll be able to use that argument with him because the emails are actually from the fucking killer himself!"

He held out a hand, a hand which was shaking, and Flynn reached across to the table and picked up his mobile. He clicked through a few screens while Anthony waited with apparent suppressed violence and then handed it to him. Flynn did the same to his laptop. When he'd finished, he looked up at into glittering and impassioned hazel eyes that didn't look anything like the man he loved.

"There are no more passwords on them." Flynn took a deep, jagged breath. "He didn't text me on the phone at all anyway, so you won't find anything on there."

"I'd like to check that for myself under the circumstances," Anthony muttered through clenched teeth. He tucked the phone in his trouser pocket and picked up his jacket from the back of the chair, tucking the laptop under his arm. He pointed a finger at Flynn.

"You—stay here. Don't go anywhere. Lock the doors and make sure that spare mobile is at hand. The one that's always in the kitchen on charge. I don't want to leave you without one. I'm going to have a police car come over and watch this place and you. I can probably justify that now again. I'll see if my friend Ernie can take care of Kieran for a short time until we get this fuck-up sorted out. I'm going to try and see if I can fix this mess you've caused and keep you out of gaol. Don't wait up for me. I'm not sure when I'll be back tonight."

Flynn heard the unspoken "*if* I'll be back" and closed his eyes in anguish. When he opened them, Anthony had gone.

Chapter 15

Anthony sat at his office desk, staring blankly at the laptop screen in front of him. He'd arrived back at the office to some curious glances from the late-nighters still there, obviously wondering why he was back. It was close to nine o'clock and he was tired. He was also scared, his emotions swirling around inside him like heavy laundry in a washing machine, making him feel nauseous.

How the hell was he supposed to fix this? Tell his boss that his boyfriend had been receiving secret messages from BTK, messages that may have helped them in the investigation. Keep Flynn from being arrested—even though it probably wouldn't stick given that he'd been a victim and had every right to fear for his life; it was an added complication they didn't need. And of course, their relationship had just taken a huge hit. How could he trust Flynn anymore? That thought alone made him cold with despair.

I don't want to lose him.

Even though Anthony wasn't convinced himself that there were really any particularly useful bits of information in the emails BTK had sent—the man was far too clever for that—the hints at his past and the names of the supposed victims he'd mentioned might have helped them narrow down the search. The one thing about having little random bits of information was that you never knew where they would lead or how they would eventually fit together. And he'd no doubt that Masumi had been dead probably before or shortly after the poem had even been sent. But still.

"Anthony? What the hell are you doing back here? You look like shit, son." Fred Winslow's voice cut through his thoughts. Anthony felt his heart lurch as he looked up into the appraising eyes of his superior.

DCI Winslow perched his large backside on the corner of Anthony's desk. "I've also just been told that you requested a new security detail to be assigned to Flynn. I've approved it because I know you wouldn't have done it without a good reason, but I think you need to fill me in. Has something happened?"

Anthony took a deep breath.

"Yes, sir. I wasn't sure you were still here; I didn't see you in your office when I got back in."

Winslow grinned wryly. "When you get to my age, your bladder has a mind of its own and you have bowels that need to evacuate more often than a prostitute lays on her back. I was in the can. Tell me what you have."

"Can we do this privately, sir—in your office?"

Winslow regarded his face and then nodded. "You're scaring me, Anthony. What kind of mess have you got yourself into now?"

He sighed and heaved his bulk off the desk. It creaked as he stood up, relieved no doubt that the pressure was off. The DCI wandered slowly over to his office, Anthony following behind him, laptop clutched in his hands. Once they were inside, Winslow indicated to Anthony to sit down, shut his office door, and then settled back comfortably in his chair before turning his piercing glance on him.

"Right. Tell me all about whatever fuck-up we're facing now. Because from the look on your face, that seems to be the problem."

Anthony wasted no time in succinctly bringing his superior up to date. He heard the anger in his voice at Flynn's actions as he related his story. He watched the steadily darkening expression on Fred Winslow's face. Anthony finished his story and sat back, feeling a sense of relief that the story was shared. Winslow leaned forward, steepling his fingers on his desk.

"This, my friend, is a monumental fuck-up. You know that, don't you?"

Anthony regarded Winslow steadily. "Yes, sir. I know that. And I'm sorry. I should have known what was going on and I didn't. I feel responsible for this mess."

DCI Winslow looked at him thoughtfully. "And just how should you have known this, DI Parglietto? Do you perhaps have telekinesis or the ability to read people's minds that you should have been able to see into the computer or your boyfriend's head to see what was going on? Because if you do, son, then you're more valuable to this unit that a nugget of cereal to a starving Ethiopian. And I'd be pretty pissed off that I didn't know this all before."

Anthony's face flushed. "No, sir. No super powers. But—"

Winslow held up an admonishing finger. He leaned forward and spoke quietly.

"You need to cut Flynn some slack. I can hear you're upset with him. But he's not a police officer. He is a victim of BTK. He was abducted and someone threatened to kill him. Now the psychopathic bastard is threatening to do it again only this time he also wants to harm you and the ex-lover as well. The man must have been shit scared. I know I would have been. And I think I might have done the same thing as he did. It's not right but I understand it. What we have to do—and I mean you and I; I want no one else to know about this—is find a way to fix this. You haven't told anyone else about this, have you, especially that moralistic bloody sergeant of yours?"

Anthony shook his head, feeling a sense both relief and guilt at Winslow's words. Relief that he now had a powerful ally and a growing guilt over the fact that perhaps he'd been too harsh with Flynn.

His DI nodded in satisfaction. "Good. We need to think about how to get this information you've found out to the unit without anyone knowing it's been sat on for a week or where it's been. Any ideas?"

Anthony sat back, his brow furrowed. "We'll have to stay as close to the truth as possible or we could trip ourselves up in the details. My suggestion would be to simply say that someone on the outside has just come forward with some information that BTK has been sending them. But we just don't say who and we don't release the full details, just what's pertinent to the investigation. We class them as a CI and then hopefully we can get away with it."

A CI—Confidential Informant—was an accepted police practice, an anonymous source protected by various legal shenanigans from ever being revealed. The best they could hope for was that this would never get questioned. If the worst came to bear, and Flynn was discovered, Anthony could always say he'd been his CI all along. But it wasn't worth exposing that fact now though if they could get away with it any other way.

Winslow nodded. "I had the same thought. Let's create a CI then." He grinned faintly. "With any luck, people will think it's that tosser, Bowminster. It's not a stretch by any means of the imagination. BTK's already contacted him once and the bugger hasn't been backwards in coming forwards on telling everyone about it." He sat back with a self-satisfied smile.

Anthony stood up, stretching his arms above his head and as he dropped them, he looked at his boss and spoke quietly.

"Thank you, sir. For not taking this further and helping me out. I appreciate it."

Winslow regarded the younger man sympathetically. "Anthony, you and Flynn have been through hell. I'm also still not happy that this psycho seems to want to target you personally any way he can and we still don't know why. I know you're looking out for yourself but still, you need to be careful, son. Watch your back. He's not going to be happy Flynn has told you about him if he gets to figure it out. I'll keep the protective detail on him as long as we can. I'll justify it a while longer to upstairs and take the flak. Just find this miserable bastard soon."

He stood up and moved around to Anthony, laying a comforting hand on his detective's back. "Now get off home and go and sort things out with your man. I'm betting you and that temper of yours had something to say to him about all this and you need to put it right. God knows how he's feeling thinking he might have contributed to killing his friend." He sighed. "I hate that. Saying something like that when there isn't even a body yet. But you and I both know it's probably the case."

Anthony felt an even deeper twinge of shame at Winslow's words.

Christ, I was so busy thinking about how to fix this and getting all angsty about the fact he'd lied to me, I didn't even think about how he must be feeling about Masumi. Flynn is still trying to get to grips with what happened to him and I just ranted all over him because he cared enough not to get me hurt. I'm an arsehole.

He nodded as he picked up his jacket, slipping Flynn's phone once more into his pocket and picking up the laptop. He was anxious to get home and talk to Flynn.

"Thanks, sir. I'll get these items to evidence. I've printed all the emails out and sent copies to my work email account. I've no doubt as soon as we start poking around into BTK's background, the details of his school and where he lived, not to mention those other victim's names, he'll find out we know about these emails. God knows what he'll do then. My priority is keeping Flynn safe." He frowned. "He made threats against his ex, Kieran, too. I'll have to arrange protection of some sort. I have a friend I can perhaps use to do that for a short while because I doubt we'll get anything organised officially."

Winslow nodded. "That might be difficult. The threat is too far removed for the pen pushers to sign another protection detail. See what your friend can do and if you struggle, then let me know. I might have some ideas too."

Anthony clutched the phone and laptop against his chest and left DCI Winslow's office. He had a lot to sort out and given the sense of guilt he felt inside, justified or not, he'd rather be home with Flynn than sitting in his cold, unheated office wondering how he was. Best get home and face the music.

It had almost gone ten p.m. when he got home. The flat was in darkness with only an uplighter left on in the corner of the room. He checked the kitchen. The spare phone was gone from the charger. He hoped Flynn had it with him. Anthony made his way through to the bedroom. It was dark and he could vaguely see the huddled form of someone in the bed. He undressed quietly and then slipped under the covers, naked. He lay down and turned to face Flynn. He needed to see if Flynn was properly sleeping or could be jolted into wakefulness for a talk. As he faced Flynn, he was assailed by the smell of brandy and his nostrils flared.

Jesus, it smelt like a distillery. How much had he bloody drunk?

He flicked his side light on. Flynn was deep in sleep, face turned toward him, pale and waxy. Anthony reached out and gently moved a wayward strand of hair off his face. As he did, he noticed the empty brandy bottle on Flynn's side table and lying beside it, a few curled up and rather alarming looking empty blister packs of some tablet or another. Anthony's skin prickled and his breathing sped up. He shook his lover's shoulder gently, watching the blanket fall off, exposing Flynn's chest. He breathed a sigh of relief as he noticed the rhythmic fall as he breathed.

"Flynn? Wake up."

There was no response and Flynn remained as still as ever, not even a flutter beneath his eyelids.

Anthony laid his hand against his face. "Babe, please wake up." There was still no reaction. He reached out and grasped his shoulder tightly, shaking it more vigorously. "*Cazzo*, would you bloody wake up? I want to know you're all right!"

His voice was louder now and he knew he was probably panicking but he couldn't help himself. Flynn opened his eyes and stared at him, his eyes unfocused. He had a look of confusion on his face.

"What's the matter?" His tone was slightly slurred but Anthony didn't know if it was from drinking or from sleep.

"I saw the pills by the side of your bed and the brandy. I was worried."

He watched as Flynn struggled up and sat back against the iron headboard, plumping up his pillows behind him as if he were punching someone. Anthony had a feeling he knew who the unfortunate "punchee" was.

"I'm fine." Flynn's voice was quiet, his face pale. "I needed something to help me sleep so I took some Panadols. I washed it down with brandy because I thought that might help too." His voice was defiant.

"How many pills did you take and how much brandy did you drink?"

Flynn's face darkened. "Enough. I didn't really think you'd care. What's with all the sudden solicitousness anyway?" There was a slight sneer in his voice.

"Christ, of course I bloody care! What kind of a stupid comment is that to make?" Anthony's temper boiled just beneath the surface and he fought to keep it there.

"When you left, it was if I was some sort of pariah that you couldn't bear near you." Flynn muttered. "I'm surprised you're home, to be honest. I expected you to stay at work and sleep there. It wouldn't be the first time."

Despite the fighting words, Anthony heard the vulnerability beneath them and he wanted nothing more than to pull Flynn close and tell him it was all going to be okay. But you didn't do that with Flynn. He'd probably push him away. Anthony had to choose his timing.

"Have you found Masumi?" Flynn's next words threw Anthony; he'd not been expecting them.

He shook his head gently. "No. I checked earlier. She's still not home and we haven't heard anything else. But we haven't stopped looking."

"She's dead, isn't she?" Flynn's voice trembled. "He's got her."

Anthony sighed heavily. "It's looking that way. I'm sorry. But if it's any consolation, I don't think anything you could have done, like telling me about the poem earlier, would have done any good. He probably had her by then."

"That's not what you said earlier." Flynn's tone was accusing.

Anthony rubbed his eyes tiredly. "I said a lot of things earlier that perhaps I shouldn't have. I'm sorry. I truly am. I was scared for you. I had visions of having to put you in handcuffs and take you down to the station." His attempt at humour didn't seem to help as Flynn looked at him steadily. His blue eyes were stark with guilt.

"I know I fucked up. But I didn't want him to hurt you, or Kieran. I don't want him coming back for me. I thought I was keeping us all safe. I never thought he'd take my friend. I didn't ask to know all this stuff about him. And now you know, and he'll know, and no one will ever be safe again."

Flynn's fists clenched and he lay back on his pillows and closed his eyes. Anthony felt a lump in his throat. His chest ached and he reached out to pull Flynn close but he slapped his hands away hard. Anthony pulled them back, his eyes wide.

"Don't touch me!" Flynn hissed, anguish in his voice. "I don't deserve to be touched. You come home to a man who's a liar, some psycho killer is using me as his fucking postbox and Masumi was my friend and because of that he took her. And now she's probably dead."

There was such pain in Flynn's voice that Anthony threw caution to the wind. He reached over, pulling Flynn into him, ignoring his attempt to pull free. He needed the power he had to hold him close, as Flynn's body fought the embrace, his stiff arms pushing him away, hands braced against Anthony's chest in a gesture of defiance and defeat. Anthony used his own considerable strength to fight Flynn's onslaught. Finally, Flynn gave up with a low, agonising groan and melted into him as he rested his face in Anthony's neck.

"I've fucked things up totally." His voice was bleak and Anthony's heart broke.

"No you haven't." He gently smoothed loose hair back from Flynn's face. "He's the mess-up. Not you." Anthony kissed his forehead softly, his mouth planting small kisses against his hair, ear, cheek, anywhere he could think of to try and tell this man that he loved him and they'd overcome this together.

"I'm so sorry for what I said earlier, *cuore mio*," he whispered as he stroked Flynn's back. "I overreacted, but it's all going to be okay. I promise. I've spoken to DCI Winslow. We've come up with a plan. It will all be fine. He's not going to get you again. I won't let him."

Flynn's blue eyes regarded him. "What about Kieran? Is he going to be safe?"

"Yes, he'll be safe. That mate of mine, Ernie, the one I was going to ask to watch you? He's watching Kieran now and I've organised another police detail for you. They're outside now. Come over here. I'll show you."

He climbed out of the bed, naked, walking over to the large floor-to-ceiling picture window. He beckoned to Flynn to come over and he clambered out of the bed, clad only in his boxers, and joined him by the window. Anthony pulled back the curtain and motioned down into the street.

"There's the unmarked car, the Volvo on the other side of the street. Justin and Rob are two of the best we have at this sort of thing. They'll look out for you wherever you go. You won't even notice them, they're that good."

In his anxiety to show Flynn said protection, Anthony suddenly became uncomfortably aware that he was standing, totally nude, in front of the window. He hoped fervently that his colleagues weren't looking up at him. He'd never bloody live it down at the station. He hastily pulled the curtain back over and looked back at his lover. Flynn reached up a hand to caress his cheek and Anthony felt a sense of sheer relief that he was performing even that simple gesture.

"What have I done to deserve you? You've fixed it. At least as much it can be fixed." Flynn smiled sadly. "But neither of us can fix whatever might have happened to Sumi. Please tell me you'll catch him."

Then Flynn reached up and took Anthony's mouth in a kiss that made his groin burn and his stomach lurch as he kissed him back, despite the strains of the evening. Flynn's tongue slid into his mouth, and Anthony groaned, his cock swelling hard and fast up against Flynn's stomach. Flynn's lips still tasted of brandy and Anthony drank him in, savouring the softness of his lips, breathing in the sighs he made. Flynn finally released his mouth and Anthony stood feeling bereft. Then with one quick movement, Flynn pulled him over to the bed and pushed him back onto the covers. He slid his boxers off and stood there, half-mast and with a look in his eyes that said he knew what he wanted. When he spoke his voice was husky.

"I know we shouldn't be enjoying ourselves like this but I really need to feel you."

Anthony knew that this sex was probably a simple primeval instinct to drive away the demons that plagued them both, coupled with the relief that both of them were there, safe together. He was more than willing to be Flynn's solace if that was what he needed.

Their lovemaking was raw and animalistic, all push and pull, flesh against flesh. As Anthony thrust his tongue deep into Flynn's mouth, as they struggled in their desire for each other, their teeth knocked together in their passion, and not for the first time he marvelled that this true moment of sexual bliss was all because of Flynn. He'd never felt this level of intimacy or passion with any other man before. Flynn straddled him, Anthony's cock buried deep inside him as he rose and fell with the cadence of his lovemaking.

"I want to watch you," Flynn whispered. "I want to keep my eyes open all the time so I know it's you always. Watch me back, Tony."

Anthony looked up into Flynn's beloved face and nodded. "Always, *amore. Sarò sempre vegli su di voi.*"

Flynn groaned as he bounced up and down, causing Anthony to gasp as his cock slid in and out, and the pressure in his groin increased. "God, I love it when you speak Italian to me in bed. What does it mean?"

Anthony smiled softly as he kept up his own momentum, feeling the familiar signs of his impending climax prickling in his buttocks and spreading warmth to his groin.

"It means I will always be watching you."

Flynn moaned softly, leaning forward as he took Anthony's mouth again in a fierce kiss. Anthony's fingers were wrapped around Flynn's cock as he stroked him and watched his face change in his orgasm, loving the sight of Flynn's come as it coated his hands and arm and belly. Anthony wasn't long behind him, the sight of Flynn's opened mouth, half-closed eyes as he jetted copious amounts of come onto both of them Anthony's body shuddered and shook with an intensity he'd not felt for a while. Flynn uncoupled himself from Anthony and rolled over to lie beside him. He grinned sleepily.

"I guess that means we're not arguing anymore," he whispered. "I like the way we make up."

Anthony chuckled tiredly. "So do I." They lay cradled together, Flynn's head against his shoulder as he stroked his arm drowsily.

"Winslow is on board with me having a CI coming forward and giving us all the stuff you had. I'll try and play it down but Rupe's not stupid. He'll probably know it's come from you. Let him think. He won't be able to prove anything."

Flynn shifted next to him. "You and your DCI are really going balls to the wall for me on this. It could get you both into serious trouble. I'm sorry—"

Anthony forestalled the apology with a hard kiss. "Enough. Let's not talk about it anymore. What's done is done. Tomorrow we'll start working through all the emails and all the details he's given us. Maybe, just maybe, he's slipped up and given us something we can use to track him down."

"Meanwhile we just wait to see if another body is found." Flynn nibbled his shoulder softly, his hands spread across his stomach.

Anthony sighed. "Don't give up hope. Maybe we've misread the situation altogether." He heard the soft sigh as Flynn settled into sleep against him. Anthony knew these were brave words and he didn't believe them himself but he had to try and give his tortured lover some solace that his friend might still be alive.

Chapter 16

The following morning Anthony got to the CID offices around lunchtime. He'd spent the morning at the hospital morgue, spending time with Graham Manning, going over all the forensic evidence they had to date. The pathologist was always amenable to the detectives from the team sitting with him in his office and reviewing the case files. Anthony had always found him to have a tremendous insight into the world of science and the enigmas that were the dead bodies of his victims. There'd been nothing new really, just the grim facts of the cases rehashed and Anthony's growing frustration that BTK seemed to leave no discernible trace of himself.

The detective walked through the office to his desk, noticing the grins and sly glances of the rest of the office as he moved across the floor. His skin prickled with unwelcome apprehension. Normally this sort of attention signified a prelude to some sort of practical joke, something that he already knew he probably wouldn't like. As he reached his desk, Anthony saw what was waiting for him and uttered a loud groan even as his eyes darted around the room trying to find the guilty face of the perpetrator.

"Jesus Christ!" He glowered at Rupert who sat at the opposite side of the desk with a wide smirk. "Whose bloody idea was this then? It can only be Justin or Rob. I suppose they've bloody told everyone about seeing me last night in the altogether. Where the hell are those two jokers anyway?" Anthony looked around the room suspiciously as he tried to ignore the three-foot white, plastic and very naked statue of David by Michelangelo placed strategically in the middle of his desk. He had no idea how the guys had managed to find such a thing so soon but he assumed it was in deference to his naked stance at the window last night—the one he'd really hoped no one had seen. But he supposed ironically that a protection detail was paid to be observant.

Rupert cocked an eyebrow at him. "Personally, I don't think the statue does you justice. I've seen you in the change rooms at the gym and I have to say I think yours is—"

"Shut the fuck up." Anthony growled as he stared ferociously at his sergeant. "I'd suggest you don't continue with that bloody sentence if you value your own balls."

Rupert sniggered along with the rest of the office. Anthony shook his head and removed the statue, placing it in the waste bin at the side of his desk. He bowed to the giggling room.

"Very funny, you lot. Let's see how amusing it is when I decline your overtime chits and give you the task of sorting out the drunk tank. Maybe you won't find it so funny when you're all up to your ankles in vomit and crap."

The room finally exploded in loud laughter despite his threat and Anthony sat down at his desk, grinning from ear to ear. The incident had certainly bought a little bit of light relief into what otherwise would have been a fairly morose room of people. He was glad of it, even if it had been at his expense. He looked forward to telling Flynn about it later. He'd find it hilarious. Anthony looked across at his still-amused sergeant, feeling his mood sober. Time to break the news.

"We have some leads." Anthony watched Rupert's face carefully. "I spoke to DCI Winslow last night. We've had someone come forward who's been receiving emails from BTK. They kindly let us know late last night and have sent us the correspondence they have. It might help us find this son of a bitch."

Rupert's face was watchful. "Really? Can you tell me who it is?"

Anthony shook his head, knowing his colleague wouldn't be satisfied and feeling like a heel for lying to him.

We're supposed to be partners in this whole thing for God's sake.

"We want to keep the identity secret. DCI Winslow has assigned them CI status. For their own protection. So we work with what they've given us but only the DCI and I will be in contact with them."

Rupert leaned back in his chair with a thoughtful nod of his head. "I see. So, this person then—BTK has been sending what to them exactly?"

Anthony motioned at his computer. "You should have a message in your inbox. I'm surprised you haven't seen it yet. You're a bit behind, Sergeant. I sent it last night."

Rupert flushed. "I get hundreds of bloody emails a day. I'm still working through them all." He leaned forward and typed something on his keyboard. "Was it marked as urgent, something to be addressed immediately?"

Anthony shook his head. "No. Subject line was simply *New Information*." He'd deliberately not marked as a priority or with any reference to BTK because he'd hoped that he'd be in the office when Rupert finally got to it. He knew Rupert's rather dilatory approach to checking his emails would work in his favour. He would have a lot of questions and Anthony wanted to be there when he saw the email for the first time.

Rupert nodded. "I see it. There look to be quite a lot of them." He looked at Anthony and the DI could sense his disapproval in not being informed of the identity of the CI. "They appear to have started arriving about a week ago if the dates on the sheet are anything to go by. But there's no email address or body as such, just the text of the emails themselves. I suppose that's to protect your CI source?"

Anthony had carefully screened each and every email, ensuring no reference to Flynn's email address remained and added them together into an Excel spreadsheet. He'd also removed the first email from BTK mentioning Flynn and their encounter. He sat back, not answering his sergeant's querying look.

Rupert frowned, seeing he was going to get no reply. "Why did this CI not come forward at the beginning?"

"They were scared. Maybe they thought they'd be implicated. Who knows? The fact is we have some snippets of information that we think might help us narrow down the search for this bastard. I want you and the rest of the team to start following up on every bit we have. See what you can find out."

"Why would BTK do this?" Rupert's voice was quiet. "Why would he send personal information to someone, knowing they might give us the information and help us find him? It doesn't make any sense."

Anthony had had the same view originally but had recently changed his mind. "It's a game. Contacting this person, sending bloody Japanese poems to Bowminster—he's playing a game. He doesn't care if the information gets to us because he doesn't care whether we find him or not. Maybe he wants us to find him, so he can show us all just how fucking clever he is. He's taunting us, taunting me, giving us clues. Because he doesn't really think we are able to track him down. He's arrogant and overconfident. And that might be his downfall."

Anthony stood up. "I need to see DCI Winslow about something. Get cracking on that information;, pull the files on any of those first names, see if you can match them up with what he say about how they died. Look at the timelines; see if you can spot any trends. It's a long shot but it's all we have. I also want someone out in Great Dunmow, tracking down this school teacher he mentions. Mr. Armandsone. Perhaps he might remember a psycho little boy that scared the shit out of him. I want everything on that list checked and triple checked. I'll expect feedback later tonight."

Anthony could feel Rupert's eyes on his back as he walked towards his superior's office. He sighed. It wasn't going to be easy keeping Rupert's curiosity and suspicions at bay. After all, that's what made the man such a good policeman.

Chapter 17

Marshall Cunningham was fractious, fed up and ready to explode. He'd had a shit journey home from the hospital on the tube, when he'd been groped by a man twice his size, to the extent that his balls were still tender. He'd been coughed on by some homeless woman as he walked along his street, and had to clean her disgusting phlegm off his new and very expensive Gucci coat and now, as he stood in his kitchen, the final straw was seeing the mess that the kitchen had been left in, obviously after some culinary effort Blair had created. Empty pots were strewn around the kitchen top. There was some sort of red sauce everywhere, one saucepan still had the burnt remains of something tarred to the bottom—Marshall wasn't sure what—and the sink was piled with dirty dishes. Blair was nowhere to be seen.

"Christ almighty," Marshall muttered through gritted teeth as he started cleaning up. "What the hell has he been doing? It looks like he had a full-blown party in here." He grimaced as he found a dishcloth covered in some sticky goo firmly stuck to the kitchen top, to the extent he had to physically yank it off, leaving shreds of the fabric behind.

"Fuck!" Marshall threw the dishcloth angrily at the open bin, narrowly missing it, watching it land on the tiled floor as he clenched his teeth. The next twenty minutes were spent cleaning up the mess his lover had left for him. When he finally sat down in his easy chair with a glass of white wine and a plate of cheese and biscuits, Marshall began to feel a little mellower. He switched on the sound system and selected his music choice. The soft strains of Alex Clare wafted through the air and Marshall sighed in satisfaction. Not for the first time he wished the man was gay. With a voice like his and a little more care of his beard to reduce it to a more sexy designer stubble, he'd definitely want the man in, up close and personal. He was still fantasising about this when his mobile rang. He frowned when he saw who it was.

"Blair? What the hell did you do to my kitchen today? It looked like a bunch of home invaders had been through here wrecking it."

"Sorry, I had to leave in a hurry." Blair's voice was slightly out of breath and Marshall wondered what the hell he'd been doing. "I'll make it up to you, I promise. Just not tonight."

Marshall felt very put out. "I thought we were going to the movies tonight? I came home especially early so we could make the seven p.m. show."

"Not going to happen. I have some personal stuff to do so I doubt I'll be over tonight. I'll be going back to my own place. I'll call you tomorrow though and we can make another plan." It sounded as if Blair was in an empty room with the echo of his voice in the phone.

"Where are you anyway?" Marshall asked curiously. "You sound as if you're in a warehouse or something. There's a real echo."

Blair's voice was smooth. "Nowhere that you need to worry about. I can't chat. I've got to go." His lover rang off abruptly, leaving Marshall scowling at his mobile.

Jesus, first he leaves things in a mess, now he can't make our date tonight! The evening was just getting bloody worse.

As he lay his phone down in a temper on the side table, he noticed a rucksack in the corner of the room. It was a grey satchel, quite large and looking as if it was stuffed with various bits of paper and documents. Marshall hadn't seen it before. He stood up and went over to examine it. He picked it up and took it back to his chair, sitting down and laying the rucksack on his lap as he looked at it. It had to be Blair's. He pondered whether to look inside it. Blair was intensely private, almost never giving anything away about himself. Marshall knew Blair's parents had died when he was younger, that he had no family to speak of and was fairly wealthy due to an inheritance he'd received on the death of his parents. Other than that, and the fact he was an Aries, with a birthday at the end of March, Marshall knew little about his childhood or his time before he'd met him. Perhaps what was inside this item might give him a clue.

Marshall felt a frisson of anticipation as he pulled open the straps and pulled out a sheaf of documents. He was a little disappointed at what he found. They appeared to be some sort of boring financial report on some investments or other. The amounts were fairly mind boggling but Marshall already knew Blair was rich—by his standards anyway. Another document appeared to be a deed to some old property out on the outskirts of London, a residential property from the sounds of it. 22B Southern Street, in Newham in London. It appeared to be in the name of a company called Mainwaring Associates. Marshall knew Blair owned a property but he'd said he never went there as he had a management company looking after it. It was apparently not in the most salubrious of places and his lover had made it very clear he'd didn't like the area at all. Marshall felt a little let down. He'd expected something a little more personal. He rummaged around in the sack a little more and frowned when he found an old till receipt. The till receipt was dated 20th December from B and Q, the local DIY and hardware store. Marshall frowned as he looked at the list.

Heavy Duty Gaffer Tape Black 25m £8.98
Blue Stranded PP Rope 8mm x 30m £29.34
General Purpose Cover Sheet Clear 3m x 4m £69.80
Chipboard Floor (L) 2400 x (W) 600 x (T) 22mm £59.40
Damp Proof Membrane Blue 1000 Gauge 3m x 4m £58.44
Stanley Titanium Sports Knife £15.98

What in God's name was Blair doing with all this stuff? And from the look of it, there'd been multiple bought of certain items. Marshall was no DIY man himself, but he'd bet his arse that a plastic cover sheet didn't cost nearly seventy quid for just one of them.

Marshall grinned in amusement. It looked like a shopping list Dexter might have. Marshall certainly couldn't remember having any DIY project that he or Blair had been busy with just before Christmas last year when they'd first met. Perhaps Blair had been doing something at this old property he owned. Marshall shrugged. He knew better than to mention to Blair that he'd been snooping. He'd be punished to an extent that even *he* couldn't quite face, despite his newly discovered masochistic tendencies. He decided not to give into temptation and look any further and packed everything back in the bag, putting it back in the corner of the room. Marshall sat back down in his armchair, unzipped his trousers, slid his hand inside and went back to his fantasies of Alex Clare singing whilst standing butt naked in front of him. It was a pretty good fantasy as they went. It might tide him over until he saw Blair again.

*****

At the same time Marshall was acting out his fantasy in his armchair, Blair Malcolme was finishing up his latest kill. His cold, green eyes observed the tarpaulin-wrapped bundle on the floor of the old house he used for his projects.

"Time to drop you off somewhere, sweetheart," he murmured as he regarded the still bundle in front of him. "Where to do this for best effect, I wonder?"

He scratched irritably at the bandage on the wound on his arm, wanting nothing more than to rip the bandage off and scratch it until it bled but knowing that wouldn't help. It was healing and it itched like hell. He'd been happily cooking his veal mascarpone at Marshall's house when the call from his eyes and ears on the ground had come in. Barry "Brick" Smith, the former leader of the gang called "Mr. Smith's Boys" had been in Blair's employ for over three years, keeping an eye on his dilapidated and boarded-up house in the centre of Newham in London. Newham was one of the most deprived areas, notorious for teenage gang violence, and Brick was instrumental in telling Blair when there was any activity near his killing zone. The last thing Blair needed was a bunch of teenagers breaking into his empty house to do drugs, or simply hang out and subsequently find what he had in there. He wasn't ready for that yet.

When Brick had called him and told him there was a bunch of kids hammering on his boarded door, shouting abuse and looking as if they were about to enter the property, Blair had told him in no uncertain terms to keep them away by any means possible. He had no qualms about what that would mean. Brick was a fellow psychopath—Blair was under no illusions about what *he* actually was and welcomed it—and he knew Brick and his team would do what was necessary. But he'd hightailed it down there anyway to make sure his precious secret remained such. When he'd arrived at the house, it had been eerily quiet, but Blair had seen the fresh blood stains on the ground outside. They'd been covered with sand and dirt, but they were there nonetheless. He was a hunter himself; he knew the signs. Brick had taken care of the problem.

The other thing Blair liked about Brick was his absolute lack of either curiosity or morality. Brick simply had no desire to find out Blair's secret and why he protected an old, ramshackle house and would do anything he was asked to do as long as he was paid. It was a strange honour amongst killers' code that seemed to work for them both.

Blair certainly paid him enough to remember that and if the time ever came to tie up loose ends, a bullet to the back of head from behind would probably be all Blair would need to take care of the old warlord who ran this area of the city. Blair didn't fancy taking on Barry Smith one on one. The man would probably crush him to death with his huge arms.

BTK regarded the tarpaulin-wrapped body thoughtfully as he pondered the best place to dump it. He smiled as he remembered the fun he'd had with this one. It had been easy enough accosting her in her flat, knocking her out then stuffing the dead weight into a very large suitcase he'd bought specially for her. He'd been well dressed in a suit and tie, looking for all the word like a successful business man going on a trip when he'd left her place and gotten to his van parked on the street. But he'd never thought such a little woman could fight back so strongly. Once he'd got her back to the house, it had felt good having her struggle against his naked body, feeling her frenzied efforts to keep him away, but he'd won in the end. He always did. It excited him when they struggled, when they were so determined to live. This one had been very tight and he'd taken great pleasure in fucking her until he was breathless. Then he'd turned her over and done the other end. He'd even heard her screams through the gag, she'd been so loud. When he'd done and she lay there all bloody and finished and barely conscious, he'd calmly carved the symbols on her stomach, taking his time as he wanted them to look right. Then he'd slit her throat. He was feeling benevolent by that time and decided to make it quick. She'd never seen that one coming. Unlike him. He'd managed to come twice, one after the other. Front and back.

He laughed softly at his own wit as he picked the body up and hauled it effortlessly onto his shoulder. Blair took it over to the waiting little red ex-Royal Mail van that he used, parked outside on the grass at the back of the house. He'd bought it for seven hundred pounds from an auction. All the sign writing had been removed when he'd got it but it still looked like a post office van. People saw it and even though it didn't have the logo, somewhere in their minds, they still saw the little LDV Pilot Crew van as a mail carrier. They made associations based on what they thought they saw and given that the population of the area he operated in had an IQ less than the temperature in Celsius on a sunny London day, he'd gotten away with so much through their sheer stupidity.

As he got into the front seat and started the engine, ready to drive around onto the street and join the mass of humanity, he hummed to himself. He had time to kill. He might even surprise Marshall later and sneak into the house with a good red wine. Perhaps they could try out that fantasy he'd had of Blair being a rock god and finding his sexy and eager fan waiting in his dressing room, naked and ready to rock and roll. Blair was going rock hard just thinking about it. He grinned at all his puns.

Yes, I will definitely follow that idea up later.

Chapter 18

Anthony was having a well-deserved lie in on Saturday morning when the call came in at six thirty a.m. His mobile rang stridently and he swore loudly, his left hand reaching out to answer it. He groped for the phone and raised it to his ear as he looked blearily at the bedside clock.

"Parglietto."

Flynn stirred beside him. One hand had been flung over Anthony's chest in sleep. He reached down tenderly and moved the arm, then sat up and swung his legs out of bed. Sickness rose up in his throat as he listened to the news.

"Is it her?' he asked quietly and closed his eyes at the answer. "Give me half an hour. I'll be there." He laid his mobile down on the side table and passed a hand over his eyes. He took a deep breath and turned to shake Flynn awake gently. He sighed deeply and his eyes opened. The slight smile of welcome on his face faded on seeing Anthony's expression.

"Tony? What's happened?"

Anthony shook his head. "They've found Sumi." He swallowed at the look of dread on Flynn's face. "She's dead. Her body was discovered at an industrial estate in Wembley about an hour ago. I'm on my way out there now."

Anthony stood up and pulled on his trousers, taking a clean shirt out of the closet, silently dressing. He saw and felt Flynn's pain in the tight muscles of his face and the hands that clenched and unclenched unceasingly. Flynn stared at him with a look of sheer despair, his lips white. Anthony felt a sense of helplessness but more importantly, he felt the slow burn of rage that seemed to start in his chest, radiating outward like a slow-burning fire, consuming him and making hate acidic in the back of his throat. This killer was destroying everything he held dear. He had hurt Flynn both physically and emotionally. There and then, Anthony Parglietto vowed that no matter what, when he caught up with this man who was tearing his world and his city apart, he would show no mercy.

Forty-five minutes later, he stood beside Rupert, who despite his dark complexion looked less hearty than normal. The man's face was drawn and there was a slight tic at the corner of his mouth as he looked down at the mortal remains of Masumi Teragaya.

Anthony had seen a lot of dead bodies in his time on the police force but this one was particularly disturbing.

The young woman lay on her back, her eyes open to the dark morning sky. The black and white ornate ribbons around her neck made a mockery of the deep slash that almost cut to the spine. Her body was completely nude, the small breasts flattened against her chest, blood stains covering her front. It had pooled in her belly button. Her legs were streaked with red and Anthony could see bruises and deep bites on the soft skin between her thighs. Her stomach had been slashed, the knife strokes looking like some sort of Japanese writing. Anthony crouched down beside her, his eyes taking in the injuries, his face dark. He knew he shouldn't touch the body until Graham got there, but it took all his self-control not to gently caress her cold cheek and say a short prayer for the woman who had been Flynn's friend. He stood up as he heard a commotion behind him, turning to see Graham Manning approaching. The pathologist blanched slightly as he saw the woman's body.

"Jesus Christ." He knelt down beside the body and opened his kit, taking out what he needed. "This is a real mess, Tony. This bastard is escalating."

Anthony nodded. "He went to town on this one. I have no idea what that is on her stomach. Letters perhaps?"

Rupert nodded. "I've taken a picture in the meanwhile and sent it over to the geek squad at forensics. If anyone can tell us what it is, it'll be Moony and his team." Moony Adamec was a diminutive Czech of indeterminate age with an IQ of close to 140 who ran his small back office computer team like a mini Gestapo officer.

Graham waved a hand at the two policemen. "Help me turn her over, please, gentlemen. Let's see what wonderful surprises this pervert has for us there."

They weren't disappointed. The woman's back was marked with the same sort of letters or symbols seen on the front, only more of them. Rupert took more pictures for the Geek squad. Graham's face darkened as he saw the finger bruises on the woman's buttocks, as if someone had spread her cheeks apart with some violence.

"This one was sodomised too," he said quietly. "I'll check it out when I get her back to the lab. These cuts were made when she was still alive too, judging from the look of them. This poor woman really suffered."

He grimaced as he stood up and stretched. "Anthony, I'd say she died early yesterday, give or take a few hours, but I'll know more later."

"We caught a bit of a break on this one," Rupert said quietly.

Anthony looked at him sharply. "What do you mean?"

"The old guy over there is a little bit more with it than the usual witnesses we get to interview," Rupert remarked drily, waving in the direction of the police van toward a somewhat bedraggled man with a grey beard. Anthony figured he called the warehouse floor home. "He used to be in the armed forces and was with the military police. He says he was here late last night around ten and the body wasn't there at that time. He went off to 'make nice with a lady,' he says."

Rupert grimaced in distaste. "He came back here about midnight. He saw the body then but was apparently 'too wasted' to be curious. When he woke up at about five this morning and decided to investigate, that's when he called us. So at least we know the body was dumped between ten and twelve last night. That'll narrow it down a little bit. He also says he left his mate sleeping here when he went off to make nice and he'll ask him if saw anything. Apparently his mate scarpered when he got back at midnight but he'll be back later."

Anthony nodded. "That's something I guess. I'll have a word with him myself." The detective looked down sombrely at the dead woman. "Graham, could you get her back to your realm and see what you can get? I need as much information as I can. This is going to blow sky high later with the press. Four people dead and we're no bloody closer to catching the bugger," he growled. "Sergeant, I want everyone you have deployed on those emails we have from the CI. One p.m. today I want a progress report and it had better have some good news. I'll be back at the station to help you in a little while. I want to speak to that guy who had the lady friend last night and try and find his friend. Tell the constable to hold onto him until I get over there. Maybe he can tell us a little more. I want you to canvas the area around here as well and see if there's any CCTV cameras we can pull. I'm not leaving this fucking place until I have something—anything."

Rupert nodded and moved away toward the watching crowd. Graham took final look down at the woman at his feet.

"Come on, darling. Let's get you back so I can find out more about you. You deserve that at least."

He wandered away with his bag, leaving Anthony standing on his own. He glanced over at Rupert who was talking to the constable. She nodded in Anthony's direction and he felt satisfied his witness would be there when he was ready to speak to him.

The sun had risen to give off a lukewarm light and the faint rays passed over the dead woman's face, giving it an unearthly glow. Anthony stood quietly for a while, listening to the sounds of the area, absorbing the atmosphere. He closed his eyes and, not for the first time, tried to imagine he was the killer.

What would I see? How would I feel? Gloating and obviously fulfilled. I've just ripped a woman to shreds after having sex with her—forcible, violent sex.

Now I'm cocking a snook at the authorities, dumping the evidence of my crime in an industrial estate frequented by hobos and winos, the dross of humanity.

I have to be in a car or a van in order to transport the body. I stop, go to the back of my vehicle, take out the body. Is it wrapped up or not? The other bodies all had traces of blue thread on them, tarpaulin, so probably wrapped up. I'd lay the body down, unwrap the tarp and then pick up the body, taking it over to where she was found. I'd lay the body down. Are the ribbons already around the neck or do I do that here? It's more of a risk stopping to tie the bows out here, they're quite elaborate so the bows are probably already on the neck when I unwrap her. I fix them, make sure they're positioned properly.

I stand back, admire my handiwork. She's nothing more to me than a rag doll. I feel nothing for what was once a human being. I didn't even feel anything for her when she was alive. I make sure she's displayed properly and I take one last look. Perhaps I even take a photo of my artwork. Then I leave without looking behind me. My work is done. I get back in the car and I disappear.

Anthony opened his eyes. For a while, he'd got so caught up in his role-play, he could almost taste the evil in the air. He took a few deep breaths and then slowly walked around the area, his eyes darting into crevice and underpass he could find in the hope of finding a camera. His search yielded no results. This particular area was definitely not covered by CCTV. Just like every other area of a body dump. This killer knew his stuff. The detective sighed and looked at his watch. It was eight-thirty. Time to see if the old hobo could answer his questions. Perhaps his buddy was back.

Anthony walked over to the police van where a dishevelled old man sat. The police constable watching him was chatting with him. She turned and nodded at Anthony. "Morning, sir. Your sergeant said you wanted to talk to Mr. Mitchum here. He's been waiting for you."

The old man held up a polystyrene cup and nodded at Anthony. "The young lady was kind enough to give me coffee." His eyes were a shade of murky blue looking out of his weather-beaten face. Anthony was reminded for a second of his lover's eyes that morning, lifeless and bleak, all joy drained from them.

Anthony gathered his thoughts and smiled at the hobo. "Mr. Mitchum. I'm Detective Inspector Parglietto. I was hoping to pick your brains a little bit more about last night. "

The man chortled. "An Eye-tie. You have the look; I'll say that for you. I once sang a song that was recorded later by an Italian."

Anthony was confused. "I'm sorry. I didn't quite get that?"

The old man waved his cup around, sloshing liquid over his hand. "You never heard of the Robert Mitchum song, 'Little Old Wine Drinker Me'? I recorded that when I was still a young man in 1968. Dean Martin went on to sing it too. He was I-talian wasn't he? So there's your connection."

The police woman threw a sympathetic smile Anthony's way. "He thinks he's Robert Mitchum, sir," she said under her breath. "The American actor."

Anthony groaned quietly. *God, someone else who's a bloody loony. Why do they have to crawl out of the woodwork at murder investigations?*

He nodded. "My colleague said you left last night around ten p.m. and got back at midnight. He also said you'd noticed that there was no body there when you left, but it was there when you got back. Are you sure about that?"

The old man looked at him. "Son, I may be a drunk and I may be old, but I'm not stupid." He grinned, showing stumps of teeth. "I got lucky last night with another lady down the block. We made the black mamba together and then I came home."

Anthony didn't even want to ask what the black mamba was. The policewoman stifled a giggled and he stared at her fiercely before addressing Robert Mitchum again.

"And you're sure it was twelve o'clock when you got back? And you saw the body but I understand you were in no condition to look at it. Exactly what condition were you in, sir?"

The old man cackled. "I had a half a bottle of whiskey down me and a pecker that just wanted to go to sleep. I saw the young lady but it was dark. I thought she was just sleeping and I didn't want to disturb her. So I crashed down at my shack and slept until the morning. Then I needed a pee so I had to come outside. I saw the lady lying there and remembered I'd seen her the night before. I thought she might be hurt and when I got close…I was sick all over the bushes in the parking strip and then I called 999."

"How did you call 999, sir? Do you have a phone?"

The old man looked indignant. "Course I have a phone! I have a really nice phone that I found in the trash over there." He pointed a finger in the vague direction of the bins along the far wall. He looked sly. "It was just lying there. I didn't steal it. I found it a couple of days ago."

"The phone has no credit, sir but it allows you to make emergency calls." The policewoman murmured quietly. "I've taken it off him and bagged it for evidence. I thought perhaps it might be useful."

Anthony nodded. "Good call, Sergeant." He turned to Robert again. "I understand you had a friend who was sleeping here whilst you were out doing the black mamba."

The old man grinned in pride.

Anthony smiled back. "What's his name and where can I find him?"

"Joseph? He'll be back soon enough. He has some stuff stashed at my place and he'll want it. So he'll be back in a little while to fetch it. Joseph doesn't sleep well. He stays in my shack and looks after it when I go out. But he has nightmares."

Anthony felt a glimmer of hope. Perhaps this insomniac had seen something, hidden away in the shack along the alleyway. He turned to the police woman.

"You can let Mr. Mitchum go. Keep someone here and tell them to keep an eye out for Joseph. When he arrives, call me. I want to speak him myself." Anthony handed her his card. "The minute this man is found, call me, not a minute after. Got that?" The policewoman nodded.

Anthony turned to the homeless man. He tucked a card in the man's dirty pocket.

"That's my card. If you think of anything else, or you see Joseph, call me. I'd like to speak to him. I know we've taken your phone so I'm going to give you a phone card. Have you used one of these before?" He took out a small sliver of plastic from his wallet and handed it to Mr. Mitchum. The man looked indignant.

"Of course I've used one before! I was a Hollywood star, remember? I know what to do with it." The man thrust it into the coat pocket where just minutes before Anthony had put his personal card.

The detective nodded. "Good, thank you." Anthony grinned. "I have to say I think your best performance was in *The Night of the Hunter*. I've seen that movie a few times. It was pretty chilling."

The old man's eyes lit up. "I can see you're a man of taste, Mr. Italian Detective. I think that was my best role too. And playing opposite the lovely Shelley Winters? Now that was a woman and a half."

The two men smiled at each other and Anthony inclined his head in farewell.

"Look after yourself. And remember to call me."

He nodded at the policewoman and turned to leave. As he did, his mobile rang. He frowned at the Private Number ID but he answered.

"Parglietto."

"Detective. It's lovely to speak to you personally." The voice was male, very English and well spoken. Anthony couldn't pick up any discernible dialect. "I believe you've found my latest project. I have to say I really enjoyed this one. Even more than I enjoyed your own lovely fellow. How is he, by the way?"

Anthony's body prickled and his breathing quickened. He turned away so no one could see his expression, his words spilling out in a torrent of hate. He knew exactly who this was.

"You're nothing but a waste of a human skin," he said between gritted teeth. "And I look forward to the time I can choke the fucking life out of you, you vile bastard."

The man chuckled. "Never one to mince words, were you, Detective? You have this very admirable trait of always saying what you think—consequences be damned. I like that in a man."

"You do know I'll get you eventually, don't you?" Anthony spat into the phone. "One way or another, I'll find you. And when I do, there won't be any fucking trial. I'll put you out of my misery like I'd swat a fly for what you did to Flynn and the other people you murdered."

"My, my, you do carry a lot of anger inside you, Detective. And I'm counting on you finding me. Why do you think I keep sending all these juicy tidbits? That reporter must have creamed his underwear when I sent him that poem. He probably saw a moment of glory for himself that might surpass anything else that little fucking twat has ever done."

There was a short silence and Anthony wasn't sure whether the man was still on the line. He listened, waiting for him to speak again. He cursed the fact this call was being done here and not at the office. At least there he could have tried to trace the call. But he knew this man was far too clever to allow that -hence the call now in the open.

After about half a minute BTK spoke again. "Sorry. I was just checking something. I have to say, Anthony, you've been busy. My little hometown appears to be crawling with policeman and my old school has even been visited. That can only mean one thing. Your reporter bitch told you all about our little conversations."

Anthony felt his skin chill. "He had no choice, you deviant. You butchered a friend of his."

The man sounded amused. "I don't really blame him. I knew it had to happen sooner or later. I just wanted to see how long he'd hold out. I wasn't really going to kill him or cut his lips off. Not yet anyway. And the ex-boyfriend is safe from me for now. I'm a real student of human nature, just like you. We're the same. We play games and we both get into people's heads and manipulate them."

"I am fucking nothing like you!" Anthony paced the concrete parking lot in frustration. "I catch people like you—" He stopped, hearing the deep chuckle at the other end, knowing he'd done exactly what the other man wanted him to do: refute the allegation they were the same. The voice was musing when it spoke again.

"It's a pity your team will find that Mr. Armandsone is dead. My old teacher. He probably could have told you a lot about me. Unfortunately he was run over by a car just after I left school. Poor man didn't stand a chance. I hit him full on; spread him all over the road like strawberry jam."

"Another kill to add your list?" Anthony's knuckles were white as they clutched his phone. "Along with all the others you gave Flynn?"

"There was one kill I didn't add to the list because I wanted to tell you about it man to man, so to speak," BTK sneered. "He was always such a trusting soul, your brother. We used to play games like you and Flynn do. Handcuffs and blindfolds. He got such a thrill out of me fucking him like that. It must be a family trait."

Anthony's head spun and he felt dizzy. He reached out a hand and steadied himself against a concrete pillar while the feeling passed.

"You're the one who killed Marco?" he whispered. "You did that?"

"Not only that." The other man gloated. "He was my acolyte. I was training him to be just like me. He was quite an apprentice, my sexy little bit of Italian rough. He was really coming around to the whole idea of killing people. I had to promise him we'd only get rid of the bad people, people who deserved to die. Rapists and scum that had been let loose on the streets to roam at will. He quite liked the idea of the vigilante justice."

There was a sneer in the other man's voice. "He'd been listening to you spout off about it long enough. Of course, I didn't care if they were good or bad and he'd never have known the truth. I could make him believe anything I told him." The voice was full of pride. "Then he found out that my list wasn't what he thought it was. He actually started questioning what we were doing, what *I* was doing, wanting to kill innocent people. He called you, didn't he, asking for advice. Do you remember that conversation, Detective?"

Anthony did remember the day Marco had called him. His brother had been more subdued than usual, asking him the unusual question, "If you know someone's doing something wrong and is going to maybe harm innocent people, but you love them, what would you do?"

Anthony's answer had been unequivocal. "You give them up and stop them," had been his reply. "Love doesn't triumph over something like that, little brother. Whatever's going on, you need to stop it." He'd tried to probe his brother about why he was asking but Marco had clammed up and rung off.

"I remember." Anthony said quietly. "Marco was worried for people's safety and he needed advice."

"Well, you put him on the wrong path with your sanctimonious crap," the voice hissed angrily. "He told me he couldn't let me go ahead with my plan. You understand I couldn't let that happen. It was too much of a risk." There was a silence on the other end. Then he spoke again. "He was mine and I knew him better than you. He had a dark side, did your little brother. And you made me kill him." The voice stopped and Anthony drew a deep, shuddering breath.

The voice hardened. "We used to sit in bed, me with my cock still inside him and joke about the famous 'Parglietto Prescience.'" The voice sneered. "He used to brag he had a sixth sense for picking up what's in men's minds, just like his big brother had. I'm so glad to say he had a bit of a blind spot where I was concerned. I suppose it was because he was crazy in love with me."

Anthony closed his eyes, feeling the bile rise in his throat and he swallowed it down, feeling the acid coating his throat. The 'Parglietto Prescience' had been a term he and his brother had coined to explain their unerring ability for empathy. The only way BTK could know that was if Marco had told him.

The gloating voice continued. "And then you have the gall to appear on TV and smile and accept that fucking award, the one telling everyone what a great policeman you are. I'd been mulling over what to do with you for a while, Detective. I'd been abroad, trying to enjoy myself and caught you on the news whilst I was in Bangkok. That was the final straw, Anthony. I needed to bring you down a peg or two. Make you work for that award. Give you something to focus on. And so here we are."

Anthony sat down on a stone bench as his legs gave way. He felt physically sick. This man was telling him that his brother's death, Flynn's abduction, and the other murders—they were all because of him. He knew deep down inside that this was exactly the reaction

BTK was wanting for and that it wasn't rational to blame himself. But he still did.

"I can hear your brain ticking over. You've finally realised what your contribution to this current turn of events is. I wanted to let you know that. Your fucking arrogance caused all this. I honestly don't care about your stupid man-bitch. There's plenty more like all of them out there. I just want you to see how this all started. You and I will finish this together. When you find me, I'll kill you then, I promise. Put you out of your misery. But for now, you can live with what I've told you so it eats you up inside like killing Marco did to me. I had such plans for that boy. Sweet dreams, Detective."

The phone went dead and Anthony stared at it in stunned silence. His hands trembled and he was freezing cold. He was still sitting there ten minutes later when the same policewoman from earlier tapped him gently on the shoulder.

"Sir? That other homeless man has come back. The one you wanted to see. Are you all right, sir? You don't look very well."

Anthony got to his feet, slipping his mobile back into his jacket pocket. His hands shook as he shoved his grief and his guilt beneath heated sheets of hatred and wrapped himself up in his professional persona. He took a deep breath. "I'm fine, thanks, Sergeant. Let me go see what this gentleman has to say."

He walked swiftly over to the waiting man, who looked as if he'd certainly seen better days. His eyes were rheumy and cracked at the corners, his hands constantly shaking and his mouth had barely any teeth. Anthony wondered absently how the man managed to eat. His mind was buzzing with random thoughts, images of his brother's butchered body, the mocking tones of the man who'd said he'd killed him.

The police woman looked at her superior, seeming a little worried. "This is Joseph, sir. He was sleeping last night he says, and he didn't see anything." She put out a hand and gently touched him on the sleeve.

"I'll go get you a cup of coffee, sir. You look as if you could use one." She smiled and disappeared to the waiting police van in the distance. Anthony turned his attention to the man in front of him. The man eyed him blankly.

"So, Joseph." Anthony cleared his throat. "You say you were sleeping last night when that body got here. Are you sure you didn't see or hear anything out of the ordinary?"

Joseph looked at him with narrowed eyes. "I saw nothing. I was asleep like I told you." He scowled belligerently. "I've told everyone now. How many more times do I have to tells the lot of you?"

"I suppose until I'm satisfied that you've told me everything. And until I believe you." Anthony moved closer to the man, his nostrils flaring in disgust at his smell. "Did you hear a car or a van last night? Between ten and midnight when Mr Mitchum got back from his booty call?"

The man cackled loudly. "Bobby and that slag down the road? I wouldn't touch her with a ten-foot barge pole. But he seems to have a thing for her. I tells him he's gonna get sick and die. But the geezer won't listen."

Anthony was getting fed up of Robert Mitchum's sexploits. "So did you hear a car or van last night? It's very important you think about this."

Joseph looked at him slyly. "What's it worth to you then? Am I gonna get a reward?"

Anthony leaned in closely, trying not to breathe in the other man's stench. His temper was wearing very thin.

"The only reward you're going to get, you miserable bastard, is not having my boot up your scrawny arse giving you a colon cleanse." His fierce growl seemed to surprise the other man who blinked and drew away from the detective's glowering face. "So I'm going to ask you one last time. Did you hear a car last night at any time?"

Joseph leaned back sulkily. "No need to get upset." He fiddled in his lap with his buttons on the dirty shirt he wore. "I did hear a van last night. Just before Bobby got back. I heard it idling." His voice was defiant. "I got up to take a look." He frowned. "I didn't know why a bloody van would be delivering post that time of night. It was a bit strange, like."

Anthony stared at him. "You saw a post office van out here? What, a red one?"

The man looked at him angrily. "Of course it were bloody red! If it weren't, it wouldn't be no post van then, would it?"

Anthony tried to quell the rising urge to put his hands around the man's neck and squeeze until his need stopped.

"Did you see anyone?" He could hear the desperate hope in his own voice.

Joseph shook his head. "I didn't see no one. I just went back into the shack and went back to sleep. Then Bobby came home." His voice grew whining. "That's all I saw, I promises you. Now can I go back to sleep?"

Anthony closed his eyes in frustration then opened them again. The police woman stood in front of him, proffering his promised cup of coffee.

"Sorry it took so long, sir. We had another call come in that I needed to attend to."

Anthony nodded. "Thank you, Sergeant. I appreciate this." He sipped the coffee, grimacing at the bitter taste. But it was hot and he needed it.

"If you promise me that that's all you saw, then you can go. But I'd better not find out you were lying to me about any of this. Or my boot will be stuck up your arse so deeply you'll need a miner's lamp to find it."

Joseph flapped a bony hand. "I promise, that's all I saw. Just the red van."

He ambled off in the direction of the back alley surrounding the estate.

Anthony sighed. "I suppose that's something, although how reliable that man is, I shudder to think." He smiled at the policewoman. "Thanks, Sergeant. I'm getting off now, back to the station. If anything else comes up, you know where to find me."

He walked off toward his car, parked on the outskirts of the yellow police tape. He was desperate to get back to his office and digest what BTK had told him about his brother's death. It would mean pulling the file out and reviewing everything he and the rest of his team knew about that particular death. He couldn't say he was looking forward to it.

The pictures of his little brother's beaten body with a final stab to his heart were disturbing even to a seasoned policeman like himself. He still couldn't believe that Marco would have been involved with BTK, even less that he would be involved in the man's psychopathic games of killing and manipulation. He had to investigate every lead he had and BTK had just given him another one, whether he realised it or not. Perhaps, knowing what he knew now, something might just make more sense to him than at the time of his brother's murder.

Chapter 19

Flynn waited for Anthony to come home that night. He'd tried to call and text him a few times but his phone had gone to voice mail. When he heard the key in the door around nine p.m. he stood up and walked wearily to the entrance.

Anthony smiled faintly as he closed the door and put the double lock on. "I got all your messages and texts, but I'm sorry, I just didn't have a chance to call you. It's been the day from hell as you can imagine and I really needed to focus on the job."

Flynn nodded. "I know. I didn't know whether you wanted anything to eat. I made a lasagne if you're hungry? I needed to keep myself busy so I went to work. Everyone in the office is in a state of shock." His voice was dull.

Anthony grimaced. "Not for me, thanks. I can't stomach eating anything now. Maybe later." He slung his jacket on the door hook, loosened his tie and kicked off his loafers then walked through to the lounge. He plonked himself down on the couch, leaning back and closing his eyes in thankfulness. Flynn sat down beside him quietly, waiting until he was ready to talk.

Finally Anthony sighed and opened his eyes. "I know you have a thousand questions. I know I owe you some answers. But can we just sit here for a while together and forget it all for a minute?" He reached out his arms and Flynn went into them gladly, laying his head against his chest, listening to his heartbeat and breathing in his scent. He closed his eyes, his hand gently stroking his lover's stomach and chest.

"I have *some* good news," Flynn murmured softly.

"Tell me," Anthony demanded. "I need some good news."

"Ginny called. She said she has the perfect property for us in Bloomsbury, not far from Russell Square tube station. It's a two-bedroom apartment, second floor, Victorian. It's just been refurbished and sounds perfect. It's in a cul de sac too, so off the main street."

Anthony sat up suddenly. "Jesus, Bloomsbury? How the hell can we afford to live there?"

Flynn sighed. "The rent is just over two grand a month. Between us, we can afford that. You're paying three quarters of that on this mortgage alone, Anthony. I said to Ginny we'd go see it tomorrow if work allowed, otherwise I'll just go and take some pictures and bring them back to show you."

Anthony settled back on the couch wearily. "I suppose that isn't too bad then. Go take a look and if you like it, just take it so it doesn't get snapped up by anyone else. I'll sign whatever papers you want."

"It even has a fireplace," Flynn murmured. "So we can get a huge fluffy rug, put it in front of the fire then do the dirty in front of it."

Anthony smiled wanly. "That *is* good news. Anything that involves you, me and just skin between us has to be."

Flynn snuggled up to him and was silent, as he waited for him to decide when he was ready to talk.

Anthony sighed and caressed his jaw line. "I just wanted to leave the whole sordid mess at the office. Pretend I was just a normal person with a normal life. But today just got worse. BTK called me."

Flynn stiffened and sat straight up, his eyes wide. "That fucker called you? How did he get your number? What did he say?"

Anthony leaned forward, his elbows on his knees as he buried his head in his hands.

"You know I have an open door policy when it comes to the public. Someone at the station must have given it to him. They normally vet the calls so he must have been very convincing as a potential witness or something. Who knows?" His head was bowed and his words were muffled by his shirt collar. "He was gloating about killing Sumi and the others. He also told me he was the one who killed Marco. He said he was Marco's lover and he was training him to be just like him."

Flynn paled, his stomach clenching at Anthony's words. "Jesus! Do you believe him or is he just trying to yank your chain?"

Anthony raised his face and looked at him. His eyes were haunted, his face drawn, and Flynn noticed his cheekbones were starker than usual. He hadn't been eating lately and he was sure he was losing weight.

Anthony nodded. "I didn't at first. But Rupert and I went back over the case. We spent all day on it. And it just solidified the feel my gut has that Marco wasn't just killed by some gay basher. He was murdered for a reason. What BTK said could well be true."

He went quiet. Flynn reached out a hand and caressed his cheek softly. Anthony reached up his hand and took Flynn's, holding it tightly.

"He told me it was all my fault. The reason he killed Marco, the reason he took you, why he killed those people. He blames me for making him have to kill Marco. He said Marco was his acolyte, his apprentice and I'd gone and spoiled that when I told Marco he shouldn't let him get away with what he was planning. I didn't know the full story then. Perhaps if Marco had told me more it would have been different. I could have kept him safe." Anthony's voice finally cracked and Flynn saw the sheen of tears in his dark eyes. "Marco started questioning him and he couldn't take a chance. So he butchered my little brother. And he hurt you."

Flynn's heart broke for him and he sat up, reaching out to pull Anthony close. "This is what he wants. He's playing with your head, Tony. None of this can be your fault, you know that. You weren't the one who killed your brother, *you* sure as hell didn't threaten me and you didn't kill Sumi or those other women. He's done that, not you."

Anthony looked up, his eyes stark. "From the age of fourteen when Marco came out and I was twenty-one, I was there for him, supporting him. We told our parents about it together. I used to fight with the bullies who wanted to beat him up. He wasn't an angel. He was promiscuous, did drugs and we used to argue like crazy about it. But he was my little brother and I was supposed to protect him. Where the hell was I when he really needed me?" His face was white with pain.

Flynn reached over and simply held him. "You always said there was more to Marco's death than just a gay murder, Tony. Now you know you were right. You need to find this bastard and make him pay."

Anthony's face was fierce. "He wants me to find him. Then he says he'll kill me. I told him I'd get him first. I want to kill this bastard so badly, it scares me. I know I'll kill him if I get a chance. I don't think I'll even hesitate. Doesn't that make me just like him? Isn't that what he wants?"

Flynn had no answer to that. He hugged him tightly, trying to will his love into him. "When the time comes, you will do what you have to do. And I'll be there no matter what. But what you have to do now is get over this. He's messing with you, and he wants to make you weak, make you doubt yourself. And that is exactly what I'm *not* going to let happen. You are Detective Inspector Anthony Parglietto, my hero, and you need to catch this bastard."

Flynn reached up, taking Anthony's face in his hands, kissing him deeply, as he sighed into his mouth and his body relaxed.

"I love you," Anthony whispered. "I need you so much."

"I love you too. That's why you have to be careful. He wants to kill you, and I couldn't bear it if anything happened to you. Please tell me you'll watch out for him."

Flynn felt the dread in the pit of his stomach, tried to quell the fear as he considered the danger his boyfriend might be in.

Anthony nodded his head gently. "I will. He says he won't harm you or Kieran. But he's sick and likes to play mind games. I still have the protection detail on you though. He knows about the fact you've told me about the emails because he's seen the activity somehow in his hometown. He didn't seem too bothered though."

Anthony filled Flynn in on the rest of the conversation as Flynn listened in shock. As a reporter, this whole affair had all the hallmarks of a great story, one that could catapult a journalist like him to the top. But all he could think of was how his life would change for the worse if anything happened to Anthony. Finally Anthony sat back, exhausted, his face pale.

"Tomorrow we'll take another look at everything. See if we missed anything. Either in Marco's case or in any of the others. And then we'll take another look until we find this psycho. I have to find him. I can't have another Sumi on my hands."

It was an opening Flynn had been waiting for. He laid a hand on Anthony's arm. "About Sumi…"

Anthony's face darkened as he looked away. "Don't ask me anything about that. I don't want to lie to you. Please don't ask."

Flynn knew from his expression that Sumi hadn't had an easy death. He nodded, bile welling in his throat once again at the ghastly thoughts going through his head.

Anthony's eyes were bright. "Just let it go, or it will eat you up. Don't even imagine anything, just accept the fact she's dead and whatever she went through, it's over now. It's the only way to cope with something like this. Even if you'd told me about that email earlier, it wouldn't have helped her. You deserve that comfort at least."

He stood up, reaching out a hand to pull Flynn to his feet. "Let's go to bed. I need to crawl into the covers and hold you. Just for a while. It's the best place for me to be right now."

Flynn followed closely behind as Anthony switched off the lights and together they made their way through to the bedroom.

Chapter 20

Marshall lay cuddled in Blair's arms on the couch as the two men watched a movie. Marshall had made dinner, the two men had poured themselves drinks, and Marshall was looking forward to his Sunday night in with Blair. The younger man had been extremely voracious the past couple of weeks and Marshall's arse bore testament to that. He'd never been fucked so hard and so often in all his life. After the activity two weeks ago when Blair had come home unexpectedly and literally fucked him to hell and gone, the trend seemed to have continued. Blair was definitely a man on a mission— a mission to rip Marshall in two. Not that he was complaining. Tonight, though, Blair seemed a little preoccupied.

"Penny for your thoughts," he whispered as his tongue slid into Blair's ear and his hands artfully caressed the front of the other man's groin. Blair smiled, but it was a smile that didn't seem to go far.

"Sorry, Marsh. I've had a little on my mind and I just want to relax and enjoy the movie. It's one of my favourites."

They were watching *Face Off* with John Travolta and Nicholas Cage. The story revolved around the two men literally swapping faces for the good guy, John Travolta, to ensure justice was done for the death of his young son.

Marshall sighed. "It's a very good movie, but honestly? As a medical professional I'm a little dubious at the fact that you can change faces like that. There'd be a huge amount of trauma, both physical and psychological."

Blair shifted. "I thought medical science could do anything? What's so difficult about taking some skin off and putting it somewhere else, anyway? It's done all the time isn't it, for skin grafts and stuff."

Marshall nodded. "Yes, that's done regularly. But a face is a little different, Blair. It has loads of nerves and blood vessels. It's not, like, just taking a patch of skin from somewhere and planting it somewhere else, is it?"

Marshall had to say that the grin he next saw on Blair's face was a little disturbing. His lover's eyes glittered with amusement but the expression on his face said something more. It was fairly demonic with suppressed glee.

"Actually, it's pretty easy doing that. I can vouch that it really is easy to take skin off one place and put it somewhere else."

"Where on earth did you get the chance to do that?" Marshall looked at sceptically. "Was it playing on one of those role-playing online games you like so much?" He watched Blair's face, seeing another expression cross it that he felt a little unsure of. It was as if Blair was weighing him up and finding him wanting. Blair leaned over and pushed his lover back against the arm of the couch as his hands slid down his crotch and cupped his balls tightly. Marshall thought he looked a little more cautious and was choosing his words carefully.

"Never mind. It doesn't matter. What matters, my lovely, is what I want to do to you right now."

His tone was vaguely threatening and the older man swallowed as Blair unzipped his jeans, smiling when he noticed Marshall was already hard, his erection pushing against his boxers. Blair reached in and stroked him gently.

"I'm not complaining, but I thought you wanted to watch the movie," Marshall murmured as Blair's hand grasped him tightly, moving up and down his shaft with steady movements. He felt Blair's thumb touch the head of his cock, rubbing him gently and he gasped at the sensation.

"I've seen it before. This is more stimulating." Blair continued his stroking of Marshall, watching his face with such intensity that Marshall felt like a lab specimen being observed for dissection. He had no idea why he suddenly had that impression, but the steady regard that Blair was giving him made him feel slightly uneasy. He'd noticed as well that when the conversation turned to anything Blair didn't want to talk about or ignore, sex generally tended to be his way out of it.

Blair ceased his stroking and tugged Marshall's jeans off his hips then bent down to take Marshall's silky hardness in his own warm and very greedy mouth. Marshall had to say at that particular moment in time, he really didn't give a damn.

*****

Two days later Marshall had a well-earned day off. He'd had some personal chores to complete and taking the time off was the only way to get them done. Of course, instead he'd been playing Halo on his Xbox most of the afternoon with a couple of beers at his side. He sighed and stood up from the couch, wincing as his stiff legs protested from hours of inactivity. He laid the controller down on the seat, stretching his arms over his head as he yawned. He was expecting Blair to walk in at any moment, late as it was. He'd been fairly pissed off not seeing Blair last night because of some other engagement he had and then again earlier when Blair had called to say he was going to be late because of some incident at the gym. Some stupid jock had overdone it on the exercise equipment in his anxiety to please some young, pert lass he had his eyes on. His suspected groin pull had turned out to be a hernia and the guy had been in complete agony. As a result, Blair had to call a paramedic and have the man spirited to the local A and E. Marshall grinned. He'd bet the guy wouldn't be trying to impress the ladies again too soon too quickly.

He wandered over to the sideboard and picked up the whiskey decanter, pouring himself a stiff one and taking a large slurp. He gave a sigh of satisfaction and walked to the large picture window that looked out onto the street below. For a while, he idly watched the activity in the street, sipping his drink as he pondered what the evening might bring. He knew what he hoped would happen. He'd been feeling fairly horny ever since yesterday when some amazingly sexy young footballer had come to see him for treatment for a really bad burner, a common injury in contact sports. The young man had been in agony from the pain extending down his neck into his arm and fingers. Marshall had treated it as best as he could and provided the necessary medication for pain and inflammation, but the young man wouldn't be playing football for a while.

The twenty-something man had been incredibly good looking, closely resembling one of Marshall's personal favourites, Kerry Degman, an all-American male model. Marshall didn't normally have such salacious thoughts about his patients. He liked to think he was a professional but for this one he was definitely prepared to make an exception. He'd thought guiltily that if Blair had suggested adding *this* young man to the proposed threesome mix, he may well have said yes. The thought rankled a little as it meant that perhaps he had been too quick in refusing Blair *his* little bit of fantasy. Perhaps, after all, Marshall might have enjoyed it. He intended talking to Blair about it later and saying that he might consider the idea. That would certainly put his young lover in a good mood and bode well for the evening.

He smiled as he saw Blair get out of a taxi in the street below, his ever-present backpack slung over his broad shoulder, his blond hair blowing around his face in the chilly evening breeze. God, the man looked good. Marshall felt a sudden twinge in his groin that signalled his definite interest and he grinned as he moved away from the window, ready to pour Blair one of the vodka tonics he enjoyed so much.

He'd only just got the drink mixed and was setting it down on the side table at the end of the couch when the door burst open and Blair breezed in, a wonderful study in his tight black jeans, his form-fitting white tee shirt, wearing the black Versace hoody that Marshall had bought him for his birthday. His face looked a little dark and Marshall felt a frisson of unease that perhaps the evening might not pan out the way he'd hoped.

"Blair. I made you a drink." He gestured to the side table. "How was your day?" The younger man threw his backpack carelessly down on the floor and kicked it under the sideboard, scowling fiercely. His green eyes looked at Marshall flatly and his lips thinned. The expression on his face wasn't particularly pleasant and once again, Marshall felt his spirits sink lower.

"It was shit, thanks for asking." Blair turned abruptly and stormed off. "I'm going for a shower. Don't think of joining me either. I'm not in the mood."

With those snarled words he disappeared into the hallway and Marshall was left feeling as if a small cyclone had just hit his apartment with a rush of bad temper and ill will. He stood there a little nonplussed, not sure whether to simply stay put or go try and find out why Blair had had such a crap day. Finally he erred on the side of caution and sat down on the couch, gulping his drink and waiting for the sounds of the shower to stop. He turned the TV on and switched it to the news. He sat watching the pictures and the commentary for a while, not really taking it in. He rarely watched news on TV, preferring to stick his head in the sand as far as the outside world was concerned. It was all bloody bad news anyway.

His ears pricked up when he heard the words "Bow Tie Killer" and he turned up the volume. The presenter was talking to a large, imposing man of what looked like Italian heritage, very tasty with mid-length curly black hair and dark gimlet eyes. He reminded Blair of some actor, but he couldn't recall the name. The man was obviously a policeman of some sort as he stood waiting for the interviewer to complete her sentence, his hands tapping his thighs impatiently. Marshall could see it was a rerun of an earlier programme.

"So, Detective Inspector Parglietto, are you telling me that you're closer to catching this serial killer, the man that's been terrorising the city and raping and killing people? I have to say, it looks to the public as if the police have been pretty powerless to date to do anything to stop this man."

She stopped and looked at him enquiringly, holding the microphone close to the man's mouth. He regarded her with a flat stare, and Marshall thought it was much the same as the one he'd seen from Blair earlier.

"No, I'm not telling you that, Miss Lucas. What I'm telling you is that we have a few leads we're following up on and I'm hopeful that we may have some more news, better news, for the public as soon as possible."

She started to speak and he forestalled her with a wave of an imperious hand.

"I can tell you, however, that he's made a few mistakes and we intend making the most of his carelessness." The detective smiled wolfishly and Marshall thought he'd never seen a man look so menacing—apart from Blair when he punished Marshall for some transgression, imagined or otherwise. "This pathetic individual—I can't call him a man or even a human being, because I truly don't believe he is one; and I refuse to call him an animal as you've been doing in your broadcasts, because even an animal has more compassion that this... 'individual' has towards his fellow men or women—has tripped up, and I fully intend to make the most of his mistakes. As soon as we've managed to investigate them further, and see where they take us, there'll be another press release. We'll keep the public updated as much as we can."

The interviewer nodded. "Have you any advice for anyone watching?"

The policeman nodded. "As you know we've had a call hotline operating ever since the first murder of Katherine Dodd. The number should be flashing on the screen below. I want to make a personal appeal to everyone out there." He turned and looked directly into the camera, his deep hazel eyes boring straight into Marshall's living room and uncomfortably into what Marshall imagined was his soul from the intensity of the stare. He felt a strange kinship with this man, this stranger. He liked his forthrightness, his disdain for being politically correct and his confident demeanour. The fact he looked like some sort of Italian stud certainly helped endear him even more to him. He wondered idly whether the man was straight. Marshall liked the Mediterranean look.

"This individual may have family, a girlfriend, a boyfriend, someone who may see a small sign of who he really is without knowing. It's true that sometimes the people closest to us are still strangers. I've been authorised to tell you that the person—the 'man' although it pains me to say the word—that we're looking for is fit, strong, is able to come and go fairly easily, is probably a London local given his knowledge of the area, and currently should have a human bite mark on a part of his anatomy. We can't confirm exactly where unfortunately. So I would ask anyone out there if anyone you know or love has recently started behaving strangely, has unexplained absences from home, and of course, has a bite anywhere on his body, that you contact the help line. It may be nothing but you might just be the person we need to help us with our enquiries. Thank you." The detective turned abruptly and walked away as the presenter turned to the camera.

Marshall felt a shiver. For some reason the air in the room had turned chilled and oppressive. He couldn't help but think about the bite on Blair's arm and the rucksack with its strange shopping list. The two reminders arose unbidden in his mind and he physically shook his head to rid himself of them. This was just what the police wanted—scare-mongering tactics to get people to spill the beans on their loved ones just because something seemed a little off. He didn't envy whoever was manning those hotlines. They'd probably be inundated tonight with crazy people trying to blame their old uncle, aunty and spurned lover for the murders. He watched as the reporter wrapped up her broadcast.

"That was Detective Anthony Parglietto from the CID here in London. Detective Parglietto has declined to comment on the fact that his significant other, a man named Flynn Parker, an investigative reporter, worked with the latest victim, twenty-nine-year-old Masumi Teragaya, at the *London Global* newspaper in central London. So far the police have been tight lipped about any possible links that may connect any of these parties or whether it's simply a coincidence, but I can assure you, we will continue asking the questions so that we can let the public know the full story. This is Tracey Lucas for London News."

Marshall sighed. So the man was gay and it was just his fucking luck that the man had a boyfriend. He'd have fancied a little bit of the Italian in him.

"Why are you bloody watching that shit?" Blair's venomous tone cut through the air like a machete swiping down in a dense jungle. Marshall turned. His lover stood there, bare-chested, hair wet and tousled, his sweatpants slung low around his hips. He looked as sexy as hell.

"It's just the news, Blair. There's some news about that serial killer—"

Blair reached across and angrily picked up the remote from the couch and tapped a button. The room went quiet. He flung the remote back down on the couch.

Marshall looked at him open mouthed. "Don't mind me. I *was* watching it. Jesus, what the fuck is wrong with you?" Marshall's temper flared. It took a lot to get him riled but Blair was making a good job of it with his petulance and bad mood.

God, was this what it was like to be in a relationship with a younger man? Teenage temper tantrums?

Blair glared at him, his eyes glinting with suppressed anger. "I had a bad day, that's all. It went from bad to worse after that arsehole was rushed to the hospital. I just want to sit quietly and watch a movie or something, not listen to the drivel that passes for news nowadays." He picked up the vodka tonic that Marshall had made for him, drained it in one gulp and went over to make another one.

"The whole city is talking about this psycho killer, Blair." Marshall said quietly. "It's the only thing anyone talks about at the hospital, that women aren't safe until he's been caught. And that detective certainly seems to know what he's talking about."

Blair froze then turned quietly, glass in hand, his body tense and controlled as he regarded Marshall with what the older man could only describe as a malevolent stare.

"You fancy him then, Marshall? That detective?"

Marshall swallowed, seeing the cold glint in his lover's eyes. God forbid that he tell him that he thought he was pretty hot.

"Of course not. He just seems like he cares about catching this killer. I like the way he thinks, that's all. But he's far too macho for my taste." He crossed his fingers mentally.

Blair nodded as he finished making his drink and took a sip, staring at his lover over the rim of his glass.

"So I imagine that you have an opinion on this case, Marsh? Do you think you know anything about it from your gossip sessions with those people at the hospital? I'd love to hear what you think. Tell me, please."

He sat down and swung his legs up onto the coffee table as he watched Marshall with a lazy stare. His earlier anger seemed to have dissipated somewhat and Marshall once again felt a little off guard at the man's change of mood. Blair patted the couch seat beside him.

"Come on, Marsh. Sit down here, my lovely, and tell me all about your thoughts on this man they call the Bow Tie Killer."

Marshall hesitated then walked over and sat beside Blair. The younger man placed his hands on his thigh, stroking it gently and holding his eyes. Marshall felt his breath leave his body at the intensity of that emerald-green stare. He cursed his traitorous body for the way he currently felt—horribly horny with a cock that was growing in inches every minute and straining against the front of his linen chinos. Blair's hand slowly travelled up and down his leg from knee to thigh, occasionally grazing his groin. It was deliberate, Marshall knew. He cleared his throat.

"I'm not a psychologist but surely you have to be very disturbed to do this sort of thing to people. Rape and kill them like that, as if they were just pieces of meat. As a doctor, I find it inconceivable that someone can do that to another human being."

Blair nodded. "I suppose that's true. But if you listen to *that detective* on the TV, this person isn't even human. He says he wouldn't even call them a man. Would you agree with that?"

Marshall winced as Blair gripped the soft flesh of his inner thigh tightly. His lover's gaze was hypnotic and was slowly focusing on Marshall's lips, lips that he now licked nervously as he realised they were going dry with anticipation. Marshall knew that predatory look and what it meant.

"I heard what he said about that. I suppose he's entitled to his opinion. I still think everyone deserves a second chance regardless of what they've done." He grunted as Blair's fingers pinched his skin again and he reached down a hand and pushed his lover's hand away.

"Jesus, Blair, that's going to bruise. Take it easy, will you!" he exclaimed.

"You normally like it when I'm rough, Marsh." Blair's voice was husky and he leaned forward, brushing his lips against Marshall's, the tip of his tongue licking Marshall's crease slightly, leaving a trail of fire as he moved over the older man's cheek and licked his jawline. Marshall swallowed again, his own need definitely evident in the bulge in his trousers and the sudden erratic cadence of his own breath. Blair caressed his erection gently.

"Rough is one thing. Pinching me like that is another." He drew a deep breath as Blair's tongue dipped into his ear.

"Christ, I never know where the hell I am with you," the older man exclaimed. "One minute you're the boyfriend from hell, the next, all you want to do is fuck. You change moods like a chameleon changes colour, you know that?"

His lover's husky chuckle sent thrills of pleasure coursing through Marshall's body straight to the tip of his already straining erection.

"I like being a chameleon. It's a pretty apt description." Blair licked Marshall's ear slowly as his hands unzipped him. He reached in and took his shaft in his hands with a squeeze and softly caressed the already leaking tip. The older man caught his breath, his eyes closing in pleasure.

"Perhaps we should take this into the bedroom," he whispered huskily.

Blair drew back his, eyes smoky and unfocused. "I can't refuse an invitation like that. It might be just what I need after today."

Marshall had to ask. "What exactly made you so upset?" he asked quietly. "Tell me about it. Maybe I can help before you screw me senseless."

Blair uttered a short laugh. "I doubt you could help. Someone said something I really didn't like and it just got my goat, that's all. Reminded me of an event in my past I'd rather forget. But now I'm here with you and I have this desperate need to fuck you until you scream. I hope you have enough lube and condoms in that bedside drawer of yours. I've a feeling we'll need them all."

He stood up and pulled Marshall to his feet. "Come on, lover. Make me feel better."

Chapter 21

Flynn sat opposite Anthony at his desk at the police station as he waited for him to finish up what he was doing. Currently he was looking extremely grim at something being said to him by whoever was on the phone. Flynn watched Anthony's eyes narrow, his mouth tighten and his fists constantly clench at his side. He bent down and made a few notes on his desk blotter. Rupert watched Flynn carefully from his vantage point across the desk on the other side of his boss's work station. Flynn wasn't quite sure what the intense scrutiny was all about. Finally Rupert's curiosity got the better of him.

"So, Flynn, what did you think of Anthony's interview early this morning? That reporter Tracey Lucas managed to broadcast the link between you and Masumi. Is Ms. Lucas a friend of yours?" He raised an eyebrow enquiringly. Flynn looked at him.

"No friend of mine, Rupe. She's a real sensationalist. And I thought Tony did very well considering his hands are tied on what he can and can't say." Flynn cast a fond look in his lover's direction, noticing the tension in his body. He'd have to try get rid of that for him later.

"But you can't fault her question about the link." Rupert said quietly. "She won't stop until she makes a connection." He regarded Flynn carefully. "It's all so personal, isn't it? First he takes you, now a friend of yours. He's really trying to make Anthony pay. I still think he's too close to the case; he needs to distance himself—" his words were cut short as Anthony banged his fist hard on Rupert's desk, causing Rupert's coffee to spill out of his mug and the pens and other items on his desk to jump furiously as if electrified. Anthony's eyes blazed with sheer fury.

"Shut the fuck up, Rupert. You have no idea what you're talking about." He turned back to the phone. "No, I wasn't talking to you, Graham. Just some wanker in my squad."

He turned away and paced around the floor as Flynn watched him, open mouthed at the sheer aggression he'd just witnessed. He looked at Rupert, whose face was white with anger. His chest was heaving, probably as he wondered whether he could get away with decking his superior.

"I'm sorry, Rupert," Flynn said quietly. "He's pretty stressed out at the moment what with everything going on. That call from BTK really shook him—" he stopped, suddenly uncomfortably aware he might have let some cat out of the bag. Then he remembered Anthony had come back to the station and told his team himself so they could re-work his brother's case. Flynn felt a frisson of relief.

Rupert stared at him evenly. "Don't worry," he said quietly. "I do know about that one, unlike other things my supposed team member doesn't choose to tell me. Like the identity of the CI he's using that got all those emails." His voice was challenging. Flynn's face flushed and he hoped Rupert hadn't noticed.

"Give him a chance," Flynn murmured. "Anthony generally has good reasons for most things. I'm sure he'll tell you when he's ready." He was aware that the observation was weak but he didn't know what else to say. Rupert nodded tightly, his eyes watching his boss as the man strode around the room like a caged tiger.

"I'm sure he will," he said drily, but Flynn could see the disbelief on his face. He turned his attention to some paperwork on his desk, watching Anthony out of the corner of his eye. Flynn thought the spat between them wasn't quite finished yet. He sighed heavily. He'd come down to the station to give Anthony and his team some background on Masumi and the day she'd not turned up for work. Flynn had signed a statement and then was planning on going home alone. His boyfriend was a man on a mission, a man with two personal stakes in this case, his brother's death and Flynn's abduction. He knew Anthony was worried about being pulled off the case. DCI Winslow was definitely not happy with the recent events and the fact everything seemed to be close to home and personal. Rupert obviously shared the same view. Anthony finished his conversation with the pathologist and slammed his mobile down on his desk.

He snarled at no one in particular. "Graham said they'd managed to decipher what those symbols on Sumi's stomach were. The bastard carved the initials BTK into her in Jap letters." Once again he hit the desk and once again the coffee spilt and the inanimate objects on the desk jumped a foot. "Christ, I'm fucking fed up with this. We're not getting much further. When in hell are we going to get a break?" He looked at Flynn. "I think you need to get off and let me get back to work. I need to organise a team meeting and get everyone refocused on where we are and what the fuck we're doing. That bloody reporter this morning as well as told the whole fucking world we didn't have a clue and we were no closer to catching him. I'm starting to believe she's right and that does no one any good. Especially the victims." He scowled. "And the last thing I want is another body on my conscience. And frankly, I wake up every day wondering whether there's going to be one. It's been a while, even for him."

Flynn stood up and nodded. "That police detail you organised already said they'd take me home so I'll get off."

Anthony winced. "I have to arrange something else on that score. Winslow says he can't get the protection detail to carry on looking after you for much longer. He's getting a lot of stick from on high about utilising police resources." He spat the words out in fury. "I need to see what else I can organise. Especially after today's press conference. I can't have him taking it out on you."

"What about Kieran? Is your friend still watching him?" Flynn searched his eyes as he replied.

Anthony sighed. "Ernie is still looking out for him as long as I need him. It's you I'm worried about."

Flynn reached out and gripped Anthony's arm. "You have to stop protecting me sometime, Tony," he whispered softly in his ear.

Anthony shook his head fiercely. "That'll never happen," he whispered back. "Not as long I live, *amore*. Now go. I'll try to get home as soon as I can."

He kissed Flynn fiercely, his lips desperate and needy, and then released him. Flynn wasn't quite sure about this open display of affection in the middle of Anthony's office in front of a lot of hardened police men. He felt a little taken aback. But nobody seemed to care, and in fact, most people looking on were smiling at Anthony's gesture. Rupert, however, was watching with a guarded look, as the rest of the squad room looked on. Flynn nodded and detached himself from Anthony, feeling a sense of loss as he did so.

"Be careful," he said quietly then turned to Rupert. "I know you two might feel a little fed up with each other but you're still partners and you need to have each other's backs. Make nice, gentlemen, and Rupert, don't let him do anything stupid. Please."

He turned to leave but not before giving Anthony a imploring look to be careful.

*****

Anthony watched Flynn leave then blew out a deep sigh. He turned to look at Rupert who was gazing at him expressionlessly.

Anthony frowned at him. "Sergeant, I'd appreciate it if you didn't blurt your mouth off to witnesses and my boyfriend in particular. I'm fine on this case. You know I am."

"Sorry, Tony, but you're wrong." Rupert retorted. "You are far too close to this one. And forgive me if I like to make sure I'm doing what's best for the department. You'd expect that from me in any other investigation so I honestly don't know why this one should give you such a bug up your arse."

Anthony's face darkened, his eyes glittering with anger as he moved forward threateningly toward the seated Rupert. "This is my fucking case, Rupert," he spat. "And if I were you I'd consider your next words very carefully. I already don't like the ones you've just spoken and this relationship could definitely go from bad to worse."

Rupert gave a short laugh. "God forbid I say something you don't like, Anthony." He stood up. "Would you like me to gather the team together, sir?" His voice was deferential but Anthony could hear the belligerent tone in it. He nodded.

"Yes please, Sergeant. Tell them to bring in anything they're working on. I want a full status update. It'll be a late one so warn them they'll be here most of the night."

Rupert nodded curtly and disappeared to round the others. Anthony took a deep breath. He knew he'd been a bastard and deep down he knew Rupert had a right to be concerned. If circumstances were reversed, he'd be saying the same thing. But he just couldn't lose this case. He sighed as he ran a hand through his unruly hair. He closed his eyes in tiredness. He had another task to do now, one that he'd put off long enough. It was time to go see Kieran Weslake.

Chapter 22

Anthony rang the doorbell of the trendy brownstone in the middle of the town of Surbiton just outside the city and waited. He heard someone moving around inside the house. Finally the door opened and a tall, slim figure with enquiring green eyes peered out at him. Sandy brown hair streaked with grey curled around an angular face. Anthony recognised him from photographs Flynn had in his memory box, in which he kept all sorts of personal knick knacks.

"Can I help you?" Kieran asked with a slight smile.

Anthony shifted uncomfortably. "Mr. Weslake, my name's Anthony Parglietto."

For a moment, the name didn't register. Then as Kieran obviously realised who he was, he scowled fiercely and stepped forward. He wasn't a big man, more slimly built and a little scrawny for Anthony's taste. He looked…*distinguished*, as if he'd be at home with people far more polished than Anthony.

"Flynn's policeman boyfriend? The one he left me for? What the hell are you doing standing on my bloody doorstep? You've got a fucking cheek."

Anthony raised a hand in a placatory gesture. "I'm aware that this is a rather unusual situation, but I really need to speak with you. I'm here in both a personal and an official capacity."

He could see Kieran wanted nothing more than to move forward and punch him hard across the jaw, but knew Anthony's size and Kieran's inherent manners were probably holding him back.

"You and I have nothing to talk about," Kieran snapped. "Now, if you'll excuse me, I have work to do."

He started to close the door and Anthony placed a large foot just inside as he looked at him in mild exasperation.

"Mr. Weslake, it's very important that we speak. Please. I'll try not to take up too much of your time."

He hated the slightly pleading tone in his voice but it seemed to make Kieran take notice. Anthony held the other man's even stare for a few seconds then Kieran gestured abruptly.

"Fine, come in. But I warn you I don't have long. I'm very busy."

He waited until Anthony had entered the flat and then shut the door.

"We can go into the lounge. Follow me."

Anthony followed him to the lounge and sat down on the one end of the couch.

Kieran glared at him. "So tell me what it is you came here to say."

Anthony took a deep breath. "Firstly, let me tell you Flynn has no idea I'm here. He'd have a hissy fit if he knew. And I'm sure I don't have to tell you a man is better off staying out of the way of his hissy fits." His voice was dry. He was heartened by the small grin forming on Kieran's face.

"Yes. I'd agree there. So he doesn't know you're here. What else?"

Anthony hesitated. "I firstly wanted to apologise to you for the way things turned out." His voice was quiet. "I never meant to take him away from you. I know it probably doesn't mean much but it happened pretty quickly." He hastened to reassure the other man. "And I can promise you nothing happened between us while he was still with you. We were friends."

He mentally crossed his fingers. He hoped "nothing" counted as scorching glances at each other across crowded rooms, instant breathlessness when they were close to each other and the overwhelming desire he'd had to grab Flynn and pound him into a mattress. They'd shared beers and jokes and the vagaries of their colleagues and both of them had known they needed it to be more.

Anthony had always felt uncomfortable at the whirlwind romance he and Flynn had started. Once they'd realised their friendship was leading to more, Flynn had refused to have anything to do with Anthony romantically or sexually until he'd broken up with Kieran. But it still rankled with Anthony that he'd been the reason for their breakup.

Kieran nodded slowly and his eyes narrowed. "That's very big of you." His tone wasn't sarcastic, but more approving. "It was a bit of a shock when he came home and told me he was leaving me." Kieran looked down at his hands. Anthony noticed they were long, slim hands so unlike his own.

Then Kieran looked up and sighed. "But you know what? After the initial shock of Flynn leaving, it wasn't as bad as it could have been. I knew our relationship was more 'comfortable' to begin with, friends with benefits, never a 'passionate, rip your clothes off' affair." Amused green eyes looked into Anthony's. "Not like yours apparently is. Any fool can hear he worships you. At least Flynn and I are still able to speak to each other with a civil tongue."

Anthony exhaled. "Thank you. I appreciate that." He took a deep breath. "Now this is the professional bit. And this is the bit I'm really going to have to ask you to understand." His voice had turned professional, steely. "Lives depend on it—yours, in fact, and probably Flynn's."

Kieran looked stunned. "What are you talking about? How can I be in any bloody danger?"

Anthony shifted in his seat, his eyes regarding Kieran intensely. "You know my latest case is the BTK serial murders?"

Kieran nodded. "Yes. I've been following the case ever since I heard you were involved with it." He chuckled wryly. "I like to know a little bit about my competition. I'm a bit of a masochist that way. From the news reports, it certainly seems as if you're the right man for the job. You have a very impressive track record."

Anthony felt a little uncomfortable at that comment. He wasn't used to having his lover's ex-boyfriends paying him compliments. "Thank you. Well, this case has a very personal connection to me. I can't tell you what. But as a result, anyone close to me could be at risk. As could anyone close to them." He stopped. It took Kieran a few second to process and when the knowledge hit him, he gasped.

"You mean Flynn could be in danger?"

Anthony nodded. "Yes. And possibly you as well, because of your past connection to him."

Kieran sat back, looking slightly panicked.

Anthony leaned forward and spoke quietly. "Flynn is fine. I have a police protective detail assigned to him. You were a little more difficult to arrange so I needed to get inventive. Police resources only go so far and because the threat was so"—he paused—"far removed for you, I wasn't able to get a team to watch you. So I got you your very own personal bodyguard instead."

Kieran looked taken aback. "Well, I'm sure that man you chose as a personal bodyguard would definitely be a man worth his salt but is it really necessary? I don't need a babysitter."

Anthony rubbed his eyes. He felt tired and wanted to get home to Flynn. "He's a friend of mine, ex-SAS, who's between jobs at the moment and offered to give me a hand until I catch this bastard. Which I will do, make no mistake. Ernie has been watching out for you off and on since this all began a couple of weeks ago. You hopefully haven't even noticed him."

Kieran stood up, his arms waving around excitedly. "I've been fucking watched for weeks? What, everything I do? And why the hell am I only hearing this now?"

Anthony closed his eyes, feeling a little guilty. "That's my fault—again. I didn't want to scare you at first, cause anything that could get into the newspapers or compromise the case. Then I thought about it and realised that if I were you, I'd want to know. It's the right thing to do. So here I am." He grinned. "Have no fear—he's only been keeping an eye on you out there," he waved an airy hand, "and watching the house when you're in here. Whatever you get up to inside your home is your business only. So all those rent boys and strippers you've had traipsing in here for your nightly jollies remain your secret—mostly." His lips twitched at the look of disbelief on the other man's face.

"I haven't had any of that sort of thing going on in here—" Kieran said hotly then flushed as Anthony chuckled. Kieran looked at him with a scowl that turned to unwilling amusement.

"If you say so," Anthony drawled as Kieran laughed softly. Anthony could see why Flynn had been in a relationship with him. He was quite a character and in different circumstances, they may even have been friends.

Jesus, I'm actually getting to like this bloody man. How sad is that, that I can form an attachment with my lover's ex?

Finally Kieran sighed. "I suppose I can understand all that. It's not an easy decision given your position in all this and the fact you're trying to get a bloody mass murderer. Thank you for protecting Flynn and me." He scowled again. "You're going to need to point this Ernie out to me, or else I'm going to be looking at everyone thinking they're the one and things might get a little awkward."

Anthony inclined his head in agreement. "I'll do that when I leave. We can play 'Where's Wally' and you can see if you spot him." He laughed. "The man's a ghost and he'll only let you spot him if he wants to be seen. I'll text him before I leave and he can wave to you."

His tone grew more serious. "I do want you to be careful. This killer is a psycho and not to be trifled with. If at any time you feel threatened, or scared, or get suspicious, I want you to call someone." He took out a business card and a pen and wrote a number on the back. "Ernie's mobile number is on the back. He might be better as a first port of call because he's closer. But I want you to know you can call me anytime of the day or night if you want to talk."

He stood up. "I'd better get off. Lots to do as well. Killers to catch."

Kieran reached out a hand and touched his arm. "Detective, I get the feeling there's something else here, something you're not telling me. Are you sure Flynn's safe?"

Anthony nodded.

Flynn would kill me if I ever told him about his abduction.

Flynn had been uncompromising in the fact that Kieran should never hear about what had been done to him. Anthony could only guess that he didn't want to worry the man and also that the less people that knew about the ignominy of being kidnapped and brutalised, the better. Flynn was a proud man.

"Yes, he's as safe as he can be, I promise." He turned to leave then turned back. "Obviously, this is our little secret. No one needs to know I've been here, especially Flynn."

Kieran nodded and Anthony pulled out his phone and sent a quick text. Within seconds he got one back. He laughed at the detail.

"Ernie says he's flattered you want to see what he looks like but you do realise that when you know, he's going to have to kill you himself?"

Kieran started and Anthony couldn't help a small giggle.

"Ha bloody ha. Very funny. You two should have your own stand-up act." Kieran grinned as Anthony opened the front door and motioned him outside. They walked up the steps to the street level and Kieran surveyed the area with narrowed eyes.

"So where is he?"

Anthony chuckled. "Patience, please. If you look directly in front of you, you'll see a man built like a wrestler with a green tee shirt and a red cap on his head. That's Ernie. Don't wave or anything; you'll draw attention to him and he won't like that."

Kieran looked over to where Anthony had casually indicated. Ernie was well hidden but he could just be seen as Anthony described him, a large man leaning against the brick wall, his hand almost raised in a greeting but not quite there. Kieran automatically started to raise his hand but Anthony shook his head and knocked it down gently.

"I said no greeting. So now you can say you've met Ernie. There are plenty of people who wish they hadn't, I can tell you. And now I need to be going." Anthony started to walk to the street when Kieran stopped him with a firm hand on his shoulder.

"Anthony, wait."

Anthony turned and raised an enquiring eyebrow.

Kieran waggled a hand at him. "Thanks for coming. I appreciate it. And thanks for looking out for me." He snickered. "It's a bit like an episode of bloody *Spooks*. Covert operations, serial killers, big, muscled detectives and SAS men in my neighbourhood. Please just keep Flynn safe."

Anthony nodded. "I'll do my best, I promise." He turned and crossed the street.

Let me have a quick word with Ernie and then I can get home and have my own secret. Flynn will never forgive me if he knew I came here to see Kieran.

Chapter 23

Flynn waited until around eleven p.m. for Anthony to come home then decided he may as well go to bed. He was awakened by a noise outside the door, a sound of something falling and he sat bolt upright in bed, his hands reaching for the small switchblade he always slept with under his pillow since his abduction. He'd had the knife since he was a teenager but never had an occasion to use it. Anthony would be pretty displeased to learn of its existence, it being an illegal weapon. He withdrew the knife slowly as he listened for further noises. The door handle turned and Flynn breathed a sigh of relief as he saw the familiar broad shape of his lover enter the room. Flynn shoved the knife back under the pillow.

"Anthony? I heard a noise. What happened?"

Anthony sighed heavily as he started disrobing, dropping his clothes as was his habit in untidy piles on the floor beside his bed.

"Sorry. I knocked against one of the pictures on the wall and it fell off." He yawned and turned over to switch on the bedside light. He winced as the brightness hit his eyes and Flynn shook his head.

"God, you look terrible." Anthony's face was pale, his eyes sunken into dark holes in his face. His hair was mussed and untidy. His cheekbones stood out sharply in the light and his normal beefy bulk was whittled down to a more wiry strength. He was still a big man but he was slowly fading.

"Thanks," Anthony remarked drily. "Always good to know I can count on you to boost my ego."

Flynn waved an airy hand. "It's no surprise. You've hardly been eating these past few days. You're obviously not eating the usual amount of junk food and when your mother sees you losing weight she's going to have a fit."

Anthony laughed softly. "Why do you think I haven't called her for a while? My mother has this sixth sense. If she hears any sound of defeat or tiredness in my voice she'll be on the first plane over. Then when she sees me, she'll be tying me to a kitchen chair and force feeding me pasta."

Flynn chuckled. "How did the task force thingamajig go tonight? Did you manage to make any progress?"

Anthony sighed. "It gave us a new sense of purpose and the hotline has had a lot of calls so hopefully we'll be able to get some new leads off that. Of course ninety-nine percent will be crap but there's always hope the one will turn into a nugget of gold." He rubbed the back of his neck then started to undress. "I just want to get into bed and perhaps take advantage of you." He shrugged out of his suit jacket and pulled the tie from his neck.

Flynn watched him with greedy eyes. "Now that's an invitation I can't refuse. A man stripping for me in the bedroom. Very entertaining." He reached down and languidly stroked his cock under the sheet, relishing the sight of Anthony disrobing and his own hands on his steadily hardening erection.

Anthony started to slowly unbutton his shirt. He knew Flynn liked to watch him undress and it seemed to Flynn that he was more than happy to perform tonight. His shirt fell to the floor by his side of the bed, and he reached down to unzip his trousers, letting them fall around his feet as he stepped out of them.

Flynn licked his lips as Anthony slowly slid his silk boxer shorts down his legs to the floor to stand fully erect in front of him. Anthony regarded him with raised eyebrows and Flynn looked from his lover's groin to his face then beckoned him over with a sly smile. Anthony laughed, a small, sexy sound that turned Flynn's bones to jelly and his cock even harder. Anthony slid into the bed and under the covers and straight into Flynn's eager arms. Flynn wasted no time in taking Anthony's mouth in a kiss that unleashed all the pent-up frustration he had welling up inside him. Teeth clicked together, lips mashed in wet, breathy pants and tongues thrust roughly into each other's mouths. Finally Anthony came up for breath, leaving Flynn aching for more.

"Christ!" Anthony gasped roughly. "I know I'm horny but if we don't get this show on the road soon, it'll be over before it's even begun." His eager hands grasped Flynn's arse pulling him over to sit astride him. He reached under the pillow and found the packs of lube they kept there then handed it to Flynn, who opened the packet and smeared lube on his fingers.

"You do it," Anthony said huskily. "You know I love watching you open yourself up."

Flynn rose to his knees above Anthony. "I rather thought tonight I might have *you*."

Anthony's pupils dilated and his nostrils flared. He enjoyed Flynn inside him but normally Flynn was happy to be the receiver. Anthony had never bottomed with anyone other than Flynn before.

"Then get me ready," Anthony growled. "It's been a while for me, so make sure you—" His voice broke off with a gasp as Flynn grinned then thrust a finger inside Anthony's tight hole.

"Jesus, babe, a little warning? That's damn cold."

Flynn ignored Anthony's aggrieved expression as he readied him to take his rather desperate cock. When he thought Anthony had had enough, judging from the moans and small sighs coming out of his kissable lips, Flynn pushed in, and slowly, thrust by thrust, buried himself to the balls in Anthony's body.

"You feel good. This was a great idea," he whispered as he made small movements, aching to pound Anthony into the mattress but knowing that he needed to take it easy. Anthony's eyes were half closed as he moved below Flynn, grasping his hips and enticing him into the deep, dark warmth of his body.

"No arguments from me," he gasped. "You just carry on, but for God's sake, move a little more. Stop being such a damn gentleman. Fuck me already."

At those words Flynn found the cord that held him back and cut it, savouring the sharp thrusts of his body into that of the willing and eager man beneath him. Anthony moaned as his own movements increased in desperation and soon there was nothing more than the sound of lovemaking, sighs, pants and moans that echoed in the room as flesh slapped against flesh.

Flynn watched Anthony's face as he smiled up at him. He savoured the smell and the feel of his man. Anthony's passion, intelligence and his unrelenting desire for Flynn had taken his heart and he was sure he would never love anyone more than him. Flynn felt himself getting to his no-return point, feeling the prickling in his groin and the breathlessness in his chest that signalled the start of his climax. He thought with a pang, even as he came with a loud groan, a groan that Anthony muffled with his hungry mouth, that the moment had been far too short-lived. Anthony was far too good at what he did, and tonight Flynn had been really hungry for him. It was like giving a steak to a starving dog—the steak didn't even touch sides. He shuddered as he came, feeling the wet spurts on his belly as Anthony climaxed too, his hands desperately pulling Flynn closer in his throes.

Anthony's warm breath in his ear and his whispered "I love you" as they climaxed together made Flynn's heart swell. For one fleeting moment, he could forget all that had happened to them both and pretend that perhaps life was going to be good for the two of them after all.

*****

The following morning Anthony left Flynn in bed and made his way to the office around ten a.m. His night's sleep had been tainted with dreams about his dead brother, the case files he'd revisited the day before bringing back terrible memories of Marco's broken and abused body. He'd seen his team looking at him with worried glances more than once and Rupert at one stage had quietly offered to review the case history if Anthony needed a break. The bad feelings resulting from their earlier argument had lessened somewhat, the needs of the case in hand being a much more urgent requirement than their personal differences. Anthony had declined the offer but thanked Rupert for it anyway.

They'd carried on revisiting the evidence, looking over witness statements and reviewing the emails that the "CI" had given them. The bottom line was that the killer had made mistakes. His arrogance would prove his undoing, of that Anthony was convinced. The bite to his body, even the emails he'd sent to Flynn allowing them to garner just that little bit more information on him, the link to Marco's killing and the witness seeing the red post van, which there was still a BOLO out on in the area. Anthony guessed that all the poor postmen in the immediate vicinity were being pulled over and thoroughly vetted by the feet on the ground. It didn't add up to much but all together the silken strands might mesh to make a spider's web in which they could finally trap the fly.

BTK had confessed to a personal vendetta, showing a weakness Anthony wanted to exploit any which way he could, hence the rather confrontational interview he'd given to the press. He hoped like hell someone out there would put some of the other strands together and call the hotline. It was all he had now.

When he reached the station his team were already hard at work, their eyes bloodshot and sunken like his. Carol Matthews, one of his sergeants, motioned him over.

"Sir, the Geek Squad has managed to make a connection between some of the killings this guy's mentioned in those emails."

Anthony felt his spirits rise. "Which killings and what connections?" He strode over to her desk intent on getting any good news he could. He saw the email printed out on Carol's desk, and the spreadsheet Flynn had put together with the chronological timeline.

Mandy was the first. Redheaded, 34C. Blended her ass till she was creamy and ready to blow.

Elliott. Aah, Elliott. He was a lovely boy. Tight, willing and very limber. Pity. I liked Elliott. It was dreadful what happened to him.

Rachael. Blonde. Nothing up front but God, what lips. I loved them round my cock. But she needed to be taught a lesson. And I'm a really good teacher.

Sandy. Did her every which way but Sunday till she screamed for me to stop. But I couldn't. I was having far too much fun. I think I might have shagged her to death.

"They used some sort of software they have to see if any of the information we have made any correlation, or had any similarities. They think they've made a connection between the killing of a young nineteen-year-old boy called Elliott Carter in March 2002 and twenty-two-year-old Rachael Windsor in September 2003. Elliott Carter was a young gay man who was studying criminology at Kingston University London. He was found in the early hours of Friday the fifteenth March '02 by a jogger. He'd been raped; from the state of his backside, quite violently, and his throat was slit. His university tie was tied around his neck." Carol checked her notes and Anthony narrowed his eyes as he listened.

"Rachael Windsor was found on Tuesday twenty-third September 2003. She'd been raped, strangled, her throat was then cut and her new Hermes silk scarf which she'd just been given by her boyfriend for her twenty-second birthday was tied around her neck."

Anthony raised a hand to stop her talking. "I'm sensing there's a pattern here then with the neck ties that the computer picked up on. Is this where you're going with this?"

She nodded. "There was another murder further down on this list, Daniele Green. She was a twenty-five-year-old law student who was found on Friday the thirteenth of February 2004. She was also raped, stabbed multiple times, throat slit and they found her old City University scarf tied around her neck."

She stopped and looked at Anthony. "She was a lesbian woman in a committed relationship with her partner for three years."

Anthony felt sick. "This bastard has been doing this forever, hasn't he? How many more did the computer match up?"

Carol's voice was quiet when she replied. "It looks as if there are at least fifteen unsolved cases similar to this MO. The guys had already run the algorithms through their software after the first two killings, to see if this MO existed. But it wasn't successful in picking up any patterns. Now, with the addition of the first names we received and some of the detail, it allowed them to drill down into the programme and work their voodoo. And this is the result. The kills were all random places, no specific victimology. He targeted straight, gay and lesbian people. No one ever connected the dots, until now."

Her hand trembled as she shuffled the papers on her desk. "We have a very prolific and long-standing serial killer here, sir. Someone who has been getting away with killing people for a very long time; some of the kills that were matched date back to 1996. Based on the profile we're working on with this guy being in his mid-thirties—even if we assume he's aged at the highest end of the spectrum around thirty-five years old—it means that this guy was only about nineteen when he started killing. And for all we know it could have been earlier. The computer's still looking at more matches but the further back we go, the less data we have."

Anthony paced the squad room. "I have the feeling this guy's been doing it a lot longer than anyone realises. He's a natural born killer, to coin a movie phrase. I can feel it." He smiled tiredly at Carol.

"That's really well done, Sergeant. Tell that geek squad I'm buying the pints when this is all over. Tell them to keep running the searches and anything we have so far. Tell Rupert to dish it out and pull the cold case files and start going over them." He frowned. "Where is Sergeant Gregg anyway? I haven't seen him this morning yet."

Carol looked uncomfortable. "I think he's around, sir. Maybe he's in the bathroom."

Her cagey tone didn't fool Anthony.

"Sergeant Matthews, where is my other fucking sergeant?"

She hesitated. "He's in with DCI Winslow, sir."

Anthony felt a slow burn start in his chest. He really didn't appreciate any of his subordinates going over his head to talk to his own boss without a very good reason and he definitely couldn't think of one related to the case unless it was about Anthony himself.

"Oh is he?" he said grimly, watching the woman squirm in discomfort. "I see. Thank you, Sergeant. Perhaps you'd better tell the rest of the team what they need to do then seeing as my own partner is otherwise occupied." His scathing tone carried around the room and others looked up from their work curiously. Sergeant Matthews nodded, her face flushed, and disappeared to do her boss's bidding. Anthony sat down at his desk and checked his mobile. There was nothing urgent on it and he put his phone back in his pocket. He'd been working about half an hour when he saw Rupert coming toward him across the office. He watched with a steady gaze as his sergeant pulled out his desk chair and sat down.

"And where have you been?" Anthony's voice was low but dangerous. "A little bird told me you were having a social visit with DCI Winslow. I hadn't realised the two of you were dating."

Rupert's face flushed. "I had something I needed to talk to him about, something personal."

"I thought I was the first line of command for you to tell your woes to," Anthony remarked silkily. "Isn't that what they do in the films—the other partner confides all their troubles in the other, they go out for a beer, end up getting rat faced together and sort out the woes of the world. For some reason, that hasn't happened here, Sergeant Gregg, even though we've been dating for almost six months now. I'm deeply hurt." His sarcasm made Rupert's face flush an even deeper shade of pink.

"I'm sorry, Anthony. But you know my feelings about your rather radical views and where you're taking this case." He fidgeted slightly. "It's not just the fact you're too close to it. You have some"—he struggled to find the words—"some fairly skewed morals. I can't in all justice let that lie."

He said this with a triumphant flourish and Anthony seethed.

"I see. Well, perhaps, *Sergeant Gregg*," he spat the words out, "You could refer to me as sir, boss or DI Parglietto in future, seeing as how we appear to be breaking up. I'm not one for familiarity with the workforce when they can't see their way to trusting me with their tales of woe and righteous indignation." He knew he was being petty but the thought of being excluded from whatever it was he and DCI Winslow had been talking about—and he had a feeling it definitely involved him—was galling. He'd tried really hard to like Rupert but it really didn't seem to be working out. The man was a moralistic, righteous prat after all. Anthony thought that he'd have his own chat with his boss and request a new sergeant to be assigned to his team.

Rupert stared at him in challenge as Anthony held his gaze. Finally Rupert gave a terse nod and busied himself with the papers on his desk and switching on his computer. Anthony turned as he heard his name being called from across the room.

"DI Parglietto. My office." The strident tones of DCI Winslow echoed like thunder through the office and Anthony stood up, casting a venomous glance in Rupert's direction.

Anthony walked over to his boss's office and entered, shutting the door behind him.

"You bellowed, sir?" he said evenly as he stood waiting for his DCI to invite him to sit down. The man looked at him and Anthony was a little taken aback at the look in his eyes. He'd been expecting censure for his irreverent comment, but all he saw in Winslow's eyes was a look of resignation, a calm acceptance about something. The man waved a hand at him.

"Sit, please. I need to talk to you about something."

Anthony sat down in the chair, leaning forward and studying his boss's face carefully. "Does said conversation have anything to do with the fact that my sergeant has been closeted in here for the best part of an hour?" he said between gritted teeth. "I have to confess I thought I was the only man in his life and I'm—"

"Anthony, shut the fuck up."

Anthony shut the fuck up and stared at his boss, his lips tight together, a mutinous look in his eyes. Winslow sighed.

"Sergeant Winslow was in here expressing his concern about your involvement in this case. He appears to think this one is too close and personal and thinks the case would be better suited to another DI to take over."

"Sir, I—" Anthony's retort was cut off by a wave of his superior's hand.

"As do I, I might say. But that's not news to you as I've expressed that concern before. But hearing it from one of your team members just makes me consider the proposition anew." He steepled his fingers and Anthony watched them as the rising anger in his body threatened to overwhelm him, fury rising through his pores like steam being released from a pressure hose. He knew better than to interrupt his DCI until he'd had his say.

"He's also expressed a concern that your views are not palatable to him. Frankly, I don't give a toss about his self-righteous, holier-than-thou crap. But I am honest enough to think he might have a point in something."

Anthony's hands clenched into fists as Winslow regarded him with sympathy.

"You know I think that you are the best officer I have in this unit. You've proven that time and time again. But this case has become so high profile that I have to consider the needs of this department against any particular individual needs. You know I've had my concerns about keeping you on this case. It's become too close to home. This killer is taunting you personally. He took your boyfriend and if you believe his words, he murdered your brother and is coming after you with a personal vendetta of some sort. He was also contacting Flynn directly, a man who is now unofficially our CI for this case. But he doesn't target you directly. He targets people you love and people close to you. I can't have that. It could put members of this team at risk."

Anthony's mouth was dry and his stomach was churning. He could see where this was heading and he cursed bloody Rupert Gregg with all the Italian invectives and curses he could muster. The older man looked at him sympathetically.

"I know this is going to be hard for you to accept but I've asked DI Gerry Mountjoy to come in and take over this case. I want you off it. It'll be better for you, for Flynn and for the department. I've probably waited too long to do this anyway and I don't want to be sitting here in a few days' time when something goes horribly wrong apologising to anyone for not doing it sooner."

Anthony stood up, his hands trembling so much that he clenched them at his sides. "Mountjoy is a complete prat," he hissed in fury.

"And as for mister fucking holier-than-thou with his altruistic outlook—you know this case is mine, sir. Haven't I been professional about working it? Have you personally got any complaints about what I've been doing?"

Winslow's voice was quiet but firm when he spoke. "Gregg is a moralistic SOB, no doubt about that. But he's got a point. You've given it everything you've got and more, son. More in fact that anyone could expect. But it's time to let go. There's more at stake here than your feelings. I have the safety of your team to consider as well. Not to mention that the powers that be have communicated to me that we could be compromised if we leave someone on this case who so obviously has a personal interest. It could queer the pitch for any future prosecutions with stories of personal vendettas or tainted evidence. You know what I'm talking about." His voice was resolved.

Anthony stared at the DI in disbelief. "This is really because of my views on crime and punishment, isn't it sir? The fact that I believe the punishment should fit the crime and this evil bastard doesn't deserve to live. And that self-righteous prick Gregg disagrees with me."

"Anthony, over the years, you've done yourself no favours being so outspoken about your beliefs. In the past it hasn't really mattered. Until now. This, as I've said, is a high-profile case and if something happens, and God willing, we get the bastard, the department needs to be squeaky clean. We don't want to be seen as advocating any sort of vigilante justice. It's politics, son."

Anthony felt his legs weaken as he considered his superior's words. He sat down and ran a hand through his hair. He knew his views were fairly strong and that he'd aired them more than once in the past but he'd never thought he'd get to this place where his beliefs were being used against him. He knew his boss was right, and even in his current emotional state he could take a dispassionate look and see where they were coming from. But to be taken off this case?

"Sir, can you not reconsider—" he could hear the pleading in his voice and he hated himself for it. Winslow shook his head quietly.

"The decision's been made, Anthony. DI Mountjoy will be here by the end of the week. That's in two days' time. I suggest you tidy up everything you can to hand over and then perhaps you can take some time off. You and Flynn deserve a break. If you don't want to do that, I have another case for you to work. The Granger Park murders. I know they'd be very glad to have you on their team."

The recent killings in the Granger Park area of South London involving what appeared to be mafia-type gangland killings was another fairly high-profile case. He gazed at his boss in stupefaction.

"I'm sure they're doing fine just as they are. Matt Blakely is a great detective and he's more than capable of doing that job. He won't appreciate me interfering with his case."

DI Winslow's voice was subdued when he replied. "Matt Blakely has just found his eldest daughter has leukaemia and he's quite happy to bow out of the case so he can concentrate on his personal life. So they are in need of a good DI. It's your choice. A holiday first then assigned to that case or a new case straight away. Those are your options, Anthony. I'll leave you to talk them over with Flynn. In the meantime, try not to kill Sergeant Gregg, wait out the time and give your current case any due attention until DI Mountjoy is on board." He stood up and moved around his desk, laying a gentle hand on Anthony's shoulder.

"Anthony. Listen to me. This is for the best. Go home, take this all in and think about it rationally. You know I'm very fond of you, son. But this is what's got to happen."

Anthony stood up, his face hard and dark. "I hear you, sir. It doesn't mean I have to fucking like it."

He turned and stormed out of the office, his hands clenched at his side, knowing his face showed his dissatisfaction in every grimace and glare that he threw across the room at his sergeant. When he reached his desk, he sat down and watched as Rupert tried to pretend that he wasn't there.

"You're a miserable piece of fucking work, you know that, Gregg?" Anthony's voice was menacing. "You shafted me, you bastard. You wormed your way into that office and like the treacherous tosser you are, you got me kicked off this case."

Rupert looked at him evenly. "It's nothing personal, *DI Parglietto*. It's just common sense. You know you're too close to this one and I for one don't want to be the red sauce in the middle of a BTK and Parglietto sandwich. Neither do any of the other team members. Plus when we find this guy I don't need you going off half cocked and ruining the course of justice."

Anthony smiled, but made it the smile of a shark circling his prey. "We have to work together for the next couple of days before I'm *replaced*. So I fucking suggest that you make sure you do everything by the book, every bloody thing I say. I expect you to hop to when I say it and make sure you don't fuck anything up. Or I'll have you hauled over the coals so fucking fast your arse will burn. Two can play at this sneaky game. And I happen to be very good at it."

Anthony stood up and picked up his jacket from the back of his chair. He left the office without a backward glance.

*****

Later that night, Anthony arrived home to find Flynn drafting an article on his money-laundering exposé. Flynn took one look at his face and opened his arms to take him in a strong hug.

Anthony leaned into Flynn, his body tense. "I got kicked off the case," he murmured. "Winslow wants me out. He says I'm too close to it all and he's worried I might damage the department eventually with my views. He doesn't want the department 'compromised.'"

Flynn looked at him in horror. "Hell, pulling you off this case is tantamount to ripping out your insides and stomping on the empty stomach with hob-nailed boots! After all the work you've put into this, they're pulling you off? Don't those arseholes know there's no better detective than you for this job?"

"Obviously not." He moved away to pour himself a drink, loosening his tie and his top shirt buttons as he moved toward the sideboard. Anthony motioned to him to ask if he too wanted a drink. Flynn nodded. Anthony poured another one and passed it over, then slumped down onto the couch and stretched his long legs onto the coffee table. He took a large swallow of his drink and laid his head back against the back of the couch, closing his eyes.

"Tony, they can't do this to you."

Anthony gave a short, barking laugh, filled with bitterness. "It's already done. There's a new DI coming into replace me at the end of the week. "

Anthony took another swig of his drink, then another and before long, the glass was empty and he moved away to get another one. This time he brought the bottle back with him and put it on the side table. He had the feeling he might even finish the bottle before nightfall.

He stared down at his hands. "I went to see Graham at the hospital to catch up on any latest developments this afternoon. Graham is as pissed off as I am about it all. He thinks it's unfair too." He gave a twisted smile. "Unfortunately, it doesn't look like I have much option."

He heaved a shuddering sigh and took another large drink of his whiskey, almost half the glass.

Flynn leaned in and kissed the corner of his mouth tenderly. "Everything will be all right, Tony," he whispered softly as he snuggled into his shoulder. "Just let today be over and we'll tackle it tomorrow. Things always look different in the morning."

Anthony nodded as he sighed, closed his eyes and leaned back against the couch.

I hope so, baby. I hope so, he thought as Flynn's loving fingers weaved through his hair. *Because I don't know what to do if they aren't. I have to catch this guy. I need to.*

Chapter 24

Blair frowned as he looked around his house in Southern Street. Brick had called him around eight p.m. telling him he'd seen gang activity around the house and once again Blair had cut short his plan of screwing Marshall after a well-cooked dinner and had to make his way down to Newham. He'd told Marshall there'd been some emergency at the gym, that someone had lost their keys and he needed to go down and drop his off so they could lock up later. The house was as he'd left it but he was sure he could see signs of someone trying to force their way into the back door, through the chains and padlocks he had set up. The windows were already all boarded up, although one had been pried slightly loose and the man cursed as he realised he'd now have to fix it. He'd checked the front door but that still looked fairly secure too. The tossers preferred the back entrance as it was hidden from view.

Fucking wankers! Pot heads, druggies and hobos just wanting to find any place where they could get high and perhaps stay off the police radar.

This house was becoming more of a problem than it was worth. He'd have to think about getting rid of it and finding another kill spot. Perhaps somewhere a little more upmarket, where people didn't really give a fuck about you because they were too busy snorting coke up their noses and bonking the neighbour. That sounded like a plan.

He'd already checked his portable generator, the one that supplied electricity and heating to the house when he needed it. It was working fine, providing him with a dim light now. Light wouldn't be evident to anyone outside as there was nowhere for light to escape apart from the small opening in the window board. That opening was in the back, though, so no one could really see. He stalked about the house, making sure his supplies were intact and finally, satisfied, he sat down against one of the unpainted and peeling walls, took out a joint and lit it up. He inhaled deeply, closing his eyes as the drug did its work.

That fucking Detective Parglietto had really upset him in his TV appearance with his bloody diatribe about not being human. That rhetoric was what got Marco killed and any reminder about it really pissed him off. The policeman had no fucking idea what life was all about. It was about control and power and doing what you wanted to do regardless of any consequences. Christ, Blair had killed his mother when he was twelve years old and he wasn't paying any piper yet. All this fucking drivel talk about karma and action and consequences—it was a pile of shit. Life simply carried on and as long as you were careful and didn't get caught, it would continue to carry on just the way he liked it.

He looked around suddenly, feeling a slight frisson of apprehension. What the hell had he done with his backpack? He remembered having it at Marshall's apartment but he didn't remember it being with him when he entered the house. *Fuck! I must have left it there. This is the second time I've done that. I'm getting sloppy.*

After getting Brick's call, he'd been so busy pulling on his pants after the blowjob Marshall had given him that he'd totally forgotten to pick it up on his way out. Blair stood up and kicked the wall in a temper, as he shouted loudly, swearing over and over again as his steel-tipped boots knocked the plaster out of the damp walls, leaving holes. That rucksack was his tool of the trade. God knows what anyone would make of the stuff he had in there. It could be his undoing one day.

Fuck, I am stupid.

One thing Blair didn't like thinking about himself was that he *was* stupid. He prided himself on his superior intellect. It was what had gotten him this far. He scowled fiercely. It was all bloody Marshall's fault. If his mouth hadn't been doing such a good job on his cock, this wouldn't have happened. The man needed punishing for that and Blair knew just how to pay him back for his momentary indiscretion. Marshall wouldn't dare look in his backpack, he thought. He was too trained for that. He knew Blair wouldn't like it, so he wouldn't do it. The man was beyond the pale pussy-whipped and he'd toe the line.

Blair took another drag on his joint and surveyed his domain. He needed to buy some more tarp if he planned on doing another one anytime soon. He had a few ideas but he'd decided to take a bit of a break and confuse the cops. The erratic pattern of his behaviour was one of his key traits and it had been less than two weeks since the Jap woman. It had been difficult not giving into the impulse to take another one and watch Parglietto's face grow even whiter and more strained but he'd managed to control himself. Instead he'd concentrated on having rough and very raunchy sex with his boyfriend. In truth, he'd decided to pay a visit to Flynn Parker again. He was going to be his bonus prize after the next one. The policeman had really upset him with his comments and it was time for a little more payback. It would take some planning as he had the guy locked up tighter than a virgin's pussy, but when he'd got his plan in place, this time he wouldn't be as lucky. He was going to end up with a bow tie around his neck as soon as Blair finished with him, and this time, he wouldn't spare him anything. The man was going to get the full treatment. This time he'd make the newspapers.

Blair's erection grew bigger and he took another hit of his joint as he sat down with his back against the wall and unzipped his jeans. Christ, he was horny just thinking about it. He reached it and took his cock in his hands, fisting it and touching the tip with his thumb, nearly coming right there with the thought of having the detective's boyfriend facedown whilst he rammed into his arse. It didn't take him long before he sprayed the room in front of him with globs of white ejaculate and sat back, totally spent, as he contemplated his plans for killing yet another deserving person.

*****

Back at the apartment Marshall was having a slight hissy fit. His dinner lay in ruins on the dining table. Not only that, but the blowjob he'd been giving his lover was rudely interrupted by some phone call that Blair had "had to take" and now his own erection was straining against his pants feeling like the monster in the movie *Alien* when the thing had shot out of the man's chest. His cock wanted to do the same thing and he was damned if he was relieving it himself. *Blair can fucking sort it out when he gets home.*

He'd had a really rough day himself. Not only had he seen more patients today than he could handle, and subsequently had to hurry himself along, something else had irritated him. He'd not been able to get rid of Angie Green at lunchtime as she regaled him with more stories about the serial killer in town. Ordinarily he'd have been very interested. Today though he'd had a shitload of patients to see, a bunch of reports to write for a conference he was invited to and a whole pile of case files to complete. He'd also wanted to leave early to get home to make dinner for him and Blair. So her stories about something to do with Oriental writing on the skin of the latest victim, whilst titillating and worthy of conversation another time when he wasn't flat out, hadn't really tickled his fancy. She also hadn't stopped touching him and for some reason today that had irked him. He'd been glad when he could get rid of her and get back to his office.

He stalked now around the apartment, bare-chested and in a really bad mood. He was fed up with all the demands on Blair's time just at those moments when he thought he'd got him all to himself. Lately Blair had been disappearing more often, or arriving late and Marshall was getting fed up. He'd even wondered if Blair was seeing another man behind his back. The thought made him stand stock still in the living room, catching his breath. He'd said he had to go the gym to drop off a set of keys. Marshall hadn't really thought about it at the time but what if he was seeing that stud from the gym, the one who looked like Brad Pitt, the one Blair wanted in their threesome? Since making the offer to Blair, Marshall hadn't heard anything about it happening. What if it was happening without him? He growled loudly and punched his fist against the palm of his hand. He'd bloody kill them both if he found out.

He prowled angrily again, going to the front door to see if he could hear anyone coming up the corridor. The corridor was silent and as Marshall turned to go back into the lounge, he spotted Blair's rucksack under the hall table, looking innocuous but obviously put there under the table to be out of sight. Blair was very protective of his man bag and Marshall had only ever had the opportunity to look inside once. With the level of his current aggravation and the fact he had the suspicion about another man, Marshall felt fairly self-righteous about wanting to take a peek inside the bag. He made sure the front door was locked so he'd hear Blair using his key if he came in then picked up the rucksack and went and sat down on the couch. He took a deep breath as he regarded the inoffensive sack and then unclipped the straps holding it closed.

Five minutes later he was feeling fairly disappointed but relieved. There were still the old papers he'd seen last time, the deeds to the house in Southern Street, Newham, in the name of Mainwaring Associates. He supposed that was the property agent or someone. There were various other lawyers' letters advising that the property taxes were due, a phrase book of some sort, which he put to one side, and various other documents that didn't look particularly interesting. There were no condoms, lube, or other tell telling evidence that Blair was fucking someone behind his back. No men's underwear, Kama Sutra instructions or dirty pictures of his boyfriend or anyone else for that matter. Marshall felt a little better. He picked up the phrase book idly and frowned when he saw what it actually was. It wasn't a phrase book at all, but instead a book advising how to draw Japanese symbols. Why on earth would Blair need a book like this? He didn't even speak Japanese, not that he knew of anyway. Something lurked in the back of his mind, something to do with Japan that he'd heard today, but for the life of him he couldn't quite remember what it was.

Marshall shook his head in bemusement, and not for the first time, wondered exactly what he did know about his lover. He found something crumpled up at the bottom of the bag. Curious, he took it out and smoothed it out. It looked as if it had been scrunched up deliberately. He grinned when he saw what it was. It was a parking ticket. He imagined that Blair had got it and had a temper tantrum and tossed it into the bottom of his bag. *Poor baby.*

Marshall frowned as it hit him. Actually, he'd never even known Blair had a car. The man he knew travelled everywhere by the three T's—train, tube and taxi. The ticket was for parking on yellow lines on Southern Street in London. That was where Blair owned the old house. The one he said he never went to. How could he have got a ticket there if that was the case? Marshall felt a prickle of unease. What if this house wasn't as bad as Blair said it was and instead was a fuck pad? Maybe that's where he disappeared to when he did, to meet another man at his cosy little *pied de terre*. He made a note of the registration number and the vehicle make—an LDV van— on a piece of paper then plunged the ticket back into the depths of the bag and made sure everything was back more or less as he'd found it. He re-fastened the straps and put the bag back under the table. Marshall tapped his fingers against his thighs as he contemplated what to do. Finally he made a decision. First, he was going to go down to the gym on the pretext of seeing if Blair was there and surprise him with a hot latte. Then hopefully, if things panned out, he'd get fucked in the sauna, and possibly even do a little bit of sly digging afterwards to see if he could get at the story behind the ticket. Having a plan made him feel a little more cheerful and when he left the apartment twenty minutes later, he whistled as he walked down to the street.

Half an hour later, Marshall was definitely no longer whistling. His face like thunder, he sat on the street outside in the gym, in the bus stop and thought about his next actions. Billy, the manager in charge tonight, had said Blair hadn't even been in the gym tonight and no one had definitely lost any keys. Marshall hadn't missed the faint look of pity the man had thrown his way when telling him that he'd lost his lover. The latte he'd bought sat going cold on the bus bench beside him and in a fit of anger, Marshall swatted it, and watched the creamy coffee spill out onto the seat and drip onto the cold stone below. A woman sitting on the opposite side tut-tutted at the mess and he glowered at her fiercely.

"Mind your own fucking business, lady!" he snarled as he stood up and strode down the street. It was time to take this one step further. He was going to find this mysterious house on Southern Street and see whether anything was going on. He found a waiting taxi and tersely told him the address. 22B Southern Street, Newham. The taxi driver looked at him with raised eyebrows.

"Are you sure you want to go there, mate?" he asked, looking a little worried himself. "Them's bad ganglands and not a good area to be this time of night."

"I'm aware of that, thank you," Marshall said between gritted teeth. "Please just do your job and get me there."

The taxi driver shrugged his fat shoulders and started the car. Fifteen minutes later, Marshall was standing on a dark street in the middle of a very notorious London bad spot as the taxi idled nearby. He'd had a job to convince the man to stay and wait while he did his little look around, but he thought that at least having someone there that knew he was here was a good plan. If anyone gave him trouble, he could always run like a hare back to the taxi. What he planned wouldn't take long—probably not long at all, in fact, he reflected gloomily, as he surveyed number 22B. It was a shit hole of a house, all boarded up with chains and padlocks everywhere he could see. It certainly didn't look inhabited. The driveway on the right-hand side was empty with a long narrow dark path on the other. This was certainly no fuck pad, a fact for which Marshall felt eternally grateful. He kept an eye on the taxi, wanting to make sure it didn't drive off, and the man waved at him.

"Hurry up, you!" he shouted. "Five minutes and I'm out of here."

Marshall nodded as he walked around the side of the house on the left, stepping over bits of wood, concrete, debris and grass as high as the Serengeti bush. He saw used condoms, needles, cold drink bottles and various other unsavoury items as he teetered across the uneven landscape, making sure he didn't touch anything. He got to the back and heaved a sigh of frustration. It was all boarded up too. There was a small red van parked at the back, reminding of him of a post office delivery van. It had the same registration number as the one written on piece of paper in his wallet. Perhaps Blair had been moving things or fixing things up and needed a van. He remembered the shopping list he'd found weeks ago. He peered inside curiously. It looked messy and it was locked. There was definitely nothing going on at this house. As he turned to leave he noticed that one of the window boards was slightly loose. He wandered over to it and pulled it gently. Might as well take the opportunity to see if he could see anything inside if he'd risked his life coming here in the first place. He was surprised to see a faint trickle of light emanating from the house which meant, perhaps, that someone was inside. He swore as the board sprung back, the sharp edge cutting his finger and he winced as he sucked at the cut. But he persevered with the board, more carefully this time and finally, he was able to hold it back long enough to peer inside. The room was dimly lit and in the far corner he could see a shadow. He narrowed his eyes, wanting to see what it was.

The shadow moved and with another curse, Marshall stepped back, his heart pounding, as the board dropped back into place. He stood there for a minute, hoping he hadn't been seen. He felt a little ill. Along with the shadow in the corner, he had seen a large table, complete with leather straps at the top and the bottom, and a whole bunch of blue tarpaulin and plastic in the corner, neatly folded. It reminded him very uncomfortably of Dexter's lair in the television show. He wondered why that TV programme was familiar. He'd had reason to think a similar thought recently but couldn't quite remember when. He took a deep, shuddering breath, not liking the place he found himself in and quietly, he sidled away around the side of the house to the front. He hadn't realised he was holding his breath and he released it in relief when he saw the taxi was still there. Marshall walked quickly over to the waiting man who scowled.

"You made it just in time. I was just about to leave. Seen enough now, you plonker?"

Marshall nodded. "Yes. Just get us out of here. Back to Battersea please."

The man snorted. "A little bit different to this place, innit? Oh, how the mighty have fallen."

The taxi pulled away and Marshall leant back in the seat and closed his eyes. He had no idea what he had just seen but he didn't like it one little bit. It reeked of something evil, something tainted. He wanted to shower and let the clean water roll down his body and wash away the stench of what he'd just experienced. He wasn't a superstitious man but this had really spooked him. He'd started dozing off and on as the taxi made its way through busy traffic when he finally realised where the image of Dexter had come from. It was the shopping list he'd found in Blair's rucksack, the one with the strange items on it. He also recalled where he'd heard the Japanese references today. Angie Green had told him about the oriental carvings on the latest victim's body—Japanese symbols, he now remembered her saying.

Marshall's body chilled. His mind was working in a way he really didn't want it to. He sat up, his thoughts feverish and sporadic. Everything he'd learnt about the serial killer known as BTK had some sort of tenuous connection to his lover. The house he'd just seen owned by his boyfriend with what looked some sort of torture table; a van he hadn't known he owned; the Japanese symbol book; the tattoo episode, Blair's comment about the removal being easier that anyone thought; the bite to Blair's arm and his lover's lies about where he'd been. His reaction to the press conference and the Italian detective. Separate, they all seemed so inconsequential. Together, they formed a picture he didn't even want to think about. He felt bile welling in his throat and muttered to the driver.

"Stop the car, please; I'm going to be sick." He felt the hot acidic vomit rising from his stomach and just made it outside before he was violently ill in the road as the taxi driver looked on impatiently. Marshall retched everything he had up and finally when there was no more, he leaned against the side of the taxi. His chest was heaving, his hands were cold and his eyes were wild. The taxi driver looked at him in concern, as did the passers-by who'd just been subject to the sight of a grown man hurling his guts up on the side of the road.

"Here, mate, you look terrible. Is everything all right, do you want a hospital or anything?"

Marshall shook his head as he pulled out a twenty-pound note and pressed it into the driver's hand. "I'm okay. That should cover the trip. I'll walk home from here."

The driver shrugged his shoulders. "You know best, mate. Hope you feel better."

He disappeared as Marshall straightened up, his stomach sore from retching and his body feeling as if he'd been put in a fast spinning cycle in a washing machine. His head hurt and his heart hurt even more. The suspicion that had taken hold of him in those last few minutes had done its damage. He couldn't go home with that hanging over him. He wouldn't even be able to look at Blair with this terrible thought in his head. He had no idea what he was going to do now. Feeling so tired that all he wanted to do was lay down on the nearest park bench and sleep, Marshall sat down in the doorway of a closed shop and pulled his bomber jacket tighter around his shoulders. Someone walked past and threw him a coin and he looked at it dazedly. He huddled deeper into the recess of the shop door as he tried to gather his thoughts.

Could he really be a fucking a bloody serial killer? Could his Blair, his young, sexy and attentive boyfriend, actually be the man the police were looking for? He remembered the words of the Italian detective" *"this individual may have family, a girlfriend, a boyfriend, someone who may see a small sign of who he is really is without knowing. It's true that sometimes the people closest to us are still strangers."*

Those words for some reason had stuck in his mind. Did all these small signs put together make something else? Who would know? How in hell would he find out? He sat in a daze in the shop doorway, his mind racing with thoughts. Marshall had two choices. He could go home and forget about it all. He could pretend he'd never had these suspicions, that he was nothing more than a fucking idiot and go back to bed with Blair. If he did that and something else terrible happened, and it *did* turn out to be Blair, he'd have to live with it. Or he could try and find someone to talk to, someone who wouldn't think he was a fucking idiot and who would listen. The detective he'd seen on the telly immediately sprung to mind. He'd seem reasonable, approachable. Perhaps a chat with him might help Marshall allay his fears. Perhaps the man would laugh and tell him he was being stupid, and to go home and fuck his boyfriend. Marshall's head was starting to spin, a blinding headache starting to form. He couldn't bloody well sit here all night in a shop doorway. Next thing you know people would either be chucking money at him or some toothless git would be kicking him out of his sleeping spot.

There was only one thing left to do. Marshall took out his mobile phone and dialled a number. He heard the ringing on the other side and then the brisk answer of the phone

"999. Marcie speaking. What is your emergency?"

Marshall couldn't speak, the thought of what he was about to do destroying his soul and his sanity.

"Is there anyone there? Can I help you?"

Marshall cleared his throat. "Yes, I'm here." He felt slow warm tears trickling down his cheeks as he pressed the phone close. "I need to speak to Detective Parglietto please. The man in charge of the Bow Tie Killer serial killings. I have some information for him."

Chapter 25

Anthony was in DCI Winslow's office when the call came in. He'd been once again arguing with his boss about his leadership of the case and they'd just got to a point when he thought Winslow was about to hit him out of sheer frustration.

"Jesus fucking Christ, Anthony, it's still no! God, I've never met such a stubborn bastard as you." Winslow's face was puce and Anthony wasn't quite sure if he was provoking a heart attack. A part of him didn't really care. One of the desk sergeants who sat outside his boss's office rapped smartly on the door and stepped into the room. Her face was set.

"Sir, there's a call for you—"

"Sergeant, don't fucking knock then just walk in!" His superior's face went an even deeper shade of puce and Anthony watched him curiously, sure the man was going to explode. "The purpose of knocking is to let the other person say whether they want you to come in and I don't remember doing that!"

The young sergeant sighed, no doubt used to her boss's histrionics. "There's a caller on the line who says he has information about BTK, sir. He wants to speak to Detective Parglietto."

Anthony sighed. "Another nutter, Marge? Or someone who actually has useful information this time?"

She stared at him solemnly. "He says he thinks that BTK is his lover and he doesn't know what to do, but he needs to speak to you. He won't speak to anyone else. 999 put him through. The man sounds upset but he doesn't seem like a nutter."

Anthony observed her steady blue eyes. Marge Connolly was a pretty good judge of character and if she thought it might be worth a conversation, he was game. He raised an eyebrow at his boss. "I'm still on this case until tomorrow, sir. I'd like to talk to this man."

Winslow waved an agitated hand. "Then fuck off and talk to him. Far be it from me to tell you what to bloody do. I'm only your boss after all."

Despite the situation Anthony grinned slightly. He followed Sergeant Marge Connolly out of the office and she smiled at him.

"He's in a right state, sir. What on earth did you do to the man?"

Anthony shook his head in amusement. "Told him a few home truths and how much of a tosser he's being. He didn't take it too well."

They'd reached the hotline centre now and Anthony picked up the headset that Marge passed to him.

"This is Anthony Parglietto. I understand you want to talk to me?"

There was silence on the other end of the line. Anthony raised a quizzical eyebrow.

"He's still there, sir. He hasn't rung off." Marge nodded her head. Anthony nodded back. She mouthed at him. *"We're tracing the call anyway to find out who owns the mobile and its location."*

He nodded again. "I understand you might have news about the serial killings. Can I ask you your name at least?"

The voice, when it came, was quiet and shaky. "If you thought your lover was a sociopathic killer, Detective, what would you do?"

Anthony felt like the bottom had dropped out of the floor. This conversation was too close to the one he'd had with Marco a year ago, the one that if BTK was to be believed, had led to Marco's death. He had to handle this one better. He wanted no more deaths on his already blood-soaked conscience.

"Probably exactly what you're doing," Anthony said softly. "Tell someone about it. Someone who can find out for sure whether it's true and stop the doubt. Before it eats you up inside."

He loosened his tie and took off his jacket, settling back in one of the desk chairs in the hotline area. His instincts told him this might be what he'd been waiting for and he wanted to milk every drop.

The voice continued. "I saw you on the television the other night. I thought you actually cared about this case, and you seemed to know what you were doing. It's why I only asked to speak with you."

"I'm pleased you feel that way. I'm not particularly good at talking to the press. The boss has a hernia when I open my mouth." He heard a slight noise, perhaps a swallowed chuckle, perhaps a sob. "What's your name, by the way? I need to call you something. *Hey you* doesn't really do it for me, I'm afraid."

He waited patiently.

"Marshall. My name's Marshall."

"Marshall, I'm Anthony. So why is that you think you know who this man is?"

There was silence then a sigh. "It's a bunch of things really. He disappears and lies to me although as a boyfriend I guess a lot of people have that problem. He has a bite on his arm which he's never let me see. And I'm a doctor. He has a book of Japanese symbols in his backpack. He spoke about how easy it was to remove a tattoo and put it somewhere else." His voice faltered a little. "I happen to know that's what happened to one of the victims. And he owns a house that looks like Dexter Morgan's place. You know, the serial killer from the TV. Not only that, he has a shopping list like his too. There was also a red van parked round the back. I found a parking ticket for it in his backpack. I didn't even know he owned a bloody car. He said he didn't. Just another lie. So I put one and one together and came up with this. The reason I'm calling."

All the time the man was speaking Anthony had felt the slow slide of cold ice water down his back. This man knew things that only the killer could know. The details about the tattoo, the Jap symbols, the red van—none of that had been released to the press. This man was the genuine thing, Anthony knew it. He could even be the killer masquerading as the informant although Anthony didn't recognise the voice as the one that he'd spoken to before.

"Marshall, where are you?" he asked softly. "I think I should come down and see you, talk this over face to face. Would you be all right with that?"

Marshall sighed heavily. "I'm hunkered down in a shop entrance at the moment, because I don't want to go home. I'm scared Blair—" he cut off suddenly, obviously realising that he'd said his lover's name.

"Is Blair the man you think might be the killer?" Anthony saw Marge write the name down on a piece of paper, anxious to record anything significant that might be said.

"Yes." The other man was getting spooked, Anthony could tell. He tried another tactic.

"Marshall, how do you know about the things that you mentioned? You must know something about the killings in order to make the connections you have with what you've found out about your boyfriend. How is that?"

Marshall was quiet and Anthony could hear the heavy breathing as the man thought. "I have contacts in the UCLH pathology lab and we've talked about the case, as one professional to another." The man's voice was guarded and Anthony marvelled that even with the stress he appeared to be under, he didn't want to get a fellow colleague into trouble.

Anthony motioned for a piece of paper to write on. Marge passed him a pen and a tablet and he wrote on it.

Check ULCH—find someone called Marshall—doctor? Speak to Graham. Someone on his team is flapping their lips. Check out connections for the name Blair to Marshall.

Marge nodded and hurried away to another phone.

"Anthony? Are you still there?" Marshall's voice was worried, strained.

"I'm still here. Just letting you get your thoughts together, Marshall." He kept using the man's name to reassure him he was interested in the man and not just his story. "It's a difficult decision to make, what you're doing. Personally, I'm glad you talked to someone else about those things you mentioned. If you hadn't, we might not be having this conversation." He hoped that would put the other man's mind at ease that he was getting anyone into trouble. "Now where are you? I'll come and fetch you and you can come back to my office and we can talk comfortably. A shop entrance in the street is no place to be this time of night. Tell me where to find you."

He held his breath as the man debated on what to do. Finally there was a sigh. "I'm the one who called *you* so there's no point in hiding who I am. You've probably traced my number anyway and know exactly who I am by now."

Anthony smiled slightly. The man might be upset but he wasn't stupid.

"I'm at BB's Property Consultants on Battersea Park Road. My flat isn't too far from here; I wasn't feeling well so I got out the taxi and I was going to walk. But I'm so bloody tired and I just don't know where else to go." The man's voice was faint and Anthony felt a surge of sympathy for the man.

"I'm coming to get you, Marshall. Just me, in a plain car, no sirens, no police cars. Will you wait for me? It'll take me about fifteen, twenty minutes with the traffic. My sergeant will take all your details, like your full name, where you live and we can talk when we get back here. I'll call your phone in a couple of minutes so you have my number. Then you can get hold of me directly. Promise me you'll wait for me, Marshall."

"I'll be here." The voice was quiet.

Anthony passed the headset back over to Marge who'd come back. "Talk to him, keep him occupied. Get as much information as you can. Hopefully he won't bolt."

"Sir, you need some backup. What if this is the actual killer? You know how he's been threatening you—"

"I'll be fine. This isn't the same man who called me. If it is the killer, well he's going to get to meet me face to face instead of being a bloody coward and hiding behind emails and phones. Stop worrying."

Anthony picked up his jacket and his car keys and left the office.

Chapter 26

Marshall was starting to feel really cold as he waited. It was closer to forty minutes later when a car pulled up at the entrance to the bike shop. For a moment, Marshall thought he might just lose his nerve and run. Then he saw a broad-shouldered figure get out of the car and he recognised the man as the one on the television. Anthony Parglietto moved toward him with an easy smile.

"Marshall? Thanks for waiting. The fucking traffic was terrible. God, you must be freezing. Here."

The detective went back to the car and picked up a long greatcoat from his back seat, which he wrapped around Marshall's shivering shoulders. Marshall pulled it closer, needing the male smell of the coat and its warmth. The policeman gestured to the car.

"The passenger seat is all yours. Get yourself in. We'll go back to the station, give you coffee or tea if that's your choice of poison, and talk. Then you can tell me what's been going on."

Marshall nodded and walked over to the car, opening the door and settling himself in the passenger seat. He noticed the older man watching him carefully as he got into the car. He seemed very edgy and alert. In person the man was even more attractive than on the television. Marshall had no idea how he could feel a surge of attraction for another man given his circumstances and he cursed his fickle emotions. Perhaps it was the fact that this man seemed so approachable, that he actually seemed to care about what happened to Marshall. After all, he'd come to fetch him personally and he could have sent someone else.

He watched as Anthony drove the car through the busy streets with an air of devil may care. The man was an aggressive driver and was in total control of the car. A very nice car, Marshall had to admit. It was a fairly fancy VW Passat, very spacious and comfy.

"This isn't standard police issue, this car, is it?" Despite his stress, Marshall reached out admiringly and stroked the dash and the control panel. Anthony laughed.

"God, no. This is my own car. I don't use it often, but I prefer to drive this when I need a car. The standard jalopies they give us are bloody useless." He manoeuvred a corner expertly but cut another driver off then raised a middle finger at the driver who hooted at him.

Marshall grinned slightly. The man had just done something illegal in his race to get to his workplace and the other driver got flipped the bird. He liked that.

He saw Anthony look across at him. "We can leave it for the office, but if you want to tell me anything now, feel free."

Marshall could hear the underlying tension in the man's voice. He shrugged and proceeded to tell Anthony the skeleton of the story of what he'd been doing today up to now, including his visit to the house in Newham and what had happened to put him scurrying into a shop porch. The detective listened avidly, grunting every now and then and frowning at certain parts of the story. Finally Marshall finished and he sat back, exhausted, glad his telling was over.

"Did you manage to see who was in the house?" The doctor could see the detective's mind ticking over, probably wanting nothing more than to share all this information with someone at the office, perhaps even sending some sort of task team down to the Newham house. The man was a barely suppressed bundle of energy, just itching to get started.

Marshall shook his head. "No. I wanted to get out of there. It felt wrong. Afterwards, like I said, everything seemed to just hit me all once and I needed to tell someone. Someone who can tell me that I haven't just betrayed someone I'm seeing and accuse them of being a psychotic killer." His voice was husky. "He phoned me while I was sitting waiting for you. Blair. I couldn't answer it. I didn't know what to say. He left a message asking me where I was and told me to get my arse home ASAP to catch up on what we were busy doing when we were interrupted, when he had to leave. He's phoned me twice more since then. He's getting pretty angry."

Anthony glanced at him. "I don't think you're being a drama queen if it's any consolation." He coloured slightly. "Sorry, I didn't mean that the way it came out—"

"It's all right." Marshall flapped a hand at him. "I'm not offended." He smiled. "I have no objection to being a queen where you're concerned." He managed a slight grin at the other man's low chuckle, despite his tiredness and his stress.

"I'm flattered—I think." The detective smiled. Marshall felt more at ease. "When you've signed all the statements you need to give, what do you want to do?" Anthony's voice was soft. "Obviously the man is innocent until proven guilty and that's our job to do, not yours. We need to take what you give us and see whether it pans out. Perhaps have him in for questioning. But there is one very important factor here. I want to listen to the voice mail message he left you. I've heard this man's voice. He's called me before. I'll be able to tell you if it's him just by listening."

Marshall stared at him, his heart beating faster. He placed a protective hand over his coat pocket, where his phone was. He didn't want to do this. He didn't want to play a message that was meant for his ears only and be told it was the voice of a murderer or a rapist of women for God's sake, something he'd been busy trying to factor into his fairly incoherent thoughts for some time. He remained quiet, watching the city streets fly by until finally, they pulled up at the Met Police Station and Anthony drove the car into the underground parking lot. The two men walked into the busy room of the squad office a few minutes later. Anthony strode over to his desk, motioning Marshall to follow him.

Rupert Gregg was sitting at the opposite desk and he looked up as Anthony drew out a chair and gently pressed Marshall down into it.

"Sit here. I'm going to get you something warm to drink. Are you a tea or coffee man?"

"Tea, please. Milk, no sugar." Marshall's hands pulled Anthony's coat closer around him as he looked around the police station with wary eyes. Anthony nodded and disappeared. Marshall sat and took a deep breath. He was glad to be off the street and to be honest, he felt safe here. He could see the curiosity on the other policeman's face as the time passed. A few minutes later, the other man appeared to be opening his mouth to speak and Marshall heard a loud angry bark behind him.

"Sergeant Gregg. Keep your mouth shut. This man is my witness and I'll have no one but me talk to him."

Anthony appeared with a face like thunder and any words the other policeman had been about to utter were swallowed by him closing his mouth and taking a deep breath. He didn't look happy, Marshall thought curiously. He thought these teams all worked together to a common goal but the antagonism between the two men was evident.

"Let's go somewhere a little more private." Anthony glared at Rupert. "Bring your tea with you." He stalked down the corridor, beckoning for Marshall to follow. Soon they were settled in a small, airless room equipped with two chairs and a steel table.

He sat down and placed his steaming tea on the table top while he waited. Anthony sat down in the chair opposite and held out a hand. Marshall looked at him in confusion.

"You want the tea—"

"No, I want your phone, Marshall." The detective's voice was gentle. "I need to hear that message."

Marshall put his cup down slowly on the table and reached into his jacket pocket for his mobile. He clicked a couple of buttons to unlock it, found the voice mail and handed the phone silently over to the waiting man.

Anthony took the phone and worked the menu options to get to the message. Marshall watched as the detective's face paled and his fingers tightened around the phone. He knew by the look on the man's face that the mistake he'd been hoping for in accusing his lover of being a killer had gone. The detective's shoulders tensed, his face frighteningly dark and he glanced at Marshall as he disconnected the voice mail service.

"There's no doubt about it," he murmured quietly. "That was the same man that called me to tell me he'd murdered my brother and abducted my boyfriend."

Marshall felt the world close in around him. He raised a trembling hand to his mouth as he bit his knuckles, trying to feel something, anything. He felt dead inside. And he hadn't missed the fact that DI Parglietto had a boyfriend.

So he was gay too.

"Murdered your brother and took your boyfriend?" He looked at the set face of detective. Anthony nodded.

"My younger brother, Marco was killed a year ago. He was gay too." He smiled rather humourlessly, Marshall thought. "What are the odds of my folks having two gay sons?" He frowned and leaned forward. "According to this man," he waved the phone with a grim face, "He got into a relationship with your friend Blair who killed him. I won't go into the reasons because it won't help you at this stage. But he butchered him and made it look like some gay rage attack."

He heaved a deep breath. "Then about three weeks ago he kidnapped my boyfriend, assaulted him intimately and sent him back to me as a message." His voice was raw with pain. "But that's not public information. I trust you to keep that to yourself."

For the second time Marshall was sick. His stomach heaved and he vomited all over the floor beside his chair, although there was very little to bring up. Anthony was up in a flash, pulling a wad of tissues from a box on the desk, kneeling beside the younger man with a look of compassion etched on his face.

"Jesus, Marshall, I'm sorry. I shouldn't have told you that. I'm a bloody idiot."

Marshall gasped. "No, I'm all right, honest. I haven't been feeling well anyway and that just got me going again. It wasn't your fault." He laid a cold hand on top of the other man's, who covered it with his warm one. Marshall felt the tears start to build at the man's obvious concern.

Soft eyes regarded him. "Are you all right to carry on, to tell me everything from the start?"

Marshall nodded. "Yes, I'm okay. Sorry about that, I'm not usually so gormless." He laughed harshly. "It's not every day you find out the man you've been fucking is a serial killer."

Anthony was quiet. Marshall heaved a deep, shuddering breath. The policeman took a small Dictaphone out of his jacket pocket and clicked it on.

"Do you mind if I use this? This room doesn't have the official equipment but it's private, and my memory isn't what it used to be. I prefer playing back my interviews later and making my notes."

Marshall nodded. "I don't mind."

Anthony placed the machine on the table. "Whenever you're ready. I need the details now. Start with when you first met this man and take me through everything since." He grinned faintly, "Within reason of course. I'm fairly open-minded but even I draw the line at some things."

Marshall could see he was trying to put him at ease and he smiled. He opened his mouth and let the words flow. He told Anthony everything. His first encounter with Blair, their relationship, Blair's personal life—what he knew about it anyway—the finding of the rucksack, his visit to the gym, the meetings at UCLH with Angie and the events that led up to them sitting here now. Anthony was attentive, asking questions, making notes on a pad the desk sergeant had given him. He stopped every now and then to disappear out of the room. Marshall supposed he was asking colleagues to check something for him. Occasionally the police constable Marshall had seen before would come into the room and whisper something in Anthony's ear or give him a piece of paper. Anthony would look at it and his eyes would deaden, his fists would clench and for a few seconds, Marshall felt scared at what he saw on the man's face.

It was almost an hour and a half later that Marshall sat back with a tired sigh and contemplated the other man. He was exhausted. He'd also noted that the mobile in his pocket hadn't stopped vibrating. Marshall had turned the ringer off and he just knew it was Blair looking for him.

"Is that him calling you all the time?" Anthony asked quietly. "I can hear it vibrate from here."

Marshall nodded dully. "I expect so. He'll be pissed as hell."

Anthony stood up and stretched his tall, broad frame and even in the mood he was in, Marshall could still appreciate the action.

"My priority is going to be keeping you safe and sound," the detective said quietly. "Once we establish Blair is definitely BTK—in my own mind there's no doubt, but I need to follow the evidence to make a clear case—you're going to be my key witness in a potential multiple murder trial. Your safety is my biggest concern not only from that perspective but from the fact that I won't let this bastard hurt anyone I know again."

His voice was deadly and Marshall pitied Blair for a moment, fleetingly. He was starting to get his bearings back, feel the sense of betrayal and anger at being duped by a lover who was probably only using him for cover. He didn't think he'd ever really loved Blair, madly, deeply, the way he should have. Something had always kept him back from that emotion. He supposed he should thank God he'd trusted his instinct and not gotten too emotionally involved. The sex had been fantastic but that was all it had been. As he'd been telling his story, the fury and the shame at being used seeped from his body like toxic waste in a stream.

"How do you feel about staying with a friend of mine for the night?" Anthony regarded the other man carefully. "You look as if you need a good night's sleep, and Dan will take good care of you. He's the very large sergeant sitting in the outer office, built like the Hulk and partial to breaking noses. You can go with him and then in the morning we can figure out what you want to do. I don't think it's a good idea to go home in the state you're in. If Blair is there, he'll know something is up and I don't want you getting hurt."

Marshall looked at him, feeling fairly dazed. "My life is going to change, isn't it?" he whispered finally, closing his eyes. "My job, my home, my whole fucking life has just gone down the toilet."

Anthony reached out and clasped his shoulder tightly. "You're doing the right thing. I know you don't want to hear that but it's a fact. Four people we know about and countless others have died because of this man. It has to stop. You can help me do that. Just stay strong a little longer for me."

Marshall nodded tiredly.

A loud voice interrupted Anthony's conversation "I think Mr. Cunningham should go home."

Anthony turned impatiently to see who it was. A tall, spare man stood at the entrance to the room, his grey hair slicked back, a stern impression on his face. DI Gerry Mountjoy was a hard-arsed policeman, close on fifty, who ruled his team with a rod of iron. He was very big on doing things by the book and had no time for people who worked outside the system or operated independently. He and Anthony therefore didn't get on very well.

"Gerry. I heard you were only coming in tomorrow. This is still my case until then." Anthony said flatly. The tall man smiled a smile that didn't reach his eyes.

"I'm aware of that. But a little bird told me you had what appears to be a key witness here in the office. Of course that piqued my interest."

Anthony felt a scathing retort wanting to burst out of his mouth but he clamped his lips together firmly. Nothing good could come of antagonising the man just yet. He was sure the little bird had been Rupert Gregg.

Mountjoy moved over to Marshall and laid a gentle hand on his shoulder. "I think that what you're doing is a great service to this city. I appreciate it. But we need to talk a little more before we decide what to do."

Anthony stepped in front of Marshall, his large frame obscuring the younger man from the DI's view.

"It's too bloody dangerous for him to go home. In his current state, he'll never be able to pull off the fact that he doesn't know his boyfriend is a killer." He glanced at Marshall who watched him wordlessly. "Forgive me, Marshall, but you're a bit of a mess."

DI Mountjoy's eyes glittered. "If we have any hope of hell in catching the bastard we need all the evidence we can get as soon as we can get it. You identifying his voice as the one who spoke to you isn't strong enough. The other things are all circumstantial. We can't arrest the man yet, only bring him in for questioning. I understand from the desk sergeant outside that there's a rucksack with important information in it that could give us some decent evidence. We need that rucksack. Marshall can get it for us. Can't you, Marshall?"

Anthony stared at him in disbelief. "You read my fucking notes?" He'd made a few important notes on a piece of paper for the desk sergeant to start logging including a request to check out the house in Newham Street. The final interview details would have been completed later by him when Anthony had seen Marshall into safe custody and could sit down and make sense of it all from his Dictaphone.

Mountjoy shrugged. "Don't get your panties in a bunch, Anthony. This is my case from midnight tonight and to be honest, we're not far off that time anyway. Just a few hours."

Anthony's hot temper welled up in his chest.

Mountjoy carried on. "I thought we could make a nice story for the boyfriend about Marshall here was mugged and spent the night in A and E, unable to answer his phone. We can fabricate a hospital report. Then he can go home later and see what he can do to get that rucksack for us. Along with some DNA evidence we can use to match against the skin cells in the woman's teeth—the one that bit him."

Marshall was shaking his head, white faced.

Anthony was livid. "Everything you've suggested was on my list of things to do, Mountjoy, but without endangering the witness. I had another play in mind, the one where we bring the bastard in for questioning, get a warrant with what we've got so far, search his apartment for the bag and DNA evidence and keep Marshall away from him. He's going to know it was him that spilled the beans. This man is many things but he's not fucking stupid."

Mountjoy scowled. "You won't get a warrant based on what we have. It's too circumstantial. Second-hand testimony from an emotionally involved witness— a story about tattoos, a book, a deed to a boarded-up house and a bag that no one else has seen. We need the hard evidence. And the voice evidence isn't really strong enough either."

"That's all true and I'm not saying it will be easy. But I've done it before. I can do it again." Anthony was adamant. "I may not always play by the rules, Mountjoy, but I don't want Marshall going back into the lion's den. We'll work around it. Follow this bastard, tail him, find out where he goes. Get something on him we can use. DNA is easy enough to get—we can go to his home when we interview him and find something—"

"That 'something' may not be admissible and will take time and resources we don't have when we have someone sitting here who can do that for us much quicker. This man needs to help us."

Anthony finally erupted. "Are you fucking joking? That's too bloody dangerous. How is he supposed to pull that off?"

The other man waved a hand airily. "We put a bug on him to make sure we can listen to the conversation and keep him safe. He goes home, bides his time until he gets the bag, hands it out to one of my men in the corridor when he's ready and then gets the hell out of there."

Anthony's voice was sheer malice when he spoke next. "You forget that I asked a team to go out and take a look at the house in Newham. What if Blair's seen that activity? He'll know straight away that something's up and all fingers will point at Marshall. He'll have been the only one that might have had access to that bag to find out that address other than the killer."

Mountjoy smiled, showing his teeth. "That's why I called the team off, Anthony. No point in tipping the man off until we have what we need. I told them to stand down."

Anthony's jaw clenched and he had the overwhelming desire to punch the man in the gut and watch him double over. "You countermanded my instructions? You fucking tosser, Mountjoy. You've overstepped the mark now."

Mountjoy shrugged, not looking very worried. "Stop being such a bloody Eye-tie, Parglietto." He said it as if were an insult. "This man is the only one that can help us nail this prick. He's our only hope. He needs to work with us to get us what we need."

Anthony took a step forward, white faced and it was Marshall that stood up and held out a strong arm to hold him back.

"It's all right. I need to do this and help you guys catch Blair. He doesn't know I've been here. He's got no real reason to suspect anything is wrong." Anthony could hear the slight apprehension in his voice. "I took some acting classes when I was younger." He smiled weakly. "I wasn't all that good. But I think I'll be able to last the night out if you need me to get that bag. As long as you have my back and you come fetch me if anything goes wrong." His voice broke a little and Anthony shook his head.

"I don't like this idea at all. What if Blair's found out you went looking for him at the gym? He'll know then that you know he wasn't there. Won't he get suspicious?"

Marshall sighed. "I'm a gay man with a slight tendency to be a drama queen, by my own admission. I'll be able to convince Blair I was jealous and just checking up on him." He flushed slightly. "Blair had this idea of having a threesome with a young man from the gym."

Anthony could see he was uncomfortable telling this story but he trooped on valiantly. DI Mountjoy looked at him as if he was some sort of pervert and Anthony wanted to hit him again.

"I can say I thought he might be having a twosome instead so I went to check it out. I know Blair. He'll find some excuse that he'll expect me to believe as to why he wasn't there when he said he would be. And I'll pretend to believe him." He swallowed. "He knows he can usually convince me of anything. Look how well he's done so far." His tone was bitter and Anthony felt a dark cloud descend over him. This whole thing stank and he was scared for Marshall.

Mountjoy was beaming from ear to ear. "That's the spirit, Marshall. I'm confident you can manage this based on what you've just said. We'll get you wired up, put a couple of plasters on your face to make it look as if you've been mugged and then I'll get someone to drop you off home. We'll have a team outside lead by Sergeant Gregg who'll make sure they can hear everything going on. If anything sounds even a little off, we'll be in there in less than a minute. You try and get your hands on that bag and your boyfriend's hairbrush or toothbrush and anything else you think might help us, then you and the bag leave that apartment ASAP. Job done."

Marshall nodded and Anthony felt sick. This was not how he'd envisaged it playing out.

"Marshall, you don't have to do this. I have a bad feeling. We can find another way."

The younger man shook his head vehemently. "I need to do this. Blair has been fooling me for all these months. Well, now it's my turn. I'll see what I can find and hopefully that'll be enough."

He turned to DI Mountjoy with straightened shoulders and a determined look on his face.

"I'm ready when you are. Tell me what you want me to do. But with one provision." He gestured at Anthony. "He's there with me too. I trust him."

Mountjoy looked a little nonplussed. Anthony stared at him waiting to see what he said.

"It's non-negotiable," Marshall said quietly. "Your call." He glanced at Anthony who inclined his head slightly in thanks.

Mountjoy scowled. "Fine then, although I think it's a bad call." He turned and motioned imperiously at Marshall. "Come with me and we'll get started."

Marshall reached out and touched Anthony's arm. "Thanks for the concern. But I'm sure it'll be okay." He squeezed his arm gently then followed Mountjoy out the office. Anthony watched them go with a feeling of complete helplessness.

*****

Blair threw his empty glass against the far wall in temper and watched in satisfaction as it shattered into tiny pieces. It was nearly ten o'clock and he still had no idea where his lover was. He'd left message after message and even been down to the gym to see if he was there. Billy had said that Marsh had been down there looking for *him*. He'd no idea why his man would be checking up on him but he'd find out. He needed a cover story though to explain why he hadn't been where he was supposed to be. Blair swore loudly. This was getting too complicated. He didn't need to have the extra effort of concocting cover stories. It got too messy. He hoped Marshall wasn't going to prove too difficult.

He heard a click of the door and strode over to the entrance to see Marshall coming into the apartment. His face was pale, his eyes haunted and he had a large plaster over his forehead, and another on his neck. Blair hurried over to him.

"Jesus, what the hell happened to you? Where the fuck have you been? I've been calling you all bloody night!"

His lover looked shattered and flinched as Blair reached in to hug him.

"I was down at A and E all night, so I had to have my phone off. I got mugged and the police wanted me to get checked out."

"You were mugged? Who the fuck would do that—did they hurt you?" Blair forgot about his bad temper in the worry of seeing his property beaten up by someone else. That was *his* prerogative.

Marshall smiled wanly. "Just a hit to the head and a nasty scratch on my neck. Nothing serious." He moved away, his body tense, and Blair frowned.

"Are you sure nothing else happened? You seem a little strange."

Marshall started then shook his head tiredly. "I just want to relax, Blair."

He disappeared into the bedroom and Blair heard the thump of his shoes as he threw them across the room. He stood there for a while then went into the bedroom. Marshall was sitting on his side of the bed, and he spun around as Blair came in. He didn't miss the faint look of apprehension on Marshall's face as he crossed over the room and sat down beside his lover. Marshall sat still, his body tense, his eyes looking down at his hands.

"What were you doing at the gym looking for me?" Blair searched his lover's face for any telltale signs he was about to lie. Marshall swallowed.

"I told you where I was going. Why did you feel the need to come looking for me?" Blair reached over and took Marshall's hand in his, slowly stroking his thumb down the side of his hand, feeling it cold and limp in his.

"It was a surprise. I bought you a latte then I was going to suggest we go for something to eat afterwards." Marshall's voice was quiet, hesitant. Blair grinned and gripped his hand tighter, causing Marshall to wince.

"That wasn't the real reason, was it? You were checking up on me weren't you? You know I don't like it when you do that."

Chapter 27

Anthony sat in the lobby of Marshall's block of flats, fuming at the conversation he could hear in his earpiece. He knew that outside in the police car, Sergeant Rupert Gregg and his new partner, Sandy Tolman, sat in an unmarked police car also monitoring the conversation between the two men. He heard Tolman snigger.

"Bloody poofters. Christ, what does a man see in another man? Bloody fudge-packers, the pair of them."

Rupert sighed. "Stop being such a bloody homophobe, Sandy. And remember that Anthony is listening in. He won't take kindly to that kind of remark given he's in a relationship with a man. I'd watch my step if I were you."

Sandy snorted. "Whatever. It's wrong, is what it is. Bloody queers think they can get away with anything nowadays, getting married, having kids. It's a fucking disgrace. And as for them spreading that AIDS around—"

Anthony's blood was boiling, his fist clenched in his lap as he observed the comings and goings around him.

Obviously Rupert had had enough too. He might have been a righteous son of a bitch but Anthony being gay had never been an issue for him. "Shut the fuck up, Sandy!" he exclaimed. "You're being damned disrespectful and you're asking for it. Hold your noise, will you."

Anthony tried to shut Sandy's vile nonsense out of his head. He heard the tinny sound of Marshall finally telling his boyfriend that he'd been jealous and wanted to see whether Blair was cheating on him. Something about a threesome and as Anthony strained to hear, Sandy opened his mouth again.

"Jesus, they do that as well, bloody perverts. Honestly, they take the cake, these two blokes."

Rupert flapped a hand at him. "Shut the fuck up," he hissed. "I can't hear anything."

Anthony tried to ignore everything else and concentrate on Marshall's conversation. He'd been secretly pleased at the small triumph of being back on the case thanks to Marshall's insistence that he be involved. Mountjoy had not been pleased with that but he'd had no choice but to agree. In some way Anthony felt responsible for Marshall's well-being, which was strange seeing as how he didn't really know the man. *****

In the apartment, Marshall watched in trepidation as Blair looked at him through narrowed eyes.

"So you thought I might be diddling Luke, did you?" Blake mused. "Not a bad idea, my lovely, but I told you I wanted to do it with you. I haven't organised it yet because he's been out of town on some bloody tour with a rock group. But I was certainly going to have a word with him when I got back." He reached over and caressed Marshall's jaw tenderly.

"I don't like you sneaking out behind my back but I do like the idea of you going all alpha and jealous on me. It's quite a turn-on."

His hand moved down to Marshall's groin and he felt his lover stiffen, but not in the right places. The older man's body went rigid and he closed his eyes. His breathing was getting shallower and Blair looked at him in puzzlement.

"You really are in a mood tonight," he murmured. "Something has you all spooked."

"Being mugged tends to do that to me," Marshall said quietly. "The man was a bit of an animal. I'm sorry, but I think I just want to kick back and watch a movie. Do you mind?"

Blair shook his head slowly. "No, Marsh, you go watch a film. I'll join you in a minute."

Marshall nodded and stood up, a little unsteadily and walked out of the room. Blair watched him thoughtfully. Something was definitely not right. His mobile buzzed in his pocket and he pulled it out. He scowled when he saw who it was and moved over to close the bedroom door.

"Brick. You'd better not be telling me you want me to come down to the fucking house. Deal with the little bastards. Get rid of them."

"It's nothing happening now, Blair. It's what happened earlier." Brick Smith's heavy London accent was anathema to Blair's ears. He hated the sound of the man's voice.

"Some geezer was snooping around your place this afternoon. He went round the back and my guy saw him trying to lift that board that's loose and look in. I told you to get that fixed."

"Tomorrow, Brick. It's being fixed tomorrow. What did this guy look like?"

Brick chuckled nastily. "Nice from all accounts. My guy said he wouldn't mind giving it a fuck himself. But I can go one better for you. He took a photo with his fancy new phone. He's just got this bloody amazing gadget that can do everything but cook your bloody dinner for you—"

"Brick, I don't give a fuck about his phone. Send me the picture. That's why you called isn't it?"

"All right, there, don't get bloody shirty. This one'll cost you though. An extra hundred in the caretaking fee for next week, seeing as how this sort of thing seems to be happening more often."

Blair felt the red mist rise in his eyes as he listened to a fat, smelly, uneducated crook trying to extort yet more money out of him. *God, what he'd give to have his knife at the man's throat now, tying him a bow tie.*

"Just send me the fucking picture. I'll sort you out."

He heard the man's snort of laughter as he disconnected the call. A minute later his phone bleeped with the promised missive. Blair opened it up and all the hairs on the back of his neck prickled in a wave of disbelief. He looked at the very clear picture of Marshall coming out from the back of his kill house. Not only had Marshall been checking the gym, he'd also somehow got wind of the property and decided to pay it a little visit. And the only way he could have known about that was if he'd looked in his rucksack.

The rucksack that was currently here in the bedroom, under his side of the bed. After being careless with it last time, he wanted it with him at all times. There were hidden pockets in there with things he really wouldn't want being found. Although it looked like that ship had sailed. Marshall had probably thought he had a lover at the house too and decided to check it out. Blair's hands were trembling with anger as he realised he'd been betrayed. That explained Marshall's behaviour tonight. He was feeling guilty for having gone the extra step, probably, and worried that Blair would find out.

"Too late, my lovely," Blair said to himself softly. "If you looked in my bag, what else might you have seen? How can I trust you again? Oh, Marshall, you silly boy, look what you're making me do."

He opened the bedroom door and went into the lounge. Marshall was sitting there, his eyes focused on the TV, but Blair could see he wasn't watching. The man's body was so tense it could have been used as a concrete railway sleeper.

Blair leaned over and kissed the top of his head. "I'm making coffee. Want one?"

Marshall nodded. Blair grinned. *Well, that was easy. I'll slip the drug into the coffee, get Marshall settled for a little fun, then find out what else he'd been snooping around in.*

Blair felt a sense of fleeting regret that he'd have to kill another useful lover but he didn't feel he had a choice. Marshall had forced him into this course of action, just like his mother had done all those years ago. It wasn't everyone who could say that their mother had tried to kill them by trying to strangle them with their favourite scarf. His mother had been a high-strung soul at the best of times. When she'd come into his bedroom when he was twelve years old and asked to speak to him, he'd had no idea she was going to wrap a bloody scarf around his neck and try choke the life out of him. Blair remembered her staring eyes, her spit on his cheeks as she'd hissed at him that he was evil and had to die. He'd fought back with all his strength and finally managed to fight her off, hitting her across the head with a paperweight he kept at the side of the bed, one his father had given him. It was a clear crystal one with the tiny figure of a shrunken head inside that his father had picked up somewhere on a business trip. He'd smashed it across her head, leaving her stunned and bleeding and she'd run from his room and locked herself in her bedroom. The next morning she'd told his father that she'd fallen down the stairs and son and mother had looked at each other across the dining room table.

Two days later he'd drowned his mother in the pond, holding her under with a curiosity borne of wanting to see how someone actually looked when they couldn't breathe. She'd been out walking and he'd bided his time until she stood at the water's edge, then came up quietly behind her and pushed her in. He'd jumped in after her and even at the age of twelve, he'd been stronger than she was. Her drinking and tendency to diet compulsively had kept her frail, light. He held her under the water until finally she'd gone still. He'd clambered out of the cold water, back up to the house, changed his clothes and finished his homework. He was good like that. His mother's body was found about an hour later and everyone assumed she'd tripped and fallen in, that perhaps her fall down the stairs had made her faint from her head injury. Blair thought it had all worked out quite well. And no one ever found out that he was the one who'd beaten little five-year-old Maggie Carpenter to death in the woods. His mother had known, of course. She'd always known what he did down there.

******

Marshall was feeling very tired indeed. He felt a little sick but he put it down to the stress of the day. He desperately wanted to see if he could find the rucksack but Blair had been so attentive, stroking his hair and commiserating with his "mugging" that he hadn't had a chance. He hadn't seen the bag in its usual place under the hall table and he was starting to worry if he'd ever be able to find it and get out of the flat. He drained his coffee cup, yawned and stood up. He swayed as he did so. *God, he was even more tired than he'd thought.* He'd barely gotten time for another conscious thought when he'd seen little black dots in front of his face. The last thing he'd seen as he was pitching toward the floor was Blair watching him.

Marshall awoke to find himself on his stomach, lying face down on the bed, blankets bunched up around him, his arse propped up into the air by pillows for all to see. He tried to move but his arms wouldn't obey his commands. He frowned and tugged at whatever was holding him down. He couldn't speak either, as something soft and silky was stuffed into his mouth. He felt the cold chill of fear rising and goose bumps breaking out on his skin. His arms and legs were tightly bound. The only saving grace he could think of in his desperate situation was that he was still dressed and Blair hadn't found the listening device.

"Sorry, Marsh, for this little inconvenience," Blair's voice drawled. "But you shouldn't have snooped, my lovely. I can't have anyone meddling in my affairs. I have too many secrets and too much to lose." He chuckled drily. "I'm afraid I'm going to have to break up with you."

Marshall felt his heart thudding. The small, circular wire device that the police team had put on his chest would be smothered by his position. There was no way anyone could hear what was going on.

The police were just outside. Anthony would save him, he knew he would. He'd soon realise something was wrong, wouldn't he? A wave of despair washed over Marshall and he struggled against his bonds, trying to cry out and being frustrated by his inability to make any articulate sound.

He felt his trousers being tugged down over his hips and he kicked back with his legs, determined to make things as difficult as possible. He shrieked in soundless pain as he was viciously hit between the legs, in his scrotum, a fierce blow that left him retching and feeling sick.

"Don't be a hero, Marsh," Blair said viciously. "If you're sick with that gag on, you'll choke to death. It's not a nice way to go. I have other plans for you, my lovely. That drug is an absolute miracle worker, it drops you in a minute, and I have you back in the same time. It's wonderful when you're in a hurry. A chemist friend of mine synthesises it especially for me."

He stroked Marshall's backside tenderly. "I'm truly sorry about what I have to do, lover. I have my reasons."

His voice hardened as Marshall strained once again at his bonds. "You've totally fucked up my usual MO, Marsh. I have to improvise here and I'm not a great fan of that. It means more risk. I wasn't sure who else you'd told about the house so I can't take you back there yet, so here will have to do. Once I've finished with you, I'll go and fetch my van and then, my friend, I need to find somewhere to dump you."

Marshall felt further panic rising in his chest and he was struggling to breathe. His mind was sluggish with the aftereffects of whatever Blair had given him and he was lying here being told he was about to be murdered.

He tried to slow his heart rate down and work the gag out of his mouth. It was an impossible task, though, as it was tied around the back of his head.

"I'm sorry it came to this, lover," Blair said regretfully as he took out a small but fairly wide rolling pin that had come from Marshall's kitchen and held it where Marsh could see it. "But you've just become the latest victim of the crazy killer terrorising the city. So this will hurt. I'm sorry. But you shouldn't have—fucking—spied—on me."

Blair grunted and Marshall screamed loudly as something was thrust deeply into his arse, splitting him in two. The pain was inconceivable and he felt bile work its way up into his throat and soak the scarf. He heaved deep, shuddering breaths at the agony in his backside as he felt his lover twist it again, causing even more sensation to stab through his to groin, his stomach and into the rest of his body. He sobbed, his eyes filling with tears as he begged silently for Blair to stop.

He felt Blair standing beside him, and then felt his head being pulled back as Blair crouched down to look at his face,

"You thought you were so clever, Marshall, looking in my bag and going to my house. Well, look where that got you. Spread eagled on your bed with a fucking rolling pin in your arse. If you'd just left well enough alone, that could have been my cock and it would have been a damn sight more enjoyable for both of us." Blair punched Marshall on the cheek, making him jerk back, and making the object inside him move and cause fresh agony

"What did you think you were doing?" Blair's fist punched him in his ribs and he retched again, fresh waves of agony echoing through his body. He wished he could just pass out so Blair could kill him and get it over with. His brain felt as if it was going to explode and his whole being was wracked with pain. Blair punched him again, in his kidneys, and then again with both fists on his back. The blows rained down anywhere Blair could get to him, his face, his shoulders, his backside, causing him to scream again with the agony as the object in his backside moved. He could feel wetness between his butt cheeks. Even his legs were subject to a constant barrage of abuse and when Blair once again punched him in the scrotum, Marshall knew he couldn't take much more. He heard Blair breathing heavily and sensed him come around and stand next to him. His head was pulled back and the gag was removed from his mouth. He heaved a great gasp of air, glad at least to have that sense back.

"If you make a fucking sound other than to answer my question, I will cut your lips off." Blair's voice was implacable and deadly. "Did you tell anyone else about the house, Marshall, or anything else you might have found out about me?"

Marshall shook his head, his eyes wet with tears. His head was pounding. "No," he whispered. "Blair, I'm sorry I spied on you. I was just jealous. I wanted to find out if you were seeing anyone else.

I don't know why you're doing this, please, Blair, just stop. It's not too late—"

Blair ignored his entreaty. "Are you sure? Do I have to push that thing in your arse any further to get to the truth?"

"God, no, please don't. I promise I didn't tell anyone else." Marshall knew if he told Blair he knew who he really was and that the police were in the area and almost outside the door, he'd be killed there and then. Blair would have nothing to lose. Marshall needed to wait, wait for the cavalry. They had to be there soon, surely? Anthony was only downstairs.

"Good. That's a good boy. Do you know why this is happening to you, Marshall? Do you have any idea at all?"

Again, Marshall shook his head. "No. I don't, please just stop—"

"Just look where your nosiness got you," Blair said, his tone flat and dangerous. "I have to protect myself, Marshall. It's what I do. You shouldn't have been so fucking nosy. This is all your fault."

Marshall felt Blair climb onto the bed beside him and he tensed, expecting another blow. Blair laughed softly and Marshall could hear the madness in that sound. He closed his eyes in despair.

"I'm going to have to put the gag back in. I need to cut you a little, and I don't want any noise. I'll make it quick, I promise, Marsh. One quick thrust in your heart, in the right spot, means a quick end for you, minimal blood and less cleanup for me. I'm a little out of my usual comfort zone here. I'll have to slit your throat later before I dump you and grace your weeping throat with my beautifully tied bowtie. I'm also going to need a really good plan to get you out of here when I'm done. Decisions, decisions."

He snickered. "The whole change to my MO is going to make the cops crazy. And if the cops find out about you and me fucking and come to tell me about your horrible demise, I can play the grieving boyfriend. It will be an Oscar-winning performance, I promise you. They won't have a fucking clue…" His voice was gloating.

There and then Marshall resigned himself to his fate. Anthony had been right. He should never have come back to this maniac who was now sitting beside him.

Chapter 28

Anthony was worried about the sudden lack of conversation. All he could hear were faint sounds, scratching and deep, rhythmic sounds that made no sense.

"I don't hear much, Sergeant. Is that bloody equipment still working?" he muttered.

Rupert's voice echoed in his ear. "It's working. Not sure why it's gone quiet."

Sandy's voice broke through. "They're fucking," he said excitedly. "That's what the buggers are doing. They've made up and he's giving him one."

"It's a pretty quiet fuck," Rupert said doubtfully.

Anthony closed his eyes in mortification at the conversation. He was as perturbed as they were about the sounds and it may well have been that the two men were getting it on, but it didn't quite feel right to him. He listened carefully, trying to gauge what was going on.

"I should get in there." he muttered.

"You stay where you are, DI Parglietto," came the gruff tones of Gerry Mountjoy, listening in from the command centre at the Met. "This is my operation and you do what I say. Give the man time."

"He's had time, Gerry. Something's not right."

"Keep the hell away, Parglietto," Gerry snapped. "That's a bloody order."

"Anthony, do what Gerry tells you. Just for a few minutes more, son. Then we'll re-assess the situation. It's only been ten minutes." DCI Winslow's tone brooked no argument as Anthony sat back in frustration.

Five minutes later Anthony was standing outside the apartment door. He'd again requested to go in and again been told in no uncertain terms to stay the fuck out by Mountjoy. It had been too quiet now for too long and he had the distinct feeling all was not well.

"I'm going in right now, I don't care what DI Mountjoy says," he said quietly to the men waiting in the car. "Something's wrong. It's too quiet." He could almost imagine Mountjoy having an apoplectic fit at his words.

"That's 'cause they're fucking," Sandy muttered. "Let them be. They're getting their jollies."

"Fuck *you,* Sandy," Anthony snarled as he tested the door. It was open and he thanked God again that Marshall had done what he'd told him to do, leaving it unlocked.

"Anthony, don't go in. You could ruin the whole thing." Rupert's voice was petulant.

Anthony grinned wolfishly. "You don't get to tell me what to do, Sergeant," he spat. "I'm going in to take a look. Screw anyone who disagrees. That's an order. I don't want the guy to get spooked and hurt Marshall."

"Anthony, you can go see what's going on but only when you have backup. That's an order. Sergeant Gregg, get up there. Now." The quiet tones of DCI Winslow overrode the expostulations of DI Mountjoy.

Anthony slipped quietly into the apartment. He had no time for wait anyone else to get up there. He needed to act now. His only weapons were his CS spray, his baton and a Taser which he was authorised to carry. He held this now, ready to strike if necessary and give himself the time he needed to defend both himself and Marshall. Not for the first time, he wished he had a gun.

He heard a low muttering from one of the rooms off the entrance and walked swiftly to the half-open door. His hackles rose as he recognised the voice of the man who'd spoken to him on the phone all those days ago. He peered cautiously around the door and saw the scene from hell that Blair had created. Marshall was face down on the bed, turned toward the door, his trousers round his ankles, some implement jutting out from his backside, his legs reddened. He was still in his shirt. He saw the back of a young blonde man sitting on the bed beside Marshall holding a long silver blade.

Marshall's eyes turned toward him, and they fluttered as he saw him, a faint spark of hope flaring on his pain-filled face. The detective's throat was dry, his heart beating wildly as he looked at the mangled man on the bed and the gloating figure sitting over him. It made him even angrier than he had been before. He took out his baton, flicked it straight and quietly approached the seated figure.

The man sensed something just as Anthony raised his baton. He started to turn and Anthony hit Blair as hard as he could against the side of the head. The younger man yelped, falling sideways over onto Marshall's beaten body and Anthony felt the surge of rage as he raised his weapon again and brought it down on the back of his head, as the man toppled off the bed onto the floor at the other side.

Marshall's eyes fluttered again and Anthony reached out a comforting hand and placed it on his back. The man winced and Anthony removed it hastily.

"Hold on for me, Marshall. Just hold tight. Let me take care of this piece of shit for you." His voice broke slightly at the sight of the broken man on the bed and Marshall nodded weakly, closing his eyes. Anthony strode swiftly around to the man on the floor, who was now sitting up, his knife held in front of him in a stance that said he knew how to use it.

Blair snarled, his face contorting in pure malevolence.

Anthony regarded him quietly. "It's over, Blair. Marshall found out all about your new career as the city serial killer and he decided he wanted no part of it." Anthony moved toward him, keeping himself between Marshall and the bed so the killer couldn't get at him. The younger man stood up in a fluid movement and stood with his back to the picture window looking out into the street, the knife held ready in his hand.

"You won't get away. There's a police car downstairs with a backup team on their way in. We've been monitoring everything you two have said. Ever since Marshall came home in fact."

Blair looked over at the man on the bed. "Well, Marshall, I underestimated you. You're one helluva actor actually. I don't know how the fuck you put all the pieces together or where I made the mistakes but you've been a real clever boy, haven't you?" His tone was vicious. "Detective, I didn't realise you two knew each other so well. Is this tit for tat—I take your fuck buddy and you fuck my boyfriend?"

"It's over, Blair. If that's even your real name. Your personal vendetta against me has ended. I'm not letting you kill anyone else." Anthony said between gritted teeth.

Blair grinned. "I had a very good run, Detective." He spat the words out. Spittle formed on the edges of his lips. Anthony heard a moan from the bed and his eyes flicked to Marshall. Blair saw the glance.

"Poor Marshall. Such a good fuck and now look at him. Just like your brother. He begged me to stop hurting him too. Eventually he was cursing me and I had to shut that pretty little mouth up. I made it quick though. Just like I was going to do with Marshall here. I'm not that much of a monster."

Fury surged through Anthony's body. He looked back at the door, waiting to see if his backup was there. The doorway was empty.

The younger man smiled as he shook his head slowly. "You and your comrades can take me in, Detective, if you can get me of course, but there's no way I'll ever see the inside of any prison cell. I'm crazy, don't you know that? I'll be given a nice, quiet place somewhere in the country, where I can get better and then one day, when no one's looking, I'll get out of there and come back to finish off this job," he waved at Marshall on the bed, "and of course your man. I'll fuck the shit of him before I kill him. And as a bonus, I'll get you too. You'll never be safe, Anthony. You'll always be looking over your shoulder. I might even get someone else to do it for me."

Anthony felt a sense of sheer release wash over him. Since he'd entered the room, he'd wondered exactly what he'd do when he came face to face with a crazed killer and his brother's alleged murderer. Alleged only in the eyes of the law because in his own mind, he'd no doubt this piece of shit had murdered his brother.

He knew what he had to do.

He thought of Flynn and what he would make of this if he ever found out. Anthony didn't want to lose the only man he'd ever really loved. But hearing the man's gloating words and knowing that he meant every one of them meant that Flynn would never be safe. Anthony's face set with grim determination. He moved toward Blair. In an action borne of his beliefs, he knew that whatever happened he would not let this killer make good on his promise to hurt Flynn. Losing him forever would be unbearable.

Blair tutted. "Any closer, Anthony, and I *will* kill you."

Anthony reached up and took off the ear piece he was wearing. He dropped it to the floor and stood on it carefully, watching Blair's face as he did so.

"I'm counting on you trying," he said quietly, and moved toward Blair. The man growled and lunged forward. Anthony reached out a hand. Instead of moving away as any sane person would have done, he took a deep breath and stepped into the assault, reaching for Blair's hand and driving the slim weapon into his right side, almost up to the hilt. He needed proof that the man had tried to kill him; it would make his story stronger.

Anthony cried out in pain as Blair's weapon punctured his flesh, and he felt the warm rush of his own blood over his stomach.

The killer's eyes widened in disbelief. "You're fucking crazy," Blair spat.

Anthony tried to ignore the stabbing pain in his side as he slowly forced the killer's hand off the hilt of the knife, now slick with blood. The metallic tang tainted the air. Anthony could see Marshall twisting frantically on the bed.

"Anthony, for God's sake, what are you doing?" His voice was anguished, still laden with pain. Anthony ignored it as he clamped down on Blair's hand and slowly took control of the knife. He was bigger and stronger than Blair, whose surprise at his actions was still evident on his face.

Anthony wrenched the weapon out of his body, feeling a wash of dizziness as the wound opened. He pushed Blair back against the wall, trapping him, embracing him in what felt like a macabre hug. Anthony was both taller and more muscular than the killer. He gripped the hilt of the knife and turned it around against its owner.

Blair's face was alight with sheer fury as he finally realised what Anthony was intent on doing. He tried to get clear but Anthony was on a mission and men with a mission have a strength that sometimes borders on superhuman. Slowly the knife was forced upward, towards Blair's chin as Anthony fought hard to stay upright with the pain of his stab wound.

"You won't be going anywhere, you fucking maniac," he whispered, as his arms strained to guide the knife where he wanted it to go. "I'm not having you hurt anyone I love ever again, not family, not friend and definitely not Flynn. It's time you paid for your crimes, you sick fuck. I'm your executioner."

Blair was struggling madly, his face plainly showing panic. Anthony rejoiced in it. It was probably the very same emotion Flynn and all the other people he'd hurt had felt and it was good to see it mirrored in the man's eyes.

Anthony kept up the constant pressure even though he was feeling faint. He experienced a sense of virtuousness and wondered randomly if this was what it felt like to play God. His fervent Italian ancestors would be turning in their graves in despair at his unholy blasphemy. Anthony watched the other man's eyes, which were slowly growing wider as the tip of the blade approached his chin. Blair's eyes lit up with an almost fiendish light as he struggled.

"This makes you just like me, detective," he whispered. "And you'll never get to know why I did all this."

Anthony looked at him flintily. "Your victims are all dead and I can't help them. As for the why—it's because you're one sick fuck. But I can do this for the living. That's going to have to be enough for me."

Blair snarled angrily and flailed in Anthony's tight embrace. But the detective held on. With one final spurt of his strength, he sent the knife upward at an angle into the soft flesh of his neck under Blair Malcolme's chin. The man gurgled as blood gushed from the mortal wound and he flailed madly as Anthony twisted the hilt until he saw the light fade from the killer's eyes.

"I told you once before—I am fucking *nothing* like you," he whispered as he stepped back and let go, then watched the man's lifeless body fall to the floor.

Anthony held the wound on his side, fighting the lightheaded feeling of wanting to pass out as he moved toward Marshall.

He picked up a pillow and with bloody, trembling fingers, he stripped the pillow case off it and held it hard against his still bleeding wound.

He'd been sure to try and get the knife just where he wanted it to avoid too much major damage to his own insides but the stab wound still fucking hurt like hell. He used the pillow slip to attempt to staunch the bleeding then sat down beside the other man who'd been watching and listening with dazed eyes.

"Marshall, listen to me. I'm no doctor, that's you, but I'd think this bloody obscenity is better out than in. Do you agree? It's going to hurt like shit."

Marshall closed his eyes in sheer dread then nodded. Anthony laid a comforting hand on his shoulder then turned as he heard a noise behind him. He saw the horrified faces of both Rupert and Sandy staring at him from the open doorway. He was relieved they hadn't arrived sooner. He'd counted on having enough time to finish the job he wanted to do before they arrived. It had been a calculated move but it had worked. Frankly though, if they'd found him shish-kebabbing Blair, he'd couldn't have cared less. At least the sick fuck would have been dead.

"Glad you could make it," he hissed. "Where the hell where you?"

"We couldn't raise you on the mike, so we thought we'd better come up. The bloody lift stopped at every floor." Rupert gazed around in shock. "What the hell went on here? It looks like an abattoir. Tony, you're hurt. Sandy, get an ambulance here, quickly. Where's BTK?"

Anthony waved a bloody hand at the window. "Over there, on the other side of the bed under the window. I think he might be dead. He came at me with a knife and I managed to turn the tables on him."

He ignored Rupert's complete look of disbelief and turned his pain-addled attention to the man on the bed, who was waiting patiently

"Ready, Marshall? Should I do it quickly, or slowly? I don't know which way is best for you," he said quietly.

Marshall gulped, his voice weak when he replied. "Just get the bloody thing out, quickly. Wait till you hear the ambulance siren in case I bleed too much. That way they'll be here in time to sort it out."

Anthony nodded. He reached over and undid the restraints attached to the bed frame, and as Marshall breathed a sigh of relief at being released, Anthony gently rubbed his wrists, which were bruised and cut from the bindings. The other man's eyes filled with tears at the gesture. He lay still on the bed, face streaked with tears and pain. Rupert and Sandy moved around the apartment, checking the layout.

Anthony heard the shrill shriek of the ambulance as it raced to a stop outside.

Sandy nodded. "I can see it. Don't you want to wait for them, they're the professionals—"

"I want Anthony to pull it out now. They'll just do the same thing anyway. I don't want anyone else to see me like this." Marshall's voice was determined.

Anthony nodded, feeling the man's body tense in fear as the detective reached down and gripped the rolling pin.

Marshall cried out loudly, but Anthony kept hold of the implement and, holding his other hand on the man's beaten back as leverage, he yanked the rolling pin out. Marshall's scream made Rupert turn away with a shiver and busied himself about the apartment.

Anthony's hands became covered with small spots of Marshall's blood and he knew it must have been an excruciating pain for the other man to bear.

Sandy went out to the front door hurriedly, no doubt to wait for the paramedics and show them in.

Marshall sobbed quietly in pain as Anthony sat helplessly beside him, not knowing quite what to do. Blood trickled out in a steady stream from between the man's buttocks. Anthony stripped another pillow and gently pressed the slip to his backside, soaking up the slow dribbles. Marshall looked at him with an expression Anthony couldn't fathom.

"What? Have I done something wrong?" he asked in concern. Marshall shook his head.

"No. It's just that not once have you stopped to think about what you're doing. Most people would be scared of getting HIV or something. You've got my blood on your hands."

Anthony frowned and looked down at his fingers. "It wasn't something I thought about at the time."

The other man closed his eyes wearily. "I'm clean, I promise. I get tested quite often and always use condoms. Blair was insistent on that. He had a real fear of getting any sort of STD. I can see why now, seeing as how he raped those people." His voice was bitter.

Anthony winced and held a hand to his side. "It's fine. It's over now. Both you and Flynn are finally safe."

"Thanks to you." Marshall's whispered words were heartfelt. "I couldn't have borne it if it had happened like he said, that he'd be back for me." He swallowed as he turned very carefully onto his side, pulling the blood-soaked cover up over his hips to hide his nudity. Anthony imagined there was no way the man could stand right now, let alone pull on his trousers. He stood up, wincing at the pain in his body. He was starting to feel a little faint himself both from the pain and the blood loss, and he took the rolling pin over to Rupert.

"Put that in an evidence sack," he commanded. "I assume you have some in the car? Go down and fetch them."

Silently, Rupert pulled a roll of bags from his jacket pocket.

"Leave everything else to the SOCO team. They can clean up the rest of this mess. Including the garbage on the floor. And then start looking for the bloody rucksack, the one Mountjoy wanted so badly that led to this fucking mess and nearly got a man killed."

He turned toward the door as the paramedics entered. He wanted to just let go of the pain assailing his body and give into it but he knew he couldn't do that yet. The first paramedic hurried over to him and Anthony waved him away.

The paramedics eyed the blood on his stomach and hands and shook his head in disagreement. "We need to get that sorted, sir. You're losing a lot of blood."

"See to the man on the bed, first," Anthony said between gritted teeth. "I'll hold out a while longer. He's worse off than I am. By the way, I took that out of his backside. So be careful with him."

He waved at the now-bagged rolling pin and the paramedic blanched. Anthony could almost see his testicles constrict in sympathy. His had done the same thing on first sight. He decided he'd better sit down before he fell and he collapsed on the end of the bed as the paramedics tended to Marshall. Now that they had his shirt open the man's body was almost naked. They tried to staunch the bleeding from his arse and see exactly what had been done. Anthony felt sick at the level of violence that had been perpetrated on his witness.

Marshall saw his expression. "I'm alive, Anthony, thanks to you," he said softly. "That's all that matters. And he's dead." His voice was terse, filled with hate. "He was a psycho and I'm glad he's dead."

"About that." Rupert Gregg stood before them both as he watched both men carefully. "Can you tell me exactly what happened, Anthony? How this man ended up dead with a bloody knife buried up to the hilt in his jaw?"

Anthony regarded him expressionlessly. "He was about to cut Marshall here into little pieces. I hit him with my baton, he fell off the bed. I went after him, he came at me with the knife, stabbed me. I managed to get it off him and jabbed it up through his chin. That's about the sum of it."

"It was self-defence," said Marshall quietly. "Blair was crazy. Anthony was trying to get him away from me and he got stabbed."

The detective and the doctor shared a glance. The paramedic looked up as the gurney was wheeled in.

"I need to get you onto that, sir, and off to the hospital. You need urgent medical attention. You may have internal bleeding. Can you stand or would you like us to lift you onto the stretcher?"

"I'll stand and you can help me get on." The paramedic nodded and slowly, Marshall uncurled himself from the bed and stumbled to his feet. His face was white with pain but Anthony could see he was determined to do this on his own. He took a couple of staggering steps toward the gurney and then almost fell onto it thankfully as the paramedics lifted his legs and got him comfortable.

"I'll no doubt be seeing you later, Marshall." Anthony felt a wave of dizziness wash over him and the room started to spin. He heard Rupert's startled exclamation as he fell. Then he heard no more.

Chapter 29

Flynn paced the small waiting room anxiously as he wondered when the doctor would come out and speak to him. It was almost two in the morning and he was exhausted. When Rupert had called him to say Anthony was in the hospital with a stab wound and that they'd caught the Bow Tie Killer, he'd had a flood of emotions. His first one was fear for Anthony and how he was; his second was relief that it was finally over.

He'd been waiting in Anthony's apartment wondering where the hell he was when the call had come. Anthony was still in surgery and as Flynn paced, he said a silent prayer that he would be all right.

Twenty minutes later he was sitting by his bedside, clasping his cold hand in his. The doctor had said Anthony been fairly lucky, that the knife had not penetrated any vital organs but there was still the risk of infection. Flynn reached over and brushed a tendril of dark hair off his white face.

"I'm here, *amore*," he whispered, kissing his cheek softly. "You're going to be okay but you need to rest. I'll be here when you wake up." He leaned forward in surprise as Anthony's eyes fluttered open and his bloodshot eyes stared at him in confusion.

As they focused, Anthony smiled weakly. "I'm sorry I didn't call earlier." His voice was husky. "I was a little busy."

Flynn leaned in and hugged him gently. "God, I'm glad you're all right, baby. I was so frightened for you."

Anthony nodded, his face ashen. "I'm okay."

Flynn sat beside him again holding his hand as Anthony closed his eyes and sank back into an exhausted sleep.

The following morning, after spending a fairly restless night in the chair beside Anthony's bed, Flynn awoke sleepily and gazed over to the bed. Anthony lay there asleep, his face still pale but he seemed to have more colour.

Flynn groaned and stretched then turned when he heard a noise behind him. He started in surprise when he saw Kieran standing there, his face anxious. Flynn stood up, and moved over to him. Kieran reached out and pulled him in for a hug and Flynn sank into him, grateful for the comfort of someone familiar.

"I wanted to see that you were both okay. I know it might be a bit strange considering we're not together anymore but—" Kieran shrugged. "It's all over the news, that he killed this serial killer. He's the hero of the moment."

Flynn pulled away, feeling ill. "Anthony killed him? I hadn't heard that. I haven't been watching the news. And everyone's been so busy, they probably thought I already knew. It's been pretty chaotic here."

Kieran nodded. "According to the reports, he went in to save his witness, there was a fight and the guy stabbed him. How he killed the chap hasn't been released yet, they're keeping that quiet. But he's dead and the scuttlebutt in the corridor is that Anthony *was* apparently the one who killed him. It's being billed as self-defence, obviously."

Flynn sat down at Anthony's bedside again and watched his lover's face as his eyes moved beneath his closed lids and he grimaced slightly in his sleep.

Flynn reached out a hand and caressed his face. "My big bad man," he whispered. "I'm so glad you're here with me now. I couldn't bear it if I lost you."

Kieran's face was unreadable. "You really love him, don't you?" he said quietly. "I don't think you ever looked at me like that."

"Kieran, I—"

Kieran shook his head. "It doesn't matter. Leave it. I'm just glad he's all right. He's a tough bugger, isn't he?" His tone was faintly admiring and Flynn smiled.

"He is that. He can be a real pain in the backside."

As if he'd heard the insult, Anthony's eyes fluttered open and he groaned softly. Flynn leaned over him, brushing the black hair from his eyes. "Morning, sleepyhead. Don't try move too much. Just stay still."

Anthony nodded and reached out a hand. Flynn took it, his heart aching at the loving expression on his boyfriend's face.

"God, Tony, I thought I'd lost you—"

Anthony reached up and laid a finger against his lips. "I'm fine, love. It takes a lot more that what that bastard had to offer to kill me."

Flynn nodded mutely as Anthony noticed Kieran standing quietly near the bed. "Hi, Kieran. Good to see you. Have you been giving Flynn a little moral support?" He grinned weakly. "Or did you come to see me?"

Flynn looked from one man to another in astonishment. "You two know each other?" He couldn't remember the two men ever meeting. The two men locked eyes in what seemed to be a secret understanding.

"Ermm, not personally. But I've seen photos. I know who he is." Anthony muttered then coughed slightly. "Do you think I could have some water please?"

Flynn had the distinct feeling Anthony had just tried to change the subject. He nodded and reached out to pour a small amount of water in a glass tumbler. He lifted the glass to Anthony's lips and he drank thirstily as Flynn held his head up. Finally he was done and he tried to sit up.

Flynn held him down. "The doctor says you should try and stay as still as possible. They've put loads of stitches in and he doesn't want you pulling them."

Anthony ignored him and struggled to sit up as Flynn watched in frustration. Kieran chuckled behind him.

"He really does as he's told, doesn't he?" he said wickedly. Flynn glowered at him and turned to Anthony with a resigned sigh.

"If you insist on sitting up, let me help you, you stubborn bastard." Flynn fiddled with the control to slowly raise the head of the bed. Finally Anthony was sitting upright. Flynn reached around and plumped up the pillows behind him. Anthony grimaced, leaning back with a grateful sigh.

"Has anyone told you how Marshall is?" he asked quietly.

Flynn frowned. "Who is Marshall?"

"He's the man they would have brought in with me. The man BTK was trying to kill before I got to him." There was a distinct sense of satisfaction in Anthony's voice as he uttered the words and Flynn felt a shiver of unease.

"No, I haven't heard anything about him. Was he hurt badly?"

Anthony nodded. "A lot worse than I was. The man went through hell." He shuddered, goose bumps forming on his skin and Flynn wondered exactly what had gone down in that room. "Can you try and find someone on staff that can tell you how he is?"

Kieran nodded. "I can do that. I take it he had a surname?"

"Marshall Cunningham. He was BTK's boyfriend. I'm pretty sure there'll be police all over him trying to get a statement. If you find him, can you find out from the nurses whether I can see him?"

Kieran nodded. "I'll see what I can do." He disappeared out the door. Flynn watched Anthony closely.

"You two seem to know each other better than just from a photo, Anthony. You seem almost comfortable with each other, something I never thought I'd see in this lifetime." Flynn squinted at him. "You lied to me earlier. You went to see him, didn't you?"

Anthony sighed. "Flynn, he deserved to know his life was in danger. I'm a policeman. I had to tell him what was going on." He felt weary and leaned back against the pillow, closing his eyes.

"What happened in that flat, Anthony? Kieran said he heard on the news that you killed the bastard. How the hell did you find him in the first place? Can you tell me anything about it?"

Anthony looked at Flynn. "Marshall contacted me yesterday. He'd seen the press conference and asked for me. He said he suspected his boyfriend of being BTK. It's a long story but the facts Marshall had fit what we knew about the killer. I went to fetch him, to bring him into the station and once we'd made almost sure it was true, that fucking idiot Mountjoy went and sent him back into the thick of things to retrieve evidence. A rucksack with some pretty compromising stuff in it. I didn't want Marshall going back in. I thought it was too dangerous. But Mountjoy talked him into it. So we mounted a sting operation and Marshall was all wired up. Only something happened to tip the killer off. I don't know what it was. He decided he needed to get rid of his boyfriend but not before he'd tortured the poor bastard. I felt something was off so I went in. I struggled with the killer, managed to get the upper hand and stuck a knife through his chin. I got stabbed in the process. And that's about it really." He winced in pain as he moved.

"And a wonderful story it is too, Detective Parglietto." The sarcastic tones of DI Mountjoy echoed through the room. Flynn saw Anthony's scowl at the sight of the man standing in the doorway, another man close behind him.

"Great," Anthony muttered. "As if I wasn't feeling crap already, now I have another arsehole to contend with. Come to visit the wounded man, Gerry? That's very big of you considering you're the reason Marshall had a rolling pin stuck up his arse and I got stabbed."

Flynn gasped at the words delivered by Anthony with pure venom.

Mountjoy moved forward, his face flushing with anger, ignoring the statement. "Don't get up, Anthony. I need to introduce you to someone." He stood by Anthony's bedside, a smile on his face. "This gentleman," he motioned to the younger man standing beside him, "is Lucas Bellingham. He's with IPCC."

Anthony's eyes narrowed. Flynn knew that it was normal police procedure that when someone was killed in an operation. The Independent Police Complaints Commission investigated the details. But he still got a distinct feeling that wasn't all this was about. Mountjoy looked far too gloating for that. He felt his stomach clench.

"Luke needs to talk to you, Parglietto, when you're feeling up to it and get your statement about the events of last night. Of course, I've got my sergeants taking Mr. Cunningham's version of events as well."

"I understand that." Anthony's voice was quiet. "I'm happy to give you anything you need, Mr Bellingham."

"However," Mountjoy stressed the word, "there is another slightly awkward situation we have to address. Someone has expressed some doubt about the events so Luke will be asking you about that too."

Anthony raised an eyebrow. "Let me guess. The 'doubt' was expressed by a man wearing a dapper suit and a permanent self-righteous stick up his arse which can only be removed by surgery or me sticking my foot up it and shoving it further in. Because I'm pretty sure it wasn't Mr. Cunningham. He looked pretty relieved at not being killed to me."

Flynn closed his eyes at Anthony's antagonism. He wasn't doing himself any favours being this hostile.

Luke Bellingham stepped forward. "There have been concerns expressed about what actually might have happened in that room as far as the killing of Mr. Malcolme was concerned. All we're doing is making sure we have all the facts and I'm the man for that job. I assure you I will be fair. I'm not out to do any type of a hatchet job, Detective, even though I know we seem to have the reputation for doing so."

"I can assure you that Detective Parglietto was very justified in killing that man. He was going to stab me with my own fucking sashimi knife." The harsh tones of Marshall Cunningham made everyone turn around in surprise. Flynn gazed in astonishment as Kieran pushed a wheelchair into his room, with Marshall in it. He looked pale, the bruises on his face stark against his white face. Flynn winced at the sight of the man sitting on a soft pillow. His own rectum clenched in sympathy.

"Shouldn't you still be in bed?" Anthony said solicitously.

Kieran grimaced. "He wanted to come and see you, find out how you're doing. He can be quite persuasive and stubborn. Much, I imagine, like someone else we know?" He raised an eyebrow at Flynn and he grinned. Kieran left the wheelchair in the middle of the room, which was fairly congested, and leaned nonchalantly against the wall as he observed the proceedings with keen eyes.

Marshall shrugged. "It's amazing what good pain meds can do. I wanted to be here." He glared at the two other policemen. "I heard that last statement. Who's the twat who thinks something wasn't right? It wasn't that homophobic bastard that came to interview me, was it, with his pathetic innuendos and a really bad dress sense? Spastic Tollbooth or something."

Anthony stifled a chuckle. "I think you might mean Sandy Tolman," he said with a grin.

Marshall nodded. "I like my name better. I was thinking about laying a complaint against him myself for the way he conducted himself. Let alone reporting him for his lack of style." His face darkened. "I didn't realise the Met Police were still employing people like that. Homophobes I mean." He raised an enquiring eyebrow at Gerry Mountjoy, who flushed.

"I can assure you we take our duties to be an organisation devoted to diversity very seriously," he blustered as Flynn watched on in amusement and Marshall looked disbelieving.

"Then perhaps someone should tell Mr. Tolman the meaning of 'diversity,'" he said silkily.

Despite Marshall's antagonistic air, Flynn saw the creases of pain in his forehead and the slight twitch of his hips as he sat in the chair. He wondered again exactly what had gone down in the room where Anthony had apparently saved this man's life by killing another.

Time for the whole story later. And damn it, Anthony had better be ready to tell it.

Anthony sat up. He swung his legs out of bed and cursed as the hospital gown he was wearing gaped open at the back, leaving him bare arsed. Flynn didn't miss Marshall's admiring glance and the sly twitch of his lips.

So that's how it is, is it? Lucky the man was in a wheel chair or Flynn might deck him one for that look.

"Marshall, don't say a fucking word," Anthony muttered. The other men looked at him in confusion.

Marshall chuckled. "Why, Detective, I have no idea what you're talking about."

Anthony shook his head in amusement as he looked around for his clothes.

"Do me a favour, please, Flynn. Get me my bloody clothes and I'll owe you one." He smiled sweetly, trying to use his boyish charm but Flynn wasn't having it.

"You've been stabbed, for God's sake. You need to stay in bed."

"I'm fine. They've repaired me, haven't they? I really need to be up. You know me. I can't sit here and do nothing."

Marshall sniggered. "I can sit and enjoy the view all day." Anthony glowered at him.

Flynn stared in amusement. The man might be ogling his boyfriend but there was something about him that was endearing. "Is there something I should know about you two, perhaps?"

Anthony shook his head as he glared at the other man. "Just ignore him." Flynn saw the smile tugging at his lips. He supposed that when you were put in a life-and-death situation together, you tended to get a little closer than expected. But that didn't mean he wasn't going to keep an eye on the other man.

Anthony looked at Flynn with an enquiring expression. "I can either get out of this bed like this with my backside flapping out the back for everyone to see—Marshall, shut up—or you can get me my clothes and give me some privacy while I change. Your call."

Flynn knew he was serious from the expression on his face. He sighed in exasperation and reached down into the side locker to take out a pile of clothes.

"I brought clean ones over because I just knew this would bloody happen." Flynn glared around the room. "Now if you could all give us some room, I can help him get dressed." He shooed everyone out into the corridor and closed the door. Anthony pulled him into his arms as Flynn leaned over to untie the back of his gown. He kissed him roughly.

"Honestly, I *am* okay. I made sure the knife—" he stopped, looking sheepish.

Flynn Parker, quick-witted investigative reporter rose to the fore. He pulled away sharply. "What do you mean, you 'made sure the knife'—made sure of what?"

"I managed to move so that the knife didn't do too much damage," Anthony muttered. "I was lucky. I had room to manoeuvre."

Flynn looked at him in suspicion. There was definitely more to this story than Anthony was telling him.

"I see." He made sure his tone indicated that he knew he didn't believe him. "Well, you can tell me more later. Right now let's get you decent so you can go out there and tell that wanker Mountjoy to fuck off."

Anthony laughed then winced. "Fuck, that hurts. Don't make me laugh."

Flynn helped Anthony with the hospital gown. He was not surprised to see his hands trembling. His throat was dry. He'd been trying to keep it together but the reality of the situation was now setting in.

I could have lost him.

Anthony reached over and captured them with his warm ones. "*Cuore mio*, you look a bit spooked. I'm fine, honestly. I'm still here."

Flynn drew a deep breath. "I've never been so damn scared in all my life when they told me you'd been stabbed and someone was dead. I thought…" His voice choked off and he gazed at Anthony in despair. Anthony smiled softly and drew him onto the bed, tucking an arm around Flynn's shoulder. Flynn breathed in his scent—sweat, disinfectant and most of all, life.

Anthony sighed as he ran a comforting hand down Flynn's arm. "He was busy torturing Marshall when I arrived and was getting ready to kill him from the looks of it. I had to do something. I hit him with my baton, and then he came after me. He stabbed me and somehow I got the knife off him." His voice quietened. "I was pretty weak so the only fool proof way seemed to be to jab him in the chin. Luckily it worked."

"And Marshall? He seems to have taken quite a shine to you." Flynn had to chuckle the flush that flooded Anthony's face. "Why, Detective, a blush. You appear to have a real admirer there. The man clearly fancies the pants off you." He leaned in and licked Anthony's ear gently, causing him to shiver in pleasure. "Have you told your new boyfriend I'm quite the jealous type and he'll have to get past me first?" He continued his slow caress of Anthony's ear and jawline as he whispered, "Actually, I think I might get quite turned on seeing you two go at each other. It's always been a fantasy of mine—"

"Jesus, Flynn, can you shut the hell up about your threesome sexual fantasies?" Anthony pulled away from the caresses with a fierce mock scowl. "Pass me my clothes so I can get up. I need to speak to that Bellingham idiot, and find out just what the hell Rupert has accused me of. That's all I bloody need, is someone thinking that this incident wasn't kosher."

Flynn growled but passed Anthony his clothes.

*****

Even as Anthony said the words, his heart gave a slight lurch and he hoped he didn't look as concerned as he felt. He had a feeling Marshall would support him in his story if his past comments were anything to go by. He needed to speak to him though, make sure they were telling the same series of events.

As he dressed, his mind raced. Anthony Parglietto knew he'd willfully and deliberately killed another man. He refused to use the word human being, and truth be told he felt very little guilt at the fact he'd executed a monster. But he had no desire to go to prison either. He finished dressing and ran a hand through his hair, which felt like dry straw. He grimaced.

"God, I'll be glad to get in the shower. I hope they've used those bloody waterproof stitches on me or they'll be fixing me up again because there's no way I'm *not* showering when I get out of here."

He frowned. "Now I need to see those two tossers outside and sort this all out."

He walked unsteadily to the door, pulling it open and moving into the corridor. Flynn followed him out. Marshall was still sitting in the wheelchair. Kieran sat a few seats away in the waiting area, a magazine on his lap as he idly flicked the pages. Gerry Mountjoy and Luke Bellingham stood in quiet conversation a few feet away. Anthony ignored them and made his way directly to Marshall.

Flynn moved over to Kieran, sat down beside him and engaged him in quiet conversation.

The detective lowered himself gingerly into one of the other plastic chairs. Marshall looked at him speculatively. The other two policemen watched them both warily and Anthony could see them making a move toward them. He glowered at them.

"Give me a minute before you start the interrogation," he said sarcastically. "The two of us shared a very intimate moment together and I think we deserve a little privacy before you start the inquisition."

The two men backed off.

Marshall chuckled. His face grew serious as he looked at Anthony.

"I know the story I need to tell," he said very quietly. "I won't let you down."

"Jesus, that's not what I wanted to talk about," Anthony shook his head, keeping his own voice down. "I wanted to find out how you were. Is everything all right with you—no permanent damage?" His voice faltered and he felt the words were a little surreal.

He was asking another man about the damage to his sphincter for God's sake. What were the odds?

Marshall nodded tiredly. "I doubt I'll be bottoming anytime soon, maybe ever, but I'll live. It looked worse that it was. The doctor says I should be fine, but it'll take a lot of healing. My ribs aren't broken but my balls are pretty bruised where the bastard kicked me, but it could have been worse." His voice was sombre. "A lot worse. He was going to stab me in the bloody heart and slit my throat. He was wondering how he was going to get my body out of the apartment." His voice faltered and Anthony could hear the underlying note of grief. No matter how much the man had hurt him, or what he'd been, they *had* had a relationship.

"I still can't believe he went mad like that, so vicious. He just didn't give a fuck. I was nothing but a piece of meat to him at the end." He looked down. Anthony put a comforting hand on his shoulder. His voice was soft when he spoke next.

"You know you don't have to tell anyone anything that you feel uncomfortable with. I'm a big boy. I'm prepared to answer for my actions, Marshall. I can't ask you to lie for me, or protect me. You went through hell and you have the right to be able to tell your own truth about what happened. And whatever you decide to do will be fine with me regardless of the consequences. I want you to know that."

Marshall looked over at him with eyes that said he did indeed know all that. "You saved my bloody life. You pulled a rolling pin out of my backside so I'd have a little dignity when the paramedics arrived. You didn't even care that you got my blood all over you. Most people would have been, 'Ooh, don't touch the bleeding gay man.' You didn't even think of that. Then you made sure that psycho wasn't going to come back and try it again or destroy any more lives. And we both know he would have done what he promised and we'd all be looking over our shoulders as long as we lived. Don't worry, Anthony. I know which truth I'm telling."

Anthony swallowed at the words and the man's earnest expression and squeezed his shoulder.

"As long as you're sure. I wouldn't want—"

As he was about to speak he was interrupted as a shadow fell over them both. The large figure of Gerry Mountjoy loomed like a battleship ready to dock.

"Gentlemen, I love the bromance but seeing as how you're both up and about of your own accord, and time is short, I'd like you to come with us to answer a few questions. We've managed to get one of the admin offices set up for him."

Anthony snorted. "God, could you sound any more like a stereotypical bloody policeman, Gerry? Fine, Detective Mountjoy, please, lead the way. Feel free to interrogate the victim. I'll wait my turn."

Mountjoy looked down at Anthony's hand still on Marshall's shoulder and raised an eyebrow slightly. Anthony felt a surge of anger at the man's sneer. He gripped Marshall's shoulder as he stood up.

"Marshall, don't let them bully you. Just tell them the truth and everything will be fine."

"Don't worry, Anthony. I'll be okay." Marshall looked up at the fat detective with a smirk. "I suppose you'd better wheel me to the interrogation room then, hadn't you? I don't really feel like walking."

Mountjoy looked around for help and Anthony could see he didn't fancy pushing a wheelchair. But no help came. Luke Bellingham stood quietly, observing the events and he caught Anthony's eye. The detective saw a faint smile on the other man's face at the sight of Mountjoy's discomfiture. For the first time since meeting Bellingham, Anthony felt a glimmer of comradeship.

"I'll get you there, Marshall." Kieran stood up and took hold of the wheelchair. He sneered at Mountjoy. "Can't have the big hetero detective soiling his hands with a gay man's wheelchair." He grinned at Marshall who smiled back. Anthony withheld a grin. It looked like Marshall had another champion to enjoy the attention of.

Kieran grasped the handles of the wheelchair in his slim hands and began to wheel Marshall down to the office. Luke Bellingham followed him. Anthony watched with narrowed eyes as the three men disappeared. Flynn walked over to him and wrapped arms around his neck, leaning in to kiss his bristled cheek softly.

"Kieran is a good man," murmured Anthony. "I can see why you liked him."

Flynn sighed. "Yes, he is." His face became mischievous. "Although it looks like he quite likes Marshall's company. Maybe this is the start of a beautiful friendship." He mock scowled. "Although Marshall certainly lusts after your fine arse."

Anthony huffed softly. "The man is a menace. But in a good way." He closed his eyes, feeling dizzy, and Flynn leaned forward in concern.

"You need to get back into bed, Tony. You look exhausted and you'll need all your bloody strength to listen to that blowhard, Mountjoy." He regarded Anthony's face evenly.

"Anthony, why are they looking at you like you're some sort of suspect?" Flynn said quietly. "I know they investigate deaths on duty as a matter of course but why would someone think there was anything else to your story other than self-defence?"

Anthony disentangled himself from the embrace as he turned to walk back to his room. He didn't want Flynn to see his face just yet. He was feeling weak, a little dizzy and he really needed to get his story straight before he went in to give his account.

"You know Rupert," he said quietly as they walked, Flynn's hand on his arm, steadying him. "He probably thinks I didn't do things by the 'Book according to Rupe.' The man has always been a bloody stickler for detail."

"Do you think he thinks you killed that man deliberately?" Flynn's eyes were watchful as he helped him onto the bed and Anthony sat back with a sigh of relief. He felt his heart skip a beat at Flynn's perceptiveness even as he shook his head wearily.

"I suppose that's possible. Everyone knows my views. I don't keep them a secret as you know." He smiled. "But there's nothing to find. It was a struggle, I got stabbed then I killed him, that's it. End of story. I'm not going to apologise for it either."

He closed his eyes and lay back on the pillows, wincing as the stitches in his side pulled. Flynn sat down in the chair as he settled himself.

"Anthony, I'm not stupid," he said quietly. "I know how your mind works. How many times have we had a conversation about punishment and what you'd like to do to the man who killed your brother?"

Anthony watched Flynn's face, his own expressionless. He pulled the thin hospital sheet up over his waist. He felt his stomach lurch in uneasy anticipation as he waited for Flynn's next words.

"You found the man who killed Marco, abducted me, killed four other people and countless others and brutally tortured a man you obviously like. This psycho would probably have pleaded insanity to get a more lenient sentence too. I've been doing this job as a reporter awhile and I've been doing you awhile too, Tony." Flynn's blunt and wry words made Anthony smile. "I don't want to know the detail. I just want you to tell me the truth—when you're ready to."

Flynn reached over and caressed his hand, stroking his thumb slowly across his upturned palm. "I love you. Whatever you did makes no difference to me. I promise you that. I'm glad he's dead and I think Marshall is too."

Anthony regarded his boyfriend from hooded eyes, not ready yet to tell him the true story yet. Perhaps later when it was all over he'd tell him how he'd felt, how his mind had worked. But for now the less Flynn knew the better. That way there could be no mistakes.

He nodded. "It was as I said—him or me. I thought you might still want your Italian stud around. Marshall was there. He'll tell them what happened."

Flynn didn't look so sure. "That man would do anything you asked him to," he muttered. "He has a bit of a hero thing for you, methinks."

Anthony grinned. "He's all right, is Marshall." His brow furrowed. "God, if you could have seen him on that bed, all trussed up like a side of beef and in so much pain—" he winced. "He's a strong bugger, I have to say. He seems to have recovered fairly well from his ordeal, and certainly gave that tosser Mountjoy a run for his money."

Anthony felt very tired and leaned back. He felt Flynn's hand on his forehead.

"You feel a little clammy," he said worriedly. "I think you've been overdoing it. I think you should try and sleep for a little while. I'll keep the wolf from the door."

He scowled fiercely and Anthony pitied anyone who tried to get past him. He nodded and closed his eyes, looking forward to just dropping out of society for a while and dropping into what he hoped was a dreamless sleep.

Chapter 30

He was awakened by a soft hand on his arm and a gentle voice murmuring his name. He blinked blearily and saw the smiling face of Marshall Cunningham.

"Anthony? Wake up, sleepyhead. The Gestapo wants to talk to you."

The detective peered at Marshall, squinting his eyes. He'd been in such a deep sleep he still felt groggy.

"Where's Flynn?"

"He went home to change hours ago. Said his thong was sticking to his arse and he needed a shower so he could be all nice and clean for you later." Marshall chuckled. "Does he actually wear a thong? He's a real character, isn't he? I think he was saying 'hands off my boyfriend' in a very not so subtle way."

Anthony grinned. "Flynn doesn't wear thongs. He's a boxer man."

Well, not unless he's stretched out waiting for me in handcuffs.

Anthony's cock gave a little jump at that thought.

Marshall chuckled. "He told the detective squad to leave you the hell alone until you wake up. Only they're getting real antsy now and say they need to get back to the station, so I said I'd do it so he doesn't get mad at them. They seem a little scared of him." He grinned. "As they are of Kieran." He smiled. "He's a real honey. He made sure I got settled and told the police in that very quiet way he has to fuck off and give me some peace. I really like him." His face coloured slightly as Anthony lifted his eyebrows. "I have his phone number now as well. He wants me to let him know how I'm doing."

Anthony chuckled inwardly at the softness of Marshall's tone. He swung his legs out of bed, still feeling a little light headed. He stood up, holding onto the bed. Marshall watched him anxiously from the bedside chair.

"You're not in the wheelchair anymore," Anthony said. "Are you sure you're okay?"

Marshall nodded. "I'll live. It feels like I have a fucking carrot up my arse still but at least I'm mobile." He stood gingerly, his face pale as he came upright. Anthony held onto the side of the bed;

Marshall stood up and hung onto Anthony. The two men looked at each other and burst out laughing.

"Christ, we're a right bloody pair!" Anthony spluttered. "The Walking fucking Dead." Marshall seemed to find this extremely funny and guffawed loudly.

"God, please don't joke like that. It hurts too much." he groaned. Anthony stopped shaking with mirth and let go of the bed. His stitches couldn't take it either.

"So where's the Gestapo then? I thought you said they were here."

Marshall let go of Anthony to stand rather unsteadily on his own. "Mountjoy and Bellingham are waiting in the interview room." He glanced at the detective. "I told them what we agreed happened. That you and Blair got into a struggle. He made a move and stabbed you then you managed to turn the tables and stab him through the chin. I told them I couldn't see it too clearly, as I was in too much pain but I saw enough to know what happened." He swallowed. "I think they believed me."

Anthony's face darkened. "Marshall, if you don't feel right—"

Marshall shook his head. "No, I'm fine with it. Just go in there and tell them the same story and then I guess there's nothing else they can do." He shrugged his shoulders but his face was haunted. "Just tell them *our* truth, Anthony. You don't deserve getting into trouble for what you did."

"No. He doesn't." Flynn's quiet voice echoed in the room.

Anthony looked over at him swiftly, his eyes slightly narrowing. His lover stood there, an unfathomable expression on his face, hands slightly clenched at his side. He must have heard their conversation and Flynn was no fool. Anthony knew he had an inkling of the real truth. Steady eyes regarded Anthony and he met the gaze unflinchingly.

"He needs to get this out of the way so we can all move on. Go on, Tony. They're waiting for you."

Anthony nodded, moving forward and brushing past Flynn, his hand lightly touching his lover's as he deliberately moved closer. He needed to feel his nearness, feel his presence on his skin, know that he wasn't disgusted by what he might have just heard. Flynn leaned forward and warm lips brushed his. "Go. Don't keep them waiting."

Anthony walked out of the room with a sense of relief.

It was going to be okay between him and Flynn.

*****

Flynn watched him go. He felt Marshall's eyes on him watchful and careful. Protective.

"He saved my life," Marshall said quietly. "He injured himself for me and for you without caring about the consequences. He deserves to be a hero. Please don't make him a pariah."

Flynn looked at him compassionately.

How does Anthony manage to get this level of devotion from someone he barely knows? He supposed it had a lot to do with what the two men had been through together. Fear, hate, love, guilt—all these emotions brought people closer.

"God, I'm not going to hurt him, Marshall. I know whatever he did, he did for me. And for you. And for Sumi and all the others that died at that man's hand." He moved over and laid a hand on the other man's arm. "I've known him long enough and deeply enough to know he would have done what he thought was right."

Marshall nodded in relief. "You're a lucky man." He grinned. "If I thought I could turn him to the Marshall side, I'd try. Believe me. But he adores you. It's in every look he gives you, every breath he takes when he says your name. And I'm no home wrecker." He smiled but Flynn could see the pain in it. "I might betray my lover and watch him die and feel a sense of sheer relief that he's dead, but I'm not a cad." His voice faltered slightly and Flynn moved over to him and pulled him close, gently wrapping his arms around him. Marshall sank into him, his body trembling and he simply held him for a while, letting his emotions play out in his arms. Marshall didn't cry; he simply needed comfort. Finally he pulled away and looked at him.

"Thank you," he said quietly. "It's good having someone who cares."

Flynn grinned and knocked him gently on his arm. "You're lucky I'm not challenging you to a bloody duel for ogling my boyfriend. And eying out his booty. I know it's really good booty, but girlfriend, it's mine."

Marshall laughed at the words then sat down gently in the chair at the side of the bed. He looked exhausted and Flynn picked up a blanket off the bed and laid it over him gently.

"Why don't you stay here and try to catch a nap? You look as if you could do with one. I'll go see how things are going down the hall. See if Mountjoy and Bellingham need saving from my fiery Italian stallion."

He chuckled even as his eyes closed and his body relaxed.

"Sounds like a plan," he muttered and Flynn could already see he was falling asleep. All the medication he was on must have been making him very drowsy. "I'll just catch a few Z's and then we can all see where we go from here."

His voice trailed off, his breathing evened out and he was almost asleep. Flynn smiled, tucked the blanket tighter around him and left the room, closing the door quietly behind him.

*****

Two weeks later, Marshall sat at a bar in the city waiting for Anthony and Flynn to join him. He nursed his beer and picked idly at the remnants of bits left over from his two packets of cheese-and-onion crisps. He was contemplating getting another packet when he felt a hard slap on his shoulder. He turned around to see Anthony with Flynn standing behind him.

"Looking a little desperate there, Marsh," Anthony said as he observed Marshall's fingers still in the empty crisp packet.

Marshall grinned. Flynn rolled his eyes as he perched his backside onto a barstool and cast a curious eye about the venue.

"I was hungry." Marshall waved to the barman, who sauntered over. He looked like a former Marine, all huge arms, whiskered chin and hairy, barrelled chest with eyes that glinted with a promise of pleasure to come.

"What can I get you, tiger?" The barman cast a broad smile at the detective. Marshall could see Anthony was a little uncomfortable with the man's appraising and rather lascivious stare. He tried hard to stop a grin forming on his face. It looked like Flynn was having the same problem containing his amusement. The barman seemed like he could be a bit overpowering.

"Ermm, I'll have a pint of Asahi if you have it." Anthony managed at last. The bartender winked at him.

"Same for me," Flynn snorted.

The barrel-chested barman licked his lips again in Anthony's direction. "Coming up, gorgeous." He turned and almost wiggled his hips invitingly as he walked away.

Anthony turned to Marshall, his brow furrowed. "Marshall, if you've brought me into a fucking leather bear bar, I will kill you." He looked around in suspicion as if seeking out huge men in leather trousers and collars. Flynn chuckled and cast an amused glance at Marshall.

Marshall laughed loudly. "Now would I do that to the great Anthony Parglietto? Stop getting your panties in a bunch. Adonis there though, he's a bit of an institution here. He and I go way back." He shook his head in amusement at the look on the other man's face. "Not that kind of way back, you klutz. There is no way I'd let that brute anywhere near my backside. We just put up with each other. I've been coming to this bar for years."

"*Adonis*? Someone names a guy that looks like that 'Adonis'?" Anthony exclaimed. Marshall waved a hand at him.

"Don't be bloody stupid. His real name is Dwight Meerskaum." Marshall shrugged. "You can see why he prefers Adonis."

The man in question brought over their beers and placed them on the counter. He looked at Anthony and smiled, showing a set of gleaming white teeth. "Your one is on the house, courtesy of me."

Anthony nodded uncomfortably. "Thanks. Appreciate that." He raised his pint in the direction of Adonis who grinned and walked down toward the other end of the bar.

"You are a definite attraction for bears," Marshall said solemnly, trying to keep a straight face. "It must be those come-hither dark bedroom eyes—"

Flynn spat out a mouthful of beer as he laughed.

"Marshall, shut the fuck up." Anthony sat down on the barstool next to the other man as he chuckled. His face grew serious as he wrapped his hands around his glass and looked at Marshall. "So, the interviews are over, thank God. I think they just want a final psych one for us both in a couple of days."

The last two weeks had passed in a blur of constant badgering by IPCC and Luke Bellingham for numerous statements and meetings for both Marshall and Anthony, visits to police psychologists and physical therapists, and of Anthony being effectively 'grounded' while the investigation was completed. The in-depth interviews were now over.

DNA tests from the flesh discovered in Chrissie Donavan's teeth and items taken from Blair's flat had proven beyond a shadow of a doubt that Blair Malcolme and the Bow Tie Killer were one and the same. It was a small blessing to all of the men around the table that they were satisfied that the right man was dead.

Marshall had been subjected to a fair amount of cross examination as well, before he'd blown a fuse and refused point blank to tell the same story again. His exact words to the IPCC, delivered in a tone fraught with sarcasm and frustration, had been, "You've heard my fucking side of things a million fucking times and it isn't going to fucking change so why don't you all fuck off?"

There'd been a lot of "fucking" involved, without the pleasure of actually being fucked, Marshall thought. He sighed. "Yes, it's all over but the shouting now. Maybe we can back to normal. I need to find a fellow who isn't a raving bloody psychopath." He looked at Flynn, his eyes wary. "Kieran's not a psycho axe murderer, is he?"

Flynn shook his head. "He's not, no. You're in safe hands with him." He sipped his beer. "How's that whole dating thing going for you?"

Marshall shrugged. "We've had a few dates. I really enjoy his company so we'll see where it goes." The relationship with Kieran was still new but Marshall really thought it might go somewhere. Kieran was warm, funny and loving—and the sex was awesome. They hadn't progressed to anal yet, as Marshall was a bit skittish and still healing. It would definitely take a little longer to get to that stage.

"Well, he certainly seems stuck on you," Flynn remarked drily. "I don't even remember him saying such nice things about me as he does about you. It's all, 'Marshall this, Marshall that.'" He raised his beer glass in a tribute.

Anthony huffed quietly and sipped his drink. "So—I'm allowed to give you an update on the case now it's all over. I'm sorry I couldn't share much with you before."

"I know you had to keep quiet. But I really want to find out who the man was that I spent two months of my life with," Marshall said quietly. "As much as you can disclose to me anyway." He cast a quick glance at Flynn who stared back evenly.

"I've heard the full story," he said quietly. "I made Anthony tell me everything. And I'm okay with what he did." He placed a hand on Anthony's and Anthony covered it with his.

Anthony gave a short laugh. "Flynn isn't an investigative reporter for nothing. He even had the thumb screws out, and not in a nice way." He sipped his beer. "Christ, Marshall, I've trusted you with my career, my reputation, even my life. I think whatever I say to you will be kept between the two of us." He looked a little uncomfortable. "I know I've said thanks to you but—"

Marshall shook his head and swatted his hand in front of Anthony. "Don't spoil this bromance we have with repetitions of your eternal thanks on how I saved your bacon," he muttered quietly. "We both have each other to thank and I think you saving my life far outweighs anything I did for you. Let's leave that behind now."

He tried to lighten the conversation. "Someone should write a comic strip about you. Some sort of superhero thingy."

Anthony was horrified. He darted a glance at Flynn who had a huge smile on.

Marshall narrowed his eyes as he gazed teasingly at Anthony. "Maybe I should," he mused. "I'm thinking gay manga porn," Marshall murmured. "You in your skimpy underwear, with a cape around your shoulders and a raging hard-on—"

"Jesus, shut the hell up!" Anthony's face flushed. "You are bloody incorrigible, you know that?"

Marshall grinned slyly. "I'm getting hot just thinking about it." He winked at Flynn and drank his beer.

The conversation turned more serious as Marshall probed Anthony for more answers—starting with who the real man behind the serial killer had been.

Anthony toyed with his now-empty beer glass. "Well, turns out Blair Malcolme was actually Blair Mainwaring. Youngest and only son of very wealthy entrepreneur William Mainwaring, he of the 'Think Yellow' chain of personal storage facilities."

Marshall's mouth gaped. "The guys who made absolute millions? He was Blair's father?"

Anthony nodded. "William is still alive. He's in a mental facility in Northumberland somewhere. He's sixty-five now and has

Alzheimer's, and has been there for nearly fifteen years. His father lost a lot of money in some bad investments but Blair was still a very wealthy man. The whole estate was left to him. God knows where it will go now he's dead. They're still looking for a will." Anthony's face went grim. "Blair's mother, Catherine, was killed when he was twelve. They found her drowned in the family lake on the property in Finchingfield. Apparently she was a big drinker and it was ruled an accidental death. There was some concern expressed at the time that there were a few odd things about the whole thing. They were swept under the carpet. The local policeman, Freddy Moss, was always convinced that the son—Blair—had had something to do with it. I looked out some of the old police reports and Fred, bless his soul, thought Blair— and I quote—'was an evil little creature and needed to be watched.'"

Marshall shuddered. "He wasn't far wrong, was he?"

"Fred also thought Blair had something to with the murder of a young child, a little girl called Maggie Carpenter. She was five." Anthony's voice went soft. "She was found beaten to death in the woods not far from the Mainwaring estate. There'd been a lot of reports of missing animals before that and Moss thought it wasn't any coincidence. He tried to talk to the powers that be about it, but because of who William Mainwaring was no one would listen. I wish they had."

"Is Freddy Moss still around?" asked Marshall. "It would be good to tell him he wasn't wrong, that his instincts were sound."

Flynn shifted on his chair as a look of regret passed over Anthony's face. "He died in a fall from a mountain about a year after Blair's mother died. He was walking in the Yorkshire Dales and went over a mountain. They found him about three days later when he didn't come home."

All three men were quiet, but Marshall just knew they were having the same vision of a young Blair—God, he thought, he could only have been about thirteen then—silently stalking the man who was causing ripples in what he'd probably seen as his well-organised life and pushing him off a cliff to his death.

Anthony looked down at his beer glass, turning it this way and that, watching as the gold liquid moved in the vessel. "After that the suspicions died down, Blair carried on doing whatever he was doing and five years later his father was sent to the clinic. He would have been about seventeen then. He seemed to have moved to London, lived the high life and of course we all know what he was doing in the meantime. I doubt we'll ever know exactly how many people he killed, both here and in his time abroad." He shivered.

Marshall leaned forward. "You were going to tell me how that psycho found out I'd been at his house? Can you tell me that now?"

Anthony nodded. "Blair had some local warlord on his payroll. Chap called Brick Smith. He used to watch the house for him and tell him when anyone came around or interfered. It was just really bad luck that he managed to catch a snap of you at the house and he sent it on." He leaned forward on the table and picked up the salt pot, idly turning it in his hands. There was silence around the table. Marshall toyed with a paper napkin. "I suppose that's what they call bad timing. If he hadn't have done that, all of the madness might not have happened."

Flynn leaned forward and laid a hand on Marshall's. "You're doing all right though, aren't you? You're getting better?"

Marshall nodded. "Yeah, I'm fine. A little sore still all over but alive. So what do you know about the relationship Blair had with your brother?" Marshall asked, seeing the look of pain on Anthony's face at the question. "Did you get any closure on that?"

Anthony shook his head wearily. "Not as much I wanted. I have no way of knowing anything about that relationship or whether what Blair said was true about him grooming him for a life of killing. I never will now. I'll just have to accept that Marco was killed because he started to have a conscience. If I think anything other than that, it'll drive me crazy."

Flynn made a comforting murmur and Anthony smiled at him, his eyes filled with love. "Flynn told me he thinks I was trying to make amends for Marco's death by protecting you. I think maybe he has something there."

Marshall laid a warm hand on Anthony's arm. "About what you said earlier, about Marco—you weren't to blame for his death, you know that? You weren't the one who killed him. Blair did."

Anthony smiled twistedly. "Some part of me won't believe that. But thanks anyway." He raised his glass. "To Marco and all the others that suffered," he murmured quietly, his eyes sad.

They clinked glasses in remembrance to absent friends and family and Marshall felt a sudden surge of affection for the men sitting opposite him. They'd been his rocks in the past few weeks and he was even starting to get over his lustful obsession with Anthony. To a point anyway. The man still had a great arse on him, worthy of perving over, even if he did have Kieran in his bed.

They were quiet for a while, each busy with their own thoughts. Flynn reached over and caressed Anthony's jawline and Marshall knew from the look on both their faces that there was definitely going to be wild sex for them tonight.

Hopefully one day that will be me gazing into someone's eyes like that…

Anthony frowned and punched his arm none too gently. "What? You're giving us that weird puppy dog eyes look. Stop it, for Christ's sake." He sat back in his chair. "Flynn thinks this whole thing is bloody hilarious," he muttered. "The fact you have—had the hots for me. I mean, you have Kieran now and if I didn't have Flynn here, I *might* have been all over you like a rash."

Marshall sighed as he winked at Flynn. "Great to know. But that doesn't stop me fantasising, does it?"

"I don't know if I can be bloody friends with you, knowing you might be having secret dirty fantasies about me," Anthony said gloomily. "I can put up with a lot, Marsh, but that sort of takes the cake."

Flynn burst into laughter and Marshall chuckled loudly. The bartender came on over, obviously attracted by their merriment by the wide smile on his face.

"You lads certainly seem to be enjoying yourselves. Is this is a private party or can anyone join in?"

Marshall giggled even louder at the horrified expression on Anthony's face.

"No, Adonis. This man isn't into your type and he's spoken for. So keep your hands off him." His tone sounded slightly territorial. "He just happens to have to put up with me." He drained his beer and motioned for another one for them all. Flynn declined, asking for a Coke. Marshall though this felt good, sitting here with people he cared about, simply shooting the breeze. The last few weeks had been a nightmare, but finally it was over. He was back to work on Monday after some time off, back to a job he loved. He had Anthony and Flynn as friends, and he was alive and not on some mortician's slab waiting to be disposed of. He had a feeling life could only get better from here on.

Chapter 31

Later that night Anthony was very much the worse for wear from his long-winded drinking session with Marshall. Flynn was designated driver so he'd only had one beer. He managed to get Anthony into the flat, only to promptly trip over boxes and cartons from the start they'd made packing up their stuff to move. Anthony cursed loudly as he hit his knee on the corner of a box.

"Fuck," he growled. "Who the hell left that there?"

"I think that might have been you," Flynn said drily. "That's the box with all of your gadgety things in, the ones where half of them are broken but you won't throw them away in case one day you have time to fix them. And we all know they'll still be here when the world ends. I'll be glad when this move to Bloomsbury is over and we can settle and stop living out of boxes." The new flat was only a few weeks away from occupation and Flynn was looking forward to it.

Anthony peered at him blearily. "God, you look so sexy. *Mi fai arrapare.* I think we should go straight to bed and get naked." He reached out for Flynn who sidestepped nimbly.

"I think we need to get you to bed but I'm not sure you're going to able to do anything," Flynn said wryly. "You smell like a brewery." He laughed as Anthony stumbled over yet another box, smacking his head against the wall. "Come on, Romeo. Let me help you navigate this corridor of death and get you somewhere safe. It's just as well you don't have to work tomorrow. Thank God for Sundays."

Flynn took his arm and helped Anthony to the bedroom. He pushed him back on the bed and Anthony leered at him.

"Are you going to undress me and have your way with me?"

Flynn tugged his shoes and socks off, and climbed onto the bed to unzip his trousers. "I don't know about that, tiger."

Anthony snorted in laughter and Flynn looked at him with raised eyebrows. "Why is that so funny?"

"That's what Adonis called me," he giggled. "Tiger."

"Oh yes, the big bear behind the bar who thought you were rather luscious," Flynn muttered as he helped Anthony undress. "Maybe I should have let him take you home instead." He prodded his boyfriend to sit up so he could pull his NYC sweatshirt over his head. He was now clad in only his underwear and his eyes were glazing over. Flynn hid a smile. Anthony was so funny when he was drunk, so much more relaxed and vulnerable.

"Adonis really fancies me, Marshall fancies me—you're very lucky to have me, Flynn baby, what with all the competition."

"Oh, that I am," Flynn said dryly. "All my Christmases have come at once."

Anthony nodded, as his head fell back onto the pillow. "'Sright. But don't worry. I won't give in and let them seduce me." He giggled again. "Although Marshall was trying really hard. But don't worry. I'm still yours, I promise. I only love you. Always will." His eyes closed as he settled back in the bed.

"I'm glad to hear it." Flynn reached out and pulled the covers over the half-sleeping form of his lover. He stroked the hair back from his forehead then leaned forward and kissed his lips softly. "Love you too, my inebriated detective."

Anthony murmured something Flynn couldn't quite hear and he climbed into bed beside him, pulling the duvet up over him and wrapping arms around his waist as he spooned.

*****

The following morning Anthony woke with a splitting headache, a dry mouth and a desperate need to pee. The bed next to him was empty. He supposed Flynn might be in the kitchen with the papers and morning coffee, or gone for a short jog. He got out of bed, groaning at the fact he was now upright and his head was pounding, and staggered over to the en suite bedroom to the toilet. Once he'd finished, he thought he should have a shower. He could smell stale beer and sweat on him and it was offensive even to him. God knows how Flynn had slept next to the stench all night. The man had to love him.

He grinned at that thought and started the water running. He'd stepped into the wet room of their bathroom, a large, beautifully created space with a showerhead that dispensed gushes of hot and pressured water. The bathroom was full of steam, heated wisps of sheer breath that licked at the glass doors and curled itself around his body. He relished in the warm water cascading over his aching body and after ten minutes, he got out of the shower and wrapped a towel around his waist. He went into the bedroom and pulled on loose sweatpants and a tee shirt. As he did so, he heard the front door open and the unmistakeable sound of Flynn's whistling as he came in.

Anthony grinned. Flynn had a vanity that he could whistle fairly well and the high-pitched strains of "Sitting on the Dock of the Bay," a song Flynn had an affinity for, bled out into the air. He wandered through to find Flynn unpacking a small brown paper bag filled with items from the small delicatessen down the road. The smell of fresh coffee permeated the air and Anthony sniffed in appreciation.

"Gianni's coffee?" he guessed.

Flynn grinned. "I had a feeling you might need it after the alcohol you consumed last night." He stowed away fresh bread in the bread bin, what looked like a large ham in the fridge and placed a packet of Gianni's special croissants out of reach of Anthony's grasping fingers. "Nuh-huh. They're for lunch. Drink your coffee."

Anthony reached out and took the container of coffee from the kitchen top and sipped it. His heart swelled with love as he watched Flynn buying himself in the kitchen.

"Flynn?"

"Hmmm?" Flynn packed away what looked like a packet of Belgian biscuits in the cupboard—one of Anthony's favourites.

"I love you, you know that, right?"

Flynn shut the cupboard softly and turned to Anthony. "I know that, yes. What brought that on?" He smiled, a soft, sultry smile that turned Anthony's insides to jelly as Flynn came and wrapped strong, warm arms around Anthony's waist and placed his forehead against his. The woodsy, masculine scent of Flynn was one of Anthony's favourite smells in the world.

Anthony shrugged. "Just that it went a bit crazy, and then I told you the whole story about Blair and me killing him and I wondered—" He swallowed. "I know what you said to Marshall in the hospital and what you've said to me about understanding what I did. But I thought maybe you might not…" His voice trailed off.

Flynn pressed himself closer to Anthony, his hardness already evident as he brushed a light kiss on Anthony's cheek. "You thought I might look at you differently? Think you were a murderer?"

Anthony gazed into clear dark blue eyes and nodded. "Something like that. I never want to lose your respect, baby. Not yours. I couldn't bear that."

Flynn shifted and Anthony's own hardness grew at the feel of that masculine and beloved body against his.

"Tony, what you did you did to save people. I do understand that even if it was a bit difficult to hear it at first. But I don't think any less of you. The man violated me, killed your brother and killed and hurt countless other people. You protect. It's what you do. And no one will ever hear any version of events other than the one that's been told. That's my promise to you."

Flynn's hand brushed Anthony's groin and he groaned, as Flynn took his mouth in a deep, ravaging kiss that speared his soul. Anthony growled. His hands slid up to Flynn's nape and grabbed him, pulling his face and his lips even closer as he returned the kiss with a fervour that made him breathless.

He breathed in Flynn's essence, his hands moving down Flynn's body pulling Flynn's shirt from his jeans. Anthony stroked down his hips then cupped his arse. Flynn moaned into Anthony's mouth and that small sound of pleasure and desire was Anthony's undoing. He was rock hard, his cock standing at attention like a sergeant major ready to salute. From the feel of him, Flynn was too.

They melded to each other, mouths hot and slick, as Anthony gripped Flynn's buttocks, pulling him up off his feet, and Flynn wrapped his legs around Anthony's waist as he was pushed back against the wall.

"Not a position we assume often," Flynn murmured against Anthony's greedy lips. "Lucky for me all that gym work and police physical training keeps you in shape. I love your arms. So damn strong…" His tongue licked Anthony's top lip. That erotic move galvanised Anthony and he slammed Flynn against the kitchen wall. Flynn's shirt had rucked up, and Anthony heard his quick gasp at the coldness of the tiles against his bare skin. Anthony chuckled softly.

"You can be quite a bastard," Flynn murmured into his mouth, as he reached into the loose pants and took Anthony's cock in a firm grip, stroking him upward and pressing a fingertip against his slit. Anthony retaliated by letting Flynn down and unzipping him. He pushed Flynn's jeans down to his thighs and then together, they had hold of each other whilst kissing breathlessly and jerking each other off with a fever born of lust.

To Anthony it seemed like there was nothing else but this, his man and the feelings that he generated in his body. Flynn bit his earlobes, sucked any skin he could find and Anthony was sure that afterwards he'd have hickeys where he'd not had them before. Flynn was like an octopus, one hand reaching, feeling, touching, the other stroking firmly until Anthony could bear it no more. He could feel the surge of sheer pleasure welling up from his feet, over his backside and into his groin. It was made even more pleasurable by the force of Flynn's own orgasm as he gave a loud cry and shot warm fluid over Anthony's hand, his body shuddering. Anthony felt the waves of small seismic shocks that made his lover's body tremor, and as he groaned he felt swelled and came too in Flynn's hand, the smell of come and sweat rank in the confines of the kitchen. His body jerked with the sheer magnitude of his climax and he ground his mouth against Flynn's, teeth clicking together as they clasped each other in the throes of their passion. Finally it was over and the pair stood, sticky with the musky smell of semen and glazed looks in both their eyes.

"Well, I think we can safely say that took my mind off the headache raging in my skull," Anthony murmured. Flynn chuckled as he removed his hand from Anthony's now flaccid cock and looked around for something to clean his hands with. He reached over and picked up the kitchen roll and tore strips off.

"As much as I love screwing you this way, it gets bloody messy. I think I might need to shower again." In typical Flynn fashion, he cleaned them both up and then zipped up his jeans. He patted Anthony's spent dick.

"Then again, it is Sunday. We could just finish our coffee, curl up and read the newspapers and maybe shower again together later." His eyebrow quirked and Anthony reached over and ran a hand across his cheek.

"That sounds like a plan. I can't think of a better way to spend a Sunday off."

Chapter 32

Later that week Anthony let himself into his flat and made his way to the lounge. Flynn was waiting for him. His lover moved toward him as he walked in, like an anxious parent trying to get to the child, the glass of wine in his hand sloshing over the rim slightly in his haste.

"Tony. You're back. What happened at the meeting with your boss? Is everything all right?"

Anthony had had a lot of time to think on the way home about the recent meeting with DCI Winslow. He was still shell shocked at the outcome and he needed Flynn. He pulled him toward him, kissing Flynn fiercely, feeling his lips tasting of wine beneath his. Flynn's hands wrapped themselves around his neck. A light trickle of his drink dribbled down Anthony's nape as he pulled him closer.

"*Sono dipendente dei tuoi baci,*" Anthony whispered, when Flynn finally released his mouth. Flynn's eyes were smoky, unfocused.

"What does that mean?" Flynn unwound his hands from his neck and put his glass down on the side table. Arms encircled Anthony's waist again as he slid his hands in between Anthony's shirt and his bare skin. He hissed at feeling warm fingers against his naked body.

"It means I am addicted to your kisses, *amore mio*. We really need to get you to Italian language lessons, Flynn. I think you should start learning it."

"Way ahead of you." Flynn moved away from him, leaving his body feeling extremely dissatisfied at being left alone. "I enrolled in a class at work, twice a week. I started last Tuesday. I'm not very good yet, but I'm learning." He grinned wickedly. "I know what's important." He grabbed him by the shirt and pulled him roughly toward him.

"*Chiavami,*" Flynn whispered in his ear and Anthony's cock went from hard to sheer set concrete in five seconds flat.

"Jesus," he groaned in abandon as his legs threatened to give way, "Who the hell taught you that?" His boyfriend had just said "Fuck me" in the sexiest voice and rather passable Italian accent possible. It had gone straight to his nether regions. He reached out for Flynn but he moved away from him, laughing.

"Hold those intentions, lover. First you have to tell me what happened at the office." His face grew earnest. "I need to know. Am I baking you cakes with nail files in them, do you still have a job or can we just go to bed right now and *fare l'amour*?" Even his last words, "make love," were enough to send Anthony over the edge.

God he is so hot speaking Italian. Now I know how he feels when I do it to him.

Anthony gazed at Flynn in sheer sexual frustration. He saw the fear deep in those pale blue eyes. He nodded. "We can just make love, baby. No prison, no job loss. I was completely exonerated."

Flynn's face relaxed as a look of delight crossed his face. "Hell, that's such good news."

"They cleared me of any wrongdoing and"–Anthony hesitated at his next words which were sticking in his throat like acid—"the city wants to give me a medal. The Queen's Police Medal."

Flynn gazed at him in disbelief. "A medal? For going above and beyond the call of duty? God, I'm so proud of you. You deserve it after what you've been through." He frowned at Anthony's obvious lack of pleasure. "What's wrong? Why aren't you happy about this?"

Anthony disengaged himself from the embrace and went over to pour a stiff whiskey to wash the taste of bile from the back of his throat. He felt Flynn's eyes on him as he took a large sip. He shrugged.

"I just didn't want such a big deal made of it, that's all. I want it to be over. I don't see the point in giving someone a medal to do their job."

Flynn stared at him. "What's this all about, Anthony? Why is this medal thing such a big deal for you?"

"Like I said. I was just doing my job. I don't deserve—" He bit his words quickly but it was too late. The air went still and he heard Flynn moving behind him. He didn't turn round but remained staring out of the window. His voice was quiet.

"You feel you don't deserve a medal because it wasn't an accident. It wasn't self-defence."

He swallowed then nodded. Flynn was far too perspicacious for his own good. He kept quiet. Flynn slowly stroked the nape of his neck, his fingers light and caressing.

"You saved Marshall. You stopped that animal going out and killing anyone else. I know there's more to your story than you said but you know what? I don't care. I really don't. He tied me up, assaulted me and threatened to kill me. He tortured Sumi. He murdered your brother and he was going to kill Marshall. You did what you had to do and you should stop feeling guilty about it. You're already having some trouble sleeping at night."

Anthony turned round quickly and Flynn stepped back from the blazing eyes and the white set of his face.

"I'm not upset because I killed him, Flynn. Christ, the man deserved what he got. I'm upset because I'm *not* bloody upset. Doesn't that make me the same as him? No conscience, no guilt? I feel nothing at killing him. And now they want to pin a bloody medal on my chest? What kind of a man does that make me?"

His hands were shaking, his secret inner fear that he too was a monster taking over. He'd known if it came down to it, he'd be able to kill BTK. He'd no qualms about that. But he'd always thought killing someone would haunt him, keep him awake at night. He'd been prepared for that torment. Yet the only thing that kept him awake at night was worrying why he *didn't* feel guilty.

"Sweetheart." Flynn reached out, clasping his face tightly in his hands, holding him with a strength he'd not felt before. "You are not like him. You have to believe that. You are not a sick killer." He huffed in frustration. "I can say the words, but you need to accept them."

Flynn moved closer, desperate lips touching his, parting his lips, running his tongue along the seam of his mouth with an urgency that made him breathless. It was as if Flynn was trying to breathe that belief into him, by a process of osmosis that made him so horny he could hardly stand. Anthony growled deep in his throat, pulling Flynn to him and crushing his mouth against his voraciously. He had a burning need to forget reality and simply bury himself in nothing more than this man, his desire for him and his hard, willing body. It was primal and he gave into the base urges that drove him.

Whispered words of love and need, echoed murmurs of reassurance from Flynn's wonderful, greedy mouth soothed Anthony's mind, giving him solace.

"You want to know what makes a man?" Flynn whispered in his ear as his hands caressed Anthony's hardness, driving him to distraction. "It's everything you are. Love, warmth, compassion, putting someone else above your needs. What you did for me, I can never, ever forget. You risked your soul for me, Tony. How can I ever repay that?"

Anthony groaned as Flynn's skillful hands played his body and senses like a finely tuned piano, notes of Flynn's love and acceptance, wisdom and understanding floating around his mind in soft, warming melodies.

"God, Flynn, I would do anything for you," he gasped. "I'd do it all again if I have to. *Ti amo, cuore mio*. Always."

He gave into the loving attention of the man in his arms and found the sublime climax he'd been seeking. Later, curled around the sleeping and warm body of his soulmate, Anthony though he might finally have laid his demons to rest.

Chapter 33

Monday morning Anthony was back at work, itching to get back into the swing of things. He walked into the station room, heartened by the sight of the same familiar faces he'd last seen nearly three weeks ago. He made his way over to his workstation, nodding at people who greeted him, acknowledging some of the shouted cheers and congratulations that colleagues threw his way. By the time he got to his desk, he was feeling more relaxed about being back. The other chair was empty and Anthony motioned to one of his sergeants, Marge Connolly.

"Where's Sergeant Gregg? Isn't he normally here by now?"

Marge looked at him with narrowed eyes. "He's no longer working here, sir."

Anthony couldn't deny the surge of relief that washed over his body. He'd not been looking forward to coming back to work with Rupert again. He'd known there'd been a chance he might not have to and it looked like his prayers had been answered.

"I see. I suppose I'd better catch up with DCI Winslow, then. Find out what his plans are for replacing my partner."

He saw a small smile form on Marge's face but thought nothing of it. He walked briskly over to his superior's office and knocked. A brusque tone told him to come in.

When Anthony entered, he saw Fred Winslow on the phone. His boss beckoned at him to sit down. His eyes rolled as he pointed at the receiver.

"Fucking twat," he whispered, his hand over the mouthpiece. "Some city official who wants to tell me what to do in my own station."

Anthony grinned at the tone of sheer indignation in his boss's voice, sat down, crossed his legs and waited for the conversation to finish.

"I'm fucking well aware of that fact, Mr. Moolam. The fact remains that I run this division, not you. If I wish to spend money on things you consider a waste of time, that's my decision, not yours. Now, I have to go. I have an appointment and honestly can't spend any more time on this subject. I expect you to release those funds today and let me know when they're available. Thank you, Mr.

Moolam." He rang off with a firm note in his voice and scowled at Anthony. "Bloody bureaucrats. I wish we still had a stockade. I'd stick that pompous tosser in it so fast his feet wouldn't touch the ground."

He stood up and came over to Anthony, who stood as Fred Winslow clapped him on his shoulder.

"You're looking well, DI Parglietto. A few weeks' rest did you good. I take it your injury has healed or you wouldn't be back?"

Anthony nodded. "Cleared for duty, sir. Psychologically and physically."

His tone was dry. He'd hated the psych evaluations with a passion but he'd given them what they wanted and what he needed to get back in the game. Winslow nodded and sat back down in his chair. Anthony did the same.

"Good. I'm glad to have you back."

"I believe Sergeant Gregg has been—reassigned—sir?" Anthony kept his tone neutral.

Winslow looked fairly pleased with himself. "Yes. He's been 'repatriated' to one of the other divisions. He was told it was a promotion, of course, but between you and me, I wanted that self-righteous prick out of my unit."

A frisson of guilt sparked quietly up Anthony's spine. He was glad the man was gone but hadn't really thought about the aftermath of the BTK incident and investigation. At least the man had been told it was a step upward. He nodded.

"I see. And who might be replacing him?"

DCI Winslow smiled and Anthony felt a little discomfited at the wolfishness of that smile.

"I decided to change the status quo a little, Parglietto. Seeing as how you struggled to get on with DI Gregg I decided a real change of pace was in order. You've already met your new sergeant on the way in."

He waved toward the open door and Anthony turned. Marge Connolly stood there, an uncertain smile on her face as she watched his. He was a little taken aback. Anthony had never had a female partner before. But he knew Marge to be a good policewoman and they'd always got on well.

"DI Parglietto. I hope you're as pleased as I am at the prospect of working together." Marge's vice was confident, but he could hear the tinge of hesitancy in it. Her hands clenched slightly at her sides even as she stood straight and proud, waiting for his response.

Anthony stood up, his tall frame towering over the five-foot-five, slightly rounded figure of Sergeant Connolly. The woman was in her mid-thirties, with mid-length brown hair worn straight and calm green eyes. She looked capable and professional and Anthony knew he could definitely have done worse.

"Sergeant Connolly." He reached out a hand in invitation and she grasped in firmly. "Welcome to my team. It's good to have you on board. I have no doubt you've heard all the stories about me but I'd prefer you to make your own opinion."

"I have heard them all, sir. Have no fear. I don't generally let other people make up my mind for me." Her voice was dry. "My husband says it takes him all his time just to convince me of something. And we've been married nearly ten years so he should know."

"Right, now the pleasantries are over, you two can get back to work," DCI Winslow growled. "Time is money and there are nasty people out there needing to be caught. Off you go. Anthony, make nice with your new sergeant. And try not to kill anyone else too soon, please. The last investigation took off a couple of years off my life expectancy."

Anthony laughed. "I'll do my best, sir."

He turned to leave and his boss's quiet voice made him look back.

"Welcome back, Anthony. It's good to see you back in the saddle, son."

The younger man smiled. "Thanks. It's good to be back."

"Oh and Anthony? The medal ceremony next week—are you prepared for it?" His DCI's voice was wary. Anthony sighed.

"Yes sir. All I have to do is go up on the stage, accept the medal and that's it? I don't have to give any bloody speeches or anything?" He'd resigned himself to the fact that this was going to happen whether he wanted it or not, so he'd better be prepared.

"No speeches, Parglietto. God forbid you get a chance to say anything I might regret." Winslow's tone was droll and Anthony grinned.

"Good, sir. I'll even brush my hair for the occasion."

Winslow snorted as Anthony left the office and followed Marge across the floor. He pulled out his chair and sat down. He switched on his PC, hearing the familiar whir as it booted up. He'd been gone so long he'd forgotten the password to his system so he looked around guiltily and pulled open his top drawer. Anthony pulled out a grubby piece of paper that he kept under a stapler and glanced at it, noting down the password. He slipped the paper back and waited for the login screen. He typed in his user name and the password and frowned as it told him he needed to change it. He ran an exasperated hand through his hair.

Hell, I have to think of another bloody new password now?

He mulled it over, came up with a word and tapped at the keys to gain access to his system. He looked up as his new sergeant approached with an armful of manila folders. Anthony felt his stomach plummet.

"Christ, what the hell is that? Have you been bloody saving them up for me?"

Marge settled herself in on the chair opposite him. "No, sir. These are open case files that everyone in your division is currently working on. I thought you might appreciate an update on what's been going on while you've been gone."

Anthony raised an eyebrow. "And is this your new spot, then?" He murmured silkily, motioning to the desk she now sat up. "Am I to be graced with your presence?"

She looked slightly taken aback. "I thought it would be a good idea to sit nearer to you but I didn't want to be forward and do it before you knew I was going to be your sergeant." She made as if to stand up and Anthony grinned at her.

"Sit down, Sergeant. I'm just teasing you. By all means, move in with me."

Marge sat back down, a slight sense of relief on her face. She reached over and pulled out a file, her face darkening.

"There is one case DCI Winslow wants us to target as a priority. It involves a couple of murders down by the docks—Canary Wharf. Two youngsters killed within two weeks of each other. Rather nasty and looks like some sort of ritual attack. He said it was just up your street."

Anthony felt the old familiar prickle of predatory interest rush through his body. This was why he did what he did. And he knew he was good at it.

He listened as his new sergeant gave him a short, succinct overview of the case and thought at the end that she'd do. He sat forward to observe the crime scene photos and spread them out over his desk as he perused them. There was no time like the present to catch a killer. Better get started.

The End

AUTHOR'S NOTES

It's no secret, really, that I share Anthony's views in this book about the punishment fitting the crime. I know this is a contentious area, but that's never stopped me from having an opinion before. In the course of writing I did a lot of research on the subject of retributivism and got some invaluable insight into both sides of the argument. There are grey areas, and I acknowledge that. And the research led me to a fascinating study of human psychology and perceptions.

I also learnt another use for a rolling pin! But you'll know what *that* cryptic statement is about if you've read the book.

ABOUT THE AUTHOR

Susan Mac Nicol was born in Leeds, Yorkshire, in the United Kingdom. At the age of eight, she moved with her family to Johannesburg, South Africa, where she stayed for nearly thirty years before arriving back in the UK in December 2000. The first year Sue was back in the UK, it snowed on her birthday, as it did the day she was born in 19-*coughs* and she swears this was England welcoming her back.

Sue's career has mostly been in the financial services area, and she specialises in what she calls 'boring' compliance and regulatory work. That's why she escapes into the world of writing and fantasy where she chats to her characters ad nauseum and is overjoyed when they reply. It beats the monotony of legalese, contracts and legislation, and let's face it—writing hot scenes between men can only be rewarding.

Sue is a PAN member of Romance Writers of America and a member of the Romantic Novelists Association in the UK. She is also a member of a rather unique writing group called the Talliston Writers Circle, whose creator is both a bard and a shaman—which makes for really interesting evening and dinner conversation with him. She lives in the quaint village of Bocking in Essex, set in the countryside and not far from the sea should she get the yen to eat oysters.

Did you enjoy this book? Drop us a line and say so! We love to hear from readers, and so do our authors. To connect, visit www.boroughspublishinggroup.com online, send comments directly to info@boroughspublishinggroup.com, or friend us on Facebook and Twitter. And be sure to check back regularly for contests and new releases in your favorite subgenres of romance!

Are you an aspiring writer? Check out www.boroughspublishinggroup.com/submit and see if we can help you make your dreams come true.

www.ingramcontent.com/pod-product-compliance
Lightning Source LLC
Chambersburg PA
CBHW071144170626
46809CB00002B/764